ONE NIGHT IN SEDONA

THE ONE NIGHT ONLY SERIES

BOOK 2

NIKKI LANG

WTS
publishing company

SYNOPSIS

It's the most perfect proposal. So why doesn't it feel like a fairy tale?

Psychologist Carmela D'Angelo always thought saying "yes" to her childhood sweetheart would feel more... magical. But according to her heart, the guy on one knee just isn't the man she wants to marry.

So, newly single and more than a little lost, she skips town to her bestie's bachelorette — and into the arms of a charming athlete.

Professional mountain biker Parker Radcliffe has been beaten to the finish line. Again. Coming in second seems to be a hard habit to shake, but a few drinks with his team softens the disappointment considerably.

As does a smile from the gorgeous redhead in the corner...

While that one night promises something more, Carmela's family ties threaten to tangle her future with the past.

When an accident shines a spotlight on her priorities, Carmela knows exactly where she has to be. But not everybody agrees with her idea of happily ever after.

To Catie —

Thank you for proving that some friendships are indeed written in the stars...and worth the wait.

Carmie

DECEMBER, Cleveland

"I never stopped loving you, Carmela, I never will. Will you make me the luckiest man on Earth and agree to be my wife?"

Those dark hazel eyes that have pioneered every inch of my body stare up at me expectantly in the middle of my parent's formal living room. Those dark hazel eyes that have witnessed every milestone in my life look so familiar to me. I could lose my vision and still remember every unique brushstroke of green and gold in them.

Our eyes, after all, are windows to the soul. I used to look into his and see enough room for both of us in there. Looking into those windows, I saw a future, a family, and a love story that was written in the stars.

But I guess that's what I get for falling in love with the boy next door.

I look down into his dark hazel eyes one more time before I raise my chin to look at my family. The smile that covers my face is automatic, much like the motion sensor lights lining the expansive property.

If I'm being honest with myself, it's hard to tell when a smile is real and when it's a lie these days. The truth—my truth—is losing ground. It's an hourglass turned over, one grain of sand after the next slipping through the narrow crevice of my sanity.

We were in the middle of the living room when Seamus casually dropped to one knee and looked around at our guests with a smile that can only be described as pure male satisfaction. I don't see the Christmas lights, the presents under the tree, or the candles flickering in front of the bay windows.

All I see now are the faces of my family.

Senators. Doctors. Wives. Children.

The faces waiting for my answer with bated breath. I should've stayed in Nashville, but I couldn't stomach seeing Tommy and Fallon so heartbroken. Coming home for the holidays *seemed* like a good idea.

How wrong I was.

My eyes blink once, twice...a desperate Morse code I pray someone can decipher after 28 years of knowing me.

I try again.

Blink, blink, blink.

My brother Carson sends me a signal back.

The right thing is never the easiest, Carm.

His hand is wrapped protectively around his wife's waist as he rests his chin on the top of her head. He's one of the lucky ones in this family. He somehow married for love and gained our parents' approval. Luck is funny that way, isn't it? How something as precious as a relationship can feel so fated, so perfect, and then ... it turns into a curse.

Did the luck change, or did I change?

My eyes finally look down at the ring and the hands that hold the maroon velvet box. The 4-carat, pear-shaped diamond sits on a thin platinum band. It would've been a dream ring for someone else. Anyone else.

The set of hands offering the ring holds it like an olive branch three months too late. I open my mouth to suck in the festive air, but my body betrays me. Maybe it would rather suffocate and die than go through with this.

If I died on the spot, it would simply be another tally in the "Carmela didn't manage to live up to our expectations" column.

No, I'm sure my luck has run out. I'll end up living a long and healthy life repressing the unhappiness in my marriage.

Seamus doesn't even have the decency to look nervous. His broad shoulders rise and fall with an even tempo. There's no fidgeting. He's the portrait of a self-assured man, so confident that I'll forgive him and we'll go back to being the child-hood sweethearts everyone knows us to be. The sweethearts our families *arranged* for us to be, pulling at our strings from the shadows, manipulating something I once believed was pure. Love.

But right now, he's watching me drown in peer pressure.

A man I once loved with every fiber of my being.

He's watching me bite my lower lip, my obvious tell of discomfort.

A man I can barely look at let alone answer the question he's still waiting for.

The word everyone is waiting for.

But I have to do the right thing.

"Yes."

Our audience erupts into cheers, someone pops champagne, and voices compete to be the loudest in the room.

He slides the ring on my finger as I watch from a vantage point that doesn't feel like my own.

If I could, I would place bars over the windows to my soul.

Hang a "closed" sign in the window and disappear. But I don't. I press my lips into a tighter smile and play the role.

A glass of rosè from Michaelangelo's finds its way into my hand, even though I've told everyone in this room countless times that it gives me headaches.

We stand side by side as someone takes our picture. His hand wraps around my lower back in a possessive touch that forces my stomach and heart to clench. I flash my teeth in a convincing smile, but I'm mentally back in my best friend's bedroom in Nashville, wishing I took the entire bottle of pills, instead of just a few.

PARKER

April, Austria

My hand taps the hidden pocket five times. The edges of the note folded there with the words, *I'll love you till I die*, comforts—and haunts—me before I take off at the sound of the horn.

I'm taking first place today. It's my time. They can say I'm cursed all they want. I'm taking first.

My hands find the handlebars and I grip them back and forth. Five times. Always five—never more, never less. The starting gate surrounding me, much like a metal corral for a bull before a rodeo, boxes me in. Contains me. There's only a narrow gap between my pinky fingers and the padded walls. The tight frame comforts me and holds my anxiety within the four walls.

Every exhale fills my helmet and goggles with excess moisture. It's the only rhythm I'll allow myself to focus on: sharp inhale, long exhale. Over and over again in hopes that I'll be able to tame the bucking organ in my chest.

After a few rounds of that, I surrender to the adrenaline

filling my veins. I've been racing for a decade, and I'm still not used to the way my stomach drops and revolts the moment I put my helmet on at the starting line.

Don't feel sorry for me.

Downhill is a race against the clock, where we navigate fast and technical passages. It's a test of courage as well as sharp technical and piloting skills to affront tree roots, banked sections, bumps, jumps, and other natural obstacles along the way.

Three minutes and thirty-four seconds.

That's all I need to take first in the UCI World Cup this year.

Time is a funny thing though; it can slow down or speed up depending on how at risk your life is. No matter how prepared I feel, no matter how much I train, those three minutes and thirty-four seconds will inevitably be the longest of my life.

Open the gates, damn it. I'm here to ride.

I'm not supposed to be here, and in fact, my sponsors and agent are pissed I registered for this race at the last minute. They asked me not to play with fate, not to tempt the bitch who assigned the World Cup on the same day as the anniversary of my father's death.

"There will always be next year, another race, another day. Don't push your already waning luck," they said.

Swallowing past the dry lump in my throat, I tap my pocket five more times. They don't know that I have no respect for luck. I've prepared, I've trained, and I've worked my ass off to be here.

Clouds open up, and it begins to rain, the pitter-patter of it hitting the metal roof above me adding to the anticipation. After a few shaky breaths, it becomes more urgent.

Mother Nature's war drum.

She's indeed on a war path today. The conditions of the

track were already wet and dangerous. Now? She's made it a cluster fuck.

Eden is at the finish line along with hundreds of fans standing underneath the darkening sky in Austria. There are a hundred or so more sprinkled across the rough terrain of the track, ringing cowbells, holding umbrellas, and screaming for their favorite athletes.

I'm one of them. But there's only one voice I wish I could hear again. One face my subconscious mind always fantasizes about seeing on the sidelines. My eyes sting like a bitch, and I move my goggles aside to wipe at the corners.

People are watching your every move, lock it up.

Cillian taps my shoulder, making sure I'm ready to hit the start ramp and peddle into the forest. Nodding my head, I ignore the weightless feeling in my bones and wait.

Anticipation is a strong drug. It hums and sings and flies through my body. I'm addicted to these few seconds before—

The horn blows and the world, along with my thoughts, fades away.

I shoot out the gate and my bike plunges down the steep wooden ramp. Trees line and loom on the course ahead, their slippery roots ready to catapult me into the forest.

But I'm in control.

My legs pump the pedals as hard as I can before I take the first of twelve sharp turns. White tape marks the edges of the dirt course and I pass a blur of red on the way down the first leg of the race.

Red, the colors of the crash pads scattered throughout. I won't need them.

I'm in control. I work the trail smarter, not harder.

Flying out of the woods, I take a ramp at full speed, landing the jump and feeling my back tire sway in the wet dirt. Losing momentum to regain control, I can hear the snarky voice of a moderator saying, *That little mistake will cost Radcliffe a precious second in this race.*

My hands flex and re-grip the wet rubber as the cold air burns my lungs. Nothing looks the same as it did during my trial runs. Everything is darker, wetter, and a fuck-ton more stressful.

My dad's voice pounds in the back of my head, to the beat of my racing heart. *It takes an incredible amount of effort to become effortless, son.*

I've focused this entire year on learning to use my eyes when cornering. Putting in the effort to up my game, the new technique is supposed to increase my exit speed and overall momentum while riding...

But it doesn't matter much in this race, does it? The irony is not lost on me. Visibility is absolute shit as the rain stings my skin and soaks through my black-on-black USA gear.

The muscles in my hands ache as I work to control the bike again, the words *Ride or Die* hidden on my gloves, those words a motto and a possible premonition.

I'm losing momentum as I pass the sponsor banners halfway down the track, forcing me to peddle harder and faster. My bike hits the next ramp at full speed. I put all the horsepower I have into it, and I know in my gut something is wrong the moment my tires hit the dark dirt on the other side.

The chain is gone.

Looking down, I pray like hell the chain flies off instead of getting wrapped up in my bike. I can't fully turn at this speed, but I close my eyes for a millisecond and *listen* for the answer.

Rattle.

It's still on the bike.

There's no time for emotions. It's gnarly and all I can do is keep going.

I'm in control.

Even though the chain can release into the bike and cause me to crash.

I'm in control.

Even though I never should have done this race to begin with.

I'm in control, I think again, trying to convince myself.

The chain starts to jam up the drivetrain and I slow down, costing myself more time I already can't afford to lose. With only a minute left on the track, there are a few jumps with just enough pitch to help me maintain speed, and the chain might finally release.

I fly over a few boulders built into the track and start ripping it at full speed.

Tuck. Pump the jumps. Stay low, and get the backside of the jump perfect.

All of my senses sharpen the moment I catch air. For a second, I feel the freedom of being a kid again, on the first bike my father gave me. Racing down to the makeshift ramp and landing on the crash pad he spent all night building.

The rain continues to pelt my kit and it drenches through my goggles and helmet, but I don't feel it. I feel free, for the first time in five years since he left me.

But when my tires hit the ground, the world comes crashing in again, and so does the burden of racing and living and existing without him.

There's less than 100 meters to go, and I can hear my chain rattling behind me, flicking into the spokes and getting spat back out. The finish line is so close, *so fucking close*, and I might have a chance of making it in less than three minutes and thirty-four seconds.

Until—the chain wraps around my back wheel and I can no longer pretend I'm in control.

I close my eyes as I'm launched off my bike just as I make it across the finish line. When I feel my body bounce and rico-chet off the rails, I give up control. The ringing in my ears doesn't stop. My hands shake with a tremor I can't get a grip on. But my heart, it's my heart that hurts the most. I don't think I can take racing and coming in second anymore.

I don't have it in me to keep falling a hair short. To keep disappointing not only myself but the memory of my father too.

Fuck.

People cheer and go crazy by the time I stand back up. I'll never understand why people love me when I can never manage to come in first.

My body is disconnected from the storm in my head. Breath sawing in and out, I see black spots in the corners of my vision. Faces blur, noise fades away, and I walk to the edge of the course with my eyes wide.

I don't have panic attacks. I don't have emotions. I am in control.

Some say it's a miracle I made it across the finish line in three minutes and forty-*seven* seconds.

Some say I'm one of the greatest and most consistent racers the sport has ever seen and they can't wait to see me again next year. Can't wait to see me finally get first one day.

But as I listen to Connor, the winner, being interviewed, holding his first-place medal, I know it's not my bike's fault I'm not the one going home with the gold.

Crossing my arms and shoving my emotions far, far, down, I force a tight smile for my sponsors and stare blankly into the cameras snapping our pictures.

"My advice to everyone in the sport," Connor yells into the reporter's mic, his smile blinding amidst the grey storm, "is that if you're in *control*, you're not going fast enough."

My lungs empty and my knees threaten to buckle at those words.

Eden's hand comes down on my shoulder and I turn away from the podium. I did exactly what everyone expected of me today—took second. *Stay in control*. Even with the technical difficulties, and the Herculean effort to make it out alive, I took second place. Anyone else would be thrilled.

Is it bad luck, or am I truly cursed?

"Cheer up mate, second is the best, and that run was a pure crack at the track."

"If you're not first, you're last," I mutter with resentment and bitterness rolling off my tongue.

Eden shakes his head and sighs.

Grabbing my bike, and looking up at the sky, I can hear my father's voice in the back of my mind, a memory surfacing:

"You are the king of that mountain. Know what to remember and know what to forget. Forget what hurt you. But always—always—remember your name."

I stop moving and repeat his words over and over in my mind. Let them float through my body like a necessary balm. Allow them to snap me out of this pity party.

Shaking the race off, I lift my chin and throw my arm around Eden's shoulders. I'm drenched to the bone and, for the first time in five years, feel called to go back home.

"Up for some team bonding?" I ask, cutting my eyes over to him.

His eyes sparkle with mischief as he takes his drenched hat off and shakes his wet hair like a dog.

"The desert?" He asks, even though he doesn't have to.

"The desert."

If there's any place that will help me remember who the hell I am, that will help me remember my name, it's *Sedona*.

In a meeting, what's up c-bear?

Just overheard Dad in his office before I left for the airport...

I told him to stop bringing his secretary home...

He was talking to Seamus' Dad.

And?

Did you know?

Know what?

WTF, Carson?

About Seamus. About our marriage being discussed when we were kids?

I mean, yeah? We get the largest tech company behind the campaign.

You love him. He loves you. Win-win. Worse things have happened in the name of American politics.

I'm going to be sick.

And who is this fixer they were talking about?

Stop texting shit like this.

Sorry. Stressed. Don't have time to explain. I GTG.

But Carm? Grow up and start packing. Move home. We all miss you.

3 / WEDDING CRASHERS

carmie

This is my only chance to do this.

I pace outside his bedroom, winding a strand of loose hair around my finger as I consider the timing. *It has to be now*, I remind myself. Everyone in my family believes I'm moving home this weekend.

That's what my fiancé thinks, too.

Seamus proposed months ago, and the pressure to move back "home" and plan a wedding "fit for a Senator's family" pulverized my nervous system until I caved and told them what they all wanted to hear.

I tried. I need you to know that I *tried* to make this work. But the last ninety days have felt like a noose slowly inching close around my air pipe. Strangling me. Snuffing me out. I never should have said yes.

Closing my eyes, I mentally lash out in an attempt to change my mind.

You're just a pathetic little girl. Remind yourself who you are: a senator's daughter, with the ultimate advantages in life.

You are wealthy, secure, and cared for. Do you need to feel loved? How original. You're engaged to a man everyone in your family loves. A little sister to a big brother you idolize and hate to disappoint. You are educated with a PhD and published research in your name—even if your father was the one to set up that entire path for you. You can't even be grateful, can you? Poor Carmie, poor Carmie, a spoiled princess unhappy in her relationship. Run away and see how hard life can be. Go ahead, sink or swim, you'll come back, you always come back. Save yourself the embarrassment and stick it out. You can make it convincing. You can make a life with him. You can make your family proud. You can do your duty. Stop being a—

No. Pausing the invisible lacerations I inflict, I grab my phone and open up my horoscope on CoStar. Desperate for a message. For validation.

Do:

Passionate Debates. Tangled Sheets. Back rubs.

Don't:

"Just Friends." Nonchalance. Closed doors.

You might not think it when you look inside my head, but I love lists. They're neat, and orderly. The complete opposite from my emotions and turbulent, mutable, thought process.

Lists help me. Have you ever tried making one when your life is swirling down the drain? There's a beautiful grounding effect when you place a pen on paper—preferably a legal pad —and line up the numbers and words.

Seamus looked over my shoulder once as I was reading my horoscope, and he rolled his eyes, laughed, and then patted my head like I was so *cute* for believing in its nonsense. Ironically, men are the first people to discredit astrology, when they are, in fact, the subgroup of humanity who could benefit the most from it.

What was that Jared? You struggle with feeling like your life has no purpose? Have you considered looking into your

Saturn sign? No? That's nonsense? Well then! Enjoy the heaviness of your existential dread, since that seems to be working so well for you!

Of course, as a classically trained psychologist, I don't say any of that to my patients. I keep it all locked behind various automatic: *Yes, I hear what you are saying. Hmm, tell me more about those thoughts. Yes, mhm.*

Lately, I haven't been able to dredge up the same level of enthusiasm and creativity for my career as I used to...but let's talk about that another day.

Right now? I have an engagement to end.

Sliding the ring off my finger, I hold the weight of it in my palm, wishing I could melt it down and repurpose the metal for something worthwhile. Something nobody else owns. Something that is a gift from the heart, instead of an obligation.

Pushing the door open, I hear a stream of water and a terrible rendition of, "Sweet Caroline", coming from the en-suite bathroom. I perch on the corner of his bed, considering my options:

Leave the ring on his bedside table. That's obvious enough, right? No confrontation is needed.

Shaking my head, I realize that's as tempting as a slice of chocolate cake, but also too childish for a woman nearing the end of her twenties.

March into the bathroom and give him his ring back, once and for all.

Also tempting, but I have slightly more decorum than breaking up with someone while they are naked.

Stay with him.

Taking a deep breath in, I remind my heart that confrontation is healthy and normal, and we are, in fact, not facing a predator. I remind my nervous system that it doesn't need to engage the fight or flight reflex, even though

I know it's not listening to a word my professional brain is saying.

Healthcare workers are the worst patients. Hence why I don't see a therapist myself.

Seamus emerges from the bathroom with a towel wrapped around his waist, and I let my eyes sweep over his body for one last time.

You see, I'm a nostalgic woman at heart. I look at his arms and see the first time we climbed a tree together. I look at the surprised expression on his face and feel the butterflies he gave me after I kissed him first underneath the twinkle lights of a school dance.

I stare down at the wet towel wrapped around his waist and remember the first time we climbed out of our bedroom windows to be each other's *firsts*.

But as he leans down to kiss my cheek, his freshly applied cologne turns my stomach. I remember the first time I smelled his cologne on someone else...on one of our friends. She was in love with him from the very start, you see, but we all believed her feelings would eventually pass. Don't tell anyone this, but it made my heart ache for her, knowing how she felt, and seeing how unrequited it was on his end.

How messed up is that? Feeling sorry for Kathleen because *my* boyfriend didn't return the sentiment. It's why Carson calls me the "bleeding heart" of the family. I spot a wounded bird and drop everything to help heal it. I can smell someone crying from a mile away and find something to make them feel better.

A blessing, or a curse... I'll let you decide.

But I suppose Kathleen didn't need my help with her sadness. She eventually got what she wanted, all on her own. She got what she wanted, *many times*.

Seamus slides a ring on his finger, a ring with *my* D'Angelo family crest on it. The white gold catches my eye, and it temporarily blinds me from fulfilling my mission. *How the hell am I going to untangle from this relationship when he has been a part of my family for almost a decade?*

"To what do I owe this unexpected pleasure? I thought you already left for Nashville." Seamus turns to face me as he slides on a starched and fitted dress shirt. His fingers make quick work of the buttons, and I swallow past a thick lump in my throat.

Pause, please.

It's important to note that cinema is one of my true great loves.

I used to believe that Seamus was my perfect real-life Noah from *The Notebook*.

But now I see how wrong I was.

I can't let this be my story.

"Seamus."

"That's my name. Hey babe, before I forget—"

He's always doing that. Cutting me off whenever a more *important* thought enters his mind, blaming it on his non-diagnosed ADHD when it's just thinly veiled arrogance.

"I forgot to mention that your bro wanted us to do an article for one of the big magazines. You know, with an election year coming up for your father, he wants all the good press they can get to secure the votes."

I'm sure he does.

I resist the temptation to roll my eyes at another mention of my father's Senate seat and my brother's life mission of keeping our family name in politics

"About that..."

"We should coordinate our outfits, I can have Melinda send you some options to try on in Nashville. Make sure you try them on, I know you've been stressed, so the sizes might not be what you're used to, especially around the hips." My face doesn't even flinch at the insinuation that I've gained weight. He winks and turns away before looking into his full-length mirror as he adjusts his matte black Gucci belt my brother bought him for Christmas.

"Seamus, I came here," I begin again.

He snaps his fingers and wiggles his hips as he admires his view, humming the tune of *Sweet Caroline* again as he starts up a one-man karaoke show.

The polarity of our two moods, of this entire situation, is so ridiculous to me, that I burst out laughing. My hands press to my stomach as I keep laughing at the absurdity of how long I've allowed myself to remain in this relationship. He keeps dancing, wiggling his hips, encouraged by my reaction. He picks up the performance and is now singing with the song playing on his phone. But I laugh until I can't breathe, remembering how it felt to almost overdose last fall. I laugh at my delusional thinking that it had nothing to do with our impending future together. I laugh at the fact he doesn't even *know* about my life in Nashville. I laugh until no sound comes out because I know, undoubtedly, that it's *over* this time.

He dances over to me and sweeps me up in his arms. We spin around his bedroom as he sings, and I laugh, and I laugh, and I laugh—like a madwoman. Or, better yet, like a woman on the brink of freedom.

Breathlessly, I say what needs to be said.

"Seamus." He dips me low in response. "I'm breaking up with you. This engagement? It's over. You know it. I know it. We've been circling the drain for quite some time."

He stands me back up and his eyebrows draw together, confusion fighting a losing battle with outrage. I place the warm ring in his hand. We stare at it for a beat, before I close his fingers around it.

Tears sting my eyes because I can't even tolerate watching the end of movies let alone become the architect of *this* ending of our decades together. It pains me, even if it's illogical. But that's the thing about pain, isn't it? It's rarely ever simple. Pain is a complex phenomenon that often doesn't make sense to anyone but the one it afflicts.

"Carmie?" His voice is velvety and breathless, and I know if I keep listening to it, I'll lose my nerve. *Like so many attempts before this moment.*

"I'll do whatever it is you want me to do. Do you want me to share my location with you at all times? Done."

I shake my head and a deep sigh leaves my body. This is the hardest part—sticking to my decision amidst the pressure.

"Please, Carmela, I'm begging you. Don't do this!" His voice rises and he steps away from me, clenching the ring in his palm. It's mildly predictable, as if he hit the shuffle button on the five stages of grief and is letting one come after the next.

Bartering. Sadness. Anger. What next?

I can't stick around to find out because I refuse to be his therapist right now. For once, I'm letting myself walk away, unshackled from the duty of bearing the responsibility for his emotions.

My body wants to remain in this room, but if I do that, I know I'll end up tangled in his sheets. So I force myself to turn around, to ignore his pacing and near-shouting, and all of his gesturing. I shut it out and grabbed the doorknob.

Ignoring my horoscope for the day, I turn back toward him and blurt out, "Perhaps we can be just friends?" I didn't *want* to say it, but my stupid brain craves putting a big, pretty bandaid over the bleeding wound of this separation.

Seamus runs his hand through his chestnut-colored hair and huffs out a bitter laugh. We stand facing one another, stuck in a purgatory of wordlessness. Our eyes are locked, soul to soul, window to window, and a small part of my resolve crumbles.

Just like he wants it to.

Shaking my head, I break the spell with a whisper. "Actually, no. I don't think we can be friends right now. Perhaps in the future."

"You think, Carm? What a great observation, you make a *fantastic* therapist. Please, tell me your other obvious thoughts on the current situation, since you're the expert."

My eyebrows lift, and I wish I could say that I'm shocked by his condescending tone. It's not a tone he ever takes in front of other people, it's a special subtle cruelty he reserves just for my company. That comment is merely one in a string of typical Seamus statements I deflect, ignore, and straight up bury in a mental graveyard of my own making.

No, you couldn't be a comedian, you're not a funny person, Carmie. That reference isn't as smart as you think it is, just saying. What would you do without me? Oh yeah, you'd turn all your clothes pink in the laundry!

"I didn't mean that babe, please—" he takes a step toward me.

The tears come fast, but I don't step toward him because I'm committed to having healthy boundaries from here on out.

"I will be in Sedona for Fallon's bachelorette next month. Please don't contact me, I need space and you will only push me further away if you keep trying to contact me."

Finally taking the hint from CoStar, I leave the door open behind me and refuse to look back.

carmie

MAY, Sedona

Five stripper poles.

That's the first thing I noticed about this dance studio. The walls are painted black, a leather armchair sits in a corner, the wood floors gleam with fresh polish, and there are fancy speakers hooked up in every corner. I recognize the brand because Tommy set the same ones up all over his and Fallon's new house in Nashville.

They're loud and obscene, and we christened them by playing break-up songs in honor of me giving Seamus his ring back. Riley muttered around a lit cigarette dangling out the window, *We're doing this again? How many times is she going to dump him?* as we played "Torn", "Fuck You" and various Adele ballads on repeat.

We arrived in Sedona this morning and Elyse, the self-appointed HBIC of Fallon's wedding (Head Bitch In Charge, for your information), planned the entire *Till Death* bachelorette weekend. She booked a sensual dance and women's empowerment workshop for our group tonight and only one thing is missing, alcohol.

After signing a few waivers, we are told to get comfortable and wait for our instructor. Dee slips her shoes off and starts skipping around the room, long box braids swaying with the movement. She slides down a pole like it's not her first rodeo. Elyse loops her arm through mine and I want to pinch her for picking something so out of my comfort zone.

Pole dancing? Really? How is this going to be empowering?

I agree with Tommy when he says, *I support women's rights and* wrongs. But the idea of moving my body in public, in front of my friends, in a new way, makes my head fuzzy with fear.

Biting my lip, I try to get my breathing under control. I look over my shoulder at Fallon and remember that this weekend is not about me. But, if she's uncomfortable with the studio or the workshop, maybe we'll be able to leave ...

Walking toward her, my eyes snag on the raw, emerald cut, salt and pepper diamond sitting on top of her ring finger. Underneath her ring, however, is the true sentiment. In tiny black letters, in all caps, her tattoo reads, *TILL DEATH*, and it makes my chest ache.

That's what I want. All-consuming, life-and-death, part-nership.

Fallon moves her body, albeit subtly, to the music. She's lost in thought and a small smile graces her face. I give up my mission almost immediately. *Of course*, she's going to enjoy this. If anyone wants to get lost in the music, it's Fallon.

A presence sneaks into the studio. I can feel her before I hear her.

"Ladies! Welcome, welcome. My name is Lina, and I'll be your tour guide through the sensual waters of femininity! This is my assistant, Jasey, and she'll be assisting me." My eyes widen as I look at the petite pregnant blonde by Lina's side.

"This will be *so* good," Elyse whispers to me, "They were featured in *GOOP* last year!" Elyse jumps up and down on the balls of her feet, radiating a sense of devilish wonder and glee.

Lina is giving us a brief introduction to the difference between sensuality and sexuality, but I'm not paying attention. I can't stop looking at the pregnant woman. She's freaking me out... How is she going to do this workshop? Is it even safe for her to be doing this? I'm worried about her, and I don't even *know* her.

Fallon nudges my arm and I snap out of making the pregnant woman the center of my thoughts. It takes a concentrated effort for me to turn off the "concerned for everyone" part of my brain, but I follow my friends and find a seat in the circle they've created on the floor.

Lina pauses, looking each one of us directly in the eye, before dropping her voice and beginning. "We sit in a circle because it's the symbol of our feminine energy, the womb, and the cycles of life. There is no hierarchy here, there is no beginning and there is no end. Remember, the only priority tonight is to drop *into* your body. There's no right or wrong, no audience, and no reason to judge your fellow sister—" Lina looks at me and pauses, "and no reason to judge yourself if you discover something new in the process."

Heat rushes to my cheeks and I look away, trying to evade her direct and penetrating gaze. It's unnerving. How am I supposed to open up to the experience when someone is staring at me and seeing right through me? My palms sweat, but I keep reminding myself, that *this isn't about me. It's Fallon's weekend, get it together*.

"Close your eyes. All you need to do is follow the sound of my voice," Lina commands the room and her voice is syrupy and thick. I follow her orders immediately, retreating into the safety of my inner world.

Someone turns off the lights, and the soft glow beyond my

eyelids tells me a few candles are being lit on shelves around the studio.

"Hear the music but don't move. Let the anticipation build before you feel the need to respond."

Her voice is hypnotic, and I find my breath deepening. "Work" by Charlotte Day Wilson rains down around us and my body sinks deeper into the sound. Her voice brings tears to my eyes, for a reason I can't quite pinpoint. I don't feel the floor underneath me, I'm weightless, floating through sound and space, lost in the container with my friends.

"Bring your palms to your body. It's ok to be nervous or to feel silly. Let them explore and sweep across the territory of your neck. Let them travel, wander, and discover new sensations. Let them come *home*." Lina's voice sounds closer to me, but I don't open my eyes to check.

My hand shakes as I place it on my heart, feeling the steady rhythm underneath my ribs.

"Sensuality is about exploring our *senses*—it's not about a partner. Explore the texture of your clothes, the smell of the surrounding air, the changing music...let yourself sink into the experience."

Experimenting with pressure, my fingertips graze my collarbone and I shiver in response. The music inspires me to sway, and I feel the first knot I didn't realize I had, relax. The end of that knot unravels and uncoils and floats away the more I drag my hands across my body.

What if I look stupid? What if I'm doing it wrong? My eyes fly open, yanked out of the experience by my intrusive thoughts.

"Trust that what you're doing is right. Trust that what you desire is right. You don't need anyone else to validate your beauty, your timing, your heart." Lina's words slide under my skin and I close my eyes again.

My hands float across my hips, feeling the softness I've

gained while living in Nashville. Something in my stomach clenches, and it feels an awful lot like shame. But my hands float to the soft space below my navel. I stay here in this new space with my hands on my skin and something magical happens. The instinct to avoid my own body—is silenced.

"Cringe" by Matt Maeson drips down the walls and into my bloodstream.

We're led through an entire Pilates-style warmup, and after forty minutes, sweat cools the back of my neck. I'm working hard, but I've never felt this connected to my body before. The music then shifts, and we all cry out in celebration. Elyse looks like she's ready to combust with excitement as Rihanna's, "Pour It Up", pounds around us. Lina looks at everyone before she drops her head, bends a knee, and rolls up her spine, snapping her head up in a gorgeous hair flip.

"We don't stand up in this studio, ladies. We *rise*."

Clapping, we all practice the signature move and I pull my hair out of the tight knot for extra emphasis. Jasey meets my eye and whistles before following suit, a goddess growing life *and* owning her power.

We're guided through a short routine that involves the wall, the pole, and the floor. The steps aren't complicated, but I'm thrust back into my head, self-conscious and nervous. Most little girls took dance classes or gymnastics growing up, but I wanted nothing to do with being center stage.

I had enough eyes on me at home. I stuck to the arts and moved my body in private to keep up the D'Angelo physique.

"When I dance, I dance for *me*," Lina yells over the music. Her voice gives me goosebumps and I close my eyes, placing my hands on my body to anchor myself into the present moment again.

Lifting on my tiptoes, I roll my hips in a circle as I lean against the wall.

"I dance so that I can strip away who I'm told to be, who

I'm supposed to be, and then I am left with the only thing I desire in this life—*freedom*."

Fallon lets out a rare "*woo*," and my smile can't be contained.

"There's a woman inside of you begging to be free. Let her out! Let her move and take up space!" Lina yells.

Sliding down the wall, hands tangled in my hair, I melt into the rest of the routine like butter on warm bread. The more I point my toes as they reach up to the sky, the more I thrust my hips in a bridge, I feel the wind of change calling my name. I roll onto my stomach and slowly reverse-grind my way up to a kneeling position.

But when the song shifts into a dark, haunting, melody, I feel the box I've built around my true self start to buckle. It's so unexpected, this dark beat, but it's a siren song flooding my blood. And then, it *clicks*. The darkness and the movement and the sounds hold me in a way the box I confine myself in never did.

"YES," Lina cries out and I know it's in response to all of our breakthroughs happening across the room.

Leaning on my hip in a "Covergirl" position, my right hand drips down my neck and I repress the urge to open my eyes. Passing my breast, and my waist, I lift a leg and tip my head back.

The song builds, the bass so strong, somewhere in the corner of the studio a glass shatters, but I keep going. With eyes closed, wrapped up in the euphoric embrace of the moment, my palm slides down my stomach, and lands on my inner thigh.

"Don't stop, ladies. Go *there*, worship yourself, give yourself the gift of being the love of your damn life!"

Before I can stop myself, I roll onto my back and reach my legs up to the sky, spreading them at a slow and agonizing speed into an open straddle. My hands travel, down, down, and then.

They stop.

My palms won't pass my inner thighs and my head is thrust back into the waters of anxiety.

Why can't I be free? Why can't I feel uninhibited like everyone else, once in a while? Why? Why? Why?

"Work Song" by Hozier thrums around us as we finish the dance portion of our experience.

The music begins to fade. Even with the small mental blip, my muscles are shaking, my heart is pounding, and I feel like I just had a spiritual experience, but instead of *leaving* my body, I was *introduced* to it. It wasn't for anyone else's pleasure. It was for myself.

We gather again in a circle on the floor. Part cool down, part discussion.

"So what are the leather chairs for?" Dee asks, with a sly grin.

"Ah! You'll have to come back for part two. We cover lap dances and sacred partnership principles in an eight-week series!"

"What do you learn?" I ask, and everyone turns to look at me with surprise.

Jasey responds. "It changed my life. I learned how to connect with my body and my desires without needing to be in a relationship."

Nodding, I thank her, mulling over how different my life would be if I had something like this back in Nashville.

We all sit in a tighter circle and connect hands. With our eyes closed, we send a pulse and squeeze the message to the woman next to us. Tears prickle behind my eyelids and I feel so connected, so whole. I wish I could hold on to this feeling forever.

After, we take a few group photos around the poles. We pour energy drinks, laugh, and run around like children.

"Please don't post these," I beg Dee. If my father or brother sees them, I'll get the full lecture on how it reflects poorly on the campaign during an election year.

Fallon rolls her eyes, used to this request, and clicks out of the post. I catch Elyse sending a video of Fallon to Tommy, and I smile.

Fallon is wearing a white cut-off T-shirt that says *BACH TOUR* with two hearts and drumsticks under it. Tommy made it for her on a Cricut machine, since she said she wouldn't be caught dead in a crown or sash this weekend.

That's a man who knows his woman.

Before we leave, Lina calls out to us, "Ladies! A word to the wise. You just created powerful feminine energy in here. It's not unheard of for wild things to happen after these workshops. You can be pushing a grocery cart with this energy and cars will start crashing in the parking lot. Remember, with great power, comes great responsibility."

My eyebrows lift. *Well, that sounds promising.*

"Come on, we're just getting started," Elyse continues, "Plus, now that we did Fallon's activity, we can focus on Carmie," Elyse yells to me on her way over to the rental car.

I stop, mouth dropping open like a trout. "No! This is Fallon's weekend!"

Fallon rolls her eyes and nudges me, "Yeah, ok. I would rather *not* do a bachelorette party in the first place, no offense. So guess what? You can give me the gift of having fun tonight and getting your rebound on."

Dee pipes up, "Oh, I heard rebounding is *amazing* for your lymph system."

If my jaw could, it would unhinge completely and land on the blacktop.

"I don't need a hookup with a random man to make me

feel better!" I ball my hands into fists and resist the urge to change my flight home and leave. Right. Now.

Dee laughs and threads her fingers in mine. "Come on, let's make a deal. If we make a list of every quality and attribute you'd *love* in a future relationship, and those qualities *happen* to come waltzing into your life tonight, you take advantage of it. No questions asked."

Considering it, I smile because there's no way I'd ever be that lucky. I spent almost two decades of my life with a man who no doubt only has a few qualities from my "ideal partner" list.

"Alright, fine. Let's get ready and then we're making that list," I point at them all.

But before I get into the car, I look over my shoulder and see Lina standing in the doorway of the studio. I wave to the woman I'll never see again, and her words echo back to me, *There's a woman inside of you begging to be free.*

Driving away, I glance up at the stars and feel a version of myself knocking on the door, asking to play. She wants to be free, and for the first time in my life I feel like I have the power to grant her that permission.

It's only one night, so to hell with insecurities and acting sensible and responsible.

I'm going to walk in my power—consequences be damned.

Carmela. I miss you. This is ridiculous.

Please pick up the phone. It's ok that you freaked out about the wedding. We can figure it out.

🙂

I'll call you when I land back in Nashville. Please respect my boundaries...

Boundaries only keep people out. Stop pushing me away. Pushing our love away.

Come on, baby.

Carmela?

Carmie

MAY, Sedona

C hewing on my pen, I stare at the view beyond the fence of this patio. My heart skips a beat as I make eye contact with the red mountains surrounding us. How small we must seem to them. How insignificant.

We're all huddled around a firepit with drinks cradled in our hands and acoustic music playing on a stage to our left. I can see why Elyse chose the *Red Wall Lounge* tonight. It's right up Fallon's alley.

It's heavenly.

"There is no such thing as a perfect man, honey." Dee grabs her straw and toys with it for a minute, thinking. "But women, now women I can get behind. Or underneath. Doesn't matter to me—"

"We get it, Dee, thank you." Fallon huffs out a laugh before crossing her bare feet underneath her on the leather booth. Her jeans are rolled up to her ankles, the baggy boyfriend fit complimenting her tight white crop top with the subtle, *Till Death* embroidered in black right over her heart.

Tucking a strand of hair behind my ear, I lean down and take a sip of my Paloma. It tastes *horrific* because I asked for no jalapeños, but, I would rather run into traffic than send a drink back.

There are two types of people on this planet. Those who send food back and those who don't. Scrunching my face and choking back a cough when I swallow a jalapeño seed, I add another quality to my list. It would be nice to have someone confident, but polite, by my side to notice when I hate something I order.

"What do you have so far?" Elyse asks from across the fire pit.

"Not much. It's harder to build a boyfriend from scratch than I anticipated," I sigh.

Elyse stands up and snatches the list from my hands.

"Hey!" I snap.

She waves her hand at me in a clear dismissal, and she begins reading my pathetic list out loud.

"*Tall, smells nice, has a job*. Carmie, this list is SAD!" Elyse's eyes pop out of her head as she shakes it in exasperation.

"Have you no imagination? This is your dreamiest and most juicy list of desires and qualities for a partner?"

Elyse leans over the fire pit and drops the list into the flames. I watch the paper crinkle and burn, the ashes of my love life floating up toward the darkening sky. They disappear and, with them, my hopes for finding a man worth my time... and my heart.

"God, you're such a brat," Fallon laughs at Elyse before smacking her. "You're harder to please than my mother."

"That's not hard, your mother is dead." Dee shoots back.

"Touché, ok, you're harder to please than Carmie's brother." Fallon plucks the cherry out of her mocktail and sucks the cola off it before winking at me.

Ugh, don't remind me of my brother. I still haven't told my family I gave Seamus the ring back.

"Carm," Elyse looks at me. "That list was barely scratching the surface of what's out there in the great sea of single and willing men."

"Are you afraid you'll be disappointed?" Dee asks.

Biting my lip, I realize, *Now I am, thanks.*

"Oh, I know!" Fallon snaps her fingers, "You're putting too much pressure on that list. Don't make a list for your next *partner*, make a list of qualities required for you to say *yes* to doing the dirty with someone." Fallon beams, proud of herself.

Elyse nods in approval at Fallon. "Yes, that's it. Take the pressure off finding your next love, and inevitably, the next *loss*. Keep it simple and just focus on something temporary. Something fun. Brilliant, Fallon. I'm so glad we adopted you."

"What do you want me to put down?" I throw my hands up, heat prickling the back of my neck. "Must have long schlong? Will make me pancakes in the morning and leave without lingering? Gives good head?" I whisper the last few words, looking around to make sure nobody hears me.

"Sure! Let's start there, with the last option." Dee grabs a new piece of paper and yanks the pen from my hand.

"I'm *not* putting that down." I narrow my eyes at Dee's perfect handwriting flying across the paper. "Fine, Fallon, you were right. It's hard for me to see a relationship with someone beyond Seamus. Too difficult to get my brain to re-write the future I've mapped out for years. But... I can do a rebound."

My friends cheer and we get to work.

"First on the list is obvious, and I'm disappointed you didn't have it already." Dee looks at me and pouts.

"MUST HAVE GREAT HANDS!" Fallon and Elyse yell in unison.

Laughing, I roll my eyes and nod my head in approval. "Add it."

"Oh, ok. Here's one I love that Tommy does," Fallon leans forward, a secret smile in her eyes. "He doesn't ask for permission. *Ugh*, that's the biggest turnoff when a man is all like, *Can I kiss you?* I don't know! *Can you?* I want a man confident in his ability to read the room and will go for what he wants."

"Add it," I nod and sip down the smoked tequila and grapefruit, hating it a little less with every second.

It would be lovely to be tossed around a bit.

"I'll write that down!" Dee winks at me.

Shit, I didn't realize I said that out loud.

The drink begins to mix with the growing euphoria of conspiring with my girlfriends, and I feel like I am someone new. Someone bold.

I hesitate but then add my own two cents, "He has to have a body that says, *I do something dangerous*. I don't care if he climbs electric poles, rides at the rodeo, fills potholes, or plays sports. I want a man who *earns* his body." I say.

"Now we're talking," Dee sings.

We move through more items, ranging from sexual prowess and physical attributes to insanely specific personality traits. There's no way in hell I'll find a man who ticks every box, but it's the most fun I've had since ending my engagement.

"Ok, shall we keep going?" Dee asks our group.

"How many do we have?" Fallon asks.

"Eleven," Dee cheers in response.

Elyse makes bedroom eyes at our server, and he races over, fulfilling our next round. I laugh and wonder what it would feel like to be so unattached to intimacy. Or, better yet, so *comfortable* with casual intimacy.

"So how many boxes does a man have to tick before I let him ... you know?"

Everyone looks at me and speaks at the same time.

"Make love to you?" Fallon rolls her eyes.

"Fuck you senseless?" Dee damn near shouts.

"Knock boots? Get lucky? Do the nasty? Score? Make whoopee? Bump uglies? Tumble? Bonk? Get frisky?" Elyse counts them all on her fingers.

My hands lift to my ears and I shake my head laughing.

"Stop being a prude." Dee tosses an ice cube into my drink, splashing my legs.

"I'm not a prude, but, don't tell anyone..."

"Who am I going to tell?" Fallon asks.

"Tommy," we all sigh.

"Fine, circle of trust." She sticks out her hand and we link up.

"Ok," I begin, taking a massive breath. "I have only ever...*done it*...in one position. Seamus didn't like me to be on top," I say.

I open one eye and brave their reactions.

Fallon's straw is lifted halfway to her mouth. Elyse is shaking her head. Dee coughs into her elbow, "Little dick energy."

"For *twelve years*?" Elyse finally hisses at me in disbelief.

"It was fine. You know? It felt good, but yeah. Twelve years of good ol' missionary." I try to make it into a joke, but my friends can read my face like a damn book.

"Well, ladies. This changes the game. We have a list to *lengthen*." Dee squeezes my hand in sexual solidarity and I nod my head with a small grin.

Even though I doubt I'll ever find the enigma of a man who lines up perfectly with this list, I smile.

What a gift, to be able to unburden your heart with a select few people.

What a gift, indeed.

6 / HITCH

PARKER

May, Sedona

Tomorrow, we start training. Tonight, we sit packed like sardines in the half-moon booth under the dark sky.

The bar is packed inside and out, but the patio at least provides fresh air. That's my only requirement when going out with Eden and the boys. Fresh air. This is one of our usual haunts when we're in town, but they've made major improvements from the dive it used to be. I sling my arm along the back wall of the leather booth.

A waitress places my drink down in front of me and I hold her eyes for a moment. She smiles back before retreating. But as my finger catches a drop of condensation dripping down my glass, I realize she's probably like the rest of them.

People look at me in one of two ways after I tell them what I do for a living.

One, as if I'm a character in a movie, something they can watch and witness, but a story they could never for themselves claim. I'm a novelty. Someone they can say they met once upon a time.

Two, like I'm a vagabond bum because I didn't bother buying into the lie that every person in this country needs a college degree. There's always an awkward pause in conversation when people outside this life find out about my lack of formal schooling. My social credit score plummets and it's all they need to know to confirm my worth. To confirm that I'm crazy.

Sipping my tequila (on the rocks, with a single orange slice) I almost smile. Do you want to know what's *really* crazy? Thinking that a person's worth or intelligence or work ethic can be printed in black cursive letters on a piece of cardstock. It's *crazy* to think the best years of your life will only be for four years at University. Plus an extra two if you're going for "gold" with an MBA or advanced degree.

It's crazy to think that everyone is jealous of where you are but never jealous of how you got there.

People drink, party, socialize, and experiment, borrowing from their future selves without even realizing it. They look at that small chapter of their lives in college as worth every penny of the hundreds of thousands of dollars of debt they'll acquire —writing it off to keep up with society's standards.

I can see it now. The group of young men and women dancing on the stage will wake up one day and realize their current life pales in comparison to what they *had* in the past. Or they'll realize, at some point, that they went down the river and couldn't swim against the current of our culture's expectations.

That realization will happen one morning while they are scrolling social media or eating breakfast or being nagged by their boss. By then, they're so far downstream from a fulfilling life, they fall into a pattern: *Work, autopilot, drink, autopilot, disassociate, reality TV, autopilot, scroll, settle. Repeat.*

Instead of using those years to sacrifice, work hard, and make something of themselves, they used that time to wake up an insatiable beast called freedom. The irony is, that freedom gained without self-discipline always disappears.

They need their distractions.

They need the once-a-year vacations.

They need the security of a vanilla marriage.

All because they believed in the lie and looked at *me* like I was the crazy one.

Draining my drink, I laugh, causing Cillian and Eden to look at me over their shoulders. Shaking my head, I don't go down the rabbit hole of my thoughts with them. They shrug and do what they inevitably always do, look at women.

Cillian grew up in what can only be described as a hovel in Ireland with a drunkard for a father. It sounds like a harsh stereotype and yet, it's still true. The story is incomplete, but I don't push on it. He's on my dig team, helping me prep for specific rides or documentaries. He's also a fellow *Red Bull* athlete and I'm closest with him after Eden. I'm told by the women in our sport that he's a dark horse with his black hair, grey eyes, and ability to stare into your soul.

Eden grew up in Australia with his grandparents, and they allowed him to be as reckless and wild as he wanted to be. The truth is, he would be a better athlete than me if he gave a damn. But he's content to keep sponsorships and be the party boy the world loves him to be. He's my number one.

Smacking his back, I give him a nod of my head, and he returns it. I've never known the love of a brother until I met him.

"I'm going in." Eden smacks the other men in our group to slide out of the booth.

"Where to?" I ask even though I don't need to. The look in his eyes tells me he has his sights on more than a few women tonight.

"Trying my luck with what *might* be a hen-do."

"They don't call them that here. Might want to get it right before approaching." I mumble.

"*Bachelorette* sounds dumb. I'll call 'em' hens and charm their pants off."

I bark out a laugh because while Eden and I don't share the same propensity for charming women, I can't help but be entertained by his constant antics.

"You know, you could give it a go?" He looks over his shoulder at me.

"The next time I open up is my autopsy."

He rolls his eyes and walks away, refusing to argue with me.

Here we go. From my position, I can watch the exchange go down without interference.

Eden snags a waitress before the women at the fire pit see him. He orders everyone another round before he slides his way onto the bench next to a woman with dark hair and a white shirt. I can't read what's on the front of it, but I *can* read her facial expression as she looks at Eden like a venereal disease.

Laughing, I steal Cillian's abandoned drink to enjoy the rare show of a woman being immune to Eden's charms.

Her face scrunches up, and she shakes her head, scooting over in the booth so that not a single inch of her body is connected to his. Holding up her hand, she flashes the ring, as the other women laugh. On any other night, Eden wouldn't care about a ring on a finger, but he has options.

The waitress sets the drinks down in front of them, and the bride-to-be takes that as her moment to leave for a phone call. She gets up and walks over to the fence by my table. Her face is hard and annoyed. I make out something like "I told you I didn't want to come here without you," but instantly softens as she listens to whoever is on the other line.

She laughs, and I know in my gut that we're all invisible to her. Not just men, but a collective *we*, anyone who is not the voice in her ear right now. She says goodbye while nodding her head, agreeing to something.

When the phone is back in her baggy jeans, she looks up at the stars and traces her fingertips over a tattoo on the back of her arm.

It unearths an unknown feeling in my chest.

My eyes follow her back to the table, and she takes a seat next to a woman who looks a tad younger. She has red hair that reflects the dancing flames like a perfect mirror. She grabs a drink Eden paid the waitress to bring, takes a sip, and *grimaces* like it's the worst thing she's ever tasted.

Eden, being the emotionally stunted douche that he is, asks her if she likes it. She nods her head and gives him a weak smile before mouthing, *Thank you, it's so good.*

He beams at her, and her friend smacks her arm with wide eyes.

The redhead objects by shaking her head from side to side. But her tiny friend ignores the motion and pulls out a piece of paper, waving it around like a winning lottery ticket.

The redhead sighs and leans back into her seat, nursing that horrific drink with floating jalapeños.

I can't stop watching them.

By now, Eden usually has sealed the deal. With one or two women on his arm, his next step would be to bring them back to our table, where I would be forced into the ritual of boring small talk to prove that Eden isn't a serial killer.

Women like that, and I don't blame them.

They'd sink into the booth or table with us and ask us questions we've all answered a thousand times over since this game began ten years ago:

Yes, we ride bikes. Yes, it's so dangerous. Yes, we're sponsored. Yes, Eden is the most stand-up citizen we've ever met. No, he's never been in love, he's looking for the one. *Yes, that* one *could be you.*

Please.

The women ask Eden something, and I watch his confidence falter for a moment. Nobody else would catch it, but I notice the tightness around his eyes. The way he rubs at the corner of his nose before smiling at them with all the charm of a modern-day Lucifer.

They ask him a question, and he holds out his hands.

A woman leans toward him and flips his hand palm side up, assessing it. She rubs her long nails over the lines and the small callouses, then shakes her head.

Then, they all laugh.

No fucking way. Now, this *is priceless.*

I tap Cill to slide out. I'm rising from the booth to go over and witness Eden getting rejected but the thump in my chest gets louder and more frantic. I'm halfway there when I stop, barely able to handle the weightlessness flooding my muscles. Looking around, I wonder if there's danger lurking in a corner because I refuse to admit adrenaline is pumping into my system right now.

My body, my *heart*, only does this before a race. It's the physical reaction I can't control.

Tapping my thumb and index finger together five times, something I *can* control, I close the distance between me and my destination. Swallowing past the dryness in my mouth, I realize a second too late that my little trip over here wasn't about Eden after all.

He's on the other side of the fire pit, a glass lifted, in the middle of his speech he stole from a movie: "Never lie, steal, cheat, or drink. But if you must lie, lie in the arms of the one you love. If you must steal, steal away from bad company. If you must cheat, cheat death. And if you must drink, drink in the moments that take your breath away."

All eyes are on him.

All of them except the two in front of me.

No, walking over here wasn't about Eden.

Wetting my lips, begging my heart to calm down, I walk willingly into the dancing flames waiting for me in her eyes.

Holding mine out for inspection, I choke past the gravel in my throat and ask her—and only her.

"What about my hands?"

Carmie

MAY, Sedona

The Australian, who barely checked five of my boxes on The List (it should be a proper noun by this point), pauses his toast and must be staring at the new arrival.

"What about my hands?"

I can only blink up at him with my lips parted. Looking to my left, and my right, I realize I'm at bat. Nobody else is going to answer for me. I get the feeling this man wouldn't even look their way if they did.

"They're steady." I grab my drink with my fumbling fingers and take a long sip of the worst flavor combination to ever be created. I wonder if the bartender *knows* and is worsening them deliberately.

With his hands still held out, he catches the eyes of another server, and orders a drink. His voice is so stable and steadfast. There's no comedy, lilt, or accent for that matter.

"Is that the only requirement? Steady? Of course, Eden didn't pass the test. He's as twitchy as a toddler on a sugar high," he says with a little light in his eyes. Something tells me that it's his version of smiling.

The Australian, Eden, scoffs and cozies up to Elyse.

She lets him, but still makes him work for it.

"Let me get a closer look." I tilt my head to the now-open seat next to me. Fallon stood up at some point during this strange exchange and escaped to the fence to text Tommy again.

He slides in and instead of being overwhelmed by the smell of cigars or cologne that every man in finance wears, I smell something so much more alluring. I smell *Earth*. Everyone talks about the smell of the ocean or the smell of a new spring day. But this is so much better. If I were to die and then was granted a single day left on earth: this is what I would want to smell. It's dry air, dirt, open skies, sweat. *Freedom*. It's so subtle, so faint, and yet masculine at the same time. It's every season wrapped into a walking form.

"They're also strong. Mark off number seven," I say to Elyse.

Dee pops up behind me and whispers in my ear, "I'll bet you a first-class seat upgrade that he can indeed do numbers seven and eleven. He can *definitely* throw you around—"

I'm about to silence her with a withering look when a drink is placed in front of me.

"It's a tequila sunrise. Orange juice, grenadine, and of course, tequila," the man with the hands next to me says in a low voice. I stare at the drink for a moment and can smell the sweetness from here. My skin gets hot and prickly when I realize what he did.

Or, *why* he did it.

"My other drink was just fine." I narrow my eyes at his *straight* tequila with a single orange slice crushed at the bottom.

"You hated it, but you were either too polite or too passive to be honest about it." He lifts his glass and takes a drink. The brown eyes that hold my gaze over the rim of said glass are unapologetic.

Scooting over, I feel defensive about his observation. His level of honesty, and his comfort with expressing that honesty, is shocking. *I didn't ask for his opinion, his drink, or his hands.* Well, I guess I did and the Universe delivered.

His thigh shifts and I tense, until I realize he's working to give me more space on the bench in front of the pit. I catch his profile out of the corner of my eye as he answers a question Eden shouts from across the fire. But my mind is spinning.

I take a drink, and it's just as he said. It's sweet and smoky and feels like the sun saying good morning after a long night.

Swallowing, I say, "Alright, let's see those hands again. That's the first step."

He turns to look at me, and his eyes are so dark they remind me of the heavy sky hanging above us. Sunburnt lips tilt up in the corner before he asks, "First step?"

"I'll explain if you make it past the first few...boxes. Hands, please." I bite my lip and fight the urge to laugh. It's the tequila making me bossy. *Definitely* the tequila.

He shows them to me, and I don't stop myself as I run the pad of my finger over his rough and wide palm. *How much of my body can you grab with that?* I wonder. Flipping his hand over again, I pretend to deliberate, but when I look at him biting back a laugh, I clear my throat. *Holy shit look at these hands.* They're the type of hands that *grab* life and manipulate it to their will. They're hands that have muscles and scars and stories. They are hands that would surely light a fire along my skin if they dragged across my back, the friction creating sparks of desire *everywhere*.

"Don't get cocky. That's only one." I'm trying to be serious, but I can feel my boundaries disintegrating around me. I can feel everyone and *everything* else disappear entirely.

It's Mr. Perfect Hands, the fire, and my uncharacteristic behavior.

"How many do I need?"

Blowing out a breath, I unfold the paper as an answer. He leans forward, trying to get a peek at my list. Holding it to my chest, I smile at him and smack his chest.

"Don't be impatient. Hands, check." I pretend to check off a box. "Name?"

"Everyone calls me Parker." He extends that same hand out to mine, and I stare down at it in contemplation. Meeting someone new, out in the wild like this, is a first.

"Carmie," I say.

His eyes hold me as tight as his palm does before he asks, "That's not your full name is it?"

I ignore him and check off the next item on the list.

"Check. *Non-douchey* name."

"How is that fair? We don't choose our names," Eden calls out, clearly offended.

"The smart ones do," Parker cryptically mutters with a smirk.

"Boring, get to the good stuff!" Elyse yells from the other end of the booth. She's sitting in Eden's lap, and I'll be surprised if her next vacation isn't to the Australian city of *Boneville*, population, two.

"Yeah, go on, have a craic," Eden calls, before nuzzling Elyse's neck and whispering into her ear.

"Do you have *Must have good hands* on the list before someone's name?" Parker asks before swirling the ice in his drink, amusement sneaking onto his carefully controlled features.

"Absolutely," Dee whispers in my ears, and I roll my eyes at her eavesdropping.

"Names, like you said, can change. But a man's hands? Those are a dealbreaker. Muscles, hair, and charm can change with time. But hands? Those are forever. Carmie wants a man with good hands..." Dee pauses before Elyse cuts her off.

"And she wants a man who knows *what* to do with those hands," Elyse sings while Eden plays with a lock of her hair.

"What do you do for a living?" I ask Parker before letting my eyes sweep across his defined forearms.

"I'm a professional athlete. Downhill racing."

He holds my gaze, waiting for something to cross my face, but I just say, "Check" with a shrug of my shoulder.

"Boring!" Elyse calls out again before letting Eden shut her up with his mouth.

I inch closer to Parker and drop my voice. Crossing my leg, squeezing my thighs tight, my foot brushes his calf. I don't move away—and neither does he.

"Girlfriend?"

"No."

I don't bother saying *Check* or looking at my list. I dive headfirst into his presence. He feels like a weighted blanket, a balm to my scattered nervous system.

"Have you ever cheated on someone?"

"Never."

Nodding, I run my tongue over my teeth, beating back the memories of that particular pain.

"If you were a song, what one would it be?"

"I'm more into movies."

I smile, and he rolls his eyes. "That was a trick question, wasn't it?"

"You passed with flying colors," I whisper, before plucking a surprise cherry out of the bottom of my drink. Lifting it to my lips, I pause and look at him.

No phone in sight.

No shifting.

His awareness and attention are fully dedicated to *me*.

Flooded with surprise and satisfaction, I pull the cherry into my mouth and savor it.

"How would you pleasure a woman?" My words are barely an exhalation, but he somehow hears them.

"It depends on the woman." He leans in, and I can smell the sun and the sky in his damp hair. He showered, but the smell lingers as if it's a strand of his DNA, unable to be altered.

"Well," I close the distance between us and scoot closer, "indulge me." I bite the corner of my lip and his eyes track the movement.

The atmosphere thickens, gravity no longer conforming to the physical laws of nature. It thickens and bends to *his* will.

"Well, if I knew she had a thing for, my hands," he looks at me before moving a strand of my hair away from my cheekbone. "I'd make sure every inch of her body felt them. I'd let them travel to places she's been too polite, or passive, to ask other hands to go. There wouldn't be a place, *inside*, or out, that would go untouched."

He pauses and my breath catches. The surrounding air becomes even warmer, the flames almost too much to bear. Parker's hand lands on my thigh, and he shifts my legs so that they're now draped across his lap. Rough hands run up and down my exposed shins, but he doesn't go higher.

"Call us if you need us," Dee whispers in my ear before walking away with Fallon. They're looped together, arm in arm, and I fight the niggling guilt at being so selfish.

Fallon must see it in my eyes because she smiles and shakes her head. Blowing me a kiss, she walks off with Dee. Glancing over my shoulder, Elyse and Eden are giving everyone in the bar a lovely chance to participate in voyeurism.

"What else is on your list?" Parker's voice breaks me away from my thoughts.

I shake my head and fold the list up before putting it in my purse. "They don't matter anymore."

"And why is that?" His hands stop moving.

"Because of how I feel right now," I whisper, "and I know how these things go. You're just a guy in a bar, and I'm the girl. We won't have forever. We'll have right now, and go our own way."

"And how do you feel right now?" He asks, and it's the first time I've heard anything but confidence in his voice.

I look at him, on the edge of his seat but trying so damn difficult to look composed, and I decide to be honest. Or maybe, I feel empowered by his honesty and can't help myself.

"I feel like...a sunrise on the inside." I tap my heart and then look away because it's poetic and sappy and sweet and not what I should be saying to the man with good hands—the man I'm considering for a rebound.

Parker, who marks most of those forgotten boxes.

But I feel his strong fingers on my chin, turning me back to face him.

I exhale and force a smile to my lips. I'm so out of my depth. So out of my element. Ten years too late to this game.

"Well, Carmie—"

I cut him off before he can reject me more than I reject myself.

"It's ok, you don't have to say anything. I can get an Uber back to my place. Thank you for, indulging me. Sorry... I ah, sorry," I blab, dimly aware of my self-sabotaging.

Standing up, my legs buckle for a moment, but he rises and steadies me. His hands hold my hips and I hold my breath.

"I feel it too." I barely hear him, too shocked to register his admission. "But I have to be honest with you. I only have one night to give." His eyes are so intense as they look at me with hunger.

I don't wait for my mind to catch up to my body.

"Well. I'll give you tonight if you can give me something in return."

He nods, not even bothering to ask what my condition is.

My hand reaches out and presses flat to his chest, over his heart. Over the erratic rhythm betraying how calm he looks on the outside.

"Give me a sunrise, Parker."

In all of my life, I've never seen a man smile like that. And I fear—as he carries me out of the bar over his shoulder like a caveman—I'll never see one quite like it again.

Ok, I know I said I would give you space and "respect your boundaries." I'm trying here, Carm.

Here's a playlist. It's how I feel about you. Listen to it here.

Please listen to it…and please come home to me.

I'll talk to you when I'm in Nashville. Stop texting me Seamus. Please.

Fuck, I miss you. I'm sorry! I'll be a better man. I love you…

Don't leave me. Damn it Carmela.

Carmie

MAY, Sedona

The stars are high in the sky and my phone won't stop vibrating in my back pocket. It's either the group text with Fallon, or *him*, and do you know what? I refuse to let *him* ruin where I'm going next.

Parker's palm is warm and strong on my thighs as he carries me out of the bar. The silence between us is comfortable, his presence the perfect anchor and reminder of the new life I've chosen for myself.

I'm going to have my cake and eat it too, and nobody from my past will ruin it for me.

He drops me to my feet and taps his keys, a large truck lighting up in front of me. I shake my head from side to side and submerge the laughter threatening to break free. Parker looks down at me and his eyebrows lift.

"What's so funny, Carmie?"

There's nothing soft about his voice, his hands, or the way he makes my heart race in my ribs. God, even the way he says my name, *Carmie*, rolls over his tongue like a salted caramel.

"I like this truck," I say before reaching the passenger handle. He beats me to it, opens it, and I hop in with a little ruby-throated hummingbird flying in my heart.

Before he can close my door, I turn to look at him and admit, "One day, I'll have a jeep or a truck or maybe even a Four Runner like this. My dog, preferably a white Swiss Shepard in the trunk, will whine for me to roll down the window for him. We'll play *Florida* by Taylor Swift and Florence, and I'll drive my way up and down the West Coast. It will never be clean and it will most likely always be out of gas."

Parker leans against the doorframe and smiles at me, "A white Swiss Shepard, huh? At first glance, you seem like the type to carry a dog in your purse."

I wrinkle my nose and blurt out, "First of all, how dare you!" He tilts his head back and laughs before shutting my door. As he walks around the hood of the truck, I see his profile lit up within the fog lights. There's something so unrefined about this man, something so natural and raw it makes my blood race in a frenzy.

"So," Parker slides into the driver's seat and grabs his white hat from the dash. He positions it on his head so that it's backward, and I can see the *Red Bull* logo on the side.

"So," I smile and spin myself in the leather seats to face him.

"I don't normally—"

"I'm sorry, but this is new for—"

We both talk at the same time and laugh awkwardly.

"You go," he nods to me.

Shifting, I pause and debate how much to tell him. "Well, I just got out of a serious relationship." I hold my breath. I'm cursing myself for not stealing Elyse away before I left the bar to at least ask her what the hell she would do.

I know what she would do, and it absolutely does not involve talking.

"I travel a lot for work and have a demanding schedule for the majority of the year, so this isn't exactly something I'm used to either," Parker offers me a lifeline and I grab it.

"Isn't that lonely for you?" I ask, my hair falling into my face as my head tilts to the right.

His hand reaches out and tucks my hair behind my ear. Where his skin contacts mine turns hot with a blistering need to be touched more.

"I travel with a group of guys, sometimes with a few more or less. But Eden is my ride-or-die. Even when I try to get rid of him, he shows up again like my damn shadow. I'm alone, but I'm not necessarily *lonely* if that makes sense?"

I nod my head, content to let him believe that. But the slight pinching of his eyes as he looks out the windshield betrays his declaration. He shakes his head and turns the key in the ignition. The truck roars to life as he pulls out of the parking lot.

My hand flies out and lands on his forearm. "Wait, are you ok to drive? Didn't you drink more than me?" I ask, eyes wide.

"Would it make you more comfortable if I didn't?" He asks, hand hovering over the key. The rumble of the truck fills the silence.

"I don't want you to get in trouble, even if you think you're under the legal limit."

"So you're only concerned about my well-being? Not yours?" He tilts his head and my face flames hot.

"It comes with the territory I guess," I mumble looking out the window. "It's a therapist thing."

"Alright, then let's go." He smacks my thigh before turning off the truck and popping out of his seat.

"Wait!" I open my door and he's there already, eye level with me, leaning on the door frame.

"Where are we going? What are we doing?"

Truthfully, I thought we'd be...you know...in the backseat already.

"The only thing to do at this hour." He gives me a serious look that's brimming with heat and tension.

I swallow. "And that is?" I struggle to maintain eye contact.

"Stargazing. Of course." His face turns playful and I decide I like this side of him.

His left hand reaches out to me. I take it without hesitation and hop down from the lifted truck.

"You can tell your friends we're going to Doe Mountain," he tells me before heading for the trunk. Before opening the door, he hands me his phone and asks me to pick a song from the open playlist.

"Top 500 Movie Scores of all Time," waits for me. As I scroll through the options, I save the questions burning on my tongue for another day, like, *What movie made you cry for the first time? What images, lines, or sounds, do you carry with you? If you could only watch one movie for the rest of the time, what would it be?*

However, there might not be another day, right? We're just two strangers meeting at a point that will never repeat. He's a man who made his way past my list.

The rebound.

Hans Zimmer fills the space around us, and I grant the music permission to slip underneath my skin. I let it settle to my bones and the nerve endings that haven't stopped buzzing since he grabbed my hand. My body settles deeper into the anticipation and I let my mind wander.

This is one of those moments, one of the ones that will flash before my eyes like a scene from a movie before I die, and I'm going to give myself something worth watching. I will relish being underneath the night sky with him.

Parker is rooting around in the trunk for supplies and I can't see his face when I ask him an impulsive question.

"Would you board the Titanic if you knew it was going to sink, but your soulmate was on board?" The question rushes out of me, from a quirky place in my brain I only let out when I'm with Riley or Elyse.

"No," Parker answers and adjusts his hat as he stands up with a backpack in his hands.

"Why?"

"Why, what? Isn't it obvious?" He asks as he double-checks the bag.

"No, it isn't. Why wouldn't you go? Your *one* true love is on that ship. How many great loves do you think you'll get in a lifetime? What if it's only one?"

His hand grabs another blanket, then shoves it in the large Patagonia bag, while he chews on my question, or maybe he's ignoring it.

"Because love like that? It's only for assholes," He answers with a tight smile before slamming the door.

Fluttering my lips, I realize this man could use some therapy, but it's not my job to fix him. Fallon rolls her eyes because she thinks I'm the Snow White of people in pain. They all end up on my doorstep with their big sad eyes, which is ironic because *she* was one of them.

It's one night. It's one night. It's one night. Don't pry—

"Tell me why you think love is reserved for assholes." I inch closer to him and inhale deeply. Being out here, away from the smell of alcohol, it's like I'm dunked in a tank of his essence. His hand reaches behind his neck and tugs his short-sleeved shirt off before rummaging in the trunk for a replacement. He leans forward, and I watch his ribs and the corded muscles of his arms flex.

Catching my eyes, he huffs out a laugh and shakes his head.

"Didn't anyone ever tell you it's rude to stare?" He pulls the black, long-sleeved shirt on, offering me a cheeky grin once his head pops through the top.

"Well, in the words of Emma Stone, I wouldn't be staring if you weren't photoshopped. What the hell is that? How do you, how do you look like that? It's not fair to the rest of the male population. You, and Ryan Gosling." I wave my hand up and down his body.

He shrugs and reaches into the trunk again, this time emerging with a bike and an extra hoodie. "Not sure why it's such a big deal, it's just a result of the work I put in. If more guys got off their ass and committed to changing, they'd look like me too."

The slam of the trunk startles me and I cross my arms, feeling a defensive swell of emotion rise in my chest. But instead of swallowing it down and keeping the peace, I go to bat for the unnamed strangers he's referring to.

"It's not that simple, Parker."

"Why not?" He tilts his head and gives me a puzzled look before swinging a leg over the seat of the bike. "People have agency, Carmie. They can change if they want to. The truth is, many people are content to live a mediocre life. If they want extraordinary, they have to do *extra*. Making excuses and feeling bad for them doesn't do them any favors. It hurts them."

My lips part, and I'm about to argue back, but I realize there's a point to his assessment. There was a long summer when I would set Seamus' alarm clock for him every morning because he refused to be responsible enough to do it on his own. It was something I did to make sure he would make it to work on time for my father because I wanted to keep the peace between everybody. But it never made him more responsible. If anything, it made him need me more.

Stepping forward, I refuse to confuse being *needed* with being *loved* ever again.

"Is this the bike you compete on?" I ask. But what I want to know is, *Are you showing this to me and then putting it back in your trunk? Please put it back in your trunk.*

"No, this is just for fun. We can ride to my spot." He tosses the hoodie at me, and it hits me in the chest. I'm assaulted by the smell. I've never been so attuned to my five senses before. I blame that dance class earlier this evening.

His hoodie smells like it hung outside all day to dry. A smell that will never be replicated, just like nature intended. *Just like this moment.*

"And this is your solution to not drinking and driving?" I take a step back but maintain hold of the soft material.

"Yes." His left foot props up on a pedal and his thigh flexes with the motion.

I thread my arms into the oversized sweater and pull it on. When my head pops out, my hair is all over the place, but I see his hands flex on the handlebars and catch my attention.

"I'm not a huge fan of bikes," I say, hoping he didn't catch my eyes roaming his body.

There's a long scar on my right knee where my brother Carson accidentally ran me over during a race. I couldn't ride a bike at the time, so I bet him that I was faster on foot and he, always the money-motivated older brother, took me up on it. I veered into his path, just a hair ahead of him, and he was unable to brake quickly enough when my heel bounced off the front tire. The world went upside down and was filled with the sound of my skin peeling off my body on the harsh concrete. The pain was so intense I held my breath until my face turned blue in his arms as he sprinted for the house, tears streaming down his face as he mumbled, *"I've got you, Carmella, I promise. I got you"* over and over again. He kept that promise, until this year.

My hands slide over the smooth matte black metal of the bike in front of me and I keep my breath locked in my chest. Parker's eyes never leave my face when he lowers his voice, "You're safe with me, I promise. I've got you."

A little breeze tickles my face and I suck in a breath to appease my lungs.

"Alright, Parker. Prove it." I allow him to get me situated on the handlebars, his hands finding any excuse to adjust my waist.

Looking back, I catch his smile and can't help but mirror it back to him. I wonder if thinks he won something far greater than getting me on his bike because as we ride away, into the dark, I can feel his smile the whole time.

9 / INTERSTELLAR

PARKER

MAY, Sedona

Carmie turns toward me on the blanket and leans her head on her hand, "So."

Her knees curl up toward her chest, and I roll onto my side to face her. My body, an instrument I mainly use to serve my goals, mirrors her movements without my permission.

It has a new master now, and quite frankly, I'm not sure how I'm supposed to feel about that.

"So," I send back, our favorite word hanging between us.

We stare at one another and there's no buffer or distractions. No cell phones, no friends, *nothing*. The anticipation is addicting. It's like launching off the line down a mountain during the first race of the year. It's the millisecond of thought before my body and bike go upside down in the air.

It's all the heavy and loaded pauses between me and this unexpected woman staring right back at me. It's the lack of control over the entire situation.

New, but highly addicting.

"If you could go back in time, to tell yourself something,

anything," she starts, "what would it be?" I notice her eyes drop to my lips.

"Nothing."

She blinks a few times and then rolls her eyes with a smile.

"Let me guess, your younger self wouldn't listen to what you had to say anyway?" She grabs the brim of my hat and places it on her head.

I shrug, content to let her assume what she wants.

The truth is, I'm more interested in my future than I am in looking at my past. Or, I'm more interested in *her* than looking too closely at my life before this moment. I'm interested in the way her red hair spills out of my black hoodie. The small pout her lips make when I don't answer her questions right away. And eventually, the way her eyes catch on the stars above us, drinking them in like she'll never get the chance to see them again.

"What would you tell yourself, Carmie?" I ask. She tosses my hat back to me, rolls onto her back, and interlaces her hands behind her head.

"Hmm."

I remain on my side, staring at her without shame, and I've never wanted to crawl inside the head of somebody as badly as I do now. I'm thriving on the anticipation of not knowing what she's going to surprise me with. What I'll surprise myself by saying in her presence.

"I would tell myself to get up from the table when love is no longer being served," she says to the sky more than she does to me. She must feel my eyes on her because as she slides her eyes to meet mine, I see the whole sky reflecting in them. They're like being out on the ocean at night, ripples of stars and movement, darkness that swallows me whole.

"Even if that means I'm alone when I do," she finishes.

Sighing, I run my hand through my hair and then roll onto my back. Vulnerability is supposed to be a two-player game. I know this on a conscious level, but I've never been a team player. When I try, it comes out disingenuous, and I typically make an ass of myself.

She laughs a little to herself, and my head turns toward her again.

"This is not a sexy conversation," she breathes more than says, and it's softer, sadder. "The pathetic truth is, this is probably the most romantic setting I've ever been in, and I can't stop feeling like I'm out at sea, floating away from any stable ground I once had. I'm sorry for ruining the mood." She gives me a nervous laugh and I hate it.

"Has anyone ever told you about the myth of having different colored eyes?" I ask looking into her one mesmerizing green eye before bouncing to the blue one.

She shakes her head *no* and sighs as if the conversation is the last one she wanted to be having.

My body, no longer following my brain, reaches toward her. I close the distance between us and there it is again—the anticipation. Instead of telling her what the myth means and who told it to me, i bask in the energy between us. Our chests are so close, our inhales sync up, the rise and fall becoming a singular motion.

"What do you want tonight, Carmie?" My voice comes out all wrong, it's rough and cracked at the edges. Almost as if her conversation and questions and soft skin are chipping away at the exterior I give to everyone else in the world.

"Don't think. Don't try to give me an answer you think I want. Don't try to please other people. Just answer."

My hand slides up her thigh and back down again, another unconscious movement neither of us object to.

"I want to feel like I'm not alone, even when I'm in a room full of people." She gives me her truth in a rush of words. "I want someone's love written in big neon letters ... translating their heart to the world. I want someone to pick me, choose me, and *love* me the first time around. Not after they screw up, not after they lose me. I want it from the start. Actually—" she sits up and the fire in her eyes makes me weak.

Her words bend my body and I lift to lean on my elbows.

"I want... I want you to kiss me until the sun comes up and burns away every star in this sky. I want your hands—those distracting, perfect, ridiculous-looking hands—on my body. I want this night to be a pivotal moment in my life, even if I never see you again. I want. I want something from the movies," she confesses. "Do you think you can give that to me, Parker?"

She's breathless, and her eyelashes flicker in rapid succession.

My heart surges, and I say, "The movies aren't real, Carmie. Why do you want to chase something that isn't possible?"

Lifting her chin, as if she's the only person left on the planet defending the notion, she speaks.

"Because the possibility of magic existing, the possibility of *love* existing in that form is enough to make me get out of bed in the morning. It's enough to make me walk unbothered into a crowded room of people because there is at least *one* soul in this world who knows me. And because, Parker, I would rather be temporarily disappointed by the absence of love than never believe in it in the first place."

A heavy, intoxicating anticipation builds between us, and then she crawls toward me until she's nearly seated in my lap. She's looking down at me, and I resist the urge to pull her closer so that her frame rests on top of mine.

"So tell me, Parker. What do *you* want?"

I sit up and reach my hands out, framing her face. Her lips part as my thumbs trace and sweep across her bottom lip... everything in nature pauses for me to say these next few words: "I want to show you that you never have to please someone else unless it pleases *you* to do so. I want to show you something better than the movies, Carmie. I want to show you something *real*. I want the sunrise. With you."

The moment I say it, I can feel the truth in it, for both of us. It might not be what she wants, but I'm certain as hell it's what she needs. Leaning down, my lips meet hers in a slow, seeking kiss. The heat between us is a brand searing this moment into the history of our lives. She crawls into my lap so that her legs wrap around my waist, and we eliminate all doubt that we want the same thing.

Her hands, her hands. They are inescapable and inevitable as a storm moving over water. They travel and dance and skate across my skin until they're dragging me under the surface of common sense. Every inch of my body bends to her command due to the friction, softness, and those breathy little moans that echo around us underneath the veil of her hair.

Please. Have mercy and give me more.

She arches her body into mine, fulfilling my wish, and I fill my palms with her curves. Instead of letting my hands roam, I hold her steady, anchoring her to me. *If I'm going down with the ship, you're coming with me.* Her kisses swim up and down my neck before they become frenzied, the rolling of her hips into mine, demanding.

We sink onto the blanket and abandon the idea of coming up for air.

She gave me the passion of every star in the night sky, and I gave her the view of the sunrise in my arms.

Just like I promised.

10 / TITANIC

Carmie

May, Sedona

Red dust hides in every nook, cranny, and crevice of my body. It spirals down, down, and slides into the drain with the rest of the water.

"I got a text!" Dee screams as she runs into my bathroom, holding *my* phone. Elyse barges in next and Fallon lingers in the doorway with her coffee cup cradled between her hands, the only friend in the villa with a scrap of decency.

Elyse peers over Dee's shoulder as they both read it. I return to my shower because it's futile to stop the "meddling train" once it leaves the station.

"Carmie. You cannot fall for the rebound guy!" Elyse hops onto the marble vanity and waves my phone in the air like a piece of damning evidence in a murder trial.

Just as I'm wrapping a towel around myself, Fallon walks deeper into the bathroom and steals the phone from Elyse's hands. She reads the message, or *messages*, and bites back a smile.

"I mean, who cares? As long as it's not Mr. Dumb-Fuck Extraordinaire, I don't care who she falls for." Fallon slaps my phone into my waiting palm and flips her long hair over her shoulder.

"Don't call him that," I grumble. "He just wasn't the right guy for me."

"Honey, he ain't the right guy for anyone. Trust me." Dee adjusts her top in the mirror and gives me a look.

"Why am I the one under a microscope? Elyse spends the night with men ALL THE TIME!" I throw my hands up and toss my phone into the bedroom, far unreachable from my friends.

Fallon hops onto the vanity next to Elyse and rolls her eyes before draining her coffee and saying, "Because that's on-brand for Elyse. The more men, the more believable. If she were to call me tomorrow and tell me she was getting married, we wouldn't be putting her under the microscope, we'd be strapping her into in a straight jacket." Fallon elbows Elyse as Elyse gives an annoying nod of approval.

"Yeah, ok. I'll remember this," I mutter as I run a brush through my hair.

Dee walks over to me and pushes me down onto the stool. She takes over brushing my hair, which is a special type of torture, before parting it with her long neon nails to start the braids.

"Carm. Nobody is saying, *Stop trying every position in the Kama Sutra*, but we are saying, *Don't fall in love with the first guy to give you an orgasm in over a decade*."

They laugh while something ugly twists in my gut.

"Stop lecturing me. Don't you think I already feel like a moron for staying with Seamus so long? Don't you think this is hard enough for me? I know what he did during our relationship—more intimately than any of you do—yet I'm the one left with phantom limb pain. Even though I cut him off, I feel his existence, his *presence*, everywhere. So give me a fucking break." I narrow my watering eyes at my friends, and they all pause at my out-of-character outburst.

Fallon sucks in a breath, Elyse's eyes go wide, and Dee stops braiding my wet hair.

"Well, judging by the mess of your hair, you had one wild ride last night. So, I'm proud of you. Tell us everything." Dee breaks the tension with a soft smile in the mirror, and I finally exhale.

"Yeah, if you don't spill the details, I will indeed snap a photo of that hickey on your collarbone..." *Oh god.* I look down and see it tattooed right above my left breast. "...and I will not so accidentally send it to Mr. Dumb-Fuck Extraordinaire." Fallon shrugs her shoulders like she suggests we all get pancakes.

Elyse gives her a high-five in return.

My lips tilt up, and I start to spill all the details of one of the best nights of my life. Not long after Parker and I came together on the mountain, twice that is, we rode down to his truck and started the process all over again.

Heat rises to my cheeks at the memory, but I will never, ever, let go of the vision of my hand sliding down the foggy window as Parker wrung out every ounce of ecstasy from my body.

He checked off boxes number five, seven, and thirty-three last night.

"I've never experienced anything like it. I mean, I knew sex could feel *good*, but I never knew it could be...like that. That I could be...wild," I say with a smile that cracks my face open.

"Baby girl, you've always had the juice. Now you just know what to do with it." Dee finishes my braids and I reply with a confused, "Thank you?" She waves me off.

"Alright, alright. I can tell we're not going to get much else out of you." Elyse rolls her eyes at me before barking the rest of her orders. "We have massages, manicures, facials, and tarot readings this afternoon. *Chop-chop!*"

Everyone files out, and I'm left with the million feelings I've left unexpressed inside my chest. They're multiplying at an alarming rate, and I'm afraid my ribs will snap from the lack of available space.

Joy. Pain. Shame. Pride. Confusion. Freedom.

"Carmic."

My head snaps up, and I catch Fallon's warm gaze from the door again. "Are you ok? Do you need someone to talk to, privately?"

You are such a selfish friend, look how you're making your friend worry during her bachelorette trip. Get it together, Carmela. Stop drowning in your thoughts and feelings. Get it together.

I pinch my lips together and jump up in what I hope looks like excitement for the day ahead. Clapping my hands, I breeze past her and shout over my shoulder, "Nope! Thanks for checking in. You're one of the most sincere friends I've ever had, Fally. Thank you."

She doesn't buy my lie and I avoid her narrowed eyes following me around the room, watching every outfit I toss over my shoulder in an attempt to find something to wear. Just as I'm about to toss on a cheetah print romper, strong arms circle my waist, and I feel Fallon give me the tightest hug of my life. All I can do is blink back the tears because I can count on one hand the times Fallon has hugged me.

It only lasts a heartbeat, and then she whispers, "Your heart is a deep ocean of secrets, but I'm not afraid of going there with you. Promise me you'll talk to me when you're ready?"

Nodding my head, I feel her arms loosen and watch her leave my room. She's right. There are so many secrets submerged in this heart of mine.

Parker jumped into the deep end. And I'm afraid I don't remember how to swim.

11 / FORREST GUMP

PARKER

MAY, Sedona

My hands run through my hair, *again*, and I catch Eden's sideways glance at me before he sips from his extra hot and bitter matcha latte.

"Spit it out. What's eating you, bruv?" He sets his drink down, and I'm surprised he also sets down his carefree vibe. The other men walk over to join us, but he flicks his chin up and redirects them to their table.

"Do we have room for one more person to join us..." I can't even finish the statement.

"Join us?" Eden attempts to put the missing pieces together without me.

"Never mind." I wave my hand and cross my arms. "It was a ridiculous idea anyway, I don't know what I was thinking, and I haven't even heard back from her."

"Wait," Eden sits up taller. "Are you talking about bringing that bird on our film expedition? To the race? I'm imagining things, right?" His eyes bug out of his head and I slide his latte away from him. I don't understand why he insists on drinking caffeine, he never needs it.

"Forget it," I mumble and look out the window of the coffee shop. The red rocks are mocking me, looking down at me for the vulnerability I displayed last night.

"Mate. I mean this with all of my heart. If you told me you were running off to Vegas tonight to marry her, I would be less surprised than you asking me if it's a good idea to bring her along to Europe." He shakes his head as if he needs to wake up from a bad dream.

"I didn't ask you if it was a good idea. I asked if we had room." I narrow my eyes on him, pissed off at his inability to listen.

"No, I think you were asking for my opinion on the matter. You can crunch numbers yourself and figure out if we have *room*." He puts the word room in air quotes, and it only pisses me off more.

"My opinion, since you didn't ask, but need it, is this. I love that you're embracing a little chaos, loosening the reigns on what you call a life. Your bloody hands must be a wreck from how hard you constantly grip the rope, trying to control every damn thing. So yeah, I think it's a great idea. Bring her."

I blink once, twice. He smiles in return and shrugs his shoulders.

Surprise and then relief floods my lungs.

Clearing my throat, I say, "She hasn't said yes yet, so, don't get your hopes up."

"Jesus, you're such a fuckin' wanker, always expecting the worst of situations and people." Eden swipes his latte back and drains half of the grass water in one go.

"Expect the worst, and you'll always be prepared for the worst," I smirk.

"That is *so* not how that expression is supposed to go.

Even I know that." He shakes his head and lifts his head to bring the rest of the guys over to the table.

"I'm not a smart man ... but I know what love is!" Cillian slaps my shoulder, sending my black coffee over the rim of my cup.

"Stop eavesdropping, or I'll make you dig the line by yourself on the mountain next week." I shoot him a death glare that he waves off.

What is it with Europeans? They don't take any threats seriously—it's all banter to them.

But, God. He's right. The idea of traveling and having her with me has already taken root in my mind. It's invasive. Every dystopian movie harps on how contagious hope is...but I disagree. Hope can be extinguished. But ideas? They can be footprints in wet cement. If you don't get rid of them fast enough, they harden, and you're stuck with them.

For better or worse.

She stuck her hand right in that wet cement and I didn't wash it away fast enough. Now I'm stuck with it.

The only left to do is wait for her answer.

As I look up at the red mountains around me, I feel a familiar sense of foreboding. Her answer, as much as I hate to admit it, will either define or destroy me.

Carmie

MAY, Sedona

My phone burns a hole in my *Blair Ritchey* white leather purse. It might as well be a ticking time bomb until I give Parker a response. I swear to God, if someone were to make a movie of my life right now, they'd say, "Add in the special *tick-tock* sound effect right here! Perfect suspense, make sure she feels the pressure!"

Assholes.

Today 7:15 AM

Come with me to Europe.

Parker…

It will take a few weeks, tops. You can take a break from your life. Get some perspective.

That's what mountains are for. Think about it. Then call me.

I'm about to respond, let Parker down gently, something like ... *That was an incredible experience last night, but I can't ride along for a month in Italy and Austria and wherever else the wind blows you while you risk your life on the side of a mountain. Thanks for the offer and good luck! Don't die, please.*

Or maybe something like *Good luck, pencil me in for the next trip. I'm sure I'll be a more enjoyable and mentally sane person by then.*

Groaning, I keep my phone in my purse and get out of the car. I follow everyone into the purple brick building with a large mural of a crystal ball on the side of it.

> Are you asking me, or telling me to come with you?

> I'm asking, Carmie. I'm asking you to come with me ... please.

> I thought you told me to stop being a people pleaser.

> Touché. But Carmie?

> Yeah?

> I promise the entire trip will be focused on pleasing you instead of the other way around.

Swallowing past the lump in my throat, I look up at the twinkling bell chiming our arrival in the clean, white lobby of the building. Ahead of me is a reception desk, to the left is a large pair of raw amethyst wings that take my breath away, and a row of chairs to the right.

We file into the chairs and I have an automatic smile on my face, a pleasant mask, as I work to untie the massive knot in my chest without detection.

"Carmie? Are you ready?"

A woman with a shaved head and large hoop earrings in her ears stands in front of me. I didn't even notice that all of my friends already headed back to individual rooms for their readings.

Dee chose a spirit guide reading.

Elyse selected a psychic cleansing.

Fallon picked an energy clearing.

I decided on a tarot reading.

"I'm Willow. Follow me!" The woman radiates sunshine and instantly eases the tension in my muscles.

Following her through the brightly lit hallway, I turn into her office decorated in rich earth tones.

Do you want to know a secret? I used to love tarot cards. I used to keep a secret deck and hidden library of mystical studies underneath my bed when I was in high school. Asking for a deck of cards felt safer than asking anyone in my life for advice, so I learned the hidden meanings and symbols on each card. Everyone except Carson of course, my oldest brother, who even occasionally indulged in my mystical little tricks. I guess it's because, since the day I was born, he took me under his wing. Literally. When my mother put me in his arms after I was born, he refused to give me back to her.

A few years ago, I asked him to choose a card before he proposed to his now-wife, and *The Tower* came up. He stopped indulging in it after that day.

Anyway. I loved my deck until Seamus found it one night. My intuition screamed at me to *protect the cards!* But I shoved that instinct down and pretended like I didn't know what they were in the vain hope he would lose interest.

He held the cards the way a toddler does—as if they know something is precious to you yet they're going to destroy it anyway. I lacked the courage to tell him that my emotional fingerprints were all over the pentacles, cups, and swords. That it offered me more guidance and support than the people I shared DNA with ever did.

So he ended up flicking each card across the room in the trash, thinking he was impressing me with his card-throwing skills before he went back to choosing a movie for us to watch.

"So, Carmie. Do you have a specific question you'd like to bring forward today? Or would you like to see where the cards take us?" Willow looks at me with big doe eyes and I nod my head. My palms start to sweat, and I rub them on my thighs.

"I suppose. I suppose I do have a question."

There's a reason I don't go to therapy. It's encouraged for every therapist to have a colleague in the profession to talk to.... after my near overdose last year, I stopped going. I don't like the role reversal of sitting on the other side of someone.

Or perhaps, I just haven't found the right avenue of healing yet.

But, I suck in a big breath and word vomit the question at the bright yellow cards in front of me.

"Am I supposed to go with Parker on this trip? Even if it means I leave everything I've ever known? Even if it means I'll officially be ending the only relationship I've ever been in? Because if I go...and I'm not saying I will...it'll be the final domino tipped over. It'll be the butterfly effect and that terrifies me. So what I'm asking..."

Willow's hands shuffle the deck, and she smiles at me with more warmth than I feel I deserve.

"What I'm truly asking is. Do I go, even though I don't know where it will lead? Do I owe myself that? Or is that selfish? Should—"

Willow stops shuffling and clears her throat. I close my mouth and take a breath.

"I think the cards understand. I felt so much energy radiating from them while you were speaking, they're ready. Cut the deck for me, please."

I grab a pile of cards and split it in half.

Willow asks me to choose a pile, and I bite my lip.

"What if I choose the wrong one?"

She tilts her head at me and asks, "What makes you think there is ever a right and wrong choice? They are merely neutral options. *You* assign meaning to them."

I close my eyes and attempt to *feel* my intuition. But it's like walking into a dark room, feeling around for the light switch. I *know* it's there, but I can't connect with it. There's no lightbulb moment, I'm fumbling around in the dark, disconnected from my higher intelligence.

So, I pick the left pile because the cliché "left is always lucky" might hold. Maybe.

Willow fans the cards out in front of me.

"Do you like poetry, Carmie?"

I nod my head.

"This is called the Robert Frost spread. You strike me as a gal who likes to get deep." She smiles, clearly pleased with the direction of this reading and her functioning intuition. Unlike mine.

"*Two roads diverged in a yellow wood*, choose two cards. They will represent each choice of the path. Keep them face down right here," she taps in front of me.

Annoyed by my inability to find my inner compass, I think of my dilemma and select two cards at random.

"*I doubted if I should ever come back*, now pull a card to represent what you need to leave behind and never come back to."

I follow her lead.

"*I took the one less traveled by*, pull a card to indicate which option is the least chosen of the two, or what less-traveled may look like in your decision."

My fingers roam over the spread and a warm buzzing sensation fills my palm. Thinking it's a fluke, I move my hand away, and the feeling disappears. Pursing my lips, I hover my hand back to the original card and feel the warmth. I grab that card and put it off to the side.

"*And that has made all the difference*, what difference will it make if you pick the less traveled path? That's what this last card will represent."

A card calls to me and I grab it faster than the others.

I finally smile. Pressing the record on my phone, I get ready for Destiny to reveal herself.

Willow flips the cards and explains their more profound meanings. With each major and minor card shown, my heart beats faster. I nod my head and bite my cheek.

But on the inside? I'm fuming.

I pay and walk out of the building without another word.

It's just like what Carson used to tell me, "Flip a coin and the moment it's in the air you know exactly the answer you were hoping to get. That's your decision. It doesn't matter what the coin lands on."

The moment I watched her purple nails turn over each card, I realized I wanted to see my future with Parker written in the stars. I wanted to see a blazing, *Yes! Go with him to Italy! To hell with your family, your job, your past entanglements.*

I wanted those weathered and magical cards to prove to me that I could be the main character in the movie of my life.

But that's not what they spelled out for me, at all.

And you know what? I'm sick of it. I'm sick of trying to help everyone around me. I'm sick of trying to keep everyone happy, a balancing act I never succeed at. I'm *sick* of asking for permission.

Ignoring the warning from the cards, I pull out my phone and text Parker.

Yes.

13 / WHIPLASH

PARKER

JULY, JFK Airport

It feels like yesterday Carmie shocked the hell out of me by agreeing to join me in Europe for a few weeks. Not only do I have the biggest race of the season, but I'm filming a documentary with my team in the Dolomite Mountains of Italy.

Even though it's been three months of long-distance, I feel like the luckiest man in the world. She's offered me friendship, romance, and everything in between. It feels like she's been in my life much longer even though it's the last day of July.

We took turns visiting each other over the last eleven weeks. I flew out to visit her condo in Nashville in June, and her friends welcomed me with open arms. She came out to visit me in Arizona a few weeks ago, before filling her schedule with patients and clients preparing for her vacation time.

I'm waiting at gate D28 in front of the sunrise. It feels like a full-circle moment. *Sunrises will always be our thing.*

"We'd like to welcome boarding group one to Flight 3470."

Any moment now, I'll spot her hair out of the corner of my eye. *Red, Red, and Red*. It'll probably be a little messy as if it refused to conform to any singular style. I hope she's wearing more than one pattern, carrying a bag full of books, candy, and treasures.

We agreed to meet at JFK before we fly off to Europe. Together.

Looking down at the small bunch of peonies in my hand, I start to get nervous. Not about the flowers, I know they're her favorite, and I paid a small fortune for a greenhouse to have them ready, but I'm nervous about traveling with someone.

It's so...intimate.

What if she likes to talk through the entire flight? What if she sleeps and her mouth never closes, and she drools all over me? What if she's one of those women who complain about every single little detail?

But what I'm most nervous about is, *What if she can't stand being with me all day? What if she thinks she made a mistake?*

As I stare at the sun rising over the horizon in New York, I shake my head. I know, in my gut, that my nerves are wrong. It's the same before a race. There's such a fine and finicky line between fear and excitement.

I remind myself that I *know* Carmie. We've talked every single night since she flew back home after that first weekend in Sedona. I call, a ritual and routine, just to listen to her talk about her day, the hospital, and how she wonders if there's anything *more* out there for her beyond being a therapist.

"Group two passengers, please step forward."

You know, most people think God can only be found in a church. But, between us, I can tell you that God is with me the moment I hear her voice pick up the phone. God lounges in the comfortable pauses between our conversations. He's filled with pride every time Carmie tells me, *I've never told anyone else that before, thank you*. God doesn't have to shoulder her burdens during those few hours because I gladly wear them around my neck like a cross I was born to bear.

I don't ever offer her advice, even when she asks. I just listen. Maybe there will be a day or a time when the roles are reversed, and I catch myself telling her exactly how I feel. But for now, I keep my cards held to my chest, content to let her voice be the best bookend imaginable for my day.

I begin to pace a little in front of the windows and I check my phone. I feel a pressure building in my chest, but I walk faster to ease my paranoia. She operates on a different standard of time compared to the rest of the world, and while I find most of her quirks endearing, I struggle to view the concept of time as loosely as she does. She tells me I'm a Capricorn as if that means anything before she uses being a Pisces as an excuse.

I'd take the middle seat for that woman, and that's saying a lot considering how tall I am. And if she asked me to be a pretzel for the long journey, I'd gladly bend. But if she makes me miss this flight, I might be forced to reconsider her company. A man has his limits, after all.

That's a lie. I'd get the next flight, give her the silent treatment until she wore me down, and then move on. I'm an absolute fool for her.

Instead of flying with my bike and the rest of my kit for the film project, I sent it along early via a special freight service. Eden and the boys flew out yesterday to receive it at the pickup spot. They insisted I come with them. They assured me Carmie was an adult and could make it on her own. Truth is, I wanted to start the journey with her. Even if she does cut it dangerously close.

My heart starts to race as I watch the last few rows of eager travelers line up at our gate.

"Last boarding call, I repeat, *last* boarding call for all passengers."

I'm dialing her number before the announcement is finished, praying she'll come skipping around the corner waving her phone in her hand as if she meant to give me a heart attack and this was all just a sick joke.

Pick up, Carm. Come on. Where are you?

She texted me when she was at BNA about to check her bag. What the hell happened?

"This user's mailbox is currently full, you are unable to leave a message. Please try again later."

I crush my phone in my hand and dial again. And again. And AGAIN. Each time I reach the same automated message, my blood pressure skyrockets as my heart plummets.

This can't be happening.

"Sir?"

"Just wait a second!" I snap at the flight agent.

Pinching the bridge of my nose, I try her again.

"Sir, we're about to lock the gate. If you're boarding..."

"For the love of all things holy, please just wait a fucking minute," I say to the agent.

I look down the hallway leading to our gate and feel a burn spread behind my eyes. Pulling up the location she shared with me last night anticipating the trip, I see the blue dot...*moving*. There's only one reason she'd be going north instead of east.

Correction: one *person* she'd be going North for. Only one person on this planet with a gravitational pull stronger than our connection. One person, I will never, ever, accept coming in second place to.

Fury and embarrassment burn hotter than the desire to get an explanation from her.

"Sir, this is your last chance."

When I confirm for the third time where the dot is headed, my mouth drops open in disbelief and my heart full-on stops. Turning my phone on silent, I throw it in my bag and take a breath. Walking up to the gate agent, I hand her the peonies and apologize.

"Were you waiting for someone?" She asks before smelling the fresh flowers. I head down the tunnel and say over my shoulder, "Yeah, I was. But I won't make that mistake again."

Ever.

14 / SWEET HOME ALABAMA

Carmie

AUGUST, Cleveland

S taring at the monitor, at the steady rise and fall of a
heartbeat across a horizontal line, I wrap my arms around
my ribcage and turn away.

Looking out the window, I think of Zach Bryan and
Maggie Rogers singing, "Dawns." I'm haunted by the lyrics,
but I'm equally haunted by the sight of this sunrise.

Instead of viewing it from the window seat, next to the
man my heart *wants* to be with, I'm viewing it from a hospital
room next to a man my head convinced me to be with. The
man obligation chained me to.

The moment I stepped into BNA early this morning,
Carson called me in a panic. Carson, the cool-headed future
politician, was *breathless*.

"Seamus has been in an accident. It's bad, Carm. It's terrible. You have to come home...please." My gut twisted and I
jumped into action. Unconsciously. I didn't stop to think. Or
rather, I didn't stop to *feel* my way through the situation. I

moved on autopilot, those two decades of my past waking up from hibernation and guiding me back to Cleveland.

Time paused long enough at the ticket counter for me to turn over my shoulder and see my suitcases for Italy lined up behind me. Two bags, packed to the brim, my passport resting in my palm, so I wouldn't forget it.

That was Parker's idea.

He said *I can't imagine this trip without you. So please, Carmie, put that passport where you can see it because I know you, and every so often your beautiful brain doesn't remember where you put things. If you can handle getting here, I promise I'll take care of everything else for the rest of the trip. You can let go and just* be.

Tears filled my eyes as I turned my back on the promise I made him. As I sped to my new gate, the scar tissue Seamus left on my heart began to ache. Matter of fact, it burned with a sense of urgency, a sense of duty, and perhaps, even a little fear.

Please don't die. Not like this. That's all I kept thinking. *Please don't die.*

So imagine my surprise upon arriving at The Cleveland Clinic this morning to see Carson and Seamus laughing in his recovery room.

I stood there, about twenty paces outside the door, just looking at them. Seamus had a cast on his wrist and there were a few lacerations on his forehead that were already stitched up. Do you want to know what this "life and death" situation was?

A small car accident.

I doubt Fallon would even declare it as a trauma. She'd probably pass the case off to a resident, and that resident would hand it off to a student.

But the moment Seamus saw me, he crumbled. Carson fell quiet and left the room, giving us space. He gave me a quick hug on his way out and went to get coffee for everyone.

I lingered on the threshold of the recovery room. Seamus began to sniff and wipe at his eyes with his uninjured hand. He held it out to me, a silent plea for support.

What is it about men crying? Why is it so difficult to turn away from them when it happens? I know I'm being manipulated and yet our history, our scars, and that phantom limb guide me forward, desperate to be reunited with their counterpart.

His hand found mine, and I hated that I sighed in relief at the contact. We didn't say anything for the first hour. I sat next to him as he closed his eyes and fell into a deep sleep. My father was the one who insisted on getting Seamus a full work up—making sure he treated him like the second *son* that he is to my family.

As my adrenaline faded, I felt my emotions drift to the surface of my consciousness. When somebody is in a state of fight or flight, or survival mode, their nervous system is smart enough to repress their emotions.

But now? There's a neon *Open for Business* sign flickering over the window of my heart, and I'm afraid of whom I'm going to see walk through first.

Anger. Regret. Fear?

The emotions all sweep in at once, searching for someone to blame. I almost buckle at the onslaught of their intensity. One emotion I'll do anything to avoid makes the bell jingle above the door in my chest as it stomps through.

Shame.

Shaking my head, I realize I never had a chance. I will always be weak when it comes to my family and the people they've brought into my orbit. Perhaps it's my destiny, to abandon myself so that I can serve other people. That's the big argument, isn't it? Individualism vs. family responsibility?

A small voice in the back of my mind that sounds suspiciously like Parker disagrees. I silence it.

Carson enters the room with a tray of coffee. His smile is too bright for my unstable mental state. He wakes Seamus up, and they start talking about business, politics, lobbying, the market, literally *everything*, except the elephant in the room.

I'm staring at them, lost in a storm of my thoughts before Carson turns to face me. He offers me a coffee and then pinches his eyebrows together at my outstretched hand.

"Why aren't you wearing your ring?" There's a bit of a fatherly bite to his tone, and it startles me back into the moment.

"What ring?" The cup burns my palm, but I don't move. I don't even dare to breathe.

Carson rolls his eyes and says, "I don't have time for games, C-Bear. Where is your engagement ring?"

My eyes flick over to Seamus, and he gives me a smug smile that makes my spine crawl. *No.*

I ... may ... have avoided telling my family about the broken engagement and this little shit is now capitalizing on my avoidance.

"I ended the engagement." I stand up as tall as I can, preparing for battle.

Carson's bottom lip drops for a millisecond before he steels his expression.

"It's fine. This is fine. This can be managed. You're here, so obviously you still care. Nobody has to know you ended it."

"But I know!" I nearly yell. My hand shakes and small droplets of coffee drip down the sides of the cup. "I'm here because you made it seem like he," I point to Seamus, "was two seconds from dying! And don't talk about my future like it's some political move. I am a human being, I don't need to be *managed.*"

Seamus' mouth tilts down as he looks at the coffee stains on my cream pants. "Carmela, you're making a mess. Control yourself. This is why I didn't mention anything, Carson. She hasn't been herself, and I would rather not worry you. I've got it under control, keep the wedding date and the plans your family has already made."

My breath lodges in my chest and I feel like the room is caving in on me. Carson looks at me with a crease between his eyebrows before rising and walking over to me.

"Is this true? Are you having your...episodes again?"

Episodes, as in, *taking pills to escape your life. Avoiding your family to avoid your future.*

Shaking my head, he ignores me and guides me outside the room by my elbow. It makes me feel like a child, but I have nothing left in my energy reservoir to deflect him.

Carson shuts the door behind us and faces me with an empathetic look on his face.

"Carm. I know you two have had your *issues*, to put it gently."

That's it. That's what snaps me out of my spiral. "Our *issues*? He cheats on me. ALL the time! That is not *my* issue, Carson. It is his *choice*. I have no issue with it because *my* choice is to leave!"

"You know you can't just walk away, Carmela. This has been planned for a long time. It's just a happy coincidence you two enjoyed one another's company. Do you think Dad's campaign can survive without Seamus' family funding him? Do you think we can keep our lifestyle without the backing of the multi-conglomerate tech business we've partnered with? That's all because of Seamus ... and it hinges on you being a good girl and doing what's necessary. It's a win-win for everyone involved."

"You are forgetting someone! Me!" I nearly shout.

Carson's eyes widen before he schools his features and looks around at the staff in the hallway.

"Keep. Your. Voice. Down. You are making a *scene*." He smiles, "You've loved him your entire life Carm. What more do you require? The illusion of freedom? A little rebellion? Seriously. How long is that going to last? You're going to give up everything you are, everything you've been, to escape your fate? How do you know you won't be even more miserable on the other side of this fantasy of yours? The grass is *not* greener, Carm. I can tell you that right now. So please, grow up. *This* is your happy ending." He waves to Seamus behind the glass window. "This is the romance you've always dreamed of. So come back to Ohio and stop messing around!"

His words settle into my bloodstream, and each breath I suck in feels like a tiny paper cut slashing across my windpipe.

Shaking my head, I mumble, "I don't want to. Please. Just *listen* to me. Just *see* me." My vision begins to fade, and I know, I just know, I'm going to end up at the mercy of those pulling the strings in my life.

With another ragged breath, the world gets quiet, and I land in my brother's arms, the *Open for Business* sign above my heart, officially flickering out.

Carmie

AUGUST, Cleveland

T his time, the screen I stare at is my own. My steady
      heartbeat marches across the screen, one breath at a
time. Sometimes, I wish it would just stop.

It's exhausting.

"What if I were to tell you that I didn't want to marry
someone who sleeps with other women? What if I were to tell
you that I'm not in love with Seamus like I was as a child?
What if I told you I was done? I want to be *done*."

I whisper the words as I stare at the screen, not bothering
to see if Carson is sitting next to me. There are two universal
truths in my life. One, the sun will rise every morning despite
the tragedies that happened the night before. Two, I can count
on Carson to be there for me in a time of need—even when I
hate him.

His voice holds no anger or bitterness as he responds and
indulges in this merry-go-round of a conversation.

"Then I would tell you that sleeping with other people
isn't the sin you've made it out to be. Marriages contain

different definitions, you just need to find the definition that works for both of you. I would tell you that you are right—"

Hope blooms in my chest as I turn my cheek to look at his profile.

"—about how being in love with someone at ten, or sixteen, is different than loving them at thirty. I would also tell you to grow the hell up, Carmela. This isn't a movie. I would tell that you don't have a choice...being *done* isn't an option. Do you want everyone in our family and our community to think you belong in a rehab facility? These erratic decisions of yours are making you look unwell."

There it is, the trump card. He always comes back to it—either because he's afraid he's going to lose me for good one of these days or as a way to control me. But it's a confusing thing when everyone in your life reflects an image of yourself you don't recognize.

Why would everyone think I need help if I don't? Why would everyone insist on this marriage if it wasn't going to work out in the end?

"Enough." My lower lip wobbles and I close my eyes.

Carson turns toward me, plants a kiss on my temple, and is about to leave the room when the nurse practitioner walks in.

"Good morning! Gave us all quite the scare, Carmela. Is this a good time to review your lab reports?" She smiles at me and I wonder if her life is exponentially less complicated than my own.

Carson has his head down on his phone and one foot out the door before Nurse Perky stops him.

"You'll want to hear this too, being the father and all!"

Both of our eyes snap to her so fast and the emotional temperature in the room plummets. Nurse Perky drops her smile and glances down at my paperwork again.

"It says here, Mrs. D'Angelo, and that would make you—"

"Ms. D'Angelo, Not Mrs." I croak out.

Nurse Perky finally picks up what everyone else is putting down and laughs like a blithering idiot. I've worked on more than a thousand charts over my tenure as a therapist and I've never—not once—made a mistake like this.

"Well, ah, congratulations. We ran your blood work, and other than being slightly anemic, you are healthy and ready to be discharged. Do you have an OB yet? We can refer you."

She keeps talking but my eyes lock with Carson and I can see him doing the math. He's staring at me, silently asking in the way only a sibling can communicate, *When did you break up with Seamus?*

I shake my head and lower my gaze, refusing to answer.

He puts his phone in his pocket and interlaces his hands behind his head as if I am the largest pain in the ass on the planet. As if his day job of trying to fix the American government is an easier task than being my brother.

"Please leave us," he whispers to the nurse, and her mouth flounders for a moment before she leaves.

The door closes with a soft, *click*, but I still jump out of my skin.

"Well," he steps in closer, his eyes never leaving my face, "this is going to be fine. We can spin this. We can ah- we can move the wedding up. Voters are progressive these days anyways. It's chic. Modern. We'll be fine."

His brain starts working overtime, the way politicians use any situation to their advantage. The way they protect their image—our *family's image*—at all costs.

The words tumble from my lips before I can reconsider them.

"It's not Seamus' baby."

Do you know what it sounds like the moment a glass breaks in a fancy restaurant? That piercing, high-pitched *crash* followed by silence. That's what my hospital room is filled with—a horrible, crushing *nothingness*.

"You have to get rid of it." Carson's voice is low and he looks over his shoulder, making sure the NP shut the door on her way out.

"Carson, you didn't even ask me—"

"I'm not asking you, Carm. I'm *telling* you. This is what happens when you play stupid games. You get stupid prizes. I told you that you weren't responsible enough to handle being on your own. How could you?"

Something hot and wicked rises in my chest, but he holds up his hand.

"Do you want to have this baby with a man who will no doubt hate his or her very existence? Seamus isn't stupid, he's going to know it's not his...and even if he didn't figure it out, could you live with this secret?"

My stomach roiling already confirms that. *No, no I could not.*

"This is why I'm telling you, I don't want to marry him. I'll be fine on my own!" I scramble, twisting the sheets around my fingers.

"You have *never* done anything on your own, Carm!" Carson gets in my face and his words are as hot as his anger. As sharp as his disbelief.

"Even in Nashville, you were set up with a condo from *our* funds. You were gifted a highly coveted position at Vanderbilt from *our* connections. Your degree, your status, your research, all of it was offered up on a silver platter! Are you delusional? Do you think you can be a single mother? Do you think whatever one-night stand happened to get you pregnant will give a shit about you in a year? In five or ten?"

Oh god, Parker.

I scramble from the bed, IVs ripping out of their ports, as I look for my phone. Catching onto my mission, Carson beats me to it and holds it up.

"Call the prick and see what he has to say. Do it. I guarantee he drops you like a bad habit." My brother lifts an eyebrow at me in a challenge and my eyes narrow in response.

"He isn't like that. He would *never*."

Even though I just left him at the airport.

"Prove it." Carson flicks my phone at me.

My stomach sinks and I fight back the urge to throw up when I see the missed calls and texts from Parker. *Fuck*. I wanted to call him, at least text him, after I checked in on Seamus...and then...and then...

I bury myself in a landslide of denial and delusion.

It's fine. I'll call and everything will be fine. I know him. He won't react like Carson says.

Tapping, *call*, I pray I get him in-between flights.

The phone rings, and rings, and rings and I'm about to burst into tears as my brother crosses his arms. But nobody answers.

I'm not sure if that's better or worse as I hang up and drop my head.

Carson's face softens and he sits next to me. He grabs my phone and puts it in his pocket, before dragging me into a deep hug.

I shudder and let the tears go.

"You have to do the right thing for our family, Carm." He strokes my hair and I close my eyes again. "That's the most important thing in this life. I'll go with you, ok?"

The tears sting the corners of my eyes as I bury my face in his pressed shirt.

How could I be so stupid? How could I forget to track my ovulation cycle before that night with Parker? It's all my fault. Everything is always my fault.

Carson pulls away and puts his palms on my shoulder, his hazel eyes meet my face. "Do the *right* thing, Carmela. Our family can't handle a scandal like this. It's an election year. Think about Dad. About Grandpa. Generations of hard-working public servants...*destroyed* by your choice." Carson makes the sign of the cross as if needing to absolve himself for being in proximity to me.

Pulling away, with the last bit of fight in my blood I mumble, "And how are those family values feeling about *this* solution? Hmm?"

He runs a hand up and down his jaw before sighing.

"Carm. There is no other option unless you'd like to be completely cut off from this family. And from the sound of it, you don't have a backup plan. What are you going to do? Burden your friends in Nashville to take care of you? Take care of a baby? I know you're not that selfish. Not that irresponsible. You won't have anyone else like Seamus to take care of you. Take the deal."

For a moment, a shadow crosses my mind as I consider the possibility of leaning on my friends. Carson catches it and uses his last line of defense.

"I need you," he says on an exhale. "Please, you have the power to save this family and the power to keep us together. Don't throw it away by leaving Seamus. Don't throw it away by having a baby born from a stupid mistake. You know what the right thing to do is."

It's the holy trifecta: *I need you. Save me. Please.*

I told you I was weak.

I didn't stand a chance.

I curl into a ball on my side and fall asleep thinking the same thought over and over again.

If this is what's right, *why does it feel so wrong?*

Carmie

AUGUST, Cleveland

"Doesn't it get old? Asking people day, after day, the same questions? I shouldn't be admitting this, but I find it tiresome as if the marrow in my bones is sick of hearing myself ask my patients these questions..." My words fade into the space between us.

"Miss, all I need is an answer to the question. I must hear you say the answer before we continue with the process."

"Of course, you agree that it gets old, what am I thinking? I waited four hours today in that waiting room out there," I tilt my head toward the door and suck down a large breath before she can ask me the same question again. "Did you know that *Guy's Grocery Games* is playing on repeat today? It's a marathon out there!" My voice escapes one octave too high, and I sit on my hands to repress the crawling urge to pick at a scab on my chin.

Again.

"*Guys' Grocery Games*, can you believe it? Beyond being an embarrassing use of alliteration, it blasted through the waiting room like an unwelcome family member at Thanksgiving. I know, *I know*, it's not anyone's fault here how long we have to wait, but can't we do something about *that*? What I need, what all of us women in here need, is to hear our name being called. That's it. Maybe some Mozart. Or perhaps, a good movie. Possibly something uplifting? Perhaps a romantic comedy? I have a list if you'd like…"

I don't give her my coveted list of favorite movies, instead, my mouth runs faster.

"It's odd, and maybe it's just me, but the relief of hearing my name was too quickly replaced by the fear of what waits for me on the other side of this door. Have you heard that before? Is that common?"

My eyes bounce around the plain room. It reminds me of the hospital where I did my clinicals.

"Ms. D'Angelo. Were you, or were you not—"

"When people come here, I doubt they are eager to learn about *Sharon's secret Caesar salad dressing* her wife taught her. No offense, but I refuse to believe that four hours of *Guy's Grocery Games* is the best this facility can do. I'm sure of it! Don't you agree? I'm sorry if it's your favorite show. What am I talking about, HA! Of course, it's not your favorite show. Who wakes up and gets excited about—"

"*Miss*." The woman across from me, where I usually sit in these situations, is losing her patience.

I can see it etched on her heavy dark brow the way a thunderstorm rolls through the Midwest: suddenly and then all at once.

Biting my lip, I offer her a moment of relief.

"I know what you are asking. I also know that it's taking my brain and my heart a moment to arrive in tandem. Please."

Her brow doesn't soften, but she doesn't ask again right away. I'm trying, I *am*. But the answer isn't just the answer. The answer is hidden between my manic rambling and the first few bars of my left ribcage where the truth remains a silent prisoner.

I've thrown away the key because I don't trust myself with it to begin with.

It's my fault.

"Would you like to know how this all happened? Why I'm here today?" I meet her eyes and refuse to blink.

Even in this circumstance, I'm more attuned to meeting her needs than my very own...

"No. That is all *too much information*. I would like you to answer if anyone—" She looks at her watch again.

"They say Sedona is a magical place. That it's *Disneyland* for the spiritual types. Are you spiritual? I'm not really. My family raised me to be Catholic which means they dressed me up in a white dress, handed me over to a stranger, and let him dunk me in the water to wash away sin. What they don't tell you is that they replace the grace with guilt. I guess that's why I turned toward spirituality. It offers me more options, less fire, and brimstone, you know?"

Thank god, she doesn't answer.

"Well, Sedona. It's this place of healing, which is why my best friend Fallon decided to do a Bachelorette trip there. She's sober, which is incredible. What she went through with her fiancé would make even the most skeptical of love believe in the potential of it again..."

"Did someone, anyone, coerce you—" she rushes in a poor attempt to get her job done.

"I'm a therapist and I think, in a way, I've spent my whole life learning how to help *treat* people. Even to my detriment sometimes, I can admit that. But Sedona, the land itself, *and* the people find a way of *healing* you. Even when you don't ask for it. Even when you don't expect it."

The woman grinds her jaw for a moment and I start to feel that Catholic guilt surface at how my story is inconvenient at best, fucking irritating at worst. But I can't stop. I'm afraid if I don't say this to the nurse across from me, I won't ever say it.

That I won't be allowed to say it.

"I met someone, and you know what? His presence *felt* healing. Or, I had been with the wrong person for so long that this new man was a mirage in the middle of the desert. A vision created by a desperate desire. I'm a fish out of water in that place, literally. A Pisces can't last in those conditions, and can't trust herself. But, he was the right person, at the very worst time. So I guess, that makes him the wrong person. Yet, I couldn't say no. I had to have *one* night, just one, where I could pretend my heart wasn't sold off to another man. A man I wanted so badly to forget. Parker was the right person for the job."

"He *was*?" The nurse asks, her eyebrow lifting in a perfect combination of curiosity and accusation.

"Was." I bite the corner of my lip.

"So, Carmela, it's time." The nurse exhales and annunciates her words with precision. The question she asks women every single day, for eight hours a day. "Did anyone coerce you into coming here today?"

My heart races and my eyes blink too fast. From her vantage point, my lips are turning white at the corners, my eyes filling and silently emptying down my flushed cheeks.

Her sensitivity training kicks in and she softens. "I have to know. We can't move forward unless I know." Her voice drops and she reaches across the small space and pats my bouncing knee with a gentle touch.

Letting my chin drop, my hair falls in front of my face like a curtain shielding me from the inevitability of this moment—if only for a second longer. A second, because it's all I need to remember how it felt underneath the stars with him. How it felt when he moved inside of me, fingers tightly gripping mine, unraveling desires I had long since abandoned. When his lips spoke my name and made every nerve ending in my body *come alive*. The way his eyes, so warm, so present, dragged me up from the secret depth of my despair.

"He was my life raft," I whisper as I look up at the beige ceiling tile and bright medical lights.

That second of remembrance is all I need before I remember how I ruined any chance I had with him.

My back is up against the wall and I know I have nobody to blame but myself. But for the first time in my life, I wish someone would reach out a hand and say, "nobody puts baby in the corner."

Lifting my chin, I meet the nurse's eyes, and lasso the lie. Holding it tight, I force it into submission and answer her so that I can get this over with.

"No. I was not coerced by anyone."

She nods her head and taps the mouse, finishing my medical chart. "Thank you, Carmela. Now let's discuss the next steps before you come back in twenty four hours for your abortion."

17 / REMEMBER ME

Carmie

AUGUST, Nashville

E lyse picks me up from Nashville three days after my procedure. I was too far along to take the medication. Carson wanted me to stay in Ohio. Seamus begged me to move back in with him. But, rather than face either of them, I just left.

Two of my specialties. Running away and hiding.

"I don't want to talk about it," I say, and yet the tears build and fall.

Elyse leans over the center council of her BMW and wipes them off my cheek with a tenderness that only makes me sink further into myself.

"We don't have to talk. We can just be together," she comforts me.

She shifts the car into drive and I reach across to take her hand. She squeezes it and I let myself come undone.

Distance doesn't make the heart grow fonder; distance makes the heart gain perspective.

The more miles I put between my family, the abortion

clinic, and the memory of that day, the more I clear the debris on the windshield of my mind. I won't dwell on the details.

I won't recall the way the doctor did an ultrasound beforehand and asked for the third time if I wanted to see the baby.

I won't recall the way I listened to one song on repeat until the conscious sedation kicked in.

I won't recall any of it.

Not right now.

"Elyse."

She stops at a red light and looks at me with knowing eyes.

"I didn't want to do it," I whisper the words.

The admission slips out with a fresh batch of tears and she nods her head.

"I just want to disappear," I manage to say.

Regret covers me like a wet blanket, weighing my eyelids down, and draining any energy I had left.

"You don't have to disappear by yourself. Just say the word —I'll be ready to go with you," Elyse whispers as I drift further into sleep.

Just say the word, and I'll be ready.

TODAY 7:00AM DAD

You have one week to return home, Carmela. I expect you in Ohio for my first press event.

Ok, love you Dad...

Don't disappoint me again.

18 / THE BOONDOCK SAINTS

PARKER

S urrounded by towering trees the color of Christmas, my eyelids flutter shut and I roll onto my back. All I can see is red. I know it's the sun beaming down on me through my closed eyelids, but I think of her anyway.

A warm breeze blows across my face and I feel the sticky blood trickling out of my mouth and down my jaw. I want to wipe it away, to move, and get back on my bike, wherever it landed in the trees.

But I don't.

Whether you played football growing up or rode down a mountain, you learned not to move your body after a gnarly crash. So I remain on my back as I hear the stunned silence of spectators. The rushing of feet toward me. Eden, somewhere close murmuring to Cillian and the boys.

Everyone in this industry accepts the possibility of this outcome. A career-ending accident. A fatal one. We can only cheat Death so many times before he collects our broken bodies and brings us home.

You know, when Carmie didn't show, everyone begged me not to race. I'd already had a shit season to begin with, but I fought my friends when they cut me open with the truth: *your tempo has been off on the turns, your legs never quite pumping fast enough to handle the terrain, and your heart ... isn't invested.*

I wanted to prove them wrong.

Wiggling my toes, I almost cry out in relief at their small and strained movements in my shoes. But I grind my teeth into dust as agony and pain register in my left leg. It's an anchor dragging me deep, deep, down into a blackout designed by my body to keep me from going into shock.

The last thing I hear before completely disappearing is Eden's voice. Praying over my broken and battered body in the middle of the track on this mountain.

"And Shepherds we shall be For Thee my Lord, for Thee Power hath descended forth from Thy hand that Our feet may swiftly carry out Thy commands. So we shall flow a river forth to Thee And teeming with souls shall it ever be."

Carmie

SEPTEMBER, Nashville

My shoes step to the cadence of, *I'm going to quit my job, I'm going to quit my job, I'm going to*—through the quiet hospital hallways. Exhaling, I shake my head and snap out of the fantasy.

Quit my job and do what? Make pottery? I've spent the last ten years of my life in school to be a therapist. Now what? People don't just take a hard left and change course. Do they?

After consulting with the resident in the ED for a few of his patients, I round the corner for the cafeteria. Since this new hospital outside of Nashville is a privately funded hospital, it has the nicest amenities, even at eleven PM. Filling up my mug —the one with 10 Things I Hate About You quotes on it—I smell her before I see her.

Elyse always smells like Prada perfume.

"Avoidance is the trademark of a Pisces, but you've made it an Olympic sport lately."

She hops up on the counter and I roll my eyes at her.

"Did you get that from *CoStar* today?" I walk away, plopping down into a leather sectional positioned in front of a few TVs.

"Hey! I could copy-write for CoStar and you know it."

I laugh, which she seems to take as an invitation to sit next to me. Pulling out my phone, my thumb taps the astrology app for lost millennials like myself and I hold my breath while reading my condensed horoscope for the day.

"Read it out loud, come on." Elyse sips her hot green tea and nudges me with her foot.

"*You're valuable outside your ability to help*. Do: Delusions of grandeur, Sleeping in, and..."

"And what? Come on!" Elyse leans over, but I move away before she can see.

I don't answer.

Waving me off like an unbothered, old Korean grandma, she says, "Ah, you'll tell me eventually. I'll just let you marinate in it until you can't take holding it in any longer."

Rude... yet true.

My eyes swing to the TV where the Ortho Jocks must have left the ESPN channel on.

"I wish this thing had Bravo," Elyse mumbles over her tea.

Grabbing the remote to change the channel, I pause as an image on the screen floods my heart with icy water.

"Carmie is that—" Elyse puts her cup down and leans forward on the edge of her seat.

Have you ever had spectacular seats at a concert? The music is loud and unbearable, but you acclimate to it. After a few hours, you don't even remember that it was too loud...too jarring...too *much*. But the moment you walk away, your body is thrust back into the normal world. You feel like you're underwater, sounds are muffled, everything moves slower and you're *disoriented*.

I'm walking away from that metaphorical concert as I watch a video of Parker being carried down the side of a mountain on a stretcher, the medics rushing him to an evacuation helicopter.

The scrolling captions at the bottom confirm that Parker Radcliffe, the world-renowned mountain biker, crashed during the World Championships and has been recovering for days.

"He's *unrecognizable*. Carmie, what the hell happened?" Elyse's breath is nothing more than a whisper.

My heart officially freezes over. Both of his eyelids are red and the size of softballs. His face is purple and ripped open, there's a small part of his skull showing. His mouth is hanging open, and he has blood dried around all edges of it. His femur is protruding from his leg, broken at an ungodly angle.

But my eyes are looking for something else.

"I can't see his chest. How is he breathing? How is he even *alive*?" Elyse stands up and gets closer to the screen.

Eden sprints to the chopper and Cillian's face now fills the screen, a reporter asking him how Parker's fans can help him recover.

His hands.

His hands, the ones I still let myself dream about in between the hours of one and four AM, are thoroughly crushed.

It doesn't take an orthopedic surgeon to see that they are beyond lifeless. It's hard to tell from the camera footage how many fingers are bent the wrong way if his wrist is where it should be...

Realistically, his hands are the least of any medics concern, especially with the potential of broken ribs, punctured lungs, and that nasty femur break, but I can't stop thinking about his hands.

It's my undoing. My fingers reach out and graze the screen, possessed.

The footage, which we now know is Cillian's video, shows

Parker being lifted into the helicopter and the entire crew holding their bucket hats to their hearts, seemingly half resigned that he won't make it. They stare off at the chopper as it whirls away to the closest level I trauma center available in that small European town.

All of their faces are the same: *will the next time we see him be his funeral?*

"Parker will be transported back home to Arizona once he is cleared for travel. He spent three days in life-saving surgeries. Fans can send their best wishes to this PO Box or can donate in his honor to his favorite foundation called..."

I turn off the TV.

"Elyse," I whisper.

We stand in front of the blank screen, our muted reflections and still bodies staring back at us.

Her head turns toward me.

"Do you want to know the last thing CoStar told me to do today?"

She nods her head, still dazed by the news.

"It told me to pack my bags."

SEPTEMBER, Phoenix

Agony is being immobile and not able to reach the remote. The last ten minutes have been a sweaty and pathetic attempt at reaching my swollen fingers toward the side table.

The little black brick is taunting me at this point, angled toward me, but just out of reach. My ribs crack, and I suck in an agonizing breath between them.

"Life is an endless series of train wrecks with only brief commercial-like breaks," the TV taunts.

You don't say?

My finger holds down the *call* button for the nurses, even though I know it's not their job to hand me a remote. It's their job to up my pain medication, so I can put on a smile and return home.

Return to my daily schedule.

Return to my trainers.

Return to my life.

Return to my sanity.

A universal remote would be preferable actually, I could click *fast-forward* and be there already.

"Mr. Radcliffe?"

"Gloria, thank god, can you please hand me the remote and—?" I cut her off because my request was more important than small talk.

"That's not why I'm..."

"And can you please do something about the pain? I wouldn't ask if it wasn't serious."

"Parker!" Gloria puts her hands on her hips, hands that are indeed not reaching for the remote.

My jaw grinds and I exhale before trusting myself to respond. "Yes, Gloria?" I glare at her from underneath my eyebrows, pain shooting through my body at a stupid speed.

"You have a visitor. Once they're gone, I can come back and give your pain meds early."

Her ugly Crocs squeak as she turns on her heel and storms out.

My head drops back on my pillow and I think, *Fuck it, I'll get the remote myself.*

Inching my right leg to the side of the bed, the entire room does a complete one-eighty on me. My left leg remains immobile but I'm regaining strength, or compensating at least, with the right. Gripping the side of the mattress, as much as my fingers in both casts will allow, I suck in slow deep breaths.

Just a little more, I reach my arm out and lean a few degrees forward. My neck is prickling with sweat and exertion, and I almost have it—

"Hi."

My arm drops, my mission abandoned.

I can't swivel my neck yet. It's too risky. But I force my spine and shoulders to turn, one degree at a time until I lock eyes with her. I don't respond because I'm uncertain of *how* I should respond. She's standing in my doorway with one blue and one green eye, arms wrapped tightly across her chest as she clings to a Trader Joe's bag as a shield.

Swallowing, adrenaline takes over and gives my body the strength to scoot back on my bed into position without looking like a broken puppet. Anger and irritation replace any pain, covering my body with its slimy and false bravado.

Carmie takes a step into my room and her gaze wanders to all the flowers and cards that I hate so much. She's giving me her back, perhaps as a courtesy for me to get settled in my bed, and it only makes me angry.

Angry that she sees you like this, weak and vulnerable? Or angry that she's here?

The latter.

Liar, the narrator in my head taunts before disappearing.

"What are you doing here, Carmela?"

She doesn't turn around immediately, and it makes my anger flare brighter. I have one of those commanding voices that tends to cut through the bullshit and get to the bottom of things. People stand up taller in my presence because they know that my attention is a gift. Time is everything to me, and I'm realizing a little too late how much I wasted it on her. Even if it was only for a short period.

"I should've brought something more impressive," she says in a small voice as she looks down into the bag in her arms. "Silly me, bringing you a care package of—well, it doesn't matter." She shakes her head, causing her long braids to sway back and forth.

She sets the bag down on the table then rolls it a few inches over so that it's touching my bed. A small and stupidly observant gesture, making my heart beat against my already battered ribs.

"Why are you here, Carmela? Also, how the hell did you get in here? I only have three people on my visitation list." My brain sends a signal to cross my arms, but my arms scream, *fuck you*, and remain alongside my hips.

Is it her fault I almost died? No.

Would it have happened if she had come with me? Maybe. But most likely not.

Going ahead with racing, against the advice of my teammates and closest friends, was probably the worst mistake I ever made in my life. I was so god-damn pissy about allowing myself to open up to someone. So pissy about being rejected that I dove into the deep end of work and became reckless.

So reckless that I might not have a job waiting for me if I don't get out of here and start training again.

"Elyse and I were at work the other night and I saw the coverage of your accident."

"So you came to gloat?"

"No!" Her eyes flash wide in horror at my accusation.

I laugh, but it comes out too raw and bitter. "Ah, you're here to pity me, then. Thanks," I lift my chin to all the flowers and cards around me, "but I have enough of that in stock already. Don't need any more."

She bites her bottom lip and I hold eye contact with her. There is something else she wants to say, but I'm not going to hold my breath waiting to hear it. She disappointed me once, broke a promise once, and *lied* to me once. I'm not going to fall for it again.

"Are you...*talking* to anyone about the accident?" Her eyes scan over my body, snagging on my hands, before moving to my left thigh. It's four times the size it should be, a very obvious elephant in the room. The femur broke, and it took the orthopedic surgeon longer than usual to fix it. The wound is open and a small tube is draining it for a few more days.

I'm not worried about the rest of my injuries. I've had broken fingers, fractured wrists, and even damaged muscles before.

But this broken femur is going to be a problem.

"No, I don't need to." I bite the inside of my cheek and count down from twenty before I call for the nurse to escort her out.

She takes a step toward my bed, looking at the only edge available to perch on. I shift my leg over to cover the area, ignoring the blinding white pain it causes me, forcing her to stand.

Her eyes narrow at me for a moment, and I feel a sick satisfaction in pissing her off. Misery loves company.

"Yes, you do. You almost *died*, Parker. You think that's going to go away like *that*?" She snaps her fingers. It's so condescending I move to push the call button.

She rips it the remote out of my hand. My throat itches to throw a tantrum, a toddler without his favorite toy, but I wait.

"The next time you get on that bike, you might not want to acknowledge what happened to you, you might think you're recovered and healed, but your body will *know*. The body keeps the score, Parker. Grief needs a chance to move through you or else it will harden."

"Stop saying my name."

"No. I'm going to keep saying it because you need to hear it you little...little..." her face gets red, and it takes her a full minute to land on her insult of choice, "entitled asshole."

My eyes fly open and then narrow into knife points.

"Entitled asshole? Do you think anything about my life is entitled? I *worked* my ass off, nearly killing my body day and night for this sport. For my *life*. I am the least entitled athlete on this planet because I have *earned* it."

"Not from where I'm standing," she takes a step back, holding the call button behind her. "From where I'm standing, I see a guarded, shut-down, shell of a man who is too afraid to ask for help. A man who is too stubborn to admit that his recovery might take *longer* than he wants. A man who will need support, but is too busy alienating himself from those who care. A man who doesn't want to do what it takes to become the best. To do the unconventional."

"Why do you fucking care about me? You don't even know me!" I roar.

If she's going to take my call button away, I'll just draw attention until she's dragged out by her long red braids.

She swallows, and I see the tears building behind her eyes. But she doesn't run out. Her eyes blink a few times as she stares up at the ceiling before putting on the professional mask. Before hiding.

Her voice drops, and I'm forced to lean *toward* her, just to hear.

"I don't understand why I would care about someone so intent on pushing people away. It's probably the gift of wanting to save everyone around me..."

"That's not a blessing, that is a *curse*, Carmela," I cut her off, shining the bright spotlight of attention on her faults for once.

She utters a "hmph" and smirks. "Fine, it's my curse. Do you see how easy that was for me to admit? It's called self-reflection, now you try it."

"Oh, you're so good at it? So, tell me, are you still engaged? Are you still asking *how high?* every time Daddy and Big Brother ask you to jump? Are you still the spineless, people-pleasing, walking-talking version of a doormat? Hmm? Or have you *reflected* on that too?"

Her face falls, and my brain doesn't know where to look for a moment—down at my hands, or up at the glassy sheen covering her eyes. My insides coil tight.

A tear escapes from her eye and she swipes at it before putting her pleasant mask on. She leans down toward me.

"That's not how therapy works. This is about *you*," she begins.

"You're not my therapist!" I yell, straining my neck to move away from her.

"Who's not?" Dick, my manager, steps into the room, his eyebrows drawing together once he senses the tension surrounding us.

I'm about to give him the SparkNotes version of why this boundary-less, promise-breaking, annoying, *share your feelings*, annoyance of a woman needs to be escorted from my room when she drops the call button onto the floor and steps forward with her hand extended.

The smile she gives him is...blinding. It's everything I'm not. Open, unguarded, sweet as the day is long. It's completely disarming, and I can see her wrapping my manager around her finger.

"Excuse us, Carmela, I need to speak to my manager," I try to usher this interaction along and control it with both hands.

"Now, just wait, Parker! This young lady wasn't leaving yet, was she?" His eyes darken and scan Carmela over, head to toe, and back up again. She giggles, literally *giggles*, and I'm suddenly watching something worse than "Deadpool." Something I don't have a remote to turn off.

"Well, nice to meet you... *Dick*, is it?" The way she says *dick* from underneath her eyelashes makes the air in the room shift with electricity, and I know by the way my insides churn that I hate her.

I hate it when she smiles when it's clear she doesn't want to. I hate it when she's near me and she doesn't smile at all. I hate that she's a politician's daughter. I hate when they don't think of her at all. I hate that she's here in my hospital room. I hate that she's there when I close my eyes. I hate how the smell of lavender makes me look for her in a crowded room. I hate that I'll never be able to look at peonies again. I hate that she's turned into this walking, talking, easy-to-digest, version of herself.

I hate how sad it makes me to remember the woman who dropped the act with me. I hate that Carmela was always a supporting character in everyone else's story. But if you ask me what I hate the most? I hate that she was the leading role in *mine*.

Dick nods, like an asshat, and she lifts her chin before sliding her eyes to me with a hint of mischief. Dick still has both of his grubby palms over hers and my fingers find the rubbery cord of the call button. Reeling it in, like a fishing line, I finally manage to push the call button five times.

"It's been a pleasure, but I believe I have overstayed my welcome. Good luck with recovery." Carmie turns toward me with her phony-ass goodbye.

She's about to leave but Dick pipes up in desperation, "Wait! Did Parker say you are a therapist? Are you available by chance? The last one, eh—didn't work out."

Her hand rests gently on the doorframe, which makes me even more frustrated because every time she moves her body it's graceful as fuck. I'm stuck in this bed, stuck in these casts, stuck in this misery.

"Well." She blinks a few times, assessing my face, before turning back to Dick. "I'm currently on a sabbatical at the moment. But I am staying in Arizona for the time being..."

"We would be so grateful if you considered working with Parker. Even if it's ah, off the books, per se." Dick winks at her and I watch her eyes cut to me before she smiles.

No, no, no, do not say it.

"Well, I do have some spare time on my hands now. I would be honored to help Peter."

"Parker," I growl.

She snaps her fingers and tries not to laugh. "That's right! Parker. Of course."

She and Dick exchange a few details before she walks out

the door without even casting a second glance back. Dick whistles and breaks his neck trying to watch her leave.

"You lucked out on that one, let me tell you. She'll even be set up in Sedona when you're discharged."

I bite my tongue and nod my head instead. It's time to be calculated and play the long game.

I'm not sure what her ulterior motive is for wanting to be my therapist, but I'll figure it out and use it to my advantage.

When Gloria finally returns and administers my meds for the afternoon, she also tosses me a disapproving glare as if she overheard my entire conversation. But the meds begin to flow and the world gets a bit warmer and a little less annoying. With the remote in my lap and an almost empty room, I can finally exhale as much as my punctured lung allows.

"Who brought you this?" Dick starts rummaging through the Trader Joe's bag, but my tongue is heavy in my mouth. If my hands weren't in casts, and I wasn't already high seven ways to Sunday, I would smack his fucking paws away from the bag.

It's mine, not yours. The thought sends a foreign feeling into my chest.

"Fresh green juice, beet juice, banana chips, mineral water, magnesium, trail mix, and wow—there's the entire health food aisle in a bag just for you. Don't you love these protein bars?" Dick uses his front teeth to rip open a foil package, and if the fogginess of medication wasn't taking over my mind, I would see red. I'm sure of it.

But I'm losing the battle, sinking further into my pillow, into what will hopefully be a dreamless and dark oblivion.

"They left a note, want me to read it? Of course, you do, what am I thinking...oh wow! There's a little oil roller in here too." Dick opens it up, and it smells like *her*. It's lavender and honey and safety and the promise of something. But I can't find the words.

119

"They say lavender softens anxiety, and I wonder whether I can plant a garden so dense in your mind that the knots in your chest unravel and never tighten again. That's a poem by Jasmine Kaur, and I wanted you to know that..."

I can barely hear the words, but they leave my mouth before I'm sucked into oblivion. "Stop reading that before I fucking fire you, Dick. *Get out.*" My tongue feels like a dry sponge and my throat works to swallow.

He chuckles and puts the note on my bedside table, pushing it just out of reach.

Dick.

"I'll be checking in on your progress with Dr. D'Angelo. Play nice, Parker. Or it's the end of an era for you and your career."

Instead of threatening him, I sigh in bliss. There's a little garden of lavender being planted behind my eyelids and I see a haze of blue, purple, and green. Warmth sweeps through my veins and I can see the appeal to so many people using painkillers every day...

It's so peaceful it almost makes me forget how much I hate my life.

I hate my life and I hate her and I hate this pain and I hate hospitals and I hate everything. But most of all, I hate that I don't hate lavender as much as I want to.

21 / BREAKFAST AT TIFFANY'S

Carmie

September, Sedona

I an is close behind Riley with two of my moving boxes stacked on top of each other. Sweat drips from their temples and I feel a bit guilty I asked my friends to help us move in this heat.

"Oy, Elyse. What's in this box? Cement?" Riley yells as he walks through the threshold.

His footsteps are light across the red Spanish tile in the entryway and his stride is graceful as it moves up the spiral stairway to my bedroom on the second floor.

"My books!" Elyse huffs from the couch.

"It should be illegal to move across the country with this much shit," Riley mutters before dropping the books into Elyse's bedroom.

"Don't be jealous that you're the only one here who doesn't know how to read." Elyse stands up, skips over to her bedroom, and winks at us before patting Riley's sweaty red cheek.

"Why didn't you ask Dean to help? I'm sure he would've jumped at the chance to peek in your panty drawer." Riley plops his hand on the doorframe and smirks down at Elyse with a knowing smile.

She slams the door and he barely moves his poor fingers away before they are guillotined off. Instead of unpacking or helping, Elyse chooses violence.

"And I know how to read!" He yells at the slammed door.

I shake my head and cross my equally sweaty arms. Elyse could at least *pretend* to be helpful moving or at least show gratitude. Riley and Ian came to Sedona to help us, but, of course, I'm here to pick up the emotional slack.

"I know you can read, Riley. Come on, let's get the last few boxes and then head into town." I drape my arm around his waist and corral his hot-headed temper outside to contend with the even hotter autumn sun.

I'm not sure I'll ever get used to this weather, or this view.

We have panoramic views of Mount Wilson and the trees that precede it. A big blue sky—that I still can't believe is real —for days. A creek runs through the property and is the perfect touch of water in the desert.

Oak Creek Canyon, Arizona is the perfect place to have ended up. Three miles from Sedona.

Elyse has a travel nursing job and I have space.

Maybe I'll take a yoga teacher training?

Maybe I'll learn how to be a masseuse?

Maybe I'll learn how to do hypnosis therapy?

Maybe I'll just sit and stare at the wall all day when I'm not sitting in a chair across from Parker trying to force something honest and true from the tiny concrete block he calls a heart.

I twist my hair into a sweaty bun on the top of my head, a new type of anxiety rising within me, threatening to rob my lungs of oxygen.

What's more haunting? Being in a tiny room, or being out in the open desert, with all that space?

Everybody wants freedom until they realize they're responsible for making something of it.

It's astonishing to see in hindsight how mapped out my entire life was up until this point. Even my Ph.D was forced on me. My father's words, *"If you're going to go into psychology the least you can do is rise to the top and make this family look good"* followed me through my postgraduate years. Even after my dissertation, I never felt like the letters after my name fit.

I wished for space and now I have it. I wished for the opportunity to make amends with Parker, and in a way, I forced that proximity on us. I've wished for many things in my life, but I made Sedona come true.

One of my first decisions since changing my zip code? Signing up for the sensual dance and empowerment series from Fallon's bachelorette weekend. The moment I registered and paid, I felt a massive relief at making a concsious decision for my new life.

That's all I need to do. Make one decision at a time.

"You match." Ian turns toward me before taking the last box into the house.

"What?" I turn.

"You and this place. You're a match. Don't ask me to explain it, I don't know how." Ian shrugs.

If Riley is a hurricane, one that you can see and feel for miles, Ian is the peace and calm after the storm. He chooses his words wisely, moves with discernment, and doesn't bother with social pretenses or customs.

"Excuse me, I have a delivery here for a Carmela?" A young man in a tan uniform walks up the driveway around the moving van.

"That's me," I reply skeptically. How would someone have

this address already? We just moved in and it's a long-term rental, not an official property in my name.

"Can you sign here please?" The man holds the box underneath his arm and extends the digital pad over to me. Heat that has nothing to do with the Arizona sun creeps up my neck.

The man hands me the box and heads back down our drive. A small kernel of hope blooms that Carson sent me a welcome package. Or perhaps the rest of our friends back in Nashville chose a gift.

"You're holding that box like it's a bomb. Who is it from?" Ian asks over my shoulder.

Shrugging, I start to work the package open, but it's taped up too tight. Riley walks forward and shakes his head. He rummages in his back pocket, flicks open his pocketknife, and stabs the damn box like Dwight stabbed the CPR dummy in "The Office"—brutally and without an ounce of grace.

"Hey!" I yank my package back, protective of the gift, before I even see who it's from. But that disapears the moment I smell *Sauvage* cologne. Moving aside the tissue paper, I spot a blue box.

A Tiffany Blue box.

My hand shakes slightly as I reach into the box. Before I open it I know what I will pull out. The white satin bow is so bright under the scrutiny of the sun, it makes my eyes water. Staring at the box in my hand, I debate leaving it as is and sending it back. Sending this type of gift in the mail is ridiculous and shows just how clueless and flippant he is about the value of things.

"Well? Aren't you going to open it?" Riley asks before lighting up a Camel Blue cigarette.

He exhales the smoke and I breathe it in, welcoming any scent that will cover Seamus' cologne.

He's trying to pee all over me like an animal, even from 1,946 miles away.

"You can open it." I hand it over to Riley before he stomps out his third cigarette of the day.

"If this can pay my rent, I'm not giving it back." He mutters and I don't have the heart to tell him how many months, or more accurately, how many *years* of rent he would be able to pay with it.

Whistling, he dangles it in front of us. "It's a bracelet." The diamonds set in platinum sparkle in the sun and Ian shields his eyes from the glare. The shine is less dazzling and more assaulting.

"It's a tennis bracelet, to be precise," I say on an exhale.

Tiffany's.

Three carats.

Twenty-two thousand dollars.

"Some gift." Ian's eyebrows lift.

"It's not a gift. It's a WASPY woman's right of passage. They are traditionally given for anniversaries...or," I pause. "As a 'sorry for fucking the nanny—again,' gift."

Riley's eyes bug out of his head and he places the bracelet back down in the case like it's the source of all the bad luck in his life. "I thought you were Catholic, not protestant."

"Doesn't matter," I mumble, still in disbelief at this whole thing. "Did you know that scene in 'Pretty Woman' was pure accident? The one where the snap of the lid makes everyone jump?" I ask with a detached voice.

They shake their heads no but their eyes are on the lid I just closed.

"There's nothing heartfelt or warm about this gift, ok? It's what I'm sure is the first of many more attempts from Seamus to get me to come back to him. When we were younger he would put his Mom's tennis bracelet on my wrist at family parties and waltz me around playing house. He would tell me, *I'll fill a jewelry box with these for you one day.* And you know what? I believed that was love. Not the promise of diamonds..."

I look off into the distance, at the mountains and the red dirt I'm already starting to love.

"But the planning of a future. That's what felt special to me. He's missing the point. *Again*."

"Well, can I have it then? I could use a new motorcycle." Riley pretends to reach for the box.

Ian reaches for it and says, "You said *rent*, not a new Harley. You crashed the last one like an idiot. Maybe it's time to call it a day."

This is draining.

"I have to go check on Parker, but let's meet at Black Panther Coffee in a few hours. I want to spend time with you guys before you head out."

They both nod and I turn my back on them. Stepping through the threshold I try to shake the sinking feeling in my gut about Seamus having my new address.

He won't show up here, right?

To be polite, I send him a quick text.

Shaking my head, I drink in the southwestern home decor, Spanish tile, and wide open windows. No, he won't be coming here. That would require him to think outside of the box and value our relationship more than he values the *appearance* of our relationship.

Riley said something on the journey here. Somewhere between Tennessee and Arizona, he sucked on a cancer stick and said, "It's time you started lifting your chin and telling anyone committed to keeping you in a box—the box of your past, or the box of who they want you to be—*Frankly my dear, I don't give a damn.*"

You know what? I don't have anything figured out. I'm almost thirty, I'm abandoning a career I made my entire personality, and I'm single in a new state. But for the first time,

I can *choose* to look around and see potential where I once only saw pain.

Looking down at the box in my hands, I repeat to myself over and over again. I'm safe here. It is safe to start over.

But a little voice chimes in from somewhere deep in my body, *you're safe ... for now.*

If only I listened.

SEPTEMBER, Sedona

G ripping the rails in the hospital PT room, I shuffle my feet forward and clench my molars together. Sweat rains down my face and a chill sweeps across my already-soaked spine. Shifting my weight into my left leg, I work to prove I'm WBAT, what I've recently learned is "weight-bearing as tolerated."

Come on, just three more seconds. Damn it. Come on.

No matter what I command my body to do, I know that it won't listen. I'm too fucking exhausted. A scream threatens to break free from my locked jaw, but I force it down, lock it up, and fight through this pain.

"Parker, that's enough man. You need to *rest*."

"I don't have the time to rest, Landon. This is supposed to be my year. I'm not letting this femur break slow me down and I'm not getting any younger. You expect me to give up my first chance to go to Rampage this October too?"

My physical therapist shakes his head and steps in my path between the parallel bars I'm using as assistance.

"It's not *just* a femur break. It's your skull fractures. It's your right wrist. It's the dozen other bones you either snapped, mangled, or damaged. It's the muscle loss from recovery. It's the mental—"

"There's nothing mental about this," I snap at him and narrow my eyes.

"Yeah, sure, and I'm not 6'2, black, and sick of your shit," he throws back.

"I can fix this. If you're not going to help, then get out, and I'll hire someone who will," I grit out, but even I can hear how my words sound between my inhales and exhales.

"Nature doesn't rush, yet all things are accomplished." Landon reminds me with a grating and patient tone.

"Stop. Quoting. Taoism. To. Me." I pant like an injured dog on the side of a road.

My eyes sting, and I can feel every unexpressed emotion threaten to pour out of me in an ultra-violent explosion. I'm running out of places inside my head to store all the shit I would rather not look at.

"Fine. No more inspiration. But you're not dismissing me, you stupid bastard. Now shut up and prove you can bear weight on your leg before we progress to higher exercises." Landon crosses his arms and plays my game.

He's been on my team for five years, which has given us time to strike this balance. He knows when to push me and when to fight to make me stop.

The moment I sink more weight into my left leg, the muscles quiver, shake, and threaten to give out. I tip my head back and almost scream in frustration, grief, and rage. Setting my eyes ahead, looking at the sign over Landon's eyes, I steady my breath and stop compensating on my right leg.

Clear Eyes, Full Heart, Can't Lose.

"Done." Landon pats my shoulder and I swallow back the thickness in my throat.

I sag all of the weight back into my right leg and drop my forehead to one of the bars holding me up.

My dad loved football, so I would often indulge in his favorite shows and movies. I can practically quote "Friday Night Lights" in my sleep.

We lived in Phoenix for most of my childhood, but one summer we took a trip up to the mountains in Colorado. I watched my first downhill race event and spent the rest of the day begging him for a BMX bike.

He told me, *no*, and I respected him too much to push it. But that was the thing about my father. He always had a card up his sleeve, and he was willing to do anything for us. To this day, I've never met anyone better at gift-giving than him. He put his heart into every exchange with someone.

On the last morning of our trip, he told us that he had another meeting and left us at breakfast. A few hours later, he met us in the lobby, a bike by his side. I've never run so fast in my entire life. But instead of going for the bike, I ran for him. Wrapping my arms around him, he knelt and hugged me with a wide smile on his face. I can still feel the starch in his dress shirt and the way our heartbeats marched to the same excited beat.

He told me that he tracked down a few of the athletes and asked them where his kid should start. They not only walked him through bikes, gear, and training—but one of them gave my dad an extra bike he had for the weekend. All black, except for a crimson red sticker reading *Ride or Die*.

As I admired the bike and felt the rubber grips in my small palms, my dad walked over to my mother and dipped her low to kiss her.

Running my palm through my sweaty hair, I nearly choke on the memory. Some people think that time heals all wounds, but I never feel joy when I think of my dad. All I feel is a crushing blackness, like an astronaut floating through space, being obliterated by the pressure. But there's never a release. I'm stuck in the purgatory.

So many of the guys I now consider brothers have dickheads for dads, and it makes the ache burn darker in my hollow chest—the injustice of it all. How shitty parents can still exist, alive and well, while my hero was ripped away from me.

Eden's dad only cares about him when he wins, often away for months at a time on his Yacht traveling the Aegean Sea. Cillian's Dad spends most of the money his son makes on drinking and gambling. The other boys have similar stories, either hyper-aggressive dads pushing them or absent ones.

It wasn't like that with my dad. Even after I was signed with my first sponsor, he only cared about *me*. Parker. Not Parker the athlete. Not Parker the cursed man to only ever take second place. He cared about me because I was his son. He always boasted, "The sun in my sky."

He was a professor while my mom went to school, and he worked at three universities and colleges just to make sure our basic needs were always met. Not only that, but he paid for every entry free, every race kit, every bike during my adolescent years without complaining. Even when I was a little shit, pushing the limits, he used philosophy and patience with me instead of using force or punishments.

"Parker? Who's that?" Landon's voice drops and knocks me out of my pity party.

My eyes drop from the sign I crudely tapped to the doorframe and look into the eyes of the last person I want to see me like this. She lingers in the doorway and her gaze sweeps over my body. Her eyes roam over my drenched grey T-shirt and the ripped grey sweatpants I reserve for only house projects and training, and then back up to the obvious discomfort on my face.

It's instinct, by my eyes do the same to her.

They soak in the crimson hair piled high on her head, a few loose curls sticking to her forehead. My eyes drink in the denim short overalls that make her look like a flower child. It's less about her outfit and more about the endless pool of hope shining behind one blue and one green eye. Hope for what, I'm not sure.

Hungry eyes aside, if she's waiting for permission to enter, she won't get it from me.

"Come on in, we were just finishing up. I'm Landon. How do you know Parker?" Landon nearly jogs over to her and holds out his hand to introduce himself.

Typical. Why is everyone enamored by her? Is it the whole mermaid vibe? The big wide eyes, wavy red hair, and irritating kindness?

But I know better. When push comes to shove, she folds and chooses what's easy instead of fighting for what she wants.

"I'm Carmie, Parker's new therapist." She smiles and that expression on *anyone* else would be too much. But on her? It just comes across as her open and friendly nature, as if she's compensating for all the darkness in the world with her smile.

Landon is still shaking her hand, and he whistles low before tossing me a glance.

"You have your work cut out for you then," he chuckles as I grind my teeth and grip the bars, trying to stand taller. "He's the most stubborn son of a bitch I've ever worked with."

Carmie lifts a brow at me, taunting.

"Isn't this a violation of HIPAA? Stop talking about me," I snap.

She laughs and Landon finally releases her hand. *World's longest handshake much?* He joins in her laughter and I start hopping toward the wheelchair.

Carmie and Landon strike up an easy conversation as they walk deeper into the treatment room, toward me, and I'm trying not to focus on how interested she seems in his life, asking him personal questions, how his day is, and *oh, you'll have to show me some of your exercises for knee pain! Sometimes when I hike, it flares up...*

Whatever. I bite back the impulse to say, *Google exists, use it.*

Trying *and failing* at not listening to them, my muscles give out and I collapse flat on my face, mere inches from the chair. There's a moment of stunned silence, and this is somehow infinitely worse than crashing on my bike. At least I'm doing what I love when I crash and tumble.

"Parker!" Carmie rushes over, but I can't see her.

My face burns, plastered to the cold checkered linoleum. I can hear Landon's deep sigh. There's nothing left in my tank, so I don't even bother rolling over or attempting to get up.

"What can I do? Here, let me help," Carmie is on her knees next to me, flustered.

Which only makes me more pissed because she can move her legs without pain. She can still do what she wants to do without every bone in her body screaming from the effort of re-learning how to function.

Waving her away from me, I feel Landon's wide hands underneath my armpits as he lifts me to get me into the wheelchair. My vision narrows, and I see spots in my peripheral vision. My breath saws in and out, and I can't hear them talking to me.

Carmie is kneeling by the wheel of my chair, and she places a hand on my arm, her mouth moving, but I'm spinning inside.

I'm never going to compete again. I'm going to be in pain for the rest of my life. All of this was for nothing. All of this was for nothing. All of this—

Her hand squeezes my arm and I snap out of it.

"Don't touch me." I push her hand off my arm and turn my face away from her. "I don't want you here. Just quit already."

"Parker," she exhales.

"I hate you," the words rush out and I don't bother looking at how the blow lands.

There's a shocked silence and I regret it immediately, but come on, what the hell did she expect coming in here? I am at my lowest and she's just... she's everywhere. I can't get *rid* of her.

She clears her throat and stands up.

"It was a pleasure to meet you, Landon. I'll see you at Parker's house when you come by for treatments and evals."

Her voice is formal and I close my eyes. In another world, another timeline, this wouldn't be happening. I hold on to my anger because I'm *here* in this world, where everything is fucked up, and I'm not healing as fast as I need to. A world where she just won't leave me alone, haunting me with every memory of her voice in my ear, of our hearts connecting on a level I never expected to find in this lifetime. The memory that she threw it all away.

Landon walks her out and then shuts the door with a loud *click*.

"Listen up, prick. You can be a dick to me all you want. It's our relationship and I know it fuels you." His steps are a *thud, thud, thud* as he walks over to me.

I open my eyes in time to see a finger being pointed an inch from my face. Then, he narrows his hazel eyes at me.

"But if I find out you're being a dick to that woman, I *will* quit, and you'll be on your own. That is where I draw the line. I won't accept or endorse any violence toward women. Verbal, emotional, or physical. There's no excuse for that shit. We both know nobody else has the patience to work with you. So get it together." Landon kicks my chair and the slight jolt makes me hiss in pain.

"Just take me back to my room, I'm being discharged later," I mutter.

"Do it yourself, big man." Landon spins on his heel and pushes through the doors, leaving me alone with nothing but the pain of the past... and the present.

Carmela.

Dad, I'm sorry. Just give me more time. You didn't need me there—you looked great. You have Mom, Carson, and your entire team...

Take all the time you need. You're cut off until you come to your senses and come home to plan your wedding.

I suggest you make up with your future husband. Or else there will be more severe consequences than just being financially cut off.

Dad...

23 / FIGHT CLUB

PARKER

SEDONA, October

The sound of knuckles knocking on my mother's front door forces Eden to pause his latest story, which is a blessing because I've had *enough* details of his sex life to last a lifetime.

It's also a curse, though, because that means the time for my first "session" has arrived. I begged Dick to find me another therapist. To find me a loophole. But my manager refused. I even told him about my history with Carmela and he waved a hand at me saying, *Stop bragging and use it to your advantage then. Get that clearance*, only proving how sparse ethics and morals truly are in the world of big sponsorships.

Eden turns his neck and yells, "Coming! I'm...I'm... COMING!" In the most high-pitched and hideously erotic voice ever.

"You are a sex addict and need help."

"Nonsense. I'm just a teenager trapped in this gorgeous vessel of a man. It's a shame that the rest of you lot on Earth are so ugly. I feel sorry for you." He winks at me and rises.

"I'll get it, just head out man."

But we both know that's a lie. My progress has all but stalled in PT and there's a small part of me that wonders if I have anything left to even fight for.

He wiggles his eyebrows at me and rubs his hands together like a walking cliché. One foot inches back, then the next, my eyes tracking the movement and narrowing.

"Eden," I warn. I know all too well how he feels about her.

"I've never had a crack at a therapist. Think she'd heal all my Mommy issues? Let me drop my crying head into her sweet bossoms?"

I will throw up.

"Are you on 'Love Island' right now? Get the fuck out of here, E."

He doesn't listen, his back to me as he jogs to the door. He swings the door open, and with far too much fanfare, I can hear his cocky accent ringing out throughout my house.

"Good aye, are you interested in a two-for-one special? Two of us, one of you—"

His words fade, and I turn my body, to get in a position where I can see them both lingering in the doorway.

I can't handle any more conflict.

Carmela looks up at him and scratches her nose. Her eyes shift around before she explains that she was hired to be my personal *Sports Psychologist* as if that title is any less embarrassing than, *Counselor* or *Therapist.*

Eden has two palms on the doorway and leans down into her face, "What are you after now? His money or something?"

"Eden," I call. He turns toward me with a smile on his face, expecting some form of praise for his behavior. Instead, I yell out, "Shut the door on your way out."

Eden rolls his eyes and mutters something akin to, "*Suit yourself. Enjoy your time, you cunty masochist.*"

Carmela walks into the house wearing a royal blue

outfit, the type where the top and bottom are connected, and she looks like a river personified. The fabric even floats around her ankles as she moves. Her eyes wander to the paintings, the photos, and the raw oak beams lining the ceiling.

They land on a painting of the *Mona Lisa* but the famous subject is standing with her hands on a bike. She smiles at it, enjoying my mother's sense of humor. It was a Christmas gift from years ago. I hate to admit it, but it's my favorite part of the house too.

I bought this home in Big Creek for my mother three years ago, and it's just as stunning as it was when I paid nearly 2 million for it sight unseen. She claimed she wanted a one-bedroom apartment since she works such odd hours. I was traveling so much, but I couldn't hold myself back from this property. It's just as much my home as it is hers.

"It's an investment, just be grateful," I mumbled to her, but she knew the truth. It was a gift, one I would gladly pay for again. A gift I thought would ease the lingering pain of my father's death but failed miserably.

"Can we do the session here? I'm already set up," I ask, but the question holds zero room for an alternative. By the way she approaches me, and looks at me, I know she caught that as well.

"Well, normally I would say no, but I guess it's fine," her eyes rake over my body, and it sends a crack through the stone in my chest.

I hate the way she's looking at me. Like I'm an injured animal on the side of the road. Like she wants to take me home to cuddle before I die in a cardboard box she made.

Keeping my expression locked down, my pain held in tight, I push my hands onto the couch and push myself up with the help of my crutches. Landon told me I'm technically not allowed to walk, but come *on*.

"Where would you like to go then?" I grind between my teeth.

If she notices me sweating and borderline grunting to move, she does not comment.

Her eyes move around the open layout of the single-story home. It's a classic southwestern design, but I love how all the rooms wrap around a central courtyard outside. She starts walking toward the sliding glass doors, and even though it pains me to move this slow, I follow her.

Fresh air helps in every situation, right?

Once I'm settled on the outdoor sectional, I curse.

"Can I get you something before we begin, Mr. Radcliffe?"

My face scrunches up at that and I mutter, "I just forgot to light the fire before I sat down. And don't call me that." She tosses me a look asking why and my eyebrows drop down, shutting her out.

It reminds me of the classes I would sit in on my father teaching. Mr. Radcliffe, even though he died as a Doctor and head of the philosophy department.

Carmela stands up, breaking our silent stare off, and navigates around the expansive outdoor fire pit as if it's a fixture in her daily life and not the first time. Once the fire comes to life, she takes a seat on the opposite end of the couch.

"I'm here to treat you like any other patient, but I can agree to call you Parker."

She tucks her feet underneath herself and positions her long hair into a twist at her nape. Without another word, she reaches into her bag, and takes out a notebook (of course she does because she's like every therapist *ever*), and uncaps a pen with a zebra on the top, bouncing wildly at the end of a spring.

"Get that from the book fair?" I smirk, going on the offensive, as every good athlete should do.

She looks up at me and tilts her head to the right.

Opening her notebook, she breaks the eye contact and looks down at the pages. Looking back up at me, her wordlessness is filled with heavy emotions. Despite a conscious effort *not* to be affected, my blood moves slower in anticipation anyway.

"No. This pen in particular is from a patient of mine who committed suicide last year."

"I'm sorry," I say automatically, because I'm not heartless, but she ignores it.

"She was my youngest one. Ten years old, if you can believe it." Her fingers stroke the pen, lost in thought.

Her pain sits right there on her face, for me to see, in all of its honest and foolish beauty. Tears line her eyes and she blows a breath out of her lips before looking up at the sky.

I can't be sure, but it looks like the familiar expression of failure I try to hide after I fall short of my goals, time and time again. Running my bandaged hand through my hair, I sigh, wondering how the hell I'm going to make it through ten required sessions with the woman who constantly makes me feel inadequate just by merely existing.

"Now, if you'd like to dislodge your foot from your mouth, I'd like to begin." She offers me a small smile and I bark out a laugh in surprise.

"My foot isn't in my mouth. I wish it was because that would mean I can move it like I used to," the admission slips out, and I lock my arms over my chest again.

"How is that making you feel? The inability to move in a way you are used to?"

Her face is empty of pain. A focused sense of curiosity replaces it, and I'm not ready to be under the scrutiny of that type of attention. I'm just not.

I glare at her and then stare into the flames.

She can't make me talk. She's exactly like the other three, all

*of their prissy notebooks and pencil skirts and heavy sighs when I
wouldn't participate.*

"Your brooding silence would be considered hot in a
movie, but it is in fact, a waste of both of our time here. So,
let's shift gears."

My eyes slide to her and I catch her smiling at her pun
about *gears*, which is annoying because I don't want to feel
anything beyond my misery.

She runs a finger down a mysterious list and purses her
lips.

"Right. Well. I contacted a colleague back in Tennessee
and he provided me a great starting point for our sessions
from the lens of clinical sports psychology.

"Pass."

Bending over, she reaches into her bag and pulls out
another sheet of paper—my copy of her mysterious list. She
leans forward and the paper hangs in the space between us. I
don't move to grab it.

"Ok. Let's start over. I'll read from the list and we can start
where you're comfortable. (A) a cursory description of the
presenting problem." She looks at me, waiting to see if I'll
jump on the first question.

Shaking my head with a terse *no*, she continues.

"Alrighty. How about (b) athletic history?"

"You can find all of my stats on the *Red Bull* bio page. Or
Wikipedia. Or any fan page online," I mutter.

"But...the whole point is to hear it from *your* perspective
Parker. Can you give me your history through an unbiased
lens? Pretend you're reporting on your career without the self-
deprecation and flagellation."

Carmie's eyes widen and she's sitting on the edge of her
seat. Her presence and undivided attention make my skin
tighten and my heart beat out of sync.

I hate it.

"Pass."

"Well, if you can't handle these easy questions Parker, we're going to be at this for months. I don't think your sponsors or agent want that. Do you?" She lifts a delicate and curved eyebrow in my direction and I bite the side of my cheek five times to keep my mouth shut.

"So. Let's move on since you love being stubborn and presenting a challenge. Here's one!" Her voice loses its innocent curiosity and is replaced by a bitter edge. "How about you tell me about (c) family and social support."

The way my eyes narrow on her and the way her lips tug into a self-satisfied smirk makes my blood boil. I know...logically I know...she didn't make this list. But she's certainly relishing how *that* question in particular will makes me squirm.

Locking my jaw down, I stare into her eyes and resist the temptation to bite back.

"Parker," she sighs and the corners of her eyes tilt down toward the patio. "I am here tonight to understand seven components of your life before I can make any real progress with you." She lifts a finger and my eyes focus on it as she rattles the seven off: "Identifying information, the reason for seeking consultation, a background of areas for improvement and concern, details of performance, life and identity outside of sport, significant relationships and support system, and self-care."

"We," I argue on a quiet exhale.

"*We*, what?" Her eyebrows scrunch and she tucks her feet into the chair. Burrowing in like she's burrowing into my goddamn brain.

"Before *we* can make any progress." I wave my hand between us, highlighting the great chasm existing there.

"That's what I said," she argues.

"No. You said *before I can make any progress*, but this isn't about you, Carmie. It's about me. I am part of the equation. This isn't on you to fix. I am not a project. I am not something broken. I am—"

"I apologize, Parker," she whispers, eyes looking big and round and full of genuine apology. But I hate them.

"Well," she clears her throat, "since you are leaving me with few options. I can think of a few beyond the checklist. Has your sense of self-worth always been connected to your job performance? How are you handling your grief?"

She looks up from her list and my hands reach for a pillow to strangle.

"What grief are you referring to?"

"What grief do you think I'm alluding to, Parker?"

"Stop doing that." I try to cut her down with my eyes.

"Stop doing what, Parker?" She asks with a head tilt.

"That!"

"Asking questions? Or saying your name? I can do both if you'd prefer, but we both know you're the one deflecting from the real topic at hand."

"Which would be what?"

Don't play her game.

"Talking about your father's death. About how your career has been impacted by it."

The pain I saw on her face when she mentioned her young patient returns. Except this time, it's for *me*. I hate it. I hate when she blinks. I can see my pain reflected there in the depth of her mismatched eyes.

"Time's up," I say.

She remains calm and quiet on the chair. Unmoving.

"Leave," I choke out, my voice echoing off the short stone walls lining the perimeter of the courtyard. It's a rare outburst and the volume of my voice surprises me.

"What I'm hearing you express is a discomfort about that topic of conversation and that you would like for me to leave."

"Wow, you're so good at your job, Carmela. Great job deducing that. Gold star."

My voice keeps rising, and yet, she's still seated on the couch. Her face pinches at that retort, but then she tucks it away.

"Could you for a moment, consider how freeing it would be to discuss the details of his death with someone? To perhaps wonder who you would be, how you would feel, *without* all of this pent-up emotion?"

"I never should have confided in you. I never should have even told you about him." The words are quiet but I put the weight of my body into them. It's betrayal, what I'm feeling. The information she already knows about me. The information she can ask about, probe into, and explore.

When a downhill race starts, there's no going back. My bike hits the dirt, and I don't look back. I'm controlled. Calculated. Effective. So what I say next, defies how I normally operate. I feel so out of control around her, that it makes my lungs shrink.

"I think you must have the lowest self-worth on the planet to be here with me, to offer help to someone who looks at you and wishes you were anyone else."

The words are equally quiet as the last ones, but I know they'll be the reason she eventually calls Dick to put an end to these sessions. I hope they leave a dirty tire track across her heart, and she packs her shit and flies home to Ohio.

Unfolding her legs, she rises from the chair and blinks a little faster. Embarrassment. Frustration. Possibly even a heavy dose of hurt feelings.

She walks over to me on her way out and looks down her nose at me. Breaking eye contact, she reaches into her bag and pulls out a notebook. She tosses it down on the couch next to me and speaks.

"Most of my patients find the idea of a therapist writing

about them in a notebook intimidating or just plain rude. I like to sit with the details they tell me about themselves...and create a notebook for them to bring to our sessions. It offers a communal effort. Shared intimacy. Trust."

My eyes glance down, and I'm grateful I've worked my entire life at hiding how I feel at any given moment.

The front of the notebook is an entire collage of my life. All of my big competitions. When I almost won the World Cup in 2019. When I *almost* won the European Ridgeline competition. Hardline back in 2010. There are pictures of me and the guys. There are quotes from interviews and exclusives.

I swallow thickly and look at my body in a few of the photos. Fuck, I miss being out there on my bike, feeling the rush of the surrounding wind. Feeling unstoppable. But I can't admit that.

My fingers idly trace over a few of the photos. It feels like I'm looking at a collage I would have made when I was young, but instead of the people I idolized, it's *me* staring back.

Looking up, I realize she's gone. The only thing keeping me company underneath the darkening sky is this notebook she took the time and energy to create.

Flipping open the cover, I catch a faint whiff of lavender oil and read the first page.

Dear Parker,

Before you throw this off a mountain or ask your friends to run it over with a bike, I would ask you to read this. Please?

My fingers trace over her cursive handwriting and I scoff at the little hearts that dot the i's like a teenager.

Let's build a little trust with one another, shall we? I can promise that I won't accuse you of having too much commitment to your sport and the lifestyle that comes with it. Not today, not ever. It is your commitment that shows me how much potential you have — not only to win — but to heal.

I get that this is an unconventional arrange-ment ... and the loss of time, the loss of progress, might seem overwhelming and crippling to you. But our lives are made to spiral. There is no such thing as a linear path.

I would love to support you. But only if you're willing to remember, "It is only after we have lost everything, that we are free to be anything."

Carmie.

P.S. Yes, that is from Fight Club and I can promise you that our sessions, much akin to Chuck Palahniuk's great novel, follow the same main rule: "The first rule of Fight Club is that nobody talks about Fight Club."

Standing up, I hop to the fire on one foot and lean a hand against the stone mantel. Resting on my forearm, I stare at the flames below me. They dance left and right, mesmerizing me. My eyes unfocus and I struggle to call upon a piece of advice from my father.

What would he tell me right now?

Squeezing my eyes shut, I try to remember the exact sound and resonance of his voice after all these years. The loss of it slides up underneath my ribs and lodges itself there.

When my muscles start to shake from the effort of being upright, that's when the darkness consumes my mind. A hopelessness that is so heavy, it's futile to fight it. It's freeing, in a way. It's freeing me from every belief and value I've upheld my entire career.

Work, strive, achieve.

Ride or die.

Tossing the notebook onto the flames, I choose to let this part of me *die*.

Sedona, October

"Being around her is like being trapped in prison," I grunt to Landon during a set of progressive gait-training exercises. If I can nail these, we move on to stairs, stationary bikes, and more advanced drills.

But I don't tell him the truth. I don't want to move on. I don't want to progress.

Shaking his head, he huffs out a laugh and glances at Carmie curled up on the outdoor couch. Why she's hanging around after our last two failed sessions, is beyond me. I told her I tossed her notebook into the fire and it gutted me a little when she didn't look the least bit surprised.

I gave her the silent treatment for the rest of the fifty-seven minutes.

"You're mad, bro. I would *pay* to be her patient. Client. Whatever. I would lick her shoes and then ask for more."

"That's because you don't know her." I struggle through the next round of exercises, barely focusing on my form.

"No, that's because I'm not a moron." He smacks my shoulder testing my balance. I wobble, and it pisses me off.

"We'd be moving faster through your recovery if you did it at my facility. Like I've been saying for *weeks*. You're at a plateau. Is that what you want?"

Yes.

"No."

But my lie is drowned out by the sound of Ms. Know-It-All chiming in.

"It's because of his pride. He doesn't want to be around other athletes or people in this condition."

She doesn't even look up from her damn book, *Women Who Run with the Wolves*. My eyes narrow on the weathered copy and I remember my father buying my mom a copy of it for her 40th birthday.

My mom was silent on our last phone call, a battle of our wills, which always unnerves me and also where I get my stubborness from. Before she hung up, she lowered her voice and said, "You know what? I don't think your father would even recognize this version of you. I love you, but don't call me again until you've worked through your shit. Preferably with a professional. I hope you find someone."

Beep.

"Why don't you make a home gym here? Isn't there a detached garage around back?" Carmie rises from the couch and stretches like a cat, exposing a sliver of skin above her hips.

I look at Landon, who's looking at Carmie, and feel a slow heat spread up my spine. My hands traveled over her skin, once upon a time, and I can't even lie to myself that it wasn't the best feeling of my life to have her smooth curves underneath the harshness of my body.

The contrast was heaven before it turned to hell.

"Because I don't want one," I shoot back like a child.

"That explains it to me so well, thank you." She smiles and walks into my kitchen like she owns the place.

Why doesn't she just go home?

"I'm going to ask her out." Landon moves a chair closer to me for our last set of exercises. His words shock me and I fight to stay standing. We stare at one another, and he smiles like he knows he struck something soft inside me.

Refusing to admit I care, because I *don't,* I tell him, "Go for it, your funeral. She seems clingy." Sitting down, I start working, eager to get him out of my house. *Both of them.* Instead of leading me, or spotting me as I pay him to, he saunters into the kitchen with a puffed-up chest. *Peacocking everywhere.*

My jaw works and my eyes narrow. I turn the volume of the movie down on the screen and try to hear their conversation. I can only see around the corner, but he's doing the classic *tuck her hair behind her ear* move. She's laughing at something he said while she pours him juice. She leans onto the marble counter and gives him these big, fuck me, mermaid eyes.

Whatever. I don't need them. I'm done with this shit.

"Do I pay you to flirt, or to be my PT? Let's go!" I yell.

They both laugh as they walk back into the room.

"From your lack of effort, hygiene, and general will to live, I would say you don't need me at all, bro," Landon tosses at me with a smirk.

He turns to Carmie as she gathers her bag. "So I'll pick you up at seven?"

"Sure. I can't wait." A small blush blooms over her cheekbones. She walks out the door with a wave to both of us. I scowl. "This is so fucked up. Come on, man."

Landon shrugs. He starts massaging some of the muscles on my left thigh. "You have no room to talk, you made your choice. *Get busy living or get busy dying*. I'm choosing to live. Plus, are *you* going to do anything about it?"

He raises an eyebrow at me and I look away, jaw clenched. He knows the answer and I don't need to confirm it. "Didn't think so," He laughs before packing up and leaving me alone with my thoughts and my pain, again.

Carmie

SEDONA, October

Flying through our house, I run down the hallway and open Elyse's door. I'm out of breath, so I don't hear the *sexy time* playlist pouring out from her speakers. Opening her door, the first word out of my mouth is not one I expected.

"Eden?!" My screech echoes off the high ceiling as I see him mid-pump into one of my best friends.

Remembering myself, I scream and cover my eyes, running away to the sound of Elyse's laughter and her directing him to, *Keep going or I'm giving you two stars*.

After a few moments, and what I'm sure was a hasty climax for all parties, they both waltz out of her room with that trademark satisfied sexy-time-glow. My stomach hollows out for a moment, missing physical intimacy like I miss my favorite hiking trail in Ohio or my favorite almond croissant in Nashville.

My skin is hot from embarrassment, but Elyse keeps laughing before plopping down on our oversized *Sixpenny* couch. Eden lingers by the counter, giving me a miniature glare. But Elyse snaps her fingers like she's ordering caviar on a yacht and Eden springs into action, grabbing her a glass of water, before digging around in our fridge for a lemon.

All I can do is watch with my mouth ajar as he slices it, squeezes it, and delivers the glass to Elyse.

"Holding grudges is low vibrational energy. Carmie did what she felt she needed to do, get over it." Elyse says. "This is our house, don't you know? *If you wanna be my lover, you gotta get with—*"

I almost start laughing at his face before he waves his hand and stops her from butchering "The Spice Girls."

"Aye, enough! Your voice is making a dog howl somewhere in misery." Eden smiles as he says it, telling me he also finds her terrible singing endearing. They look at one another for a beat and my head tilts, reading the quiet bond forming between them.

One that is more than just sex.

"Hey, I'm glad you're here." I look up at the ceiling, a little nervous about my plan before addressing everyone. So nervous I forgot to ask in the first place, "And, when did this start up again?" I wish I could hide the small emotion in my voice aimed at Elyse. It's not a feeling of jealousy, but more so, the complicated grief that accompanies the memory of my own lost possibility.

Elyse's eyes soften and so does her voice. "He saw you leaving the coffee shop with Riley and reached out to me. I've been traveling so much for work, Carm. I'm sorry I didn't tell you sooner." Which is also code for, *I didn't think I would still be seeing him.*

Nodding my head, I continue. "So, Eden, I have a favor to ask."

"Mm," Eden plops next to Elyse and plays with her long black hair. "And what would the little heart breaker like to ask, hmm?"

My eyes widen as embarrassment creeps up, but Elyse beats me to it.

She smacks him across his naked chest and announces, "You're giving me the ick. I don't sleep with people who are this petty."

"We're not just sleeping together, babe," Eden whispers into her neck.

I cut them off, "So, Parker isn't progressing in physical therapy *or* during our sessions and I had an idea."

"You don't gotta tell me about my best mate. I know exactly how he's doing." Eden points at me.

"He's given up, Eden."

His blue eyes stare me down and I can see the conflict churning in them.

Over the last month, Parker has completely caved in on himself, burying himself so deep under the rubble of his life, content to stay there. Anytime a rescue team attempts to reach out with a hand, he bites it and sinks lower into the canyon of his own making.

He doesn't show up for PT. Even when Landon comes to the house. He doesn't shave, shower, or bother with anything beyond watching movie after movie. He won't drink the healthy juices I have delivered, he won't answer phone calls, and not even his agent can put a fire underneath his ass.

"I know you don't want to see him throw his career, or his *life* down the drain." I sit on the edge of the coffee table and try to appear more confident than I feel.

Eden, looking more somber than I've ever seen him, nods his head in silent agreement.

"You could quit. He'd probably be better off." Eden's voice lacks all humor and I feel his words like the heavy cross I already bear. Elyse stands up and looks at Eden. Something passes between them before she says with a steady voice, "That is the last time I will allow you to disrespect my friend. You have a decision to make. Bury this grudge like a good boy," she winks, infusing a little humor into the conversation, "or say goodbye. I can't stand for this, Eden. I...like you. But this is my boundary and it's not going to change."

My heart pumps and I fight the tightness behind my eyes. Looking up at one of my best friends, I wonder what I did in a past life to deserve this level of love. She sits next to me on the coffee table, the line officially drawn in the sand.

"Ah," Eden sighs, his chest lifting and falling. "Alright. Go ahead."

"I would love your help creating a home gym for him, in the garage he never uses. I already talked to Landon last night at dinner on what equipment he would need—"

"Wait, you went *out* with Landon?" Elyse and Eden pipe up at the same time, the earlier conflict already forgotten.

"Not, *out* out. Just to talk about my idea." I cross my arms.

"Does Parker know this?" Eden asks, but he draws out the question.

"Probably. Why?" My eyebrows pull together.

Eden sighs and mumbles, "Bloody women, makin' absolute chaos at every turn."

Elyse smiles and leans into me. "Was he...jealous?"

"You are focusing on the wrong thing again," I point my finger at her before continuing. "No. Trust me. Parker can't stand me, and that's why I need your help with this training space."

Elyse huffs as she leans back, uninterested again.

"All I need are some pointers and a little help assembling the equipment. Please? I know you want him to compete with you again. And I don't know if he's ever going to get there. At least, not the way he is right now."

I look out our sliding doors at the creek trickling down below in the yard. Parker could very well be my last counseling patient *ever*, and I want to make an impact. It seems unorthodox, or a bit delusional, but I can't shake the idea that I'm meant to be here. That I'm meant to be doing something for him.

A small voice in the back of my mind calls me out. *This entire operation is a scam, a way for you to selfishly absolve yourself of the guilt and hurt you caused him. Don't you know it's your fault he's in this position in the first place? It's all your—*

No.

I stop the voice before it can burrow deeper into my consciousness. It isn't my fault he got hurt.

No? You weren't the first tipped-over domino leading to pain and chaos in his life?

No.

"Do you believe me walking away *again* will change his mind? Motivate him to get up and find his fire?" My voice is directed at Eden but I realize it's also for myself. "If you believe that, I'll walk away right now. That's more important to me than staying in his life. I'm not sure why I felt so compelled to help in the first place." My throat works to swallow past the thickness of those words, of the bitter truth in them. I *would* walk away, even if I hated it. Even if I wanted to stay. Even if my intuition screamed at me to.

"No, I don't believe that," Eden admits. "But I'm not admitting that to anyone but you."

Exhaling, I feel the weight lift off my chest.

"Yeah, fine," Eden sighs and runs his hand up and down his blonde stubbled jaw. "I'll help. Ok. But don't tell anyone." He stands up, stretches, and pats my head like a dog. I'm not sure if that means he forgives me, is on my side, or is just entertaining *this* idea before he goes back to hating me. He turns to look at me as he pours a cup of coffee into a mug.

"How do you plan on paying for all this stuff? It's not going to be cheap." He eyes me with curiosity.

"Don't worry about it." My lips turn up and I can feel the first real smile of the day, of the week, pulling across my face.

He sips the coffee, clears his throat, and says, "Well, come on then. Let's get our Kevin Costner on."

"And what does that mean?" I ask, feeling lighter than the altitude-thinned air.

He turns and winks before saying, "If you build it, he will *come*."

"Gross," Elyse and I mutter before jumping up and getting to work.

Sedona, October

C illian leads me back to my front door after a weekend
away in Flagstaff for an expedition. I made face with my
sponsors, met some new athletes, and had an overall miserable
time. Cillian made me shower, shave, and *show up*, which was
the hardest of all. I've never been a liar, and I was tempted to
throw in the towel and officially end my contract. End my
career. But I couldn't find the right time.

"Yeah, my recovery is moving along. Next week I should be
able to get back on the bike and take an easy run down my
home tracks." I told my sponsors all weekend as I fought to
keep my slow walking pace even, hiding my limp.

The next race season is almost here, and I'm coming to
terms with the fact that I won't be on a bike competing. Not
now, not ever. But I can't imagine saying it out loud, can't
imagine the look on my father's face if he were here. If I were
in the mood to lie to myself, I could say that my father would
be disappointed that I haven't taken first place yet. But, the
truth is quiet and it eats me alive, a slow-spreading disease.

He never gave a shit about what place I took. He only cared that I put my head and my heart in the same place. If he saw me today...I know he'd see right through me. He'd see me going through the motions, in the way only a concerned parent can.

There's little chance he would be quiet about it. He'd sit me down, on top of one of our hiking trails, and stretch the silence between us until even I couldn't stand it.

Then, I would talk. Sometimes I would pace, yell, or even cry.

But he always managed to get the truth from me.

My father used to say that *the person who has a "why" to live for can bear with almost any "how."* But maybe, he was full of shit. Maybe, it's time I stop denying the fact that my body is broken and my spirit is not too far behind it.

Cillian is bouncing on the balls of his feet, filled with a nervous energy that's making me crazy.

"Ok, Cill, I don't need a chaperone in my house. I promise I won't hang myself. Just give me some space." I unlock the front door with the code, and he pushes ahead of me.

My mom has a client in Denver, so she's gone for the next week or so.

"I'm going to ignore that you just said that, yeah? So, ah, can I use your back garage to store my new kit? Can we go look at the space? See if it's big enough?" His face lights up and mine screws up in confusion and annoyance.

"What is going on with you, today? Go home." I spin around and limp toward my bedroom. Landon checked in on me once last week and told me the limp is psychosomatic and that I'm full of shit. I could've already been climbing back to the top of my game by now. I slammed the door in his face.

"No! Wait! Come on. I need a space and don't want to pay for a unit."

Deliberating, but coming up with zero reason to deny

him, I sigh and walk toward the sliding doors. He races in front of me and that's when I notice something is off. The light in the garage is on, and there's muffled music floating across the lawn.

Nobody's been in there since I stored some of my old bikes in there. Was that last year? The year before last? What the hell is going on?

"Close your eyes!" Cillian yells before stopping at the door to enter.

"No."

"Come on!"

"No."

He sighs and rolls his eyes. "I told Eden you wouldn't be any fun. Fine, have it your way." Cillian pushes the door open and I don't know what I was expecting. But it wasn't *this*. Goodbye drab, dusty, storage space. Hello, functional, clean, training space of my *dreams*.

Taking a hesitant step forward, I realize that the space is the physical equivalent of the inside of my brain. Someone pulled out the perfect details to make this place everything I could ever desire. Except, they had the idea first. This space screams my name.

Walking beyond the row of mirrors hanging on the wall, the weights lined up neatly in their racks, the *Rogue* CrossFit materials, I stop in front of the garage door. Eden's waiting there with a smirk on his face and his arms crossed.

Behind him, large crimson letters hand-painted on the door read *RIDE OR DIE.*

"Did you do this?" I ask, but it comes out raspy. Spinning on my heel, I take in every inch of the dark garage. Matte black everything except small splashes of gold and red.

On the opposite wall, there's a *Red bull* flag hanging over a shelf of all my trophies and medals. I can't believe it's real. There's recovery equipment, foam rollers, a stationary bike, ropes, weights, a massage table, elastic bands, and even a small mini fridge humming in satisfaction by the corner. I can see through the glass door that it's stocked with green juice, my favorite water, and protein bars.

"Did you do this?" I spin back toward Eden and narrow my eyes at him.

"Who else would do this?" He waves his hand around at the garage.

"So you're telling me you spent an entire weekend doing *this garage*, instead of your new girlfriend?" I lift an eyebrow.

"She's not my girlfriend. It's ah, it's casual." Eden breaks eye contact and his ears get red.

"Mhm," I murmur.

"You did this?" I clasp Eden's hand and pull him into as strong of an embrace as I can manage. He slaps my back and pulls away, face a bit serious before saying, "Like I said, who else would have?"

He's staring at me like I'm missing the plot, but I shake it off. All three of us walk around the garage, testing the equipment, wrestling one another, and christening the space. My throat works overtime to contain the emotion nipping at my heels like hellhounds. The four walls echo and reverberate a sense of love and loyalty so strong it makes my skin break out in goosebumps. Always a fan of logic, I'm surprised by how overwhelmed I am by the *feeling* of the space.

Overwhelmed. It's the only word to describe it. As I stare at myself in the mirror, I see how selfish I've been the last two months. How stuck in my own self-pity and downward spiral. How I've had people, *good fucking people*, working to get me back. Waiting for me. Working *for* me when I stopped trying to work on myself.

I catch Eden's eye in the mirror and clear my throat. "How did you get everything in here? Did you come up with the design and layout of the space?"

"Mhm, sure." Eden breaks eye contact and bends over to grab a juice from the cooler.

"It must have been filthy before you got everything here. How long did it take to clean it?" My eyes follow his form around the sanctuary. Because that's what this is, a mental and physical sanctuary.

"Ah, I lost count. Dunno." He shrugs.

"Eden."

"Yeah, mate?"

"Did you do this?" I ask for the last time.

He drinks his juice and hops on the bike, changing the channel on the mounted TV to a Marvel movie marathon.

"Man, I love this movie. Best soundtrack ever."

I gaze at the screen and realize it's the first time he didn't answer me. Cillian starts to do some box jumps, and I pivot to stare at the words painted on the garage door. There's a flowing quality to them...a slight imperfection from the hand of someone not concerned with using a level or ruler. Someone using passion over precision.

Eden's like that. But so is someone else I know. I shake my head as if I can manually remove any thought of *her*.

Eden did this, why would he lie? He wants to see me win, has the funds, and most of all—the bossy nature to direct people around for quick renovations.

My eyes snag on the bright red *RIDE OR DIE* of the garage door and my heart pumps my blood a lot harder. Looking over my shoulder at Eden, who is distracted fooling around with Cillian, I turn back to the words. Without this gesture, without this space, I know exactly how far I would have let myself sink.

She knew it too.

Carmie saw it in our three failed sessions, probably from the first time she saw me in the hospital bed. She felt every ounce of pain I was withholding. She heard it in my silence, sitting across from her refusing to participate.

She knew I was ready to die.

That's when it hits me like the full force of the wind going downhill on my bike. There's something in this space that even my oldest friend isn't capable of creating.

Love.

Carmie

Sedona, October

P icking at the red paint underneath my short nails, I tune back into Lina's voice across from me in the circle of women at the dance studio. It's our third week in the eight-week series, and we're dropping into the juicy topics along with learning new dances and pole tricks.

"We know enough about being distracted, being entertained. But we know very little about experiencing pleasure."

Each week we have a homework assignment. They're less about getting it *right* and more about embodying a theme. The first week, we had to spend thirty minutes in the shower instead of racing through our self-care routines. Our second week was filled with exploring our five senses: tasting chocolate, experimenting with new clothing textures, and even listening to music we wouldn't normally gravitate to.

Our homework is to prove to ourselves that we can take the version of ourselves in this room, and bring her into the world where it matters. This little studio, filled with spilled secrets, soft floors, and shiny poles, has become a second home to me. It's the space where I can feel an authentic self emerging, even if I'm not ready to share that with the world yet.

Most of us women in the series come from high-stress careers: lawyers, corporate bankers, and business owners. There's even another counselor enrolled in my group. Lina is constantly reminding our group, "It's the women who lock up their femininity to survive male-dominated workspaces who need to re-learn the art of sensuality the most."

I fall into that category, but I'm also in a league of my own. It's not that I'm forced by my career to be tough. Nobody is actively encouraging me to repress the concepts of femininity, self-worth, love, and pleasure... (Scratch that. My family encourages it).

But it's that I'm still unable to carry those concepts with me out into the world, or more importantly, into my relationships.

That is *my* responsibility, not anyone else's.

I'm the one who chose to grow into a version of myself I no longer recognize. I decided to mangle myself to keep the peace, a tree forced to grow around a man-made structure. Warped and tangled.

Hopefully, over the final five weeks, I'll grow new roots. Roots so strong that I won't be tempted to conform myself around another person ever again. But, I'm the only one responsible for doing the work to make that happen. It's why I keep showing up, even when I would rather die of embarrassment instead—which is often.

"Before we move our bodies and learn the chair routine, we are going to create a list in our journals." Lina motions to us to grab our notebooks as then Jasey Rae picks up the conversation. "We're all going to make a list of all the qualities..."

My ears perk up. "A list of potential traits and qualities in our future partners?" I blurt. I still have that list somewhere, hidden in a pile of clothes in my dresser. The edges are worn and the ink slightly faded, but I can't bring myself to throw it away.

"Nope!" She pops the *p*, excitement gleaming in her eyes. "We're going to make a list of all the qualities we want to cultivate within *ourselves* before entering into a partnership again." She pauses and looks around, "And in some of our cases, qualities we aim to bring into our current relationships."

The pinched smile on my face remains, fake as the day is long. *Please don't ask me to do something like, make eye contact with myself in the mirror or take myself out on a date, please don't—*

"One way we're going to deepen these qualities is by going on a solo date this week as part of your homework."

Jasey rubs her stomach absent-mindedly as she lowers her voice. "Who are you *without* a companion? If given the chance to be alone: what food would you order, how would you walk, and what thoughts would you have? Will you hide when the world sees you without a phone or a distraction or a partner? These are the emotions and experiences we are going to work through over the next few sessions."

Lina adds, "It's about discovering the pleasure and love of your *own* company." She makes eye contact with me and holds me captive. I nod my head, agreeing to the assignment before her lips twitch in response.

"Now!" She claps her hands and rises. "Let's learn this lap dance!"

Carmie

SEDONA, October

Marching down the small hill to the garage, I gnaw on my lip in anticipation. Parker must be inside by now. The palms of my hands are raw, my nails are cracked, and my body is utterly exhausted from the marathon weekend of getting his surprise training space ready.

The back of my thighs especially burn after two hours of learning a lap-dance routine that Lina said, "*Is just for you ladies. If a man is so lucky to ever grace a chair you're dancing on, make sure you always dance for* you *first.*"

Elyse, Landon, Eden, and a few of Parker's other teammates helped me pull this project off while Cillian took him out of town. Over the three days, everyone would head home around dark, but I stayed long into the early morning hours. Three nights in a row. There was something therapeutic about working on the surprise. Brushing the floors, cleaning away dead bugs, scrubbing the walls, and painting. The long hours of manual labor were a catharsis I didn't realize my body and heart needed.

Surprisingly, clearing out the space also cleared out my head.

If you were a fly on the wall, you would have seen me creating my own little "Karate Kid" montage of chores. I played music as I scrubbed old cinderblock walls. Up and down, as the suds washed away the grime. I listened to podcasts on healing codependency in relationships as I removed old metal shelving units to make space.

Sliding, pulling, and sweating, my muscles burned with effort and motivation.

I set up the TV with the help of Landon and the boys so that I could re-watch my favorite movies while I painted.

Dip, roll, and then peel the tape.

There's a poet and artist out there who once said, if you're lacking direction or purpose in your life, go do your dishes. Get out of your head and try your hand at finishing something.

This weekend also allowed me to ask for help instead of shouldering the entire operation on my own.

By the last evening, I laid down on my back, staring out the skylight that was professionally installed in the roof. The stars winked at me. I was tempted to fall asleep right then and there, smelling the fresh paint on the garage door and the sounds of the dessert floating in through the open door.

But now, in the light of day, I'm wondering if it was too much. If Parker will even like it. Will he show up and *try to* get his shit together? Will this be a turning point?

The garage door is rolled up and I hear Landon barking orders at Parker. Leaning on the edge of the cinderblock wall, I cross my arms and smile.

Parker's face is shaved and his eyes are bright. He's wearing new compression gear and I spy a green juice, water, and coffee by his side.

"Last one! Let's go!" Landon yells in Parker's face, and I

wince before he turns and winks at me as Parker wraps up the set. I've never been the type to voluntarily sign up for military-style workout classes, and I don't think I'll start now.

Parker finishes and then pulls his shirt off with one hand. His hands are still the navigational buoys that catch my drifting eyes. I can't help it. He interlaces his strong, now slightly crooked fingers, behind his head as he lets out a gruff sigh. Sweat rains down his back and pools in the dimples of his lower spine.

Heat floods the bottomless cavern of my stomach and my mouth gets dry.

The music turns off and my eyes snap up to the mirror where Parker's eyes are waiting for me. Watching me. We're snared, and for a moment we're in a different story—where two lovers don't waste precious time.

At the very least, they don't hold back how much they want to feel calloused palms sliding up and down the softest parts of their body.

Swallowing, I look away first.

"Good morning gorgeous," Landon sings, a note of laughter in his voice.

Parker shoots him a glare. "I thought we agreed, no women in the garage."

"Pipe down—" Landon walks over and gives me a bear hug, lifting my feet off the black mats, "she's more welcome here than you."

"What is that supposed to mean?" Parker turns toward us and his eyes linger on Landon's arm wrapped around my shoulders. Truthfully, Landon feels more like Riley than a potential romantic partner. But I don't feel like proving anything to Parker. He can assume what he wants.

I like getting under Parker's skin a little. It's a sign of life. *Oh God, I sound like Elyse.*

"Because man, she's the reason—"

"Landon! I almost forgot. You left your hoodie at my place the other night. Want to swing by later to get it?"

The Earth sucks in a breath for what feels like an eternity. Landon's eyes sparkle with mischief before snapping his fingers and going along with me. "Right, right you are my little fox. Of course, I'll grab it." For added effect, he pinches my ass and makes me yelp in surprise.

"I'm out of here, don't forget to see your massage therapist today," Landon throws over his shoulder at a stone-faced Parker before he walks out.

"So, really impressive space here," I say, while walking the perimeter of the gym. It already feels different with him in here, filling it with his focused and competitive energy.

It smells different too.

Red dirt. Sweat. Open skies.

"Yeah, Eden outdid himself. It's perfect."

I smile and look over my shoulder at Parker as I keep walking, "Yeah? What's your favorite part?"

The temptation to close my eyes and press rewind on my life is almost too strong to resist. To rewind and ignore my brother's phone call. To rewind and go to Europe with Parker. To rewind, and never get back with Seamus in the first, or second, or third place.

Being around Parker is a full sensory experience. His smell, his presence, his energy, and *our* memories, create a siren call inside me. It was easy to ignore when he was being a royal pain in the ass during our sessions. But it's hard to ignore when I'm seeing him in his element.

My feet stop walking and I'm somehow standing back in front of him, my unconscious pacing leading the ship right back to the wreckage. Right back to where it started.

Waiting for an answer.

He grabs his shirt and puts it back on as if he can't leave

any part of himself vulnerable to me. He needs the armor, and the protection, and it doesn't go unnoticed.

Shrugging, he says, "I can't put my finger on any one thing that's my favorite. But when I walk in here, it feels...like being seen."

"That's because you are." The words are out of my mouth before I can hit the pause button. Covering my impulsive comment, I add, "And, I'm glad to see a fire underneath you again."

He considers me for a moment, but instead of shutting down, he tilts his head and asks me, "What's your favorite part of the space?"

Without looking around, I answer, "The words on the door."

My heart stutters and I realize my mistake.

"How did you know there were words up there?" He points to the ceiling where the garage door hangs above us like an omen.

I smile and look up, "Oh, ah, I heard Eden talking about them to Elyse."

Parker narrows his eyes at me. "Bullshit."

"It's true!" I laugh before I scratch the side of my nose.

"Bullshit." He smirks now and I think he's enjoying watching me squirm.

"How do you know that's bullshit?"

"Because I know Eden and when he's using his mouth it's not to wax on about a garage. He's more likely to use it by talking about pussy...or using it to eat it."

My mouth drops open and I suck in a sharp breath. His lips turn up at my cartoon eyes popping out of my head.

"Don't be crude! I hate that you just said that." I smack his shoulder and look scandalized. *My god, the mouth on this man.* I steel my spine so my legs don't turn to jelly.

"Bullshit." He leans in and whispers in my face. "You love

it when I talk like that. And I know without a doubt you don't hate the idea of me doing that to you either."

"No," I say, but it comes out all wrong. "I mean, yes, I would hate it." Instead of defiant, my voice is breathy and weak.

Parker steps into me and I keep my eyes on his face the entire time, I'm so focused on the confusing fire and borderline hate in his eyes, that I flinch when his palms land on my waist.

"I'll tell you what's bullshit, Carmela." He leans down to whisper into the shell of my ear. If I had any sense in my God-given brain, I would keep my eyes open or keep distance between us. But I'm a sucker.

Closing my eyes, I wait for it. I wait for his words, his breath, his touch. I don't care that my stomach is tumbling and my heart is faltering. I would spend a lifetime floating in these confusing, hot waters.

"It's *bullshit* that everyone keeps walking around here giving Eden the credit for this." One of his hands squeezes the flesh between my hip bone and my ribcage. My body bends like warm wax toward him, melting under his intensity, and my eyes fly open.

"You hate me," I whisper.

"It's *bullshit* that you're not taking credit for the single best gift anyone has ever given me." His thumb traces up my waist and lands underneath the curve of my breast.

"I don't know what you're talking about," I whisper, chest rising and falling with the weight of my lie.

Parker's thumb travels down, drawing a half-moon right over my exposed hip bone. Every time he passes over it, stroking with his thumb, my skin grows tighter. The rhythm creates a matching pulse between my thighs and I'm aware of the small droplet of sweat racing down my temple.

We don't break eye contact.

"*Bullshit*. Tell me Little Red," his gaze sweeps down my body, landing on my bruised and cut knees. "When you felt the pain from being on your knees all those hours, did you think about me?"

Oh god, I'm going to pass out.

"You're giving me whiplash."

They say when a swimmer is caught in a riptide, it's best not to panic. It's best to *let go*, swim parallel to shore, and stop fighting.

So I stop fighting.

His voice lowers, knowing damn well his effect on me. "Did you imagine me laying you out right over there?" He lifts his chin toward the floor-to-ceiling mirrors. "And going down on you as I encourage you to watch yourself come all over my tongue? I'd pin you down," his wide and rough hand splays over my lower stomach, "and start all over again if you closed your eyes. I want your moans, your body, and most of all—your eyes, on me."

My knees buckle and his grip tightens. It's funny how the brain locks up certain memories, memories that can make you question every choice. Parker's husky dirty talk is a memory of the past, unlocked and unearthed, once more. His voice was in my ear, coaxing me into ecstasy before falling asleep, a routine I fell into and never dreamed of falling out of.

"N...no—" I'm stuttering, blubbering, and a hot, *wet*, mess. My thighs squeeze together to alleviate the pressure.

It doesn't work.

His one hand slides down my body and I don't have to have good intuition to know where it's headed. His fingers dip into my waistband and...he calls my bluff.

"*Bullshit*, Carmie." My lips tremble slightly, emotion overtaking lust, realizing he hasn't called me that since that horrid day. When I left him and went to Cleveland instead.

Both of his hands drag up my body until they're on my

neck, his fingers cupping the back of my head, angling me to look up at him. There's a shadow of a smile sitting on his lips, just for me, and all I can do is blink at it.

"Why did you do it?" His lips are so close that my mouth dries out again. "Why did you let them take credit for it?" He steps toward me, only his shirt and mine separating our bodies, and I wish I dared to erase the distance, to beg for what my body wants.

With every second that hangs between his question and my silence, I watch his eyes harden, brick by brick, a wall being erected.

"Carmie, for once in your life *please* tell me the truth. Why did you do this?"

When most people beg, their voice gets high with desperation. But, Parker? His voice turns into the memory of my first scraped knee. His voice sounds like my teeth clenching together to bite back the pain. His voice tumbles through my stomach like loose rubble.

It's not that I can't say why I did this for him. I *won't*. Everything in my body is screaming at me to unburden my heart, unburden the secrets, and believe that he'll still be here standing with me when it's done... but I know better.

His hands—*god, his hands*—drop from my face. Taking a step back, he stares down at me as my phone starts ringing. I hear its tune, but I can't drag my eyes away from his face.

After the ringing ceases, my pocket buzzes relentlessly to Elyse's special text alert. A heartbeat. The sound is lodged between me and Parker, our hearts *breaking*, to that cadence.

Swallowing, I force my eyes to glance at the screen and blanch when I do.

Carson is at our house.

You're embarrassing everyone.

Especially yourself.

Are you out whoring yourself to other people? Is that why you won't call back?

Babe, I'm sorry. I'm stressed. I lost one of my biggest clients. I fucked up.

Please come home.

I'm lost without you.

Please.

29 / THE MATRIX

PARKER

SEDONA, October

Carmie's face drains of all the color she's earned since being in Sedona. Her freckles splay across her nose and cheekbones, small constellations from worshipping the sun and open skies.

She looks healthy here, the distance and desert giving her a glow that isn't dependent on being a good fiancé, a good daughter, or a good therapist.

That's the thing about any wild land, you have to work for your freedom—it can't be faked.

She swallows again, attempting to slide her phone back into her pocket. I bite my tongue until I taste metal, resisting the urge to reach out and grab the glass brick. But that's not what she needs and I'm not an animal. I've seen men become reduced to teenage boys, snooping around in their girlfriend's phones, or worse, lunging for them, and using force to get them.

Some men never learn how to reign that shit in, learn how

to control their immature instincts. Or better yet, learn to inquire *why* they feel the need to do that in the first place.

Oh, and yeah, I know she's messing with me when it comes to Landon. And also, yeah, I know he'd still shoot his shot if she gave him the opportunity.

But if you asked me why my body is fighting the urge to see her phone, I would be forced to be honest. *Because she's upset. And against all logic, I care.*

Carmie has one of those expressive faces that shows every emotion when she's honest, a multi-faceted gem reflecting the full spectrum to you.

But when she's not? She's a looking glass with the fingerprints of other people smudged and streaked on every edge. She's taught herself how to mirror emotions, and how to match mannerisms until she can be alone.

"Talk to me." It comes out more like a demand than a question.

She shakes her head and turns on her heel. This woman would rather sink than swim, would rather take in water instead of fight to paddle to shore.

All she has to do is be honest, why is that so damn hard?

My body, still broken, but finally on track, moves in front of her. Both of my hands press into the doorframe, halting her exit.

"Do you need help? Talk to me."

Her eyes follow the horizon line of muscle between my left hand and my right. It makes my heart kick a little, being desired in the way that's written all over her face.

Her lips flutter before she tips her head back in frustration.

"Carson is at my house. I share my location with him, but that's more because they're so paranoid I'm going to be targeted one of these days as a politician's daughter. He's probably the one who gave Seamus my address to send that gift," She mutters to herself more than to me.

"A gift, hm?" The hair on my neck raising at his name. "Sounds like *same old, same* for you and Mr. Boy Next Door." I can feel my mouth twist into an ugly grimace, a mirror image of my heart wrapping itself in barbed wire to defend itself.

But in the time it takes me to finish my sentence, Carmie transforms her pain into a low burning anger. With her jaw set, and eyes hard, she takes a step closer to me. Tilting her chin up in a challenge, she presses her body into my chest, forcing me to concede a step out of the doorway.

The heavy Sedona sun beats down on my back and every blood cell in my body burns.

"Yeah, a gift. That *gift* paid for this space, I'll have you know." Her fingers trail my collarbone over my shirt and I repress a chill working up my back despite the heat. "Eleven thousand, three hundred, and forty-five dollars. The rest went to a friend. You think you know me, but Parker, you know a version of me I'm in the process of actively shedding. I *wanted* you to have this," she tilts her head to the sanctuary at her back, "more than I wanted to cling to the nostalgia of my past. More than I wanted to do the polite thing. But most of all, more than I wanted to keep a *dead dream* locked up in a box."

Her words may have been quiet, but they were lined with a new strength I've failed to see in her. She ducks underneath my arm and walks to her car without looking back.

☆

I stand in the doorway for three minutes, just enough time to hear her door shut, *Florence and the Machine* blare through her speakers, and tires peel out of my drive.

> Need Elyse's address.

Hi, Eden how are you? No? Ok. Fine. Right to it.

Do you mean Carmie's address? 🫣

> ...

😅

> You can pry later. Need it now.

📍 "Elyse's hot banging pad" location has been shared with you.

By the time I park on the road outside her long-term rental, keys in my hand, one leg in the car, and one out, I realize I have no plan. Turning my head, I see her standing in front of the stained glass door, refusing to let Carson inside. She looks like she has everything under control. They're just two adults having a conversation, albeit a tense one.

What the hell am I doing here? I sit back in my front seat, key in the ignition, ready to pull out and away from the impending family drama.

But then I hear her choked-up voice holding back tears drifting through the open window. She's a dam about to break.

"Don't *touch* me."

It's all my body needs to override my brain. I'm out of the car, moving faster than I have in months, to reach her. Instead of reaching for *her*, I reach for *him*.

All I see is his hand wrapped around her upper arm, his face bent low into hers, invading her space. Refusing to take his hands off her.

I abruptly pull him back by the shoulder, but he doesn't release Carmie. He remains latched onto her upper arm and pulls her forward so that she drops to her knees on the concrete. Onto knees covered with purple bruises, cuts, and scrapes from building my gym last weekend.

My heart surges, my lungs squeeze tight as fuck. I scoop a shaking Carmie back up to her feet before he can touch her. She refuses to look at me, so I place her a few inches behind my body.

"This is family business." Carson's eyes never leave her face, but he paints on a swarmy politician's smile I know is meant just for me. I know he's dropping a mask down over the ugliness of the last few minutes to save face. He dusts off his suit jacket and slacks before he looks me in the eye again.

"Yeah?" I ask, voice growing as big as my fury. "That's not how my family handles business."

He laughs. Honest to god, he has the nerve to *laugh*, before raising his hands to the sky. "Let's start over, shall we? I'm Carmela's brother. My name is—"

"I couldn't care less, man. All I care about is how you're making her shake like a leaf behind me and how you're *not* wanted here."

He blinks a few times and makes a *tutting* noise in the back of his throat as if I need to be reprimanded like a child.

"Carmela, you can't ignore your family forever," he says to her as if I'm not standing between them. "All the missed calls, texts, and invites? It's piling up. Eventually—other people are going to start showing up here. Do you want Mom traveling all this way with her health conditions? You want our father to step away from his campaign, to talk some sense into you? Are you that selfish?"

I didn't need to turn around to know how those words struck the soft heart behind me. It's clear that Carmela is a loyal woman who gives far too much love to her family—even with no return on her investment.

He keeps talking but I tune his platitudes out because he reminds me of all the people on this planet who reap the benefit of keeping the status quo. The only role of those people, the universal *Agent Smiths,* is to ensure people in society stay in line by any means necessary. Most of the time, it doesn't come down to force. It's with coercion, manipulation, and threatening to take away a conditioned human's only desire.

To belong.

Biting my cheek and flexing my hands, I realize I have a bigger opponent here than I first realized. Carmie's still under the influence, the programming, of these people. Just like she said, she's in the process of shedding her skin but isn't quite there yet. All I want to do is scream, *WAKE THE FUCK UP.*

I tune back in just in time to feel my stomach roll at Carson's words.

"We love you, C-bear. Your wedding festivities are in three months."

"I'm *not* engaged," Carmie leans around me to affirm.

"You *are.*" Carson's eyes glide up and down my body, making it clear how little he approves of her being in my company. "Like I said, we love you, but our patience is running thin for these childish antics, Carmela Sabrina D'Angelo." Carson lowers his voice and uses her full name like a threat.

I've had enough.

"This doesn't sound like love. It sounds like possession." I take a step toward the man I'm confident has never taken a single punch to the jaw in his life. Might be the time to introduce him to it. But he surprises me, taking out his cuff links, and slowly rolling up the sleeves of his expensive jacket.

He takes a step in, meeting me in the middle of our stand-off.

Carmie slides in front of me and shakes her head. She turns and looks at me with a different type of mask than his, but a mask nonetheless. With a bright smile and cool composure. She can wear that mask all she wants, she can wipe her tears away, but I still see the salty tracks left on her face.

"Parker, I'm going to talk to Carson for a moment. Carson, would you mind meeting me inside?"

Her voice is polite and demure. I can't help the disappointment that floods my system. That dumb smile she's wearing cracks a little at the corners, no doubt sensing where my head went. My tongue glides over my front teeth in frustration, but I relent.

What was I expecting? We all have the same choice available to us. Take the blue pill, accept that your life is as it is, and remain asleep. Or, take the red pill. Leave everything behind you've ever known, go down the rabbit hole, find Wonderland, and finally live on your terms. Did I really expect her to do that?

I won't let myself be so naive again.

My eyes bounce between her left and right eye, a woman quite literally and physically divided between two worlds, between two versions of herself.

Shaking my head, feeling exhausted from the adrenaline of a situation I don't even belong in, I reach out to lift her chin up a few more inches. Ignoring our company, I drop my voice so only she and I can hear it, "If you need help, you can call me."

"Thank you, Parker." Her eyes smile back at me.

"Parker, where do I know that name?" Carson interrupts our moment.

I glare at him before moving around his thin and polished frame. He's the type of man who will never smell like an open sky or fresh rain on the pavement. With that thought, I smirk and brush his shoulder with a little too much effort.

"Ah, yes. *Parker*, now I remember." He turns back to Carmie and my steps instinctively slow. I can hear the smile in his tone, the insinuation of something I'm sure could give him the upper hand.

"Carson, why don't you come inside?" Carmie's voice lifts higher and higher with each word.

"Why wouldn't you want him to know what you did?" He presses her with a tone that reeks of victory.

I turn to look into those mermaid eyes, held so wide in fear I could drown in them. His question is less a string of words and more a barrel of a gun held at her temple. Whatever it is she's hiding, she doesn't want me to know. Would rather invite that bastard inside her new home, than let me overhear.

So I made the decision for her before her brother could hurt her any more than he already has.

I walk away promising myself that this is the last time I get pulled into the matrix of drama that is Carmela D'Angelo's life.

Carmie

SEDONA, October

E lyse is often gone for weeks at a time working her way through the understaffed and desperate emergency rooms of the West Coast. She's a hard one to pin down, a butterfly refusing to let life pin her down.

I didn't realize how much I missed her voice. She called me while I was in the process of getting ready for my date and I've yet to hang up. I just keep walking back and forth between her room and mine, the bathroom and her closet, with her on the other end but imagining she's here.

"Carm, it's true," she whines into the screen. Her Croc-covered feet are up in the air in an on-call room. No doubt she's taking a break from being the smartest person in the room.

"What's true? The West Coast is the best?" I ask, eyeing myself in the full-length mirror of her now-empty bedroom.

With Elyse's schedule, I'm here more by myself than I am with her. It's as if I moved to a new city, halfway across the country, by *myself*. My stomach churns with the salty waters of loneliness but I suck in a big-girl breath in anticipation for tonight. I buoy there for a moment—sink, float, loneliness, freedom.

"Everyone on the West Coast is terrible at their jobs," she pouts as she rips into a sour gummy worm.

Shaking my head and laughing, I step into my other role. "Elyse, what I'm hearing you say is that you are experiencing frustration at the way your co-workers do their jobs. That it's an *adjustment* for you."

"No, babe. I'm saying they're just REALLY bad at their jobs. I ask for an ultrasound ID and everyone just stares at me. Do we have a code? They *walk* to fulfill orders. It's agonizing. What the fuck is this? *Island time?* We're in the states, honey. Walk with a sense of purpose." She sighs then proclaims, "I need to stop taking jobs in California. Besides, Eden misses me."

My eyes shift to the screen just in time to see the cat-caught-the-canary grin stretched across her gorgeous, shameless face.

"So, things are heating up between you two?" I ask.

Elyse can be like a stray cat, so approaching her from a subtle angle about a sensitive subject is always more productive.

"Yeah..." her voice trails off and I catch the small pinch between her eyebrows. Lost in thought, there's a beat of silence before she perks up. "I like him, yeah, sure. All good. Now!" She claps her hands and leans into the camera. "Show me what you're wearing tonight for your sexy date."

Rolling my eyes, I remind her for the tenth time. "It's a date with *myself*, I don't know why I need to go through all of this trouble."

"Why not? Do you think the top CEOs of the world skip

out on important meetings with themselves? They treat every second of their day as if they are the most important person in their world. I don't think you've ever done that for a full day. Instead of people pleasing, why don't you try people *displeasing* for once?"

"Rude!" I chastise.

"True," she counters.

The door opens behind Elyse and she jumps up onto the bed waving her arms to yell, "Occupied, Ricardo! God!" before slamming the door back in his face.

"Don't you have a shift to get back to?" I laugh before I slip out of outfit option number five, tossing it atop the growing discard pile.

"No, it's residency and student season. They can handle it for a bit longer. *I* know what I'm doing, they need the practice." She waves the thought off.

My hand hovers over a few more options Elyse left on her bed for me, along with a tube of crimson lipstick I won't be entertaining. *Black sequins, plunging neckline. Frilly pink tutu, leotard bodice. Latex body suit, cat-woman style. Nothing here works for me.*

"Wear the red *Angelinta* one. It's underneath the white feather skirt on the edge of my bed." Elyse leans into the camera as she dumps the excess sugar from the candy bag into her mouth. The screen freezes for a moment and I take the opportunity to slip into the strapless burgundy dress.

Wow.

Blinking a few times to make sure I'm not in a fever dream, I'm taken aback by my reflection. Elyse is speaking in the background about texting someone but I can't focus. I reach my fingers up and trace my exposed collarbone. Cheeks flushed with excitement, I pull my hair into a French twist and pin it up.

That's more like it.

Over the last week, since Carson flew in and out, I've caught my features falling little by little. My dull eyes stared back at me in the reflection of a fork, the frizzy braids in the haziness of my car window, and the sharp corners of my lips stare back at me in the mirror of Parker's garage. I see that reflection in particular every day when I attempt to get him to do another talk session with me.

It didn't matter what feature I saw reflected on me, they all said the same thing. *You're losing momentum. You're losing. You'll go back eventually. You always do.*

"Hello? Carmie? Let me see, come on, I'm staring at the ceiling over here."

Shaking my head, keeping the explosive grin on my face, I hold up the phone for Elyse to see. Instead of making a joke, something about me looking like *every man's wet dream*— which I would've bet good money on her saying—she's quiet.

"Should I change?" I run my hands down the tight fabric. The swell of my breasts looks incredible in the corset bodice. Can't tell you the last time I saw the girls up and out like this, for anyone's pleasure let alone my own. The red fabric continues to spill from my waist in a long pleated skirt that moves like honey over my hips.

Sensual, bold, and yet still *me*.

"How do you feel about it, friend?" Elyse smiles at me like she's witnessing an important moment.

"I feel..."

"Try the lipstick before you answer," Elyse directs me without room for argument.

Tossing the clothes off of the bed and promising myself I'll clean them up later, I grab the DIOR lipstick and feel emotional as I read its color: *#742 Forever Sisterhood*. I swipe it across my full bottom lip then make sure I get every inch of my cupid bow.

"I feel powerful," I answer, stepping back from the mirror to admire, actually *admire*, my reflection.

My skin takes on a glow in contrast to the deep red dress and instead of washing out my copper-toned hair, it highlights it. The material is such a rich and earthy hue, at first glance, it appears to be mahogany. But my lips steal the show.

It's ironic. As much as I feared going on this date alone, I've wrapped myself up in a package that says, "*Come closer at your caution. I bite.*"

"Get on out there you little slut. I have to go make sure nobody is killing my patients."

"I'm going on a date *alone*, need I remind you." I cut my eyes over to my best friend.

"You never know," she sings as if I'll meet the man of my dreams and the manifestation of every list I've ever created tonight. "Slut is a state of mind. Plus, in your case, it stands for, *Sensitive, Loving, Ugly Crier, and Trying.*" Elyse kisses the phone and hangs up.

My phone beeps a few more times but I'm lost in my reflection. The image of this new person sends a confusing shockwave of remorse through me.

Remorse for the girl who never wore red lipstick before tonight.

Remorse for the girl who was too delusional to realize she was being fed table scraps of validation and praise from the people around her.

But there's also hope.

Hope for the *woman* staring back at me. She is with me as I light lantern after lantern, night after night, in search of myself.

Swallowing past the emotion in my throat, I soak in one last glance of myself in the mirror before I head out to the reservation Lina took the liberty of making for me.

> 8:30 pm. The chef is a friend of mine, send him my regards. 🦋

Getting in my car underneath the night sky, I smile at the name of the restaurant as I type it into my GPS.

Mariposa.

31 / MR. AND MRS. SMITH

PARKER

SEDONA, October

There isn't a bad seat in this entire place. I'm surrounded by wood, steel, glass, and the smell of Latin cuisine. Stars sparkle beyond the impressive glass walls, the mountains stand sentry around us, and the majestic night sky creates an intimate atmosphere.

But I don't see any of it.

Sitting at the bar, with an untouched Old Fashioned in front of me, I tune out the conversations of people around me. I'm irritated they don't feel the scrape of shackles around their ankles as they drag the memory of a loved one behind them. Bindings locked and tightened with each passing year.

Every time the date rolls around, I allow myself to feel the raw skin underneath the thick cuffs of my grief. Three hundred and sixty-four days a year, I shut the pain out.

But on one night—tonight—I feel it all. Preferably in public, because I don't trust myself. I don't trust that I won't take a bone saw and cut myself off completely from the memories. From the pain of it all.

Don't trust I won't follow in my father's footsteps.

Lifting the glass to my lips, I barely taste the sugary bourbon and cherry flavors sliding down my tongue. Setting the glass down, I push it away.

Ten years.

My lips part on a harsh exhale and I bow my head. If you were to see me, you might think I'm praying. But my head hangs from the heaviness of the past decade.

Submission. That's what I look like. It's not acceptance, not at all. Submission is what happens when your knees buckle and slam onto the cold and harsh ground of reality. There's no energy left to fight it, so you bow. Bend the knee.

Acceptance, I imagine, would feel worse. To accept what happened to my father would also absolve what he did to me. How could I ever make peace with his choice?

I prefer this prison of my own making. Suddenly, I hear her words floating to me on a phantom memory.

"Parker, who would you be, who could *you be without this grief?"*

My jaw tightens. She's so capable of getting to the heart and truth of a matter without cutting someone down to get there. I admired her once upon a time. Respected her. Coveted her. But my heart still has a limp. Even if nobody else can see it. I know it's there.

Don't get involved again.

A flash of red catches my eye near the lobby. I don't turn, for fear I've summoned her from thought alone. Gripping my sweating glass, I hold my breath and close my eyes. On any other night, I could handle her materializing into my space.

Not tonight.

It's the southwest, and women here wear bright colors unlike the East Coast and its never-ending mourning parade of black. It's probably a woman waiting for a date. Perhaps an anniversary of happier memories, unlike me.

Motion from the other side of the bar draws my attention. Breath abandons me. My teeth bite my bottom lip so hard I taste the color of her dress. Grief momentarily forgotten as I scramble to believe what I'm seeing.

Who I'm seeing.

She's a god-damn comet streaking through the inky dark lighting of this place. It's a once-in-a-lifetime type of sighting. Carmie doesn't just walk, she *blazes* by as the countless heads turn and lift in her presence. The shadows press in closer to the walls, scrambling to get away from the brightness. The hair raises on my arms and heat rushes through me at how she commands this room.

When the hostess finally pulls out the leather seat for her, after what feels like an eternity of watching every man in this room lose his mind over her, I'm already on my way to ensure I can get a table near Carmela.

A few words later, the hostess with her heavily greased pocket, leads me to the adjacent table. Wiping my palms on the back of my slacks, I realize I'm nervous. The black collared shirt I never wear feels like a noose. *Fuck.* Unsure of what to say, and how to start the interaction, I sit down and lift the menu, angling my body to face the night sky instead of the sunrise of a dress spilling down her body.

"May I see a dessert menu, please?"

The smile that curls across my face is as automatic as wishing on a shooting star. I'm about to turn around, to cut the shit, and join her when a wall obstructs my view.

"Dining alone, tonight?" The wall asks like a jackass.

I close my eyes to focus on their conversation.

"What gave it away?" She exhales with a breathy laugh.

With my eyes closed, I can hear every subtle emotion lingering between words. There's a smile in her words but it's not because she's entertaining this man—she's keeping a secret. She's not trying to be polite—she's toying with him.

I can't help but smirk as I let go of the breath I couldn't help holding tight in my chest since I sat down.

"Well," I hear the shifting of the man's weight on his feet next to me. "Any man leaving you alone at a table must be out of his mind."

Classy. Douchey. Won't last a minute.

"Mmm, and I suppose you'd be the man to never let me out of your sight?" She muses to herself more than to him.

My blood rushes south of the border as I imagine her breathing those words onto my neck.

"Why don't I prove it to you?" The man asks. He pulls out the chair and drops into it because it's clear his legs and ass haven't seen a leg day since he graduated college. There's little finesse in his movements at all. There's a good chance he sits at a desk. Gets happy hour with his crew before landing on the couch to binge-watch the shows his boss casually drops in conversation at the water cooler. Pathetic.

I look around and notice three or four other men at the bar watching the exchange with thinly veiled interest. All lining up, waiting their turn.

Before bachelor number one can weasel his slicked-back hair into her heart, I'm moving.

"Little Red, *darling*, are we done playing our game?" I walk to her chair and lean down to place a quick kiss on the juncture of her throat and shoulder.

Hovering for a moment, I feel her suck in a breath before a surprised little *oh* escapes her lips.

Straightening, I stare down at the man with the flapping mouth like a trout, before I tilt my chin wordlessly back to the bar.

Except he doesn't listen.

"What game?" He leans forward and places his elbows on the table as if he exists to question my intentions. Honestly, this guy proves you can have an MBA and still be a clueless idiot.

"Every year on our anniversary we take off our rings and pretend not to know one another." Carmie picks up the hand I dealt her and plays it flawlessly. "It keeps the relationship... interesting." She drives the lie home by biting her bottom lip and boiling my blood at the sight of it.

My hand moves up her neck, fingers wrapping around it in possession, a slight collaring. I drive it home by thumbing her bottom lip with my thumb. The pillowy muscle moves away from her teeth. I almost demand that she suck it...she'd do it. No doubt. Not because I said so, but because my hands are her favorite.

"So, dessert?" I ask, remembering her request.

The move was a royal flush. I win and the man drifts away like a scattered deck of cards.

My body finds the open seat next to hers and she watches me the entire time I pull the chair back to take my rightful position next to her.

When the small menu is dropped off, I watch her lips raise, twist, and turn while she deliberates which sugary meal to consume first.

Not only does her full pout look like the sun peeking above the horizon, her entire presence feels like it. If she's the embodiment of a sunrise, I'm the moment the world is plunged into the darkest night.

"I'll have the crème brûlée please," she tells our waitress.

I simply shake my head when it's my turn. We sit in silence for the better part of fifteen minutes and I relish the comfort between us.

But then, she breaks the silence.

"You know, this is supposed to be a solo date for me. It's part of my homework." Carmie looks at the dessert placed in front of her as if it's disappointed her.

"Is it hard for you to do things alone?" I ask without judgment.

She gives me a wry look.

"You love being right, don't you?" She asks.

"So? It doesn't mean I love being right at the expense of your feelings." It's genuine, but I also could have said, *I don't love being right as much as I love the unlikely turn of events tonight.*

"I suppose it's a little ironic I'm hesitant to eat alone when the majority of my life I felt desperately lonely, even in the presence of other people."

"Those weren't your people then."

"We don't get to choose our family," she responds with a slight narrowing of her eyes.

"Says who?" I counter, lowering my eyebrows and leaning in. The smell of caramel, vanilla, and fresh strawberries invades my space.

"Life is not as simple as you make it out to be, *Parker*." She bites the word out and I bite the flesh inside of my cheek.

She's trying something new and I need to remember that not everyone wants to be *pushed*. Some people want to be supported.

I sigh, then decide to switch gears. One that will honor her request and mine.

"We can be alone, together. I won't say a word. You enjoy your meal, and I'll enjoy mine. Play the game with me." I interlace my hands on the table and look out the window at the stars beyond the horizon line.

"What game?" She asks in a tentative voice.

"Let's be the old couple who doesn't need to talk to one another. The comfort of years and years of intimacy and trust living between us in silence. Let's be alone, at the same table, with no expectations. Play the game with me," I say with a drunken smile full of emotion.

Her eyes search my profile, hot on my skin like the full force of the sun.

"Please." I send that single word over to her like a caress. My grief is out of the dark box I keep it in tonight and it just wants to be in her light.

Picking up the polished gold spoon, Carmie whacks the surface of the burned sugar and *cracks* the tension right down the middle of us. Dipping her spoon into the custard, she brings it to her lips in slow motion and savors it like a last meal.

Tilting her head back, exposing the graceful column of her neck, she closes her eyes in pleasure and lets herself spill a satisfied, *hmm*, from her lips.

When she opens her eyes again and sweeps them over my anxious body, her words are as sweet as sugar.

"Let's play, Parker."

Carmie

Sᴇᴅᴏɴᴀ, October

I nstead of waiting for a reaction, I turn my attention back to the best dessert I've ever had in my life. The crème brûlée is a transcendental experience. Heavenly. There's no awkward pause after asking my companion if they want dessert and then following their lead. There's no voice in the back of my mind telling me that the sugar is going to go to my thighs and everyone will notice.

No. There's nothing and nobody here to stop the pure and sensual experience of having dessert first and enjoying every damn second of it.

Parker asks our waitress for a dinner menu and I smirk, but that's all the attention I'll give him. Sucking on the spoon, I stare outside at the stars winking down at me and contemplate the strange situation I've landed in. *Does this still count as a solo date even though he joined me?* Of course, it counts. He joined me. Plus, I'm making the rules.

Stealing a glance at him, I force my face to remain unaffected. Even though I'm foolishly and hopelessly affected.

How can my lungs not get tight when I smell the soap on his freshly showered body? How can my kidneys not send a flutter of adrenaline into my bloodstream when I listen to his carefully chosen words? How can my pulse thrum anything less than a bass in my neck by being so close to him?

Tonight, for some reason, he traded his usual long-sleeved mesh training shirt for a dark-collared one with a few buttons undone at the base of his throat. His typically messy, half-wet hair, now glows under the ambient light around us. Parker even traded in his disappointment for something else. Something I can't nail down yet, but I feel so close to uncovering it.

"So, our anniversary, huh?" I crack another corner of my crème brûlée and notice a slight flinch around his temples when I do so.

Instead of staring directly into my soul like his typical infuriating and confrontational self, he leans back and gives the reflection in the window a grimace.

"It's another anniversary today. To be honest, I'm as surprised as you are that I said it." He speaks to the distorted version of himself he's battling with.

"Would you like to talk about it?" I hedge.

Ripping his eyes away from the window, he considers my offer before picking up my spoon and taking a leisurely dip into the round dessert.

He turns the spoon vertically, so his tongue can lap up the custard in a ridiculous and tantalizing show. "Isn't that against the rules for this *solo* date?"

With the skin on my cheeks catching a blush, and my eyes glued to his mouth lined in short stubble—I forget myself.

Forget that he asked me a question.

What do I want more? The skeleton key that will unlock one door in this man's head? Or to say I went on a date successfully by myself?

I don't want to be a "good girl," a "nice girl," the "sweetest in the room," any longer. My spirit is exhausted from living two different lives. I want to flex my inner power. Make and follow my own rules. And damn it, there's nothing that makes me feel more powerful than being entrusted with one of those keys. Especially one from a habitually locked up and guarded man like Parker.

But, I also made a deal with myself, and I'm learning that the key to *my* future is about making deals with myself and keeping them. Not breaking them. If Sedona is teaching me anything, it's that life is less of a *this or that*; it's much more of a nuanced third option.

"I don't see why I can't do both. It's not like you're a renowned conversationalist anyway."

He grunts in agreement and I take it as a cue to add in another condition.

"After I get my silent, relaxing, dinner. You open up and treat the second half of our evening as if two friends happened to meet again after years apart."

He opens his mouth to argue, but I hold my hand up in a surprising show of boundaries and restraint.

"No, no arguing. It's this or kick rocks. So, decide now."

His eyes trail the edge of my face, and he leans in, voice low and rumbling like said rocks tumbling down the edge of a mountain. "Is that what we are Carmie? *Friends*?" His smile is a little loopy and I can smell a hint of smoky bourbon on his breath.

Swallowing, I shrug and continue to enjoy the first portion of our time together.

The first few moments are filled with a brutal awkward-ness I've worked my entire life to avoid. Heat crawls up the back of my neck and sweeps down my chest in mortification at how difficult this assignment is, especially now with a witness.

The silence between us, heavy and smoky, sits on my tongue like ash.

Shame, an experience I'm all too familiar with, takes a seat to my right, an invisible shadow. It whispers to me, "You're a grown woman and you can't even sit in silence for more than a few minutes without wanting to run away. Go ahead, Carmela. Run away, distract yourself. Go on."

I'm about to open my mouth, to put us both out of our misery when I witness Parker completely at peace. He's not a man who fidgets, and if he does, he's three seconds away from launching himself down a ravine on two wheels.

His controlled movements make his knife and fork move with precision as he works away at his lamb-chop appetizer. His eyes are soft, and the hard brackets around his mouth are lax. He appears to be at home with the silence as much as he is at home with his body.

I'm the one feeling dipped in fiery waters. I'm the one undergoing the baptism by fire. But with his cool demeanor next to me, I settle into my skin and get curious about whom I'll emerge as on the other side of this mini-initiation.

When the fried plantains are delivered, we both reach for a long curling chip at the same time, causing the tips of our fingers to brush.

Neither of us breaks the silence, but my skin tingles and my mind wanders back to his gym. Back to the moment I let his roughened hands roam my body.

We look at one another and a small edge of his lips turns up as he moves the basket closer to my plate.

No words are necessary. We eat in the increasingly comfortable atmosphere and I sink back into my body, into the experience of my senses. Truth be told, he overwhelms all five of them.

I drink him in as if I'll never get another intimate opportunity to do so. The weight of his eyes brushing over my body when he thinks I'm not paying attention. The sound of the ice in the bottom of his glass, swirling and swirling, as he stares down into it for answers. The scent of his laundry soap, shower gel, and the distinct stamp of outdoor air. The salty and fried taste of the food we share in communion. The memory of his lips crushing my own once upon a time.

It's inappropriate to compare people, professionally I know this, but I can't help but flip through the memories of eating with Seamus.

How busy they were. How loud. How catered they were to *his* tastes. How one-sided the questions were. How invisible I felt, even though I never got a reprieve from his conversations or his opinions.

Not only am I learning quite a lot of information about myself when I'm alone, but I'm also learning information about what I desire and need in a relationship.

Biting my lip, I feel an epiphany pull my heart out to sea with a metaphorical tide. When it sends my heart back to the shore, it's wiped clean of the past. It beats to a new and subtle philosophy—a gift and a curse offered by Parker's presence.

I don't have the words to describe this lightbulb moment, but I can feel it re-arranging me from the inside out. Parker's thigh accidentally brushes mine underneath the white-draped table, the action pulling me back to the surface.

This is the epitome of who he is as a man. Action, always. Words, rarely.

Every love song, romantic comedy, and work of poetry I've encountered is a piece of me. I've collected them, curated them, and treasured them as a hopeless romantic ought to do.

But that epiphany rising in me like a flood is peeling back the wallpaper of romanticism in my heart, one love-stained piece at a time. After ripping down the corners, I see how empty the wall is. What good are legendary words, love confessions of such magnitude, if there's no action behind them?

If Mr. Wrong offered me a lifetime of actions to prove his promises, I would gladly send Mr. Right and his empty words to the curb.

My bare ankle reaches forward and connects with his strong calf under the table. His eyes flit over to me, razor-sharp in assessment.

Tucking a loose strand of hair back into my French twist, I blink at him, *I need to be grounded. I need you.* He widens his legs in response under the table, moving across the invisible dividing line I drew at the start of our meal.

His hands drop from his utensils and my eyes watch in fascination as he bends at the waist to grip the bottom frame of my chair. My body doesn't flinch when he slides my chair closer to him, eliminating all but a toothpick's distance between our body heat. I imagine if we were in a booth, he would have stood up and joined me on the same side of the table, ignoring any social norms.

Parker is the type of man to care more about his proximity to me than he does about following the rules. My body squirms in my seat because I know that when he reaches for what he wants—this time *me*—it's equally unnerving and *hot*.

He's the match to my candle. I don't initiate, but I melt and burn for him endlessly once he makes the first move.

"My father exuded a certain magic," Parker whispers into the small intimate void between us, "When he was alive."

Fixing my hands in my lap, I keep a steady breath and pivot my heart toward his voice.

"It's why my mother fell in love with him. He was big on expressing himself. Big on putting his love up on a billboard for everyone to see." His eyes drift out the windows. "He taught a little bit of everything: philosophy, religious studies, anthropology. Most of the time, I can hear his voice when I need it most. Bumper sticker wisdom to ephemeral Taoism. His words are all there, sitting on a dusty shelf with only unopened books of sadness to keep it company." Parker takes a sip from his drink and hisses after he drains it.

"He's the one who helped my mom learn English. They would sit for *hours* watching movies. It wasn't unusual to watch them act them out in the kitchen as they made dinner, or listen to them recite monologues on long car rides." Parker's voice drops below a whisper as if all he has left is a shaky exhale to carry his next words.

I don't have to be a therapist to know there isn't a happy ending to this story.

"It's the worst type of story. The ones that are left as mysteries, left up to reader interpretation, Lil Red." He says my nickname like he's clinging to a life raft before swallowing thickly.

"I hated that in English class, you know? Just tell us already what the green light symbolizes. Stop giving us multiple explanations. Stop asking us to see a bigger picture, the metaphor in the mess. A man needs to have explanations."

"What explanation were you robbed of, Parker?" I place my hand on top of his, making it as heavy as possible, anchoring him the way he often does to me.

Leaning back in his seat, but keeping his hand underneath the safety of mine, he looks out the window again. Seeking answers in the constellations or his disappointed reflection, I'll never know. I slip my other hand underneath my thigh, forcing myself to be still.

"I'll never know why my father killed himself ten years ago. Ten years ago, tonight."

Tears run down my face unbidden but I wipe them away with my free hand. It's worse than I imagined. I had assumed a car crash perhaps, perhaps an accident, or an aneurysm. All tragic, but explainable.

"I found him. There wasn't a note." His voice cracks slightly and so do the foundations of my heart at the sound of it. "At least, there wasn't at first," he adds before sighing. "He had one delivered to me a week later." Parker taps his chest five times.

"By the time the paramedics came, by the time my mom made it home after her birth client was done delivering, the sun started to creep over the mountains. I stood in our small yard and glared at it because I didn't want to look anywhere else anymore. Watching the sunrise and knowing that Earth was still spinning, made me sick with fury. How could the darkest night of my life get lighter?"

Nodding, I force my lungs to suck in a razor-sharp breath. The sounds of the restaurant seem to fade, the lights dimming in a cinematic fashion.

"But it did. The sun rose and fell again the next day. And I think, ever since that night, I scrounged up any scrap of darkness I could find...kept an eternal midnight, a sky-filled blanket of grief, alive in my chest." He taps his sternum.

"Parker." This isn't a session, even though I can hear how close he is to a breakthrough. How cathartic this is for him.

"Sunrises," he meets my eyes in our reflection in the window and I freeze, "were the worst." His tongue wets his bottom lip before whispering, "Until I met you."

PARKER

Sᴇᴅᴏɴᴀ, October

When a woman asks, "Would you like to come inside and watch a film?" most men only listen to the words, *come inside*, and don't bother with the movie.

But when Carmie asks me, I heed the invitation and respect it for what it means. A chance to connect.

Carmie waltzes into her newish house and flicks on the vintage wall sconces lining the entryway. Low light bathes the Spanish tiles in an alluring glow. Her home is warm, inviting, and intimate. Those three aesthetics somehow follow behind her wherever she goes, like a faint cloud of perfume you can't help but notice.

"I'm not letting you pick the movie." She tosses a little crimson smirk over her bare shoulder. It lights something in me, that I struggle to ignore.

"Why?" There's supposed to be a bite to my tone, but it comes out light. Her tinkering laugh haunts me from down the hall.

I stop and stare at a gallery wall of Polaroid photos hanging by a strand of twinkle lights in the breakfast nook. Elyse, two men side by side on motorcycles, the whole gang outside a moving truck in Nashville.

A hollow pit opens up in my stomach and I have to look away.

"No, because there's no way I'm going to sit here and endure the likes of Dunkirk, Saving Private Ryan or dare I suggest," she shudders, "a documentary."

Before I can stop it, my head tips back and laughter rumbles through the house. Looking at her standing in the living room, with a matching bubblegum pink crop top with baggy sweatpants. I stop laughing and swallow.

"I hope you don't mind I changed. I can grab something of Eden's for you if you'd like?" Her fingers twist in the hem of her shirt, and she bites the corner of her lip.

And just like that, I no longer give a shit about the movie.

She walks toward me with her eyebrows raised, and I remember to respond. I shake my head no, so she shrugs and heads to a cabinet. My eyes trail to her and re-map the swell of her curves and the fluidity of her long hair flowing down her shoulder blades.

On her tiptoes, she reaches for a stack of bowls, just out of her reach. Her back dimples pull my attention, all that creamy skin exposed between her ribs and hip bones. The perfect terrain for my hands to map.

My bones begins to overheat, but I'm moving toward her, eating up the distance between us in the dark kitchen, before my palms make contact to steady her waist. I'm pressed damn near flush against her as I begin pulling down the three mismatched pottery bowls.

She whispers a throaty "thank you" but doesn't move.

We breathe in tandem. Fast inhales and soft exhales. Heat

flares between the skin on my palms and the skin of her hips. My fingers spread wider, fingertips curling toward the twin peaks of her hip bones. She tips her head back, and I'm filled with the scent of her sweet shampoo.

Her back arches under my ministrations, making her full ass press flush to my groin. My eyes drop to where our bodies connect, and I can feel my restraint slipping. With my palms massaging her waist and lower back, all I can think about is watching myself slide in and out of her gorgeous body. Taking her, right here in this kitchen.

My hands continue to massage the tight muscles of her back. In my fantasy, I would reach forward and wrap her wavy hair around my knuckles, worshipping the red leash she would all too willingly give me.

Carmie might appear sweet, but I know exactly what type of physical contact she desires the most. There isn't a bone in my body that believes she wouldn't love to explore and enjoy the plethora of ways I could bend her to my will. It's not about dominating her as much as it is about mutual ownership.

Every sexual dream, every fantasy—hell, even every delusion —could be hers. We wouldn't need to come up for air, both of us too stupid or stubborn or content to drown in the ocean of chemistry between us. Chemistry we can't deny any longer.

I can't decide if I want anything more than that. My hands slide up and down her flesh five times, a ritual and anchor, attempting to figure out what the hell I'm doing. As if reading the intention behind my movement, Carmie cocks her head to the side in contemplation.

"What are we doing, Parker?" she asks between a ragged and confused breath.

My hands stop moving. I lean down toward the irresistible slope of her neck, where her pulse meets her shoulder, and bite it. Not hard, but with enough pressure to make her muscles melt like butter.

"Don't stop," she begs, forgetting she even asked a question.

My body believes whatever this is between me and Carmie is logical, sensical, and a realistic moment between two people with needs. My brain is scrambling, desperate to put out the fires of my impulsive, and pheromone-led decisions.

I deny myself most pleasures in life—but when it comes to her? That's too tall of an order.

Leaning down, I hover my mouth over the shell of her ear.

"Did you put this on to seduce me?" Pinning her to the edge of the counter, my body presses into her curves.

"Is it working?" She breathes out, tilting her head back to look at me.

Bending down, I almost take her lips between my teeth but decide not to at the last moment. Her body trembles in anticipation and I feel it vibrate through every awakened muscle in mine.

"Yes. When it comes to you, the answer is always, *yes.*"

My lips crash down on hers and I don't wait to tease my tongue against the seam of her lips. I swallow her moan as her hand snakes up to the back of my neck, tugging on my hair to fuse our lips together. The rhythm of our movements sings out *more, more, more.*

Using my grip on her hips, I bend her over the counter. Her body undulates underneath me, both of her palms pressing into the countertop as she searches for friction, searching to relieve the tension we've strung all night long ...

My hands spin her around so I can hold the back of her head as I kiss her. With passion. With heat. With no space left between us. Pulling away, I lift her onto the counter and she wraps her legs around my waist.

"Stop being gentle," she pants. With her ankles hooked

around my lower back, she tugs me closer to her hips and squeezes her thighs.

"Your wish is my command," I say low and slow.

With my hand in her hair, I tug, angling her chin to the ceiling so I can access the delicate curve of her throat. My lips descend and I suck her pulse point, harder than I've ever done.

Her body writhes and moves beneath me, and as I continue to suck I move away from her waist just enough space to dip my fingers into the waistband.

"No lace, no thong, *nothing*?" I pull away to stare into her heated eyes. "Is it my birthday already?"

"I agreed to play, didn't I?" Her mouth reaches up to tug on my bottom lip and when my eyes close at the bite of pleasure and pain I see purple, blue, and green sparks behind my eyelids.

My hand circles around her back and grips her ass as I resume exploring her neck and collarbone with my mouth.

"Did you miss these hands?" I whisper to her. One of my hands travels up the bottom hem of her crop top, while the other moves from her ass and multi-tasks by drawing slow circles on her clit.

She still hasn't answered me, so I stop teasing her with my fingers and press the heel of my hand into that sensitive apex at the top of her hips instead. My other hand tweaks her exposed nipple, because *no bra, of course*, and her back arches off the counter.

"Yes! Why do you need to hear it?" She pants.

I chuckle, and both hands resume their new favorite pastime. Dipping one, then, two fingers inside her, I draw her wetness out and tease her with it.

She's panting, coming undone, and we haven't even made it to the movie yet.

I decide I need two hands for this job, so I lift her shirt and take over teasing her left, then right, breast with my mouth.

With my now free hand, I send it down to her hip so that I can grip and knead her ass to my delight. And *her* delight, by the sounds she can't stop making.

She's a mess, and I'm about to be in another few minutes...

Using the pad of my thumb, I find the spot that makes her eyes roll back, before adding a third finger. With the walls of her pussy clenching around me, my body vibrates with desire and my lips are magnetized back to hers. Just in time to swallow her moans as she comes around, and on, my hands.

Coaxing the last little whimpers from her, I kiss her flushed cheeks, neck and breasts again.

I wrap my arms around her upper back and pull her up so that she's seated on the countertop with her arms and legs wrapped around me. It's quiet, so I take the moment to whisper the answer into her hair.

"I need to hear it, Carmie because everyone needs a little validation when it comes to intimacy. Even me."

The ticking of an ornate clock on the wall counting down the seconds of silence between us is louder than the frantic beating of my battered heart. I'm straddling the line between an *emotional* relationship and a *sexual* one. It's not that I've thought about having a mature, adult relationship with her again. But it's like muscle memory, whenever I'm with her. My body acts like a traitor. A soft wind could blow me either way. I'd let it if it smelled like her shampoo.

"Say it to my face, Parker. Or else it isn't real," she whispers, pulling back to stare at me. There's a wobble to her voice, but her spine stiffens.

Seconds tick by and my blood freezes, slowing down my pulse. She extracts herself from my hold, hopping off the counter. Her chin lifts in defiance. For the life of me, I can't figure out why she's putting up a wall between us.

"Say it to my face. Tell me what I mean to you then. Tell

me, anything, *everything*, right here. Be intimate in a way that isn't solely physical."

"You know it isn't just physical—" I whisper. But she steps back once, then twice, and I know it's not convincing enough for her.

Her eyes water but then sharpen, narrowing on me, spearing right through my fucking soul. After an inhale, she marches over, reaches up on her toes, and tangles her long fingers in my hair before she lowers my face toward her own.

With only an exhale between our lips, I reckon giving in to her would feel like the first thaw of spring, icicles melting drop by drop, giving way to the season of re-birth. If I told her what she and I both know is true.

But I move away from her mouth. Such a small withdraw, and she catches it. Freezing us both over.

Pulling her hands out of my hair, she glares up at me with her watery emerald and sapphire eyes. "You don't get to hide from me, from what we still have." Her index finger pokes my heart as if it could *pop* and flutter to the ground like a sad balloon.

It dawns on me that she wasn't merely asking for something from me. She was *demanding* it. Challenging me to rise to the occasion, and my heart kicks with a glimmer of pride. Pride that she won't accept a crumb when she deserves the whole fucking cake. Sparkling candles, glitter, a cherry on top. Nothing less.

Shine a light on my heart, the one pretending not to give a shit, and you'll illuminate the truth I can't bear to say: Falling in love with Carmela D'Angelo feels like riding down the most dangerous mountain blindfolded.

Give up control or die trying.

I loosened the reigns the first time around with her, and look where that got me. Nobody may know, but the pain of her leaving almost eclipsed the pain of dying on the side of the mountain.

Her eyes blink up at me, begging for a scrap of monologue that will explain why I can't give her what she needs. I shake my head no, even though the muscles don't want to follow my lead.

We stand at this crossroads, and with each passing moment I don't open my mouth a wall erects between us, inch by inch. I can see the hurt and the confusion and the anger, plain as day, through it. My fingerprints are all over it. I don't have it in me to bring the wall down. Only one or two sentences would bring it down, remove the barrier between us.

"Parker." The yearning in her voice sends my heart to the bottom of the ocean.

A tear drops down her cheek and I reach to wipe it away. She swats my hand with a vicious sting, her eyes narrowing. I take a step back and instead of retreating deeper into the counter, she takes a step forward. Toward me. As she advances, I retreat, until I'm the one trapped against the opposite counter.

She's the full and glorious sun forcing the shadows to submit.

"Perhaps, you need to hear this, Parker Radcliffe." She sucks in a breath and lifts her chin higher still. "You are the second-greatest loss of my life and I feel it here, knotted around my ribcage, every *single* day. I can't find the loose end of that knot, no matter how hard I dig and dig and dig." She points at her chest, and it makes my ribs ache watching anger spread across her features.

"I fumble with this knot because it doesn't seem logical, does it? That I would be so impacted by a relationship that barely got off the tarmac, let alone took flight. But you're still here, knotted around my bones, and the empty cavern of my chest. Missing you, longing for you, feels like everyone in my family pretending to care on my sixteenth birthday. It feels like being crushed by the first boy I cared for, even though that's why they call them *crushes*. It feels like making a wish, the *only* wish I want to come true, and not being able to blow out the candle."

Tears slide down her face, an army prepared to fight.

"One day, I might be able to take a pair of scissors to the whole thing, snip you free like Clotho snips a thread of fate between two people, but I have a feeling..." her breath rattles, but her voice is strong. "I have a feeling, when I do that, the emptiness left behind once my knot is gone will swallow me whole."

My eyes burn. I feel, more than see, my father smiling beyond the grave. Smiling at the woman brave enough to have this conversation, to feel so much, even when it's agony.

"I'm not sure if I can forgive myself for not choosing you. I'm not sure if I'll ever stop punishing myself for my cowardice, for my inability to be who you needed me to be at that moment. So, I'll say this, I am sorry, Parker. I am *so* sorry. As much as it might hurt to admit this, I have to say it. If you can't find it in you to forgive me, to love me in the way I think you did, then you need to pull the emergency brake and stop romanticizing me. Neither of us deserves it."

My stomach flips like I just went over the handlebars.

"Perhaps, there will be a woman in your life one day who doesn't view your iron-clad sense of control as a wall. Maybe, she'll paint it and install a window. She'll be happy with those walls and consider it a home."

Anger rises, moving me forward to her. She doesn't give an inch.

"Control leads to freedom. Control is about being responsible. Control, is all I have left, so don't you dare look down on my greatest virtue with pity," I spit out in defense.

She shakes her head, as if I'm the dumbest fuck in the

world, and sighs. "You're not in control, Parker. You're *repressed*. Now, I'm going to go finish what you couldn't start." She heads for the living room and grabs the remote on her way.

I shake my head and blink several times for clarity. But I cling to my anger, cling to any semblance of control I have left, cling to the smell of her still on my hand and slam the door behind me.

carmie

SEDONA, October

It's nice when you can sit with someone and not have to talk. Unfortunately, that's not the purpose of therapy. Eventually, someone has to talk.

This is why I wouldn't make it as a school teacher. I don't have it in me to wait someone out.

My foot twitches. As does my mouth. So, of course, I give in and break the ice.

"Your agent called me this week," I break the tension hoping to get a sign of life from the man across from me.

Flatline.

"Aren't you curious as to what we talked about?"

"No."

Of course, he's stonewalling me. It's been one week since the, *can't handle the heat get out of the kitchen* fiasco.

"Please work with me, Parker."

"Stop saying my name, Carmela."

Slamming my notebook and zebra pen down, I glare at him.

"Just because you couldn't deliver last week, doesn't mean you have to be such an insufferable pain in my ass. Have you ever—"

"Oh, I delivered, I remember it vividly," he says with a mean smirk. Then he opens his stupid mouth again. "I'm not insufferable. You are. This entire relationship is so ridiculous. In what world would you ever be my therapist? How is that normal?"

"I'm not your girlfriend either. So what is the problem here? Why can't we talk through some of the biggest moments in your life? What's holding you back? And newsflash, you are *not* normal. You are a world-renowned athlete who keeps throwing away his future."

Was I hoping to talk about what happened between us after last week? Of course. I'm an optimist. Am I ever going to get that opportunity? Of course not, because as half-glass-full as my heart is, I'm not naïve to how half-empty he is.

"I don't... I don't know what the problem is. With you or with me." He stares at me, eyes a bit blank and red.

"Why don't we start with a rose, thorn, and bud," I suggest.

He rolls his eyes but I see a light turning on inside his head at the idea of finishing a task and getting it over with.

"Rose, going to Europe this weekend to watch Hardline. Thorn, you, per usual, right in my side. Bud," Parker stops and stares off before answering. "I'm not sure. Normally I would say the next race. But that's not in the cards right now."

"Who else do you believe you are beyond racing, beyond being the man on the bike?" I almost hesitate to ask.

"Can't you quit so I can talk to someone else?" He mutters while crossing his arms. He's dressed in a waffle henley, the light grey bringing out the rich olive tone of his skin.

"Parker," I sigh. "I thought we were at least past this. We

can be friends. You can open up to me and utilize what I have to offer to *help* yourself get over this setback."

He eyes me before his lips twitch up. "Women and men can't be friends, Little Red."

"Yes, they can," I argue, ignoring the spark at hearing his nickname for me. "Case in point, I would never date or explore an intimate relationship with Ian, Riley, or Tommy."

"Tommy is engaged to one of your closest friends," he lists on his strong fingers. "Ian seems like a serial killer in hiding, and Riley? He smokes a pack a day. I know you wouldn't be able to stand by as someone kills themselves. You want to be friends with them because it makes you feel like you understand men as a whole. It soothes that restless heart of yours. Gives you hope that one day you will find your destined movie-like love."

My eyebrows draw together in a tight line.

"Plus," he continues, leaning forward, resting his elbows on his knees. "Men don't want women as friends. They have men for that."

"Then what do my friends want from me, huh?" I snap, losing the plot and my professionalism in the same question.

"To have sex. Always. *It's doomed from the start,*" he shrugs while casually dropping a line from my favorite movie.

"Don't desecrate Nora Ephron like that."

"I can prove it. Text Riley and ask him if he's ever considered having sex with you."

"No!" I jump to my feet.

"You're beautiful, you care deeply about the people you love, you're intelligent, unique…" he keeps listing what he thinks about me on his fingers.

My heart beats faster as the anger transitions into disbelief. Disbelief sweeps into an unfamiliar sensation of being *seen* through the eyes of someone I respect.

Parker rolls his eyes. "If I have to be the one to tell you

that, I feel sorry for you. It's true. My point," he waves an open palm out, "is that at the end of the day, if you offered, any one of them would jump on the opportunity."

"Tommy would never." Defensiveness drowns out the glimmer of disbelief and satisfaction I felt moments ago.

"I don't know him well enough to say either way." He shrugs.

"If you keep shrugging your shoulders, you're going to dislocate them." Crossing my arms, I sit back down.

"Text Riley then. Go on."

"I'm not proving shit to you, Parker," I spit out.

"Ok. A forfeit is considered a loss." He grins.

Biting my lip, I decide to play his game.

"If Riley responds with any interest at all in having sex with me, I will quit as your therapist. I'll tell your agent *it wasn't you, it was me*, and move on with my life."

My words hang between us, a grenade yet to explode. His jaw flexes for a moment, but I don't stop to analyze it.

"*If* Riley, as I expect he will, doesn't want anything to do with sex, you will sit here and have a full-blown therapy session without any brooding, nastiness, or defensiveness. You will participate fully. You will reflect. You will *finally*, for the love of God, make some progress."

The perfect contour of his hand reaches forward and I shake it. Heat envelops my skin and I clear my throat.

"Make it convincing or it doesn't count," Parker points at me.

I laugh, despite the circumstances, and start banging out a text.

> Riley, I've been thinking about this for some time.

> I'm trying to quit, I promise 😔

> Actually. Would you ever consider, our relationship to be anything more than what it is now? 😬

.....

Are you ok?

> Hypothetically, would you ever have sex with me?

My cheeks flush in embarrassment under the scrutiny of Parker's intense focus. I watch Riley type and stop. Type, stop, type, stop.

To like, have a baby or something? Do you need a sperm donor? I'm not really into the idea but if it means you won't have a baby with Douchey McDouche pants, yeah, I'll donate. It would be a good-looking kid, but I'm not sure whose side of the brain they'll get. Let's pray it's yours.

But, to be clear, I would need a lot of alcohol. And therapy. But if it's really what you want, I guess I could do it 👍

> OMG, no. Just curious about the sex part. But thank you for offering your genes, they're top-tier, I'm sure.

Don't flatter me, these 👖 are discounted at best.

> ... stop that.

Ok, sex? No, Carmie. Ha, I love you.
But no.

Even though I just won, I wasn't prepared for this conversation. Biting my thumbnail, I stare at the screen and let my eyes unfocus. The idea of having a baby with anyone makes my blood run cold in shame. The secret I've been dragging behind me in the shadows whenever I'm with Parker rears its ugly head.

Whenever I acknowledge it, I get depressed and exhausted.

"I win," I say with very little fervor.

His eyes narrow on my downturned mouth and his jaw clenches. I come to my senses and jump up to dance in a circle around his chair. Ripping my hair out of my claw clip, I spin, laughing like a child, faking the noise until it becomes genuine.

Until I trip, and fall right into Parker's lap. My arms reach out and land around his neck, my hands finding the slightly curled ends of dark hair like they missed being buried in them. I'm breathing hard and my eyes look up to find his, open wide, staring down at me.

Eyes so dark they swallow me whole.

The nighttime sounds of the desert surround us. Wood crackles in the fireplace, mimicking the way my heart is jump-started to life by his proximity. My breath slides in and out.

I never want to catch my breath around him. I want to feel wild and unfiltered and free. Do you ever wish you could freeze a moment where you feel all those things? You stay as still as a movie on pause in case just one blink of an eye will burst the magic.

My bottom is planted between his strong thighs and my breathing isn't the only thing having a hard time. There's no logic or consciousness preceding it, but I nestle myself deeper between his thighs. A low groan vibrates deep in his throat and I pray for something. Anything. With my blood turning thick and sweet as honey, I fight the urge to pull his face down to mine.

You're not settling, remember?

But... I want his lips on my body. More than I want to

have a lasting once-in-a-lifetime love. My eyes lower to his heavy lips slightly parted, and I almost do it. I almost suck on his bottom lip like it's the last time I'll find a cushion as perfect as him.

"I told you," Parker whispers. "Men and women? Can't be friends. We're proof enough."

His finger tilts my chin up and I fight to stop the wobble in my bottom lip. I hate losing my damn mind around him. I thought I wanted to be free, to be wild.

Tucking my hair back up into my clip, I slide off his lap and look down my nose at him.

"I'll see you in a few days for our next session. I won, so get your house in order and come prepared to talk."

I'm too in my feelings to notice the dim sadness in his eyes as if he doesn't want me to leave like this. But like I said, my emotions are too strong. They're a violet filter covering my vision, tinting everything in muted disappointment. As I'm almost through the sliding doors, I swear my mind plays a trick on me. Because there's no way I heard Parker say what I think I did: *I'd give you the love you want...but I'm not half the man I used to be.*

35 / THE JOKER

PARKER

S<small>EDONA</small>, October

"S o why did you sit down with her at dinner in the first place?" Landon asks me between alternating rounds of kettlebell exercises and the StairMaster. Looking at my body, it would be hard to believe it's been months since an almost-fatal injury.

I'm not the first in the industry to take a beating like this though. Healing is possible with the right team and a selective memory.

"Who are you, the CEO of the gossip mill?" I laugh despite myself. It's almost impossible for me to be in a bad mood in this gym. The sweat, the hard-earned endorphins, and the calculated training plans bring me a sense of peace that's damn near close to being on my bike. Which I'm not cleared for yet.

I agreed to do some promotional work and signings in Europe this weekend because my sponsors are eager to see me in the flesh again. If I can't ride or race in the Hardline event then I might as well be there to support Eden.

"Well?" Landon slams his beefy fist down on the *Stop* button, forcing me into stillness.

"Call it a grief-induced insanity, that's it." I bite down before hopping off the machine.

"That's shit and you know it. You're making an idiot outta yourself." Landon's voice covers me like smog.

"If you're so invested in her, why don't you take a crack then, huh? Go ahead and give her the Hollywood romance she keeps going on about," I grind out between my teeth.

"Maybe I will this weekend. Nothing more romantic than Europe, am I right?" He steps back and crosses his thick arms in front of his.

"No."

"No, what?" he asks.

"No, she's not coming to Europe with us."

"Dick just called me, he set everything up already. Something about an initiative to utilize sports psychologists across the organization."

I'm about to roar out an objection when Carmie appears in the opening underneath the garage door.

The first thing I notice is her eyes. Instead of the clear, wide-eyed wonder, they're red. Crimson.

"Can I speak to you for a moment?" She looks anywhere but directly at me.

Landon walks over and wraps her up in a bear hug, spinning her around so her hair defies gravity and the pain momentarily subsides from the corner of her mouth.

"You ok, babe? Say the word and I'll bring the punishment."

Her smile is Jeff Buckley's "Hallelujah," a major lift with a minor key, before it succumbs to gravity again.

"Ah," she kicks her foot front to back. "I was just wondering. If, uhm, I could stay in the spare bedroom for a few days?"

Landon and I exchange a look. The first unified look, truth be told, when it comes to the woman in front of us. Concern sits heavy on both of our brows.

Taking a step toward her, I wipe my face with a towel and place my hands on my knees. Getting eye level requires a bit of a bend, but I need to see what's going on in that head of hers.

"Are you in danger, Carmela?" I ask so softly I feel the words leave my lips rather than hear them.

"No, no. Possibly. I'm not sure. Ah, I came home and found Seamus sitting on my porch with roses and gifts. I never gave him my—"

Standing to my full height I cross my arms. "You hate roses."

Not bothering to deny it, she nods her head. "I asked him to leave and he—he refused," she chokes out.

"Elyse is away on another work rotation, this time in Montana, and I'm not sure when she'll be back."

My mouth opens, but I'm too slow.

"You can stay with me." Landon cuts into my line of vision and grabs both of her palms with his.

She looks down at his hands and her frown gets heavier as if she's just now noticing those palms don't feel quite the same as mine.

"I've got an extra room, plenty of space. I won't bother you when you're meditating or get upset when you clutter up my bathroom vanity." He laughs lightly as if they've shared a thousand personal details over a thousand dates.

First, I'm pissed off he knows that much about her. Second, I have more room in my house and it's an obvious decision.

"No, you can stay here."

My eyes slice over to Landon and I swear I see a crinkle of delight in his face. A dimple, just for a moment.

"I'm sure Carmie would feel better if she had some separation from her *work* don't you think?" Landon pivots to me and lifts an eyebrow.

Sometimes, when I can't sleep at night, I scroll Reddit and find damn near interesting shit. Did you know that if you're in a tense conversation with someone, if you add five seconds between their remark and your response you unnerve them?

So, I wait, smile, and show a few teeth. "Why don't you let Carmie speak for herself?"

The competitor in me rises to the occasion, a dragon unfurling from slumber to protect what's his. Even if she's not technically *mine*.

She sure as shit isn't Seamus' or Landon's. If I were a better man, the kind of man who could openly admit his feelings, I might even take this opportunity to push Landon out of my garage and take Carmie for myself. For good.

Carmie looks between us, a spectator at a tennis match, and weighs her options.

"I can just get a hotel room. It's fine. I'm just not exactly, flush with cash, at the moment."

"It's not fine," Landon and I say at the same time.

"Alright," she clears her throat. "I'll stay here then, especially since we're going to Austria this weekend, right?" Carmie looks up to me for confirmation and every cell in my body is begging me to shake my head. Instead, I nod stupidly.

She smiles, just for me. It's not the one she gives to the cashier at the store. It's not the one she gives Elyse, or Eden, or even Landon. It's just for me. Don't ask me to prove it. I just know.

She waves to Landon and walks out, letting us know she'll be in the house.

"What are the chances that prick is still sitting there?" Landon cracks his knuckles and I resist the urge to do the same.

This reactive and violent impulse is new to me. It churns through me and makes the pulse in my temple throb. I'm not the man my father wanted me to be. But I'm the one he left behind. I'll do what my father couldn't. Protect the people in my life—without giving up on them.

Nodding my head to the door, Landon follows. Part of me is sick at the idea of seeing that pathetic excuse for a man. Another part is enraged.

Enraged that he can't accept *no* for an answer. Can't figure out how to live his life without her. Enraged that he can't respect boundaries, limitations, and restrictions. Especially when asked by a woman like her. A woman who rarely asks to be left alone. A woman who takes the hammer out of your hand and hits her own again and again so you don't have to feel any pain. She's the type of woman who would do it until you asked her to stop.

I look into the bay window of my home and see her standing there with arms wrapped around herself. Shaking my head, I slide into the seat and start the engine with a roar.

He might have had twenty years with her, but he doesn't have the right to the woman she's becoming.

A part of me is starting to believe that he'll never have her again. I can't tell if that's what is making me smile or if it's the promise of unleashing something darker looming on the horizon of my consciousness.

☆

We pull up in front of her house and the piece of shit is pacing on the porch, talking into his phone. He's laughing, throwing his head back. If I were a bystander, I'd think he owned the place. Except that he's on the outside looking in. Not the other way around.

"Just follow my lead," I mutter to Landon as I get out of my truck.

Walking toward Seamus, my stomach flips at the memory of Carmie standing me up in the airport. A romcom gone sour.

He's got slacks, a dress shirt, and a loosened tie that look like the type Wall Street washouts wear to Sunday brunch at the country club. Custom cuff links. Tousled hair with just enough product in it.

Seamus isn't muscular, but he's also not an idle threat. There's a raw edge to his movements that are more manic than her brother's controlled ones.

What the hell is with me and this woman's porch? Am I destined to find stray men from her life here, all the time?

Walking up to the front porch, I lift my chin at Seamus and move to the keypad.

"Carson, I'll call you back in a bit."

With my back turned to him, I smile, and punch in Eden's guest code.

"Landon, stand out here, will you? I have to get the rest of my woman's belongings. One drawer in particular I can't live without." I send a wink over my shoulder to Landon and stroll inside.

Seamus begins to negotiate with Landon, but he doesn't budge. Landon's frame fills the doorway and I know I've got a good fifteen minutes to pack her essentials and get out of here before Landon does something we'll both regret.

"Get the fuck out of my fiancé's house," I hear Seamus call from the front. His voice bounces off the stone walls and floor, giving it an unhinged combination of boredom and defiance. All I hear is how annoying this dude is.

"Your fiancé huh?" I can't help but yell back. "That's not what she was moaning last night!" I laugh, now *that* sound is unhinged.

Landon's voice finds me next. "Buddy, pack up the panties and let's roll. Getting a little tricky out here."

Grabbing an oversized tote, I start shoving random shit into it. A little of this, a scrap of that. Half-filled notebooks, a toothbrush, and of course, the red lace I promised Seamus I was claiming. Those I hold in my hand, while I swing everything else in the bag over my shoulder. Whistling a merry tune, I make my way back to the front door.

Making eye contact with the prick who shall no longer be named, I give him a wink as I brush past him.

"I'm calling the police and reporting you!" He chokes out in rage.

"For what, dipshit? Doing as Carmie asked? For having a code to her place? Don't act like someone pissed in your Wheaties, not a good look." Landon smacks his palm down on Seamus' shoulder and I almost choke on the effort it takes not to laugh.

As I unlock my truck, I call out his name for the first and last time. "Seamus!"

He turns, and if I were being my more observational self, I would've noticed the internal shift taking place within him.

I bring the red panties up to my nose, close my eyes while inhaling, and then pocket them with a grand smile.

"All mine," I mouth to him.

You see, for all his societal strength, and all his money, he has nothing to threaten me with. He's all charm and no personal responsibility.

We drive back to my place and I don't stop smiling, not even when Landon opens his fat fucking mouth.

"Bit overkill for a woman you say you don't care about. Don't you think?" He holds back a smile and I slam on the brakes, just to throw off his equilibrium.

But I don't reply. Nothing is going to stop the fog from

lifting tonight. Not Landon's truthful observations. Not Carmie sleeping down the hall.

Certainly not the feel of her lace burning a hole in my pocket.

No, definitely not that.

36 / SAVE THE LAST DANCE

Carmie

Sᴇᴅᴏɴᴀ, October

Tip-toeing into Parker's garage, I look left, then right, and finally exhale. Walking deeper into the darkened space, I face the mirrors and take inventory of my reflection.

My fingers reach up to touch my flushed cheeks. I can feel the tiny fires lit underneath my skin and smile at the *life* flowing through me. The flames of anger, embarrassment, and finally, re-invention are helping me shed this old skin.

I'm shedding it fast. Without mercy.

Seamus wants me to feel guilty.

I'm not going back.

Seamus needs me to resume my position as a peacekeeper.

I'm ready to start fires—I'm not in the business of putting them out anymore.

Seamus will tell my family.

I'd prefer he did. Maybe they can start a support group.

Laughter bursts out of me, uninhibited and free as a creature of the night. The sound rolls around me, echoing off the wall of mirrors before I slam my mouth shut and look around.

Parker and Landon aren't back yet. Nobody is using the space, so it's *mine.*

Dimming the lights even more, I pull the candle out of my back pocket and light it. My phone connects to the Bluetooth, and I'm almost ready to dance my way through the turbulent week. Normally, I'd spend my time at the studio, but Lina is out of town with a client.

The last thing we learned was the lap dance choreography, and it was the first time I felt what it meant to dance for yourself first.

Lina drilled it into us that, *If a man gets up to get a drink in the middle of my dance, I wouldn't even notice. It wouldn't crush me, I wouldn't feel rejected. Truth be told, I wouldn't even notice. That's how much I dance for myself.*

Of course, I didn't believe her at first. How could I crawl on the floor toward a chair and get lost in the music without anyone sitting in it? Without anyone to perform for?

Well, fun fact, it's much easier than I anticipated. It's my new favorite routine.

"Say It" by Tory Lanez blasts through the state-of-the-art speakers in every corner of the dark gym. I drop to my knees the moment the bass pulses through the space. The fire inside me blazes brighter the moment my hands slip under the hem of my oversized Pink Floyd T-shirt. My palms connect with the softness of my stomach, hips, and breasts. Lifting onto my knees, I pull my shirt up halfway, then drop back onto my heels, bouncing for a moment.

As I repeat the movement, I peel out of my shirt, until my sheer red bralette is exposed. Tossing the shirt to the corner of the room, my hands grip my chest. My head falls back, a devious smile pulling across my face.

My eyes are closed, but it doesn't matter. The only light I need with me tonight is the flicker of a large candle. The darkness is where I now find myself.

Dropping onto my right hip, I slide my arm out and maintain eye contact in the mirror with myself the entire time I lower down onto my side. The chorus rises and my body rolls so that I'm flat on my back, legs pointed up toward the night sky.

Taking a deep breath, I drop my legs open into a straddle. But I don't do it fast—no, sir. I go so slow, it takes me almost half of the song to be fully bared open. Tiny satin sleep shorts are the only material covering the sensitive skin of my hips and pelvis.

You are a gift, your body is a gift, unwrap it as such. Take your time and take up space.

My hands graze the heated skin of my inner thighs and caress their way back up as the song shifts to "Love on the Brain," by Rihanna. It's sultry and raw, exactly how I'm feeling on the inside. Empowered by asking for what I needed tonight, I grip that thread of courage and let my hands run up my thighs until they land on my most intimate anatomy. Pressing my palm down, I feel the heat rising from my core. Breath sawing in and out, I fight the urge to run from myself, to run from facing *all* of myself.

The song lifts my spirit and chases away the heaviness. Rolling onto my front, I rock my hips side to side, grinding into the ground, arching my back to prepare for the next move. "Wicked Games" by The Weekend blasts through the garage and a dark feminine energy coils at the base of my spine. Slower than I've ever moved, I arch my back and turn my head to look in the mirror. I watch myself the entire time as my body moves into a reverse dive, ass lifting first, chest dragging on the ground as long as I can stand it. Just before I'm on my knees, I dramatically flip my head up, forcing the clip to release from my hair. I continue dancing, rolling my neck until my hair cascades down my chest, shoulders, and back.

So wholly alive.

That's the only way to describe how I feel. Reflected in the mirror, I see my heart and my invisible scars on full display. A tear escapes, but I don't wipe it away.

Don't run. Don't rush. Feel your way through.

I listen to that voice inside of me, a voice that has guided me since I stepped foot in Sedona months ago.

As the song shifts into, "Set Me On Fire," by Estelle, my eyes look up into the far corner of the mirror. The fire in me almost stutters out. Almost, but not quite.

Parker leans in the doorway, his silhouette barely visible with the dark sky behind him. He remains silent with his hands in his pockets. White-hot energy courses through me when I see his chest rising and falling at twice the speed it normally does.

"If you're going to stay, take a seat," I call over my shoulder before continuing my dance. Here's my opportunity to practice what Lina has been preaching for months.

I'll dance for myself because when I do, everything fades away. here is no *me and Parker*, there is no me *and everyone else*. All the decisions I have yet to make—all the desires I have yet to claim—can wait until the playlist is finished.

Parker's steps are slow and timed to the bass of "Movement" by Hozier. He grabs the back of the old leather chair Eden brought into the gym last week and drags it to the middle of the open floor opposite of the mirrors. Sitting down, he opens his legs wide and leans back. His jaw flexes with effort, but he's yet to utter a single word. He doesn't need to. His dark eyes are alive and burning—for me.

My body moves to The Black Keys, H.E.R., SZA, Prince, Post Malone, and Fleetwood Mac, but it's not until "Grind With Me" comes on that I have the momentum to make my way toward him.

On my knees, I drop my head and crawl like a possessed jungle cat toward the chair. My heart races, but I force my body to slide through the air, unhurried. When I reach his knees, my palms grip them while I serpentine my hips in slow circles, all while I look up and hold his eyes prisoner.

My hands slide up his strong thighs and the friction makes me burn hotter. I take satisfaction in feeling his body shiver underneath my touch when my fingers graze his hip bones.

I crawl my way up, my chest grazing his chest as I move so, so, slowly. His hands clench into fists and in any other situation I would laugh at his Olympic-level self-restraint... but this is no laughing matter.

My knees pivot and balance on the arm of the chair. Dipping my body, I arch my back, and alternate pointing my toes. Technically, I'm perpendicular to him, hovering over his waist and teasing him as I grind the air, but I can feel how much the anticipation is turning him on.

Flipping my hair up, I spin and lace my hands behind his neck, lowering my hips down to his waist. The feel of his hard length just inches away from my shorts is enough to short-circuit my brain. Dropping my head back, I moan and sink into the most sensual and sexual version of myself.

His hands, my favorite hands, circle my ass and squeeze. *Hard.* I lift, rise, and tease him within an inch of both of our lives. "Too Deep" overtakes the speakers and there's never been a better moment for the song. This moment with Parker, all of my moments with Parker, are too deep, and I never want to be pulled out of them.

Without notice, I slide down his chest, pressing the tight peaks of my nipples into his body the entire way down. Using my hands on his knees, I rise, ass first of course, before pulling my bra off and tossing it at him.

Turning on my heels, I hook my thumbs in my shorts, and shimmy them down, before bringing them back up.

"Tease," he growls from behind me.

The leather creaks as he leans forward, elbows pressing

into his knees, but the sound is drowned out by "D.D." and The Weekend blasting through the garage.

I spread my legs, look over my shoulder with what can only be described as *come-fuck-me* eyes and bend down until my hands touch the ground. I feel rough fingers graze the opening of my shorts by my thigh. Legs shaking, I can barely take the contrast of his calloused fingers with the lightness of his touch—just a feather of sensation. One finger finds my opening and slides inside me. He pulls out and spreads my wetness through my skin before leaning back once more, leaving cold air in his wake.

Taking my time to rise, arching my back like a pin-up girl, I lift and sway my hips. I don't move to the beat, I'm dragged *underneath* the music as if I were the queen of Parker's underworld.

He might be the one on the throne, but just like Persephone, I can bring him to his knees. And after all this time, I'm claiming my place as the goddess of rebirth.

Melting to the ground, I find myself on my back again, legs reaching for the heaven and hell that is Parker Radcliffe. Pointing my toes, I widen them, just like before, agonizingly slow. My hands trace the muscle and shadowed skin of my legs... and, as I knew it would, it brings Parker out of his chair and onto the ground above me.

On his knees.

I use only a single finger to trace down the inner seam of my thighs before I land on the front of my shorts.

Parker's swallow is louder than "Cosmic Love" building and building in the background.

Using my right hand, I start to pleasure myself, until I see stars spark behind my eyelids. Skin alive and ablaze under Parker's widened and lust-filled eyes.

The darkness I became echoes around us and with one swift tug, Parker rips my shorts off and lowers his hand on top of mine. It's a weighted and grounding sensation as I continue to pleasure myself. I continue calling the shots, but the friction and warmth and searing intensity of his eyes on my body drive me to the edge.

He presses both of my hands up above my head and moves his fingers inside me as if my pleasure is the light at the end of a dark tunnel. In the far corner of my mind, I'm screaming, *We don't need the light, I'll stay in the darkness with you.*

As the tip of his finger swirls through me, tantalizing circles that make me break out in a thin sweat of ecstasy, I cry out, arching my back until I think it might break. His other wide palm flattens itself on my stomach, forcing me to stay.

Don't run, his lips say as they lean down to kiss me. *Dance to this.* He teases every inch of skin he can find with his fingers, the heel of his hand, and his thigh pressing my legs wider.

Then one hand slides up my torso until it is pinching my nipple in an unyielding grasp. His lips leave my mouth and he cracks me open the moment his tongue flicks my breast.

Wide, cracked open. There is no in-between with him, with us.

Parker prays into my skin with every movement, sending me straight into an orgasm that takes me past the second star to the right and smack-dab into Neverland.

It's when the stars fade that he scoops my shivering body up into his arms, and when he's cradling me close to the fortress of his heart, that I realize with absolute certainty: there is nothing more of my old skin to shed.

carmie

SEDONA, October

I know, without a doubt, that I do not want to be a clinical therapist any longer. But for the first time in my life, I realize I can carry that version of *her* with me, into the next season of my life, without feeling as if I abandoned her. I don't need to drop her off at a bus stop and wish her well, before driving off into the sunset. I'm not giving up. I don't have to define it as a failure.

This place, more than any I've ever been to, makes me believe that it's possible to hug that version of myself and let her retire in *peace*. The sun is lifting into the sky ahead of me on the trail and the wide-open expanse of the desert is reaching toward me, the same way my heart is reaching for it.

Breathing in the rich and sacred morning air, I smile. My body is still sore from dancing and moving and writhing around on Parker like my life depended on it ... and in a way ... a hopeless romantic way ... I suppose it did.

My life depended on moving through every emotion and

pent-up desire I'd locked under the armor of my skin for so, so, long. He just also happened to be there.

I'm waiting for Parker to get out of the car. For his stubborn streak to yield, just an inch, for our unconventional session today. Rocking forward and back, toes to heels, and back again, I pray he doesn't wait until the sun hangs directly above us.

And, look, I get it.

This isn't how clinical psychologists conduct themselves. They don't sleep (literally, sleep) with their patients. They don't engage socially with them outside of the four walls of their practice or clinic. They certainly don't go to these lengths (platonically or romantically) for their clients.

But if I were a yoga teacher and someone I loved needed a new way of moving to help decrease pain or stress, I would be teaching them. I would be there for them, ready and willing to share what I've learned.

So maybe, these aren't so much "therapy" sessions as much as they are a chance for me to expose Parker to a partner, or friend, who can be trusted with his truth in this season of his life. Someone to hold the space and bear witness to the untold stories from seasons past.

His body unfolds from the passenger seat and my eyes drink in the way his body looks so *normal* and functioning from the outside. As the door slams shut, I know in my heart that his movements are anything but easy.

There's so much determination and pride wrapped up in the way he carries his body after his accident. My eyes water but I cough and turn away, blinking the emotion back, before we begin.

"Alright, you got me here. Now what?" Parker asks.

He sounds agitated but his hands snake around my waist and he molds his front to my back. Dipping his nose down, he trails the curve of my neck and takes a shameless breath in. It's less of a breath, and more of a deep drag, much like someone taking a deep hit of their drug of choice.

Kissing the spot behind my ear, he whispers, "What are you doing to me?"

My heart skips and trembles in my chest, but I tell her to pipe down because we have work to do.

"Come on, let's go. We're doing a loop on this trail. Did you grab the backpack?" I tilt my head so I can look at him, his body still wrapped and pressed around me.

He exhales and I can hear all of the unsaid words in that one out-breath.

Yeah. But, I'm doing this for you.

Fine by me, because sometimes that's enough motivation to get someone to try something new ... and to plant the seed of a new way of being.

Walking in front of him, I repeat over and over again to myself that I won't be attached to the outcome of this hike. I won't get attached, I won't get attached. What I offer and what he does with it are two separate entities.

Our feet leave dusty red footprints behind as we step onto the wide and marked path of the Courthouse Butte vortex trail. Sedona has seven 'vortexes' and it's one of the reasons people consider this to be such a holy and sacred place in the United States. To attempt to describe their power and energy is fruitless. All descriptions online, or in words themselves, are cheap imitations only filled with limitations.

Elyse took us on a few of the hikes during Fallon's bachelorette weekend here and they were *magnificent*. To watch my friends, Dee, Elyse, and even Fallon, experience the energy firsthand, was a gift. Dee had an epiphany about moving away from her family and a co-dependent relationship with her father. Elyse led us through a meditation but I knew that was only to distract herself from whatever was coming up about her past. Fallon cried and cried and left with a beaming smile on her face.

I remember repeating, *I am ready to release all versions of myself that keep me blind to my magic. I am ready to release the fear that my family won't love me for the choices I choose to make. I am ready to disengage from relationships that keep me feeling small and codependent. I am ready...*

Before I drifted to sleep last night, I knew that I wanted to bring Parker here. Even though he grew up in Phoenix and then relocated here later on in life, I had a feeling he'd never interacted with the land in a way that wasn't just focused on what he could "take" from it.

Any relationship requires a harmonious balance of give and take—the land we are lucky to live on is included in that.

The sky is so brilliant, so blue, it threatens to take my breath away. Since my solo date assignment, I've started to hike alone. My legs, along with my lungs, have opened up to their full potential. But, I also remember, that not three months ago, Parker was near death. He's put in the work (or more like, he's been working overtime) to be able to maneuver on a trail like this.

So I trust in his healing and don't baby him.

Looking over my shoulder, I toss him an easy smile as my ponytail swings from my head like the tail of a wild horse.

"If those eyes of yours are asking me if I'm enjoying the view..." he smiles before his eyes dart to my ass in my equally swishy and short shorts, "...the answer is always, yes." His feet move toward me, a little faster, one step, then another, until his body moves into a tentative *jog* before I let him reach me.

Wrapping his palm around my ponytail, he angles my chin up, to claim my lips in a deep and searing kiss. I feel it, like a sharp ache of joy, in the middle of my solar plexus. But this journey, this hike, is about helping Parker see that although his life and his career are good, they have the potential to evolve into something *great*.

It's not too late for him, just like it's not too late for any of us, to begin again.

So, I sadly end the kiss that melts my bones into a river of lust and soul and pure want. Pulling my face away, I take note of how the sun filters through the dark lashes of his eyes and how his irises turn into the color of an old-fashioned, waiting to be savored.

His hand remains wrapped around my hair and we linger in the middle of the path, content to live in this blissful and achingly full silence of one another's company.

Sighing, he releases his grip on my hair, and I laugh at his disappointment.

"Come on, pouty face. Let's do the entire hike."

"You're very distracting, do you know that?" He adjusts himself in his training shorts and I laugh again, letting the sound carry into the cloudless sapphire sky.

Continuing up the trail in silence, I can hear his breathing regulate and acclimate to the elevation and heat.

This little experiment isn't about babying him or analyzing him. It's about *being* with him and letting my persistence and patience smooth over the harsh rocky edges of his mind.

I'm not the water crashing into him, again and again, begging him to change. I'm a calm, moving river, and he's a stone at the bottom of it. We benefit one another because of our contrasting natures. The way my nature smoothes him over, and the way his nature, brings more boundaries and structure into mine.

Up ahead on the path, there's a father with two children. They're all on mountain bikes, yelling, laughing, and hitting the brakes as hard as they can so clouds of red dust *poof* into the air.

Out of the corner of my eye, I see Parker's lip twitch, before it shuts down. His eyes look anywhere *but* the scene, so I take the moment to stop, drop, and tie my shoe.

Manipulative? Sure. But I give zero shits.

From my position, I look up at Parker and notice his eyes are glued to the scene quickly approaching us. The Dad, in the back of the group, looks utterly exhausted and equally overjoyed. The youngest, a girl, leads the group in a colorful tutu and matching rainbow helmet. She's leading the pack, with a fierce little pout on her face, because her brother keeps trying to beat her.

"I'm winning!" She screams for the entire West Coast to hear.

"You can't always win," the boy responds, before standing up and pumping his pedals twice as fast.

Both children are racing toward us and I barely squeal and lurch out of the way before they pedal out of control down the gradual hill. The father, too far back now, is calling out their names.

The entire scene happens in the span of three heartbeats.

But I watch it in slow-motion, knowing it's one of those flashbacks I'll look back on when my card is punched and I'm headed into the after-life.

The girl senses that she's made an error, and hits her brakes sooner than her brother. She calls his name, with a desperate little plea, and my heart lurches. My ribs knit tighter as panic and hopelessness flood my body. The boy, now in front of her *yelps*, before his handlebars shake, and wobble, and he loses control of the bike completely.

I'm jumping up to my feet, but Parker is already *running* toward them. He places his palm on the little girl's helmet, and commands her to, *Stay*! When he makes it to the boy, crouched and crying underneath his bike, Parker drops to his knees in the red dirt and moves the heavy frame off of the child.

The tire is still spinning, the main frame unbent. But while the child is visibly rattled, Parker is being so...stable.

Even from my vantage point, a few jogging paces away, I can see in his face that Parker isn't panicked, the way most people would be. He's calm and confident, and it impacts the boy deeply.

They sit up together and Parker takes off his shirt to dab at the boy's tear-stained, dirty, and bloody face. I could be wrong, but it looks like the boy only sustained minor cuts and bruises. Parker's lips are moving and the boy is nodding in response. Then, the boy smiles.

By the time I make it there, I can hear the tires behind me of the father and daughter.

Everyone is reunited and Parker stands off to the side, his eyes never leaving the young boy's face. The father thanks Parker and they strike up a conversation that eventually leads to the potential of all-terrain riding lessons for both children.

But I barely hear any of it.

My palm moves to my empty womb and my throat tightens. A sharp ringing fills my ears and I shake my head, once, twice, to force it away. But my body refuses to comply.

It remembers.

Watching Parker with the boy, with *both* children dancing around his feet begging him to ride on their little bikes, I feel my stomach flip. In any other situation, I would call it butterflies, but paired with my regret, it feels like moth wings flapping around. Devouring me, chewing holes in me from the inside out.

He would have been an incredible father.

The thought rings across my mind as clear as a church bell. There's an aching *emptiness* to me, and at this moment I fear the vortex and land itself will swallow me whole and digest me, churn me into compost, and leave me to rot in my shame.

Parker places a foot on the tiny pedal, and then his other one, and as far as I know, this is the first time he's been on two wheels since the accident. Except, instead of apprehension or pressure or stress, the lines on his face curve up toward the sky in lines of joy.

Of passion, and pleasure, and *purpose.*

He rides like a clown on the tiny bike. He circles and then throws little tricks where his tires go left and right in the air.

The children clap and whoop and yell, while the father applauds in tandem.

You have to tell him.

That thought enters my mind like an unwelcome house guest. It's not even said in my voice, which makes me close my eyes and tilt my head up to the sky.

Is that you, God? I ask, even though I know, without a shadow of a doubt, that the Earth herself is speaking to me.

Heart to heart, Mother to almost-Mother.

Parker comes jogging over and I open my eyes to see all three bikes riding off down the path once more. The smile on his face is ... brilliant. Imagine only ever seeing one facet of a diamond or rare gem. It wouldn't be impressive. But turn it, rotate it, shine a light through it, and you're gifted all of the multi-dimensional angles.

I love seeing all sides of this man.

My heart beats like a finger over a typewriter, *I love this man, in all light, in all angles.*

"You know what I just realized?" Parker whispers over my lips before peppering kissing over my wet cheekbones.

Sniffling, I force a smile and ask a question of my own.

"Wait, was that your first time on a bike again?"

I need to know.

He nods, his smile only growing wider. My heart kicks

and jumps and air-pumps the air in the cavity of my chest ... so, I force my confession to the bottom of my throat. At least long enough to ask, "Alright, what, did you just realize?"

His hands, those wide, work-heavy palms, find my face. There's nothing refined about Parker, he's all raw-cut rock, rough palms, and whiskey-flavored whispers.

But, I love him more *because of it.*

His palms press into my cheeks as his sun-kissed skin hovers over mine. It's a spiritual experience, lingering in this great epiphany with him, the type of experience one can only *hope* to share one day with a partner.

"That I don't have to carry old feelings into new experiences."

Then, he walks ahead, on the path, as if none of this happened.

Standing, with my lips parted, I swallow and jog after his renewed pace.

☆

We're sweaty, huffing, and thoroughly satisfied by the time we sit down on a ledge looking out over the desert. I start laughing and the lightness of it chases the remaining shadows away in my body.

"What's so funny?" Parker asks, eyebrow lifted.

My laughter subsides and I give him a shy little smile. "A good hike resembles good sex." I look at him from the corner of my eyes.

His head tips back before he laughs and laughs as if some great shackle has been obliterated and shattered free from his life.

He laughs like a free man.

Then, he leans back, his palms spread wide in the dirt. Our

bodies are close, but not touching, and yet I still feel the warm boundary of his arm posted up diagonally behind me.

We're sitting on top of our version of *Pride Rock* watching the way the wind moves across the open desert when I release the tension in my stomach and begin.

"So," I start.

Lips quirking, he finishes our tango, "So."

"I thought, after we moved our bodies, and got in the open air, we could have a conversation about your career."

"Mmm," his eyes follow a bird flying in a wide and lazy circle above us.

"Do you trust me?" I ask.

Without looking at me he gives me one swift nod of his chin.

"I'm going to close my eyes. I invite you to do the same. Feel where you are in space, starting with your lower body. Can you feel where you are plugged into the Earth?"

"Yes," he responds, with a deep and thoughtful timbre to his voice.

I suck in a breath before continuing. Feeling more vulnerable than I should.

"Focus on the way your ribs move with each breath. Let it anchor you deeper into this moment of time and space. If you'd like to imagine a color flowing down and back out again, feel free to ..."

"Red."

I didn't ask him to share it, and knowing that it was freely given to me makes warmth spread in my chest. With both of our eyes closed, I know my smile is a private one. But it's one I'll hang in the gallery of my life's favorite moments for a long while.

"Now that you're in your body, let's re-introduce you to yourself. Keeping your breath smooth and measured, I would like you to walk yourself through how you prepare for a day of practice. What type of lines do you choose to warm up on? What does your body feel when you take your first ride down the mountain?"

I let those instructions hang between us and then focus on the sound of his breath.

After a few minutes of deep breathing, I prompt him again.

"Now, acknowledge the distractions that came up for you during that exercise. Where it popped up in your body, what voices tried to interrupt you. Acknowledge them, and walk through the exercise again. But this time, perhaps add another layer. Put someone there with you. Eden, or a friend. Someone you trust. Not a fellow competitor."

"Ok."

We repeat the process with a few more prompts. But, this one will be the hardest.

"Now let's walk through what *works* for you before competitions. Your rituals, routines, and preferences. Walk yourself through, from the moment you wake up, to the time the buzzer rings and you're racing down a hill."

"I can't," he whispers.

"You can. There are *no* stakes here. No medals, or placement times. It's just me and you, Parker. Take yourself back to the start."

"If I go back to the start...of when I stopped racing with my heart, I'll see my father."

His voice shakes, but I remain steady.

"Part of my job is to help facilitate self-knowledge and self-trust. I believe that you're ready to see your father in your memories again. To walk alongside him and to hold your pain in one palm and nostalgia in the other."

There's a rustling and I open my eyes. Parker stands and begins to pace.

"Ok, let's—"

"No."

"Parker," my voice is heavy and sad. I remind myself, *again*, not to be attached to the outcome of the day.

Walking toward him, I extend a hand in his direction.

"No!" He shouts and it freezes my advance to him. I stare down at my hand, reaching toward him, before I let it hang limp by my side.

He paces for a bit, mutters to himself, and stares at the sky. Then, he pauses.

"You know. My father is the one who told me what different cultures believe about someone having two different colored eyes." He steps closer and there's nowhere, literally nowhere, for me to retreat.

Parker's voice drops low and he doesn't smile.

"Every time I look at you, my eyes bounce between your blue and green eyes...and I marvel at how fucking beautiful you are. How caring, how intuitive, how *special*." His words soothe a purple bruise inside me that never quite healed...but his tone...is something less healing.

"And then, I remember it's *him*, who told me the deeper meaning. I look at your eyes, something that would normally be so perfect on their own, and see the shadow of everything I lost the day I found him dead."

I open my mouth, but he stops me by shaking his head.

"It's not fair, it's so not fair and I'm so fucked up about this still, and you don't deserve it. But I'm telling you the truth."

His calloused thumb pad rubs across my lower lip.

I step back, just out of his reach, as I stare at him unblinking and, numb.

Sighing, he interlaces his hands behind his head and looks up at the sky as if the answer to both of our lives might appear out of thin blue air.

"I'm proud of you for telling me the truth. For even

admitting that ... but why can't you keep going? Give the truth *air*, Parker. Give it space ... I can hear it. I can handle it!" My voice raises with my rising desperation. Frustration.

He steps toward me again ... into my orbit.

"Do you have a truth, a truth buried in your fascia and muscles and every fiber of your being? A truth you can barely wrap your tongue around, let alone say it out loud?"

The skin on my face tingles, all of the blood draining from it at his words.

He steps closer.

"Do you have a truth like that, Carmie? Do you?"

Tell him. Just tell him.

My mouth opens and my mind is made up.

I'll tell him.

"Yes, I do."

He steps back for a moment, eyebrows lifted, surprise and disbelief playing across his face at my choice to be honest. My willingness to step up, toe-to-toe, and challenge him to meet me on equal playing ground.

"Well, I don't want to hear it. We're not trading war stories. I'm done with this shit." His eyebrows slam down and I feel the shackle of grief he wears around that ankle *snick* shut again. Locked tight—a weight he's choosing to drag with him.

On my long hike down, all I can think about is how Parker is the first man I've ever met in my life who needs to forget about the invisible line between two contrasting choices.

Good, evil.

Black, white.

Right, wrong.

While "Walking the line" and exercising self-control would save more men on this planet than I can comprehend—it's destroying the man marching away from me. And I'm coming to accept that he's the only one who can take the free fall—the only one who can kiss the line goodbye—and save himself.

Austria, November

Traitorous thoughts circle my mind like vultures drifting over a rotting corpse. I've only been in Austria for a few hours, and I grossly underestimated how hard it would be to be a spectator instead of an athlete.

It's...embarrassing.

The Hardline is one of the toughest downhill races, and everyone was devastated it got canceled last year due to wet conditions.

If you forced me to choose one word to describe the event, I would have to say *gnarly*. That's the only way to describe the downhill track testing thirty-five of the best riders in the world. Normally, my name would be on that roster.

Most years, I end up in second place. Which, practically everyone else behind me would be thrilled to achieve. Not me, i'm sick of second place. I guess we won't know until next year, when I can manage riding at this level again.

The event takes up to a week to complete between the men's and women's races. And with it being the fifteenth anniversary this year, it's bound to be a party. But we're not just here because *Red Bull* pays us. We're here because we're a *part* of something special with Hardline. The organizers listen to us, to our suggestions on where to build out the best track in the world, and the fans look forward to this race every season.

I looked forward to it, too. Emphasis on the past tense.

Pushing myself harder in recovery and training the last two months didn't make up for the time I lost. Landon said under no circumstances am I to get on a bike and compete in this race. Something died inside me when he delivered that message. Something attached to my core identity.

Perfect timing for my therapy session with Carmie. Did I think she'd give me a break after our little rendezvous in the garage? No. Of course, not.

After I carried her to the guest bedroom and lay next to her, she mumbled, *I'll see you tomorrow for your session. Don't be late.* I kissed the back of her head with a tenderness I had forgotten I possessed and stayed with her in bed long after her breathing evened out. If I moved, the moment would be over. So my mind replayed the evening on repeat, a favorite movie, warming my blood.

How was it watching Carmie move? Better than a sunrise after years of darkness, if you can believe it.

The shadows danced and moved with her. The music brought out a side to her that I never expected or dreamed of knowing. It's difficult to describe. But in those moments, Carmie belonged to no one but herself. She wasn't interested in appearing interesting. She wasn't angling her body to look a certain way. Her light enhanced the darkness instead of chasing it away.

Carmie was a woman possessed by her heart and spirit. She danced like the phrase, *drive it like you stole it*. That's the power of an awakened woman. She bends the laws of physics to her will.

Now that I know it. Now that I've seen it—tasted it—I can't forget it.

That's why knowledge is so powerful. You can't unlearn something that is a monumental discovery. Try as you might to force it out of your head, but a mind stretched by a new perspective can never return to the same dimensions again.

Fuck.

We continued the rest of our week in a comfortable orbit. I can't tell who is the Earth and who is the moon in this quasi-relationship. It doesn't matter. We revolve around one another. Which is good enough for me. But, I know it's not good enough for her.

"*Red Bull* Hardline represents proper racing to me. It's so wild, a proper downhill track, and to buzz with all the riders is so much fun. I never expected to win seeding and get a chance to compete in the finals." Eden's voice breaks me out of my trance. He's giving an interview after his last run, a spectacular one that filled my heart with pride.

That's the only good thing that's come from my absence on the track. Eden's wings are spread, and he's soaring toward the sun. Something has settled in him, a rock hitting the bottom of a river, since meeting Elyse.

Ironically, being with a fellow free spirit, grounds Eden. I've never seen him work hard for a relationship. But the freedom and respect Elyse gives him is motivation to keep rising to that level of love.

"The last few days have been a dream, and if somebody told me this outcome a year ago, three years ago, or even a couple of weeks ago, I would never have believed them." Eden steps away with a wink at the reporter and slings his sweaty, mud-covered arm over my shoulder.

We make our way back to the shuttle and toward the hotel

where the rest of our team and crew are staying. Where Carmie is staying. Bringing her feels like a rash building underneath my skin. I scratch at my neck, telling myself it's the altitude and the last of the sunny day burning through my skin.

"Looks like hives." Eden narrows his eyes on my neck. "Are you that stressed about being here? Or is it about...a certain someone joining us? Giving everyone attention, except you." Eden laughs and steps to the side, just out of reach of my swinging palm.

Carmie and I rode to the airport together. Silence. We boarded the plane together. Silence. Sat next to one another for the entire journey. Silence. But when we arrived and met with everyone else, she came alive.

It's a punishment.

For not giving her everything I could in the therapy slash hike session I promised her. Shit move, I know. But there's just something about sitting there and letting years of sadness and rage and pain break open that terrifies me. Of what I might say, how I might feel after I say it—and what she might feel toward me in the aftermath.

"Shut it," I growl.

"I can't bruv, you're so easy to read."

"Nobody else, literally *nobody*, else thinks that."

"That's because I love you. You're an open book. I don't know why so many people try to crack your spine and read you because honestly? You're the most boring read since *Moby Fucking Dick.*"

The journey back to the hotel is short. I'm ready for a shower, fresh clothes, and a corner booth I can relax into. Somewhere I can belong with my crew without any effort.

After I rinse off, change, and cringe at the deafening silence around me, I walk toward the door between our rooms. Either Dick (my manager trying to live vicariously through me) has a sense of humor, or the Universe does because I *would* end up one flimsy lock away from the woman working her ass off to ignore me.

I knock once, keeping it a soft tentative gesture. I wait a few breaths, then knock again, slightly more demanding. Blowing out a breath of frustration, I pound five more times. I'm starting to see *Beast's* point of view in Beauty in the Beast now. Of course he was pissed off. Belle kept shutting him out.

She can ignore me all she wants, fine by me. I lie to myself and storm out, headed for Eden's room.

My hand doesn't even lift to knock on his door before he swings it open and marches out in a collared shirt, dark jeans, and too much cologne.

"Bar," we both say in unison.

Which proves to be idiotic, because I underestimated just how committed Carmie would be to ignoring me. The lengths she would take. Honestly, I just assumed she was ignoring me in her room. *Reading a book or crying over Grey's Anatomy season one, again.*

So imagine my face when I walk into the bar and see Carmie holding court with half of the riders from the race. A stack of red cards sits in her palms, and she deals them all out with a radiant smile.

She's in another one of those romper outfits, but this time, it's sleeveless. The royal blue color only makes her hair glow brighter under the intimate lighting of the crystal sconces on the wall.

Even with the distance, I can still hear her voice.

"*We're Not Really Strangers*, is one of my favorite games to play. Find a partner and exchange a card." Carmie sits on a red velvet stool and I watch from the oiled Oak bar top as she explains the activity. An activity every single person around her is genuinely interested in.

"I'll set a timer for your conversations. Then those of you in the booth will remain seated, while everyone in the chairs will shift to a new partner after three minutes. The goal is to be *vulnerable*, as challenging as that might seem at first. Trust the process and open up. What's the worst that can happen? You've already raced down a cliff today. I think this will be cake," she laughs with them, and my heart flutters in my chest.

Eden catches the eye of two women at the end of the bar, and I smack his arm.

"What are you doing?" My eyes narrow on his dumb face, visibly drooling over the twins.

"What? I'm celebrating."

"Do you have dementia? You are in a happy and healthy relationship," I remind him.

"It's open." He shrugs, but his eyes don't match the cocky smile he feeds me.

"It is? On whose authority?" I lean onto the bar and await his answer. Nudging his elbow with mine when his attention drifts back to the double cleavage angling in his direction.

"Elyse," he responds.

"There's no way."

"Believe it," he bites out and his tone shuts down any more of my unanswered questions.

Eden is pushing away from the bar and making his way over to the women before I can grab my drink from the bartender.

With nowhere else to go, I decide to head over to the corner with Carmie, my fellow athletes, and crew members. Standing behind her for a moment, just to see if she can feel me like I can feel her the moment she enters a room. I'm disappointed to find she doesn't. No acknowledgment. No awareness of my eyes on her skin.

If I believed she wanted a physical relationship with me last week, even if that was against her original intentions, I no longer do.

The ginger and syrup slide down my throat until all I'm

left with is a snappy aftertaste. Clearing my throat, I watch her spine stiffen before she turns that proud chin over her shoulder to look me up and down with her blue and green eyes.

"Here to play?" She asks. But before I can respond, she turns around as if she already has an answer and doesn't bother with a confirmation.

"Ready for the next partner?" She asks the group, aiming her question at Cillian (that traitor) with a cherry-sweet smile. It's as if I don't exist and am not burning holes in the back of her head.

"You're not playing?" I invade her space and lean down into the shell of her ear.

"Odd number," she retorts.

"I'll play with you," I offer. It would be no chore at all to *play*, which brings a smile to my lips.

As if she heard the direction of my thoughts, she scoffs and turns her back to me.

"Carmie, I'll be your partner. Old man here can take my place," Cillian offers up smugly. He speaks to her but stares at me with hazy, drunk eyes.

"Perfect idea, Cill. Come on over," she coos to him, her velvety voice lower and thicker than it was with me.

He rises, eager as hell, and stands above her. His pupils are dark as he smiles and stares down at Carmie, who is looking up at him with wide eyes and perfect lips.

I grind my molars into dust before moving to my new seat across from a young rider named Roman.

"Why don't I make more room for us?" Cillian asks her.

Turning on my heel, I watch him lift Carmie off the stool, spin, and position her on his lap. Her arms hold on to his neck and her head tips back in laughter. Red hair cascades down, down, down, her back. All that hair begging to be reined in.

All I can do is blink at the sight.

One of my best mates, drunk, swapping secrets with the woman who could get Hannibal Lecter to open up to her... that's how good she is. That's how open her heart is.

Have I used up all of her grace? All of her patience?

My eyes burn into her profile. This might feel worse than coming in second place.

"So, what is one of the worst nightmares you've ever had?" Roman asks me, laying his red card down on the table. *Why does everything around her have to be red? Red hair, red cards, red blood pouring from my head when I was dying...and thinking of her.*

Swallowing, I shake my head.

"Come on man, I know next to nothing about you," he pushes, not bothering to read the room.

Sighing, I tilt my head in Cillian and Carmie's direction. "That, right there."

The kid *laughs* as if I just told him a joke. Letting a dry chuckle leave my chest, I let him think it is. Pocketing my card, I tell him I have to meet my agent and stand up from the small cocktail table just in time for us to switch partners.

Walking right toward Carmie and Cillian, neither of them switching partners, I hand the card to Carmie.

"You want to know the answer? You know where to find me. Offer expires at midnight."

She stares at the card in her hand and blinks. I'm already gone, headed out of the bar and down the hall before she has a chance to respond.

It's true. I keep my cards close to my chest, often to my detriment. If there's one thing her presence in my life has given me, it's the dawning realization that not all cards can be kept. Some are meant to be given away.

Carmie

AUSTRIA, November

B efore I leave the bar, every athlete and crew member signs up for a complimentary therapy session with me for the coming week. Every single slot is filled.

But I can't focus on that joy or accomplishment. All because of *him*. So, with a pit in my stomach, I head for the gilded elevators.

This isn't my first time in Europe. But it *is* the first time without my family. Without an insufferable villa. Without the suffocating pressure of filling our days with *note-worthy* and *picturesque* tours. Without trailing behind Seamus like a street dog, desperate for his scraps.

Without guards and security and meticulous planning to avoid any attempts at violence against my great American family.

Gag.

Shaking my head, I take in the beauty and charm of a hotel that has never been featured in a luxury travel magazine, let alone on my family's radar. The low lighting, rickety elevator, and ornate wallpaper all give a romantic but dark vibe. This place, if properly decorated for it, would be the perfect setting for a horror film.

Who does he think he is? Giving me that card and walking away?

I've had it with him. What we shared last week was so astronomically stupid and yet so groundbreaking. It was heaven wrapped up in a sinful red bow. A hell of my own making.

Hell. That's what it feels like inside my chest when Parker exists around me with his stoic face and lack of explanations. When I'm locked out of his interior world.

The double doors of the elevator open up and two twins appear on the threshold. They're wearing black dresses that cling to their skin and their pupils are nearly blown.

Startling, I jump back with a hand to my chest. Icy dread fills my arteries. It's not the heart-faced twins that make my chest turn into an icebox. It's the man in between them.

"Eden, what the hell are you doing?" I whisper before my eyes narrow into slits.

His eyes widen for a moment as the twins look me over.

"Come and play with us?" One of the twins whispers into Eden's ear in a thick European accent before her tongue draws a wet line down his neck. The other twin parrots the same phrase, giving me the chills.

Come play with us.

I stifle a gag and my face must show it, because the twins shrug, and Eden coughs out in surprise.

"She's going to murder you," I promise him. I'm not referring to the *redrum* twins, but to my best friend, and the look on his face tells me he knows it.

Those are my last words before I turn and take the stairs. No air conditioning. No windows. I feel trapped in the middle of a secret. In the middle of a place I don't want to navigate.

Now what?

Am I supposed to call Elyse and tell her what I saw? What did I even see? The start of something? Or maybe it isn't anything now that Eden saw me...perhaps he stopped the party in its tracks?

No, why would he do that? He's no different than Seamus. Then all of the generations and long lineage of men getting their dicks sucked by secretaries, assistants, fan girls, and groupies.

Panting on the fifth landing, I nearly retch at the memory of Seamus telling me he cheated on me for the first time. I sit down and metaphorically reach for the jar of sadness I keep shut tight on a dusty shelf in my mind. There's something about seeing Eden and those women that cracks me wide open.

Nowhere to run. Nowhere to hide. Sucking in the dry air of the stairwell, I look down into the darkness and am flooded with a random, yet visceral, memory.

That memory breaks open like a nightmare as I hurl my jar of sadness at the wall.

☆

New York, January — *eight years earlier*
"We're leaving already? But you've barely shown me how to get down the hill in one piece! It's only seven o'clock!"

He doesn't answer me, he just marches to the car and throws his gear in the trunk. Not five seconds later, he slams the driver's door and starts the engine with a roar.

Seamus convinced me to skip my classes today so we could go up to New York from Cleveland and spend our time skiing. Except, when we got here, he told me that it was time I tried something new. I held my breath because I've heard when guys say that, it's typically about branching off and trying the other hole, but Seamus held up a snowboard and helmet for me. Which, is a relief because I might be flexible with my boundaries, but that hole will forever be an exit ramp only.

Anyway. I hate snowboarders, but I loved the stupid smile lighting up his face more. I fake an easy laugh and nod my head, willing to try something new, for him.

No surprise here, but after a few hours, one bruised tailbone, two aching knees, and New York's most unhappy couple later, I'm ready to completely launch myself off a cliff and end this misery.

Seamus is normally a patient person. But there's no patience tonight. There's been a dangerous current in the air between us since we arrived—and he can tell me I'm being paranoid all he wants—but I know that I'm not wrong. A shoe is about to drop. Hard.

It took five minutes of silence in the dark car ride home for the truth to come out.

"I slept with Kathleen."

There are many types of alone. Alone in a car after work. Alone in a restaurant waiting for a blind date. Alone when someone dies and you have to hold yourself together at the *funeral. Alone when you realize that the person who loved you, loved someone else at the same time. And now there's this type of alone—alone in the car on the darkest night of the year when a secret is exposed.*

The worst part about his confession, besides being trapped in a moving vehicle on dark icy roads, is that it doesn't surprise me. If anything, it validates my intuition. That there's truth to the moving shadows and whispers of my mind that have been begging me to confront him. I always talked myself away from the nagging suspicions. Because how could it be possible for him to indulge *in her feelings? If I were a bigger woman, I would feel sorry for her. She's been nipping at his heels, begging for his heart, since we were kids.*

I guess she finally got that piece, except it's not a piece of his heart. It's a bleeding scrap of mine.

"Say something, please. It's killing me."

His voice is the sad WWII movie, the perfect picture of agony. It's winning me over and gutting me at the same time. Am I pathetic? Sitting silently in the passenger seat, tears freezing on their way down my face...Where is the outrage? Where is the fury? Where is my spine?

"Please, Carmie, it meant nothing. *It was stupid, and I was drunk, and it meant..." he pauses, but I fill the space for him.*

"Nothing," I say to the window as I feel my heart and my stomach get dragged along the pavement.

"Exactly. Nothing, baby. It was a stupid mistake. I lost my head. I let her go too far..." He threads his fingers through my own and kisses my limp hand, oblivious to my impending detachment from reality.

"I just hope...I hope you can forgive me, you know? It's just sex, and it wasn't even that good, trust me..." He glances over at me with a worried line between his brows before he decides it's probably wise to stop talking.

He pulls over into another parking lot that's about a mile long and puts the truck in park. His hand cups my chin in the most tender of gestures, and it's starting to cauterize the bleeding wound of my heart. I look at him, really *look at him, and feel a fault line form between* then *and* now. *It's such a subtle little line, it's scar tissue nobody else will see.*

But like I said. It's small enough for me to live with. For now. For me to continue living in this house we've built out of our friendship and love. Small enough for me to ignore it the way I ignore putting away my laundry. Small enough, that I can toss a patch on it, or hide it underneath an ornate rug.

He senses the shift and pulls me onto his lap. His thin upper lip leans forward and grazes my earlobe. He whispers promises and love and sweet words of commitment into the mess of my hair, into the mess of confusion swirling in my chest.

I let him kiss me. I don't think twice about his fingers undoing my pants. I don't stop his ragged breaths as he lifts and slides inside me to ease his guilt with the warmth of my body. I let him simultaneously atone for his sins while he walks through the temple of my body with muddy shoes.

☆

I let him.

My eyes focus on the endless stairwell above me. All I see is red. It's the exact tint of regret and anger. A crimson shade of all the imaginary blood spilled from my heart at the hands of my ex-fiancé.

The sick part of the image isn't the blood—but the realization that I too had a hand in the carnage. I look down at my ring finger and sigh. Even though the angry red rash faded from my skin, I can still feel the itch.

Rising, I take one step at a time, slow and determined, dragging the heavy axe of my thoughts behind me. Parker can keep his answers and feelings to himself. I'm done losing my mind. I'm done with men.

But up every step, I hear a singular word. *Liar.*

Are you in Europe? I think I saw a photo of you...

You look good. Healthy ... but good. I miss you.

Come on. You can't block all of my numbers, Carmie. You'll give in eventually.

I'll block you as many times as I need to, Seamus. It's over. It's been over.

You don't listen, do you? We are meant to be together. The sooner you realize that the easier this is going to be.

Stop being a pain in the ass.

Nobody is going to want you. You are nothing without me. Without your family.

I'm sorry. Baby. Please. Call me.

Carmie

AUSTRIA, November

S tanding in front of my hotel door, I feel no better than I did fifteen minutes ago. My palm itches to grab my key card, but my eyes keep straying to the gilded numbers hanging between my door and his.

603 and 604.

There's nothing special about those numbers. Nothing, except the fact they're paired, side by side. His room and mine.

Thin flowering wallpaper and a dark walnut door are the only barriers between Parker's bed and my own. I'm tempted to press "mute" on the rest of the world. To tangle my legs with his, intertwining vines nobody will care or dare to take down.

But a small voice, perhaps my intuition, whispers. *You don't need to sit in the front seat of the emotional rollercoaster anymore. Time to get off the ride.*

Parker's door opens. His eyes stare down at me. He doesn't step out of the doorway but stands with one hand on the door frame and the other relaxed on the doorknob. When he catches my eyes on them, he gives me a ghost of a smile.

"Change your mind?" Parker asks. His voice is whisper soft, thick red velvet seats in the shadows.

"I pour into everyone, Parker. Everyone and everything. You included. And what do I get?" My voice is sharper, and more cynical than I've ever heard it. And underneath that edge is exhaustion. Years of it.

"What are you trying to say, Carmie?" Parker leans his temple on the door frame now as if my exhaustion is his own.

"I want to be *filled* at an equal ratio to which I pour." The words are out of my mouth too fast to take them back. Parker's eyes get a shade darker and sweep over my body.

"Stop that. You know what I mean," I demand as heat moves across my neck under his watchful gaze.

My eyes snag on the slow curl of his smirk before I look away.

"I do know what you mean. And *you* also know," his hand reaches for mine and tugs me into the threshold with him, my chest now flush with his, "that I can fill you, exactly the way you want. With pleasure—"

"You fill me with pain," I snap.

He winces but his thumb rubs circles over the back of my hand. It's hypnotic. I almost close my eyes and sink into that delicious heat building between my thighs.

But I don't.

"I meant what I said. Pour yourself into me, and then we'll see about all of that filling business." Leaning in toward him, just to smell the alpine air and trees and sky, I resist reaching up on my tip-toes to kiss his cheek.

His mouth drops open at my quick retreat, but I cut the interaction short before I lose all boundaries (as flimsy as they are) and climb him like a pine tree.

"Goodnight, Parker."

Swiping my keycard on my door, I turn my back to him. Before I can enter, a smooth envelope is pressed into my other palm.

"In case you need this later." He turns and heads into his room while letting the door slam behind him with a bang.

Slipping into my room, I open the crisp folder and pull out the room key. 604 is written on the top in neat script. The plastic is still warm, and a romantic corner of my mind likes to imagine he was holding it and turning it over and over again with those hands. That he was contemplating giving it to me all night.

Turning to strip out of my clothes and shower, I glance at the envelope again and spot a few pieces of hotel stationary folded neatly at the bottom...

Carmie,

It's almost like fate, destiny, and irony are all in collaboration, having a pint and a good laugh at my life. Why else would I draw that card? Why else would those red letters ask me the one question I find myself unable to articulate?

Because of you. Somehow, since that night I met you in Sedona, it's always been because of, despite, and for you.

You are the most lovely rose-gold wrench that wedges itself in my plans. You are the instigator, agitator, and manipulator of my many moods. But most of all, you are the golden promise of a sunrise. You are the first cherry I want to taste, after years of depriving myself of anything sweet.

So I will take my time now, in the silence of my room, in the world's smallest chair, to answer that question.

What feelings are hardest for me to communicate?

I hate my father for killing himself. I hate that he took every memory of him, every philosophy, every strand of DNA we share—and tarnished it with his selfish and desperate final act. I hate how much I think of him before I race. I hate how he left without a note. I hate how this pain, hatred, and misery taste in the morning.

But what I hate the most is how I didn't see, or know, how much he was suffering. Before it was too late. I hate thinking of the times I ignored his phone call while I was training. I hate not knowing why he felt so alone, so hopeless. Why he pretended his life was fine, instead of being honest with me.

Do you know what's even more painful? He decided not to be buried. Instead of leaving us a note, he left us a will and some instructions, and that's it. There's no place for me to go, Carmie. No place for me to drop to my knees and place one of my many second-place medals. Or soft grass to place his favorite chocolates from Switzerland. There's no spot or destination for me to visit when I need to rest my forehead against a cold stone with his name etched in it. You might not find me sentimental, but if I had such a place, I would run

my fingertips through engraved letters that read,
HUSBAND AND FATHER.
Does this make me weak?

"No, Parker. Of course not," I whisper to myself.

Don't answer that. Your worst quality is being
able to see the best in me, to see that first ray of
light over the dark horizon of my life. Or maybe one
day, if I can figure out how to say the rest, answer
it to my face. Place your palm on my cheek and give
me your green and blue eyes with all of their watery
emotional depth. Look at me and say, No, Parker.
Because if one thing I know is true, it's that I
won't believe it until I hear your lips whisper it.

For what it's worth. It's also hard for me to
communicate that I feel worthless and of no value
to the world if I am not racing. Death gave me
back my body, not without a fight of course, but he
kept my identity and my pride. I don't know who I
am anymore, Carmie.

But I do know that I will race again one day.
That I will take first place. Or better yet, become a
world champion. That I will be worthy of your love,
as I was the first time we met. Or maybe, I wasn't
even worthy of it then. Why else would you go back
to Seamus instead of coming to Europe with me?
Why, Carmie? Why?

The world tilts and I feel my center of gravity shift with it.

My heart is in my throat and I want to stop reading and run to him...

> *Maybe, on the day I take first place, the day I ride faster than my insecurities and ghosts and fears, you'll be waiting at the bottom of the track for me.*
>
> *That is almost everything that I have a hard time communicating. Almost. But I feel it's an excellent start.*
>
> *— Parker*
>
> *P.S. Thank you for proving to me that a gentle nudge can be more powerful than using force.*

Tears run down my cheeks and I lean against the wall facing our adjoining door and slide down to the carpet. Holding the paper protectively over my heart, I close my eyes and sigh. I've been using an ice pick to gently tap away at Parker's exterior for what feels like decades. This moment makes it all worth it.

His words, his beautiful and honest and raw feelings, douse the flames of bitterness right out of my system. They are a testament to how being gentle and moving through the world with a soft heart pays off.

Leo Tolstoy once said, *If you feel pain, you are alive. If you feel other people's pain, you are a human being.*

That's how Parker makes me feel. So utterly and wholly human.

With my eyes closed, I lower to the ground and swing my legs up the wall. Clutching the paper to my chest, I take measured and deep breaths, lulling my nervous system into a state of relaxation.

What a gift.

Parker could have ignored the card and ignored the call to open up. Perhaps in another timeline or universe, he did. Repeating the same pattern and cycle, over and over again.

I smile. This time, *with me*, he didn't.

41 / INCEPTION

AUSTRIA, November

A sinkhole opens up and I fall into it.

Except instead of falling with the rubble, I'm tumbling through an open void of pain. Tears leak from the edges of my eyes as I flail my arms out in an attempt to grasp onto something. My nails crack, splinter, bleed, as I drag them down the side of the dark cliff face.

Tumbling, head over feet, legs over torso, I'm an abstract painting of a man, ricocheting off every surface.

I'm desperate to stop falling. To regain control. But it's hopeless.

My body falls too fast. My heart beats frantically. My mind realizes I must be near the end, closer and closer to my demise. But before I hit the bottom of the void, and before the all-consuming pain cuts my life short, I'm floating through time and space.

As if a lifeguard pulls me from the inky depths of drowning, I suck in a breath and choke on the thin air. Everything around me shifts until I register that I'm back on the top of the mountain in Europe.

Except this time, I'm not alone. My father, Carmela, and other shadowed figures stand near the edge in a semicircle.

"Just one more race, Parker." My father reaches his hand for me to grab in solidarity.

Throat tight, I try to move my mouth and scream, *No! You're too close to the edge*, but my lips won't move. Everything around me feels slow and fast and hot and cold all at once. Everywhere at once.

I'm gasping for air, dragging my cinderblock feet forward. *I have to save them.* It makes no sense that they're all here, standing at the edge of a cliff. My entire body is fighting a cosmic force holding me back, and sweat breaks out from my temples. My jaw aches as I hold it open to scream, but no sound emerges.

"I'll take one more ride down the mountain, I'll be fine, son." The words come from my father, but it's my voice I hear. The same words I used before plummeting down the mountain all those months ago.

No! I try to warn them, but again nothing comes from my mouth.

It's no use. My father is the first to go over the edge.

Dropping to my knees, my hands dig into the hard, sun-bleached dirt and stone. Full-body tremors take over and all I can do is squeeze my eyes shut, *Wake up, wake up, wake up...*

"Just one more, I can do it." Carmela smiles down at me before she tucks a strand of her hair behind an ear. "Trust me, I'll be fine." She turns her back on me and steps to the edge.

My right knee slides forward as both of my hands claw the weight of my body closer to her hanging over the edge. Crawling is all I can manage to do.

Looking over her shoulder, her smile drops, as if someone

changed the movie out. I no longer hear the variation of my words.

Everything she says is her own.

"You can't control the wind, Parker. Why not become friends with it?"

"Don't—" I barely choke the word out.

She turns to face me but widens her arms like great angel wings.

"You can learn to ride the wind, Parker. Instead of always falling, don't you want to fly?"

"No!"

Her head cocks to the side, and then she smiles at me again.

"Well, I do. I want to fly." Then, she trust falls, into the open air.

Searing pain blazes through my temples as I scream into the sky and race to the edge. Leaning over the lip of the cliff, I can't see the bottom. She didn't scream. I didn't hear bones snapping or crunching on the rock face.

Blood begins to trickle out of my nose, winding a river of warmth right onto my top lip. Wiping it away with the back of my hand, I stare down at it for a few seconds. Its pain, and its confusion, swiped across my hand like a Rorschach ink-blot of my life.

More blood dribbles out of my nose and now my eyes and ears, *drip, drip, dripping* onto the unforgiving stone beneath me. It's a countdown, grains of ruby sand slipping through the hourglass of this strange reality.

Fly, Parker.

Her voice is all around me as if it's echoing inside me, no distance between sound and space.

"Everything hurts. The past, the present, the uncertainty of the future. I can't do it. I can't let go. I can't jump, I can't —" I tell her voice.

Let go and the pain will stop.

"No, I won't be like him. I won't give up. I won't go over that edge. I have to keep trying. I can *fight* it. I can—"

Blood pools at my knees and runs like a compass to the edge of the cliff. It flows like a waterfall, a river's current ready to take me away.

Let go or wake up Parker. I'm waiting for you.

The roaring in my ears gets louder as the blood moves faster and faster over the edge. Rising on weak legs, I stumble to the brink. It feels like my femur broke yesterday, searing pain blazing through my body as I fumble, and stumble, to get there.

Knowing how it feels to fall, to lose it all, my head spins until I believe I will be sick. Hands on my knees, my lungs compress, my chest heaving in and out. In a far corner of my mind, I understand that it has to be my choice. I must willingly go over the edge and let go of it all. Even without knowing what will happen. Or who will be waiting for me.

Rising to my full height, I spread my arms and look at both of my palms. The lines and scars are etched in my flesh, roadmaps of where I've been, and where I've yet to be.

Tipping my head back, I scream the scream I wish I let out ten years ago. I don't stop, and nothing in this world can make me. The chords of my throat shake and rumble. I squeeze my stomach tight, rinsing out every ounce of pain I've hidden inside.

When the air is silent and heavy around me, I open my eyes and *fly*.

Eyes fluttering open, the first thing I see is a curtain of red hair hanging over me.

"Wake up. Wake up. Wake up," she whispers, but her eyes are closed as if lost in a trance of prayer.

I feel shaking fingers skim over my drenched forehead, moving my hair aside. Left and right, *sweep*. Left and right.

Her repetitive touch is a balm to whatever hell my subconscious forced on me in sleep.

In the dream world, it felt like hell. As if my skin were being peeled back, layer by layer. But hell has a way of stripping one's existence down to the essentials—it has a distinct way of exposing reality.

Now that I'm awake, there's a loosening of the bars in my chest, an unlocking of deeper truths.

With my head nestled and settled in between her thighs, I let out an audible sigh. Her eyes fly open, and I offer her a tiny smile. Just the corner of my lips twitching up before falling back in line.

"So," she whispers.

"So," I return. Her fingertips move off my forehead, but my hand reaches up to stop her from leaving.

"Don't stop, please. It feels like heaven." Closing my eyes, I sigh again and feel how her presence re-knits my bones and stitches up my invisible wounds.

"I heard you screaming," she starts, but her fingers lose their calming pace. "When I came in here you were thrashing on the floor. I think you broke the bedside lamp and cut your hand..." As her words trail off, I blink my eyes open and lift my neck to look at my left hand.

There's a bloody strip of the sheet wrapped around the center and tied in a bow.

"Thank you," I croak before dropping my head back into the sanctuary of her lap. "Not just for coming in here...or for... my hand." I lift it and turn it side to side in the darkness of my room. "Thank you for saving me."

My voice is so soft, and it sounds like a broken chain on a bike.

"I did no such thing," Carmie scoffs, but she slips her hands underneath the base of my skull and begins to move her fingers along the tight muscles of my head.

Groaning, I shake my head.

Her hands stop, and I use the opportunity to step up to the edge of another cliff. Turning onto my side, I sit up and take her face between my palms.

Staring into her eyes, I'm about to speak, but blood is leaking through the bandage on my palm, staining her skin.

Her fingertips reach up to wipe it away, but I use the back of my hand to wipe it. Staring at that smear, a near replica of the one in my dream, I look back into her eyes.

"I don't want to fight the wind anymore."

Carmie's eyebrows draw down, and she holds her breath in anticipation.

"I want you, and I've wanted you since the moment I walked up and offered you my hands for evaluation by the fire-pit all those months ago. There is no part of me, broken or healed, that wants to resist your presence, your body—your heart—any longer. I see you, more than you see yourself. I see you trying every new hobby under the sun to discover different facets of this new Carmie. I see you watching new movies instead of replaying the ones you know by heart over and over again. I see *you*, I want you, and—" I squeeze her face between the heart lines on my palms.

There's no need for me to get my palm read. I don't need a psychic, tarot cards, or a palm reader to tell me what I already know. They'd see her silhouette in the swooping lines on my hand. They'd feel her love etched into the fine markings of my skin like braille.

My story begins and ends with her.

"I want to let go, Carmie." My finger catches a tear that rains down from her blue eye.

Leaning in, I kiss the trail of her emotion, until I reach her eye. Placing my lips, softer than I've ever done before, over her eyelid, I linger. Moving over her face, I grace her other eye with the same attention.

Until we're nose to nose, I remain silent. Interlacing my hands behind her head, I force her to look up at me.

"I want to *fly* with you."

As if back in my dream, Carmie spreads her wings wide and wraps them around my neck. My lips crash down on hers and as our bodies move closer together, on the floor of my hotel room, I can feel the shift in our relationship.

There's reverence. And I plan to worship at her altar—all night long.

Carmie

Austria, November

I have so many questions, but now isn't the time for answers. No, now is the time for our bodies to talk. If our heads try to get in the way, if our hearts try to drag their battered remains out the door, then we'll clasp our hands and steal the night right out from under the moon.

What do I want more? His hands or his heart?

Breaking away from our kiss, breathless, I stare into Parker's equally flushed face and know, without needing verbal affirmation, that I can have both.

With him.

Crawling into his lap to wrap my legs around his waist, I place my hand over his heart, then stack his palm on top of mine.

"If your heart doesn't beat for me, or doesn't want to let me in, then I don't want your hands on my body. That is my boundary."

He stares down at where we're connected and then swallows. "Carmela. I'll give you every beat of this reserved and quiet heart. The door is open. But full disclosure, it won't swing both ways again. If you walk through that threshold, stay. I can't bear watching you leave again. That is *my* boundary."

Neither of us blinks.

"Please, " he adds quietly, and it just about breaks me. But before I can respond with an eager nod or words of affirmation, his darkened eyes light up from within.

"As for these hands?" He grips my bottom and squeezes, the breath whooshing out of me in surprise. "They're going to love you. Loud and in a way that every man in this hotel—in this world—will know undoubtedly that you're mine."

Somehow, over the last few seconds, our lips have moved closer, within the same orbit. Closing the space between us, I seal my answer with a kiss.

His lips move in a sensual and slow rhythm with my own. It's a steady build, the strings of an orchestra plucking and tuning before they perform. Without breaking our contact, I suck on his lower lip with a desperate fervor, but I can feel him holding back.

It's in the way his body vibrates with careful control.

Unhooking my ankles from his back, I rest my legs on either side of his narrow hips.

I'm on my knees for him.

Sliding my tongue along the seam of his lips, I press my chest against his and angle my hips to rub against his growing erection. I demand entry to his mouth, so I can swallow the moan he's unleashing.

The tension in his shoulders melts at my contact, and I take the opportunity to press him deeper into the wall, as my fingers tangle in the loose and wet strands of his hair.

"Let go," I pull away and beg into his mouth.

Shivering, he kisses me and opens for me. A rush of adrenaline and power floods my veins.

"Tell me what you want, Carmela." Parker pulls away before leaning forward and kissing a line down the sharp slope of my neck. I tip my head back, letting my hair tickle his fingertips where he holds on to me for dear life. "Telling me what you want is not a burden, Carmie. It's a gift."

I've never felt safer as I mentally tip-toe my way to an edge I know I'll end up tumbling over. But I won't crash. So I picture myself swinging a glorious hammer and smashing the small box of desires I've kept to myself...and tell him.

"I want you to use your control on me. Use me," I breathe while rolling my hips over his growing arousal. "I want you to *own* me."

There's no mistaking the smile that overcomes his face, except it's not one of light or joy or warmth. It's a shadow spreading from masculine jawline to sharp cheekbone, a darkness he's all too pleased to drag me into.

A darkness I'm skipping toward.

Victory rumbles through my body, every nerve ending on fire and exposed, while he brings one hand up my side at an excruciatingly slow pace. My thighs tremble, and I close my eyes, dropping into the sensation of his hand instead. It traces up my waist and drags under my breast before a thumb slides across my bottom lip. He parts it and I almost latch on to suck it, but Parker leans in and demands, "Give me a word, any word, and if you use it, I'll stop."

His thumb rubs back and forth across the pulsing heart-beat in my lower lip...

"Paloma." I open my eyes and see a mirth reflected to me in his.

"Paloma it is," he almost laughs, but his eyes drop to my neck.

Intuiting what he wants to do, and where he wishes to go with said hand, I angle my chin up and close my eyes once more in submission. The flat expanse of his hand traces across my collarbone before landing on my heart. He rests it, for only a moment, before I feel five fingers close the distance and wrap around my bare neck.

Testing the pressure, I moan and then shiver as I feel the vibration of the sound pressing into my skin. It's intoxicating...the way my head and body feel whiskey-drunk and tequila tipsy.

"Do you like this," Parker asks, "or does my sweet girl need *more*?" His other hand adds pressure onto my lower back as my hips shamelessly grind into his.

This isn't our first time in bed together, but it feels like it. I almost tip my head back to laugh at the memory of how insecure and reserved I was with him all those months ago...

I don't recognize that woman—and good riddance.

"Stop asking questions and take control, Parker." I level him with a cocky grin, and he barks out a strong laugh.

"You have three seconds before I take you over this knee and show you just how controlling I can be."

I squeal and jump up, breaking free from his grasp, and run away from his ravenous grin. Placing the bed between us, my chest heaving in euphoria and joy and a little fear, I watch Parker uncoil his body and stalk toward me.

"Come here, Little Red," he crooks a finger at me. "This wolf is hungry."

He lunges around the corner with a face full of delight, and I almost let him catch me. Almost. Jumping onto the middle of the bed, nearly evading his hands, I hop a few times and laugh with glee.

"Three seconds. That's all I'm giving you." Parker places his hands on his hips and I feel my heart beat as a countdown.

One. My body freezes.

Two. I pull my oversized concert shirt over my head and toss it at his face as a deflection.

Three. Flight instincts take over, and I give him my back, so I can retreat to my room through the door.

"Enough games," he catches my ankle just before I launch off the bed, and I'm dragged across the duvet to his lap.

I try to wiggle, left and right, but he has me pinned by the steel bar of his forearm on my lower thighs. How incredible to be chased. To be desired.

"You're right."

"About what?" I breathe out, mesmerized by the idle circles he's drawing on the cotton fabric of my boy shorts.

"No more questions." And with that, his hand delivers a sharp *slap* to my ass. My head rears back and there's a vibrating, electric, silence following the spanking.

His body shifts, so I can feel his hard muscular thighs pressing into my throbbing core. With a dark laugh, he rubs the area he struck with a featherlight touch. "What's your word, Carmie?"

"Paloma."

"Do you want to use it?"

Shaking my head, his hand retreats from my flaming skin. The cool air in his absence makes my body tense in delicious, but cold, anticipation. I can't see him, and can barely hear him over the roaring in my ears. But his long fingers, moving my panties to the side, now *that* I can feel.

"If this is what you wanted so badly, let's see the proof," two fingers slide inside me with little resistance. And I mean none, no barrier to his mind-numbing rhythm of dragging out my pleasure. But just as fast as he built the fire, he douses it by pulling away, causing a whimper to leave my lips.

"*Shhh*, until I tell you otherwise," Parker murmurs, armbar still in place. Before I can protest, there's a crackling *smack* followed by a succession of two more across my already tender skin, making me cry out in ecstasy.

I can feel Parker's arousal through his thin grey sweatpants, and my mouth waters. Never, and I repeat *never* in my life, have I been so turned on. Rubbing myself on him, as much as his restriction will allow, a wanton moan escapes my mouth.

"Oh, now you've done it." Parker leans down, so his breath is hovering over my sensitive ass cheek, and then he bites down on my flesh. As he pulls me into his mouth, his hand snakes around underneath his legs.

"The next thing I take between my teeth is this," he finds my clit with expert ease and pinches it between two fingers.

Wolf, indeed.

Whimpering, I can barely form coherent sentences, but I give him what I know he wants.

"Then do it, already."

His momentary surprise is all I need to escape his lap, but instead of running away, I crawl up to the headboard of his bed and spread my legs.

An invitation for him. A challenge for me.

It's not something that was ever on the table in my past relationship. There was a season after I met Fallon and heard *all* about her time with Tommy, that I initiated it. But ... all I got was rejection. And I subconsciously believed that what *made* me a woman wasn't desirable. Or worth the time and effort.

My heart kicks violently in my chest, and I suppress a shiver when I watch him waste no time before kneeling in front of my feminine altar.

"Say what you want, Carmela." He leans forward and runs a finger up the seam of my shorts, spreading a liquid fire of friction up through my core.

"I want you to *devour* me."

"Less poetic, more literal. Try again." He flicks me.

He must read the shock on my face because he presses a

soft kiss to the inside of my left thigh. "You asked for it, remember?" He winks before leaning back on his heels.

Swallowing, I try to find the courage to *say* it.

"I want you to take these off. Now." My eyes glance down at my shorts.

Without fuss, Parker's fingers help me shimmy out of the last barrier between his mouth and my impending pleasure.

"Now what?" Parker gets on his stomach and is at eye level with the most vulnerable parts of my body. He hooks his arms around my open thighs and scoots closer to my center.

"I want to feel what it's like," I look anywhere but him.

"What it's like?" His voice is whisper soft and hot against me. "When I do this?"

He smiles, a real one, before he closes the distance between his lips and mine, and French kisses me exactly where I want him to.

He moves in a way that defies time. A master at widening and dragging the wide part of his tongue up and over my sensitive flesh. My eyes are closed and my lips are held tight. But then, Parker stops. He places a firm hand on my pelvis, anchoring me to the bed, and says, "Now is the time to be loud. If you hold back, I'll keep you on the edge, all night."

I whine, he laughs.

He explores and savors, never coming up for air. Pulling me closer, Parker devours me savagely, thoroughly, and devoutly, for the next eternity.

Ok, it's not that long because truth be told, it only took a mere thirty seconds before I felt the wave build at the base of my spine and threaten to suck me out to sea...but I couldn't get those words of worship he wanted to hear—the ones I wanted to *scream* out of my mouth.

So here I am.

My bones melted from the inside out, and my muscles wrapped in tense, tight, barbed wire. I'm shaking, sweating, and dying for a climax. He slips three fingers inside me, and curls them, as he hovers his mouth a breath away from my skin.

"Parker, please, please, please, *please*—"

I feel his smile as his mouth finds me again and sucks me in between his teeth. It's not painful, but it fills me with so much sensation my skin feels too tight, a balloon ready to *pop*.

"Let everyone know who's making you come, Carmie."

Those were the last words I heard because if I thought Parker was trying *before*, I was woefully mistaken.

So I feel no shame or hesitation in letting him know it. As I let myself accept the pleasure Parker wants to give me. As I accept how worthy I am of a man on his knees for me.

The entire hotel now knows it. Parker doesn't stop, not even as I'm arching and gasping for breath. Perhaps, now, in the quaking aftermath of my life being rearranged, the entire universe knows it too.

PARKER

AUSTRIA, November

B ang. Bang. Bang. BANG. "Parker, someone's at the door!" Carmie whispers in alarm.

"Ignore them," I command before crawling up her body. I need my mouth on her lips, the slope of her shoulder, and any other soft terrain I can discover before dawn.

And I needed it yesterday.

Carmie's face turns into a stop sign...but the knocking makes me smile. It's a gold medal. I brought that pleasure out of her. I broke down her resistance and now someone wants us to pipe down.

"Parker! I know, I know, I know you are in THERE!" Eden bellows, his words slurred and desolate. "And I'll huff! I'll puff, and blow this place down! Now where is that damn key card I stole? It's in here somewhere..." muffled stumbling and swearing are all we can hear.

Bloody hell.

"Ignore him." I look down at Carmie in hopes we can continue, but I catch her worrying her lip instead.

"What if something is wrong? He seemed so...off... tonight," she whispers.

With a deep and frustrated *sigh*, I drop my forehead to hers for a moment and begrudgingly crawl off the bed.

I yank on briefs and toss her an extra shirt to cover her naked chest before I pad barefoot to my door. Opening it, just a crack, I see the face of my best friend and kiss my hard-on goodbye.

"Eden, buddy. What the hell are you doing?" My voice softens because the under-lids of his eyes are red and puffy and make the blue irises look cold and vacant.

"Can I come in? What am I thinking, of course, I can—" Eden moves to push past me, but I hold strong.

"I have someone in here," I put my hand on his chest, stopping his momentum. He bobs in the threshold, a buoy lost at sea before Carmie appears behind me and sneaks underneath my armpit.

"Yes! I feckin' knew it!" Eden whoops and fist pumps the air.

Looking down at her, I catch her narrowing her eyes on him in a defeated attempt to stay mad at him even though she *just* admitted to me that she's concerned for him.

I bet she falls in love with the villain in every book she reads too.

"You have ten minutes. That's final." I push my finger into Eden's sternum, but he's already waving it off and running for my bed. He plops down, face first, and then admits, "I'm so effed over here, mate. So effed."

Carmie crawls into bed near Eden, with shorts on, thank god, and pulls his head into her lap. She strokes his damp hair away from his brow and says in the most honeyed voice I've ever heard, "Tell me about it."

Before he can respond, she stops moving her fingers and asks, "Were you seriously cheating on my best friend? Because

I'm having a hard time understanding why I saw you with those women..."

Her eyes catch mine, and she offers me a glare as if she can get a sober answer from me.

"Don't be cross with me, Carmie. I'm sorry. And no, I would *never* cheat on Elyse. She is...she is—" Eden's normal confidence seems far away. The sound of this smaller version of my best friend, who is typically larger than life, is the only thing that eases my frustration.

"She is *everything,*" he chokes out.

Sitting next to Carmie, I sling an arm around her shoulders, and watch her comfort Eden, all of her anger toward him completely melting away.

"Why is love so hard, Carmie? Why?" Eden closes his eyes and releases a breath when she strokes his brow bone.

She laughs, softly, and it's like a wind chime twinkling in the dark room. "It sounds like you are trying to tell me that you are in love with Elyse. But it's hurting you?" She inquires.

"Of course I am!" His eyes fly open, and I see a spark of the defiant man I know and love.

"I see. What specifically is bringing you pain, Eden?" Carmie drifts her fingertips over his eyelids so they're forced to close and relax.

"She loves someone else." He mumbles, a twitch in his lip.

"And you know that for certain?" Carmie asks.

"No. But, why would she want to be in an open relationship with me if she didn't love someone else? Is she holding out for someone else?"

Carmie pauses as if considering this question as Elyse's friend and not as Eden's.

"I'm not sure, Eden. Perhaps you can ask her?" Carmie's thumbs work in tandem to ease the new lines of tension appearing.

"Ask her?" He mumbles.

"Yes. Elyse, above all, values honesty. She is not...the most concrete when it comes to her personal life or feelings. But I know her. It is better to face her directly instead of avoiding or assuming."

Eden's nose twitches and it makes my chest ache to see him on the brink of whatever emotion is gripping him so tight.

Shaking his head he clutches Carmie's wrist and opens his eyes. "I'm not enough. She doesn't want *me*," he whispers.

Swallowing, I bite back the urge to shake him. To recite to him the *truth* about who he is. How enough he is. How I wouldn't be breathing if it weren't for him, how I wouldn't have kept going all of these months away from racing—without him.

But before I can say anything, Carmie wiggles out of the iron grip on her wrist. Not to let him go. But so she can get closer. She threads her fingers in his hand and raises it to place a kiss on the back of it.

My eyes burn as I watch.

"Eden," she whispers, "being in a relationship with someone who isn't able or willing to meet your needs is like being stuck on a see-saw. At first, you both are level, on the ground, and it feels new and exciting." Her eyes lift as if she's staring at a re-run of the past. "But then, the scales tip. It's so small at first. Maybe you bite your tongue and swallow the blood instead of being honest with that person. Maybe, you tolerate something you know you shouldn't...because you can't imagine being in a relationship with anyone *but* that person. But eventually, you're still on the ground, and you've lifted that person into the sky. Their needs matter more than your own. Their opinions, desires, goals, and *life* are above your own."

She sucks in a breath and resumes stroking his forehead.

"But then you wake up one day and realize, you have no

idea what the world looks like from up there. What the air tastes like, what it feels like to *fly* because you are still on the ground, holding all the weight of the relationship. Doing the work for two people instead of one."

Her eyes water and I notice a matching tear slide down Eden's cheekbone.

"It's terrifying to wake up and realize that. To feel so *heavy*, all of a sudden. So terrifying because it feels impossible to fight against gravity and *get off* the see-saw. You're holding all the weight, and you would rather not let the other person, the one you've idolized and held above yourself, down. But you are also afraid of getting hurt on the way off. Maybe you've been there for so long, your legs have atrophied, and you're afraid you don't have what it takes to walk away. To have the strength to stand on your own."

She pauses, then instructs Eden, "Take a breath with me, Eden." They inhale and exhale in unison and the energy in the room shifts from chaotic storms to a warm tropical breeze.

"You deserve to feel the joy, pleasure, and playfulness, of a relationship that meets your needs. Where two people can enjoy the ups and downs and still respect one another..." she pauses. "It's not about being *enough* for someone else, Eden. It's about knowing when to get on and off that see-saw and how to bounce back when you do. How to keep a buoyant heart. How to have hope that one day, you'll know better, and choose better, in love."

He yawns, then nuzzles closer into her lap.

"I like you, Carmie."

"I like you too, Eden. I wouldn't normally make a promise like this, but I will, just for you—" she starts.

His eyes open and we all hold our breath.

"Someone, out there, is getting off a see-saw, taking off the wrong size shoe of their relationship, and risking getting hurt again. They're dreaming of their perfect partner—the person who will make them laugh when the sharp edges of life cut them. They're thinking of a man who will bring light and pleasure into their lives. This person is going to bed, just like us, holding on to hope that they find their way to..."

"Their way to?" He asks, so quiet I can barely hear him over the sound of my heart.

"You." She places her palm over his cheek, cupping it gently. "Because, you, Eden, will be someone's version of paradise one day. I promise."

And that folks, is when I fell madly in love with Carmela D'Angelo.

Carmie

AUSTRIA, November

P arker and Eden are both fast asleep. We're stuffed like sardines in this tiny European bed when my phone rings.

"Elyse?" I extract myself from Parker's arms and slide off the edge of the bed.

She sucks in a breath. "Do you remember when I set a Google alert for all of our names?"

Walking to the bathroom, I slide the door closed and draw out my response. "Yes? And?"

"I did it when Fallon was miserable without Tommy and I wanted to keep tabs on him. But then I added all of us to the system just in case Riley ever got arrested. Again."

Sitting in the dark, I feel the walls start to close in on me.

"Elyse, please, get to the point. You're scaring me."

"You came up on an alert. A lot of them." Her words hang between us.

Holding my breath, I wait for the confirmation of what I already know.

"In an exclusive interview with your father—"

"And my brother," I finish for her.

Closing my eyes, I sit on the cold toilet and wait for my heart to fall out of my ass.

"I would tell you to turn on the TV but it's online already."

Swallowing, I nod, even though she can't see me. "What does," I drop my forehead into my palm. "Or, how far does he go in the interview?"

Elyse muffles the phone and tells someone she'll see the patient in a moment.

My family typically keeps our lives private, so I know if something is said, it's for political gain. Moving pawns across a board.

"It's about your abortion," she says.

Ding ding ding.

"Does Parker know, yet?" She follows up.

The blood leeches from my face and it's replaced with tiny pin-pricks of shame and mortification.

"No," I exhale.

"Well, if I were you, I would have that conversation soon. And Carmie?" Elyse asks before scolding a coworker next to her.

"Yeah?"

"Home might have been the first place you learned to run away from, but you don't have to run or hide from us. Ever," she promises.

"Love you, Elyse."

"*Tu Me Manques*, Carmie. Bye."

The silence of the small bathroom presses in on me. I struggle to find a calming rhythm for my breath. Sucking in large pockets of air, I feel like I'm underwater with a too-tight snorkeling mask.

"What's going on, love?" Eden's groggy half-drunk voice

enters the darkness and I feel the heat from his shirtless body bending down to crouch in front of me.

Tears run down my face as my past and my shame and regret dig their claws into me.

"I have to tell Parker something. But. I don't want to." I can't look at him. Which isn't a great indication of how well I'll handle the conversation with Parker.

As if my nightmare was made corporeal, there he appears. Parker moves into the bathroom and nudges Eden out of the way to take his spot.

I close my eyes and gather as much courage as I can.

"That next day after I didn't meet you at the airport. I found out I was pregnant. My brother convinced me to have an abortion. He was, he was so convincing. So steadfast in his conviction. I regret it. Almost every day."

Parker places his palm on my knee.

Eden sighs in the doorway.

Keeping my eyes closed, I let my words roll out into the open.

"I didn't tell anyone about it. Except Elyse and my brother. And now. *Now*. He's using it. *They* are using it in their campaign. Probably to get all of the younger voters who only seem to care about abortion rights."

"That's fucked, Carm. My god, that's bloody fucked," Eden whispers from the doorway.

I open my eyes and see Parker throw Eden a murderous glare before Eden walks away to give us privacy.

Nodding, I begin to feel numb on the inside. "It...doesn't surprise me. As a strategy it makes sense. Sows empathy with new voters. Makes them appear more trusting. But what does surprise me, is that they would do it without consulting me."

"But, *is* that surprising?" Parker asks, already knowing the answer. "From the people who asked you, begged you, or coerced you, into being with someone you don't love. In getting rid of an unplanned pregnancy that didn't align with *their* timeline. In sending your brother and Seamus out to Sedona to collect you like lost baggage? Is that surprising?"

Dropping my forehead into the space between Parker's shoulder and neck, I shake my head from side to side. Letting the tears soak his skin.

"That's not love. That's politics. And you—" He brings a hand to my chin and squeezes it a touch too hard, "—you are not a pawn in their game. You are an extraordinary woman. A woman I would have gladly dropped everything in my life for had you shown up and told me the truth." His voice is soft and low and he brings his palm to the back of my head. Cradling it.

"I would have more than embraced being a father with you by my side, Carmie. Why didn't you come to me?" His eyes are closed and I can feel the emotion he's trying to hold back. "Why didn't you come to me?" He repeats it as a broken prayer, wading into the pool of sadness to join me with every word.

"It's the only thing in my life I truly regret, Parker. I'm so sorry. Could... would you.... ever—" I stutter inbetween sobs.

"Yes, I forgive you. We can talk about it more in-depth later if you need. Shh." He strokes my head. "Is this what you tried to tell me on the mountain the other day?"

Nodding, I suppress the gaping and gnawing urge in my stomach to make the world disappear for a little while. By any means necessary. Pulling back, I look into his eyes. There is so much passing over his features, that it's hard to catch up. I'm tired, it's dark, and the relationship we're re-building feels too fragile for this moment...

I don't want it to break.

Then, his hands cup my face and I feel something new forge between us. The look on his face tells me that if I were to ever break something between us, instead of tossing the pieces away, he would melt gold and line the pieces with it. Fixing it. Making it more beautiful and stronger than before.

"Let's do an interview." Parker's voice is strong but low.

There's not an ounce of contempt laced in his words. Only a slow, burning, heat of anger directed at the people I'm supposed to love and value above all else.

It's an interesting phenomenon to have someone stand behind you or, *beside* you, as you choose a new path and grope blindly in the dark along the way. It makes the lack of light a little less ominous and a lot more adventurous.

A shiver runs down my spine.

"Alright." My heart trembles and I'm flooded with adrenaline at the idea of flipping the family script. Going *off* script completely.

"It's *your* turn to be the wolf," Parker whispers into the night.

☆

BROOKLYN, NEW YORK

It's wild how fast time moves once you've decided something.

The moment Parker kissed my forehead, we all filed back into our rooms to pack. Eden told us to go, that he would get first place at Hardline in my honor (he did, by the way) and Parker told his agent he had a family emergency to tend to (which, I suppose, he also did).

I decided to go with a third-party news broadcast because everyone and their mother knows that the big networks are all owned and chained by the corporations and politicians that back them.

As we pulled up to the studio in Brooklyn, New York, I started to question if this was the right move or not.

"Getting pregnant by a man taking advantage of her

fragile state, was not her choice. She deserved medical care and options." My brother's voice lying on national TV had made my stomach flip.

I watched it. Over and *over* again. In the private airport. On the plane. In the car. Until Parker almost threw my phone out the window.

How dare he. It's all I keep thinking. How dare Carson take one of the most vulnerable moments of my life and spin it for political gain. I'm being bombarded with text messages from friends, family, and see countless mentions on social media by every Tom, Dick, and Harry from my past.

"Women, all women, deserve the choice. Despite my party being historically pro-life, I believe there is room for the state of Ohio to make exceptions," my father had declared with open palms and something he meant to look like love in his cold eyes.

Parker's thigh brushes against my exposed leg peeking out from the slit in my white dress, bringing me back to the present.

"This is on your terms, Carmie. You don't owe anyone an explanation or a conversation." But deep down, a voice reminds me that the resistance I feel is only fighting to protect me, to cling to that age-old sense of pleasing others at the expense of myself.

"It's not a limitation or failure to change your mind. Anyone who has led you to believe that isn't on your side."

Nodding my head, I suck a large breath in and grab my purse.

"Just be honest. You don't need to sugar-coat anything. You don't need to sell some digestible version of yourself. You only need to be you."

If Parker keeps up his words of affirmation *and* acts of service, I won't be getting out of this car. I'll be straddling him in the backseat like a love-obsessed teenager after prom. But, without a backward glance, I open the door and step onto the busy sidewalk. An assistant meets me at the rusty door of the reclaimed warehouse.

"Ms. D'Angelo? Thank you for reaching out. We were quite eager to discuss your family's history in American politics..." her words drift off as she climbs a spiral staircase to the right of the entrance.

The warehouse reminds me of a textile factory from another era. It sends another chill down my spine.

Parker is right behind me. Similar to a protector, but more Princess Bride vigilante and less The Bodyguard with Kevin Costner.

"Right this way, please."

I follow the woman with her chic bob and criminally overpriced outfit through the dark halls. Her spotless designer tennis shoes are silent as we wind and curve through open-concept workspaces. People turn their heads to offer me small yet welcoming smiles, but I'm too on edge to return them.

Making eye contact, I lift my chin and allow myself to be led into a quiet recording studio.

It's a good sign, I suppose, that I'm not willing to smile when I don't feel like it.

After a few moments, I'm exchanging *hello's* with the sharply dressed woman running our interview. I've seen her before, circulating social media, and I've heard quite a few insults regarding her being a black woman in media who refuses to choose a political side.

I'm intimidated.

Once the microphone is set up underneath the collar of my dress and Parker's is clipped on the inside of his (only) white button-down, it's showtime.

The lights dim, and three large cameras begin to oscillate and pan around us on a leather couch the color of bourbon.

Our interviewer, Dawn, introduces us. My ears begin to buzz while my vision tunnels out.

Instead of the lights feeling dimmer, they feel brighter and hotter on the surface of my skin. Everything within me wants to run, run, run, away from this moronic idea.

Who do I think I am? No, I can't do this— my head snaps to the right, and I catch Parker's eyebrows pull tight. His hand lands on my knee, squeezing it to a pattern, a rhythm, a wave I can follow and mimic. Five times total. My breath becomes less choppy. It evens, and slows, and eventually, I make eye contact with Dawn and the cameras with their little red lights waiting for me.

Panic rises again, once I realize I didn't hear her ask me a question, but Parker leans forward and tucks a strand of hair behind my ear. Turning to look at the camera, with the most solid and confident voice, he answers her question.

"Well, Dawn. I'm a libertarian."

I turn to look at his profile before I smile, picking up the thread of conversation. "Of course, it only seems fitting I would fall in love with the most anti-establishment man I've ever met."

The words leave my lips without effort or forethought, the way someone breaks through the surface of the water and sucks in their first breath after nearly drowning. Instinctual. Life-saving. Couldn't help it if I tried.

Parker, instead of responding or showing surprise by my confession, leans in and kisses my temple.

"Well, if you weren't America's sweetheart before, you most certainly are now."

Feeling fortified by love, I look into Dawn's eyes and say, "I'm not looking to be anyone's sweetheart. Nor am I going to sit back and become a political pawn for a party—for any party —seeking more female votes."

Dawn lifts a perfectly manicured eyebrow, part approval, part *start your engines, this is gonna be good.*

"So, can you let our viewers and listeners know whose political party you *are* associated with then?"

Instead of looking at Dawn, I stare right at the blinking red light on the camera.

"My name is Carmela D'Angelo. I'm here tonight to tell the American people that I am not *with* any political party, regardless of how they may use, abuse, and prosper from my story. I am here to remind the women in this country, and the politicians that are supposed to represent us that speaking *for* someone is different than advocating for them."

Lifting my chin, I drop the sweet girl act, show my teeth, and tell them exactly who I'm becoming.

"My name is Carmela D'Angelo and I'm not affiliated with any political party because I am with women—not the institutions that misuse and abuse us."

BROOKLYN, November

I've never watched someone I love do something *they* love.
Is this how my father felt, watching me race? Is this what my mother feels when she watches a client deliver a baby into the world?

It has to be.

Carmie is sitting on the edge of her seat, face flushed with passion, a fire alive in her mesmerizing eyes. It's her voice that sends my heart into overdrive. It's not the voice of an altruist, politician, or even the voice of an angel.

This voice of hers sounds like the moment a cage is opened and wings beat and beat on their way to freedom. Her voice is the releasing of doves. It's no small thing, a voice like that.

"If we cared about women's health in this country, we'd be prescribing and covering pelvic floor therapy. We'd have longer maternity leave and support to handle the postpartum period with grace and care. We'd figure out why our death rate for women of color in labor is astronomically higher than white women in the US."

God damn, I love her voice.

Closing my eyes, I nod my head and bask in it.

"If Republicans cared about women's health and if Democrats cared about women's health, they would stop fishing and fighting for the emotional vote with *one* hot-ticket item, and start addressing the issues that are killing women every single day."

My eyes open to catch Dawn also nodding along, encouraging Carmie to have this moment.

"They would take domestic violence accusations seriously. They would not allow women to be separated from their children and forced to give them over to their abusers. They would allow women to make choices for their health—health beyond abortion. They would stop letting corporations poison our food. Politically correct or *not*, these topics need to be brought out of the dark and into the light."

She pauses and shrugs her shoulders. "Because that's what the kicker is. Whenever we address issues that impact women, *all* women, we are merely used as a bargaining chip. But just like in casinos, the house always wins. Their concern, and let me repeat this, *all* politicians on both sides of the aisle, only want us to buy in. They don't—"

"Ever let us win," Dawn finishes.

"Exactly."

Carmie grabs my hand and interlaces her fingers in it. "I was not manipulated, coerced, or tricked into having a consensual, intimate relationship with this man. My family lied. The only people I felt coerced by were members of that same family. I can't blame them for what I chose to do..." Her eyes water and I squeeze her hand tighter.

"That choice was my own and I live with that regret. As I know many women out there do as well. Saying that I regret my choice does not diminish that I believe women should *have* the choice. But it does shine a light on how *everyone* is so obsessed with abortions and yet so ignorant as to how to make this country a safe, livable, place for women, those with children, or not. With regrets, or acceptance."

"So, you consider yourself a feminist?" Dawn asks.

Carmie pauses, chewing something over mentally. "See, this is part of the epidemic in our society—labels." Carmie looks at Dawn with conviction in her jaw.

"If I say I'm a feminist, but also say that I regret my abortion, I'll be dragged to the proverbial town square and stoned by the very people who claim to *love and support all women*. If I say I'm not a feminist, I'll be burned at the stake and called a 'trad wife' or a disgrace to modern progress. So what if instead, I am a secret third option, that has my feet anchored in the grass, with my head tilted up to the sky? Like I said, I am with women. Not the abusive systems that work to keep us fighting amongst ourselves."

Dawn asks her to expand on her political leanings in other areas, which Carmie handles with grace and equal fervor.

"How can someone expect the macrocosm to change when they don't take the responsibility to change their microcosm? I wish more people understood that. Went home and started there, then branched out. It isn't the label, it isn't our identity, that defines who we are in the community...it's how we live our values and beliefs. Some of the most charitable and altruistic people I know don't identify with a political party, religion, or movement. No ballot is required. No authority figure to praise when things are going well, or to blame when things are going down the drain. They're just...citizens of this country. A legacy that leaves their community, or family, or corner of the world *better* than how they found it," she answers.

She's still talking, with her heart in her hands, and her joy painted across her face. The world fades away as I watch her, and I feel her energy radiating toward me. There's so much we need to talk about, in the privacy of a dark room, in a warmed bed. I know that I'll never be able to untangle myself from the strings that bind us.

With exceeding clarity, I realize that I want the privilege to be by her side when she walks into a room and inevitably changes it. I want the privilege to be a stable piece of land when she feels lost at sea. I want the privilege—want it so much I fear I might need it—to watch her shed the skin of who she used to be—and become who she was meant to be, over and over again.

The privilege to hold my hands out and say, *That's my woman, my wife, re-inventing herself again. Do you see her? Do you see how she never loses heart?*

When people lift their eyebrows at my admission, I'll shrug and say—

She's not mine, in the sense that she's my property. She's mine in the same way my favorite grocery store is mine. The way my body drives to it on auto-pilot, how the people there know me and welcome me. She's mine the way my favorite bike trail is mine, that familiar feeling of being at home. She's mine in the same way my favorite movie is mine. How it makes my heart beat faster and always makes me cry, even when I know what's going to happen. None of those things necessarily belong to me, but they are stitched into me, into the fabric of who I am.

But most of all, I want the privilege to lift my chin and let everyone know, *There goes my heart, walking and spinning and beating outside of my body.*

Dawn is speaking to the camera when I snap out of my reverie.

Leaning in toward Carmie, I let my lips brush the shell of her ear as I whisper, "Will you marry me?"

Carmie

MANHATTAN, November

"Carmie, are there any last words you would like to say to our listeners today? Perhaps to your family?" Dawn's voice barely reaches the shore of my consciousness.

"Yes." But my answer isn't for Dawn. It's for Parker.

Turning my head to him, I say, "Yes, I will marry you."

I'm not sure what I was expecting, but it wasn't this. I wasn't expecting every stone to crumble and fall off the wall that protects Parker's emotions. Not only that, but I wasn't expecting his hands to reach out and cup my face with a slight tremor, before dropping his forehead to mine.

I wasn't expecting him to look into the camera, with all of his joy and pride on full display for the world, or whoever out there is watching, to see—before kissing me. Deeply. Without reservation or hesitance. Without getting anything in return, except my love.

For such a private man, to make such a public gesture, well, it's the type of movement that shifts the Earth's axis by a few degrees.

My brain rewinds the story of my life to when Seamus proposed to me. It shows me, like I'm a ghost in the room with that old version of myself, how I felt. How sick, scared, and utterly desperate I was for anyone in that room to bail me out of my relationship. The anchor of dread pulled me down into a place of no return when Seamus slipped that ring on my finger.

Blinking, once, twice, and now three times, I feel none of those things as I consider a life with Parker. All I feel is peace.

Dawn jumps out of her seat and starts squealing with joy before asking for a hug. We spend the next few minutes of the interview talking about my relationship with Parker Radcliffe. How we met. His career and what comes next.

When we close out the interview and begin pulling our microphones off, Dawn offers me a guest spot on an upcoming show she's doing on the state of women's mental health.

The rest of the afternoon is a whirlwind. From making out with Parker in the elevator on the way down to our car to sitting in his lap in said car, to making our way to a boutique hotel to lock ourselves in for the next day and night.

☆

Elyse won't stop sending a thousand messages in the group chat and my head is starting to pound. But I get a phone call from Lina before I put my phone away.

"So! When were you going to tell me you are in love with my son, hmm?" My mouth drops open, and I fear it will never close again. I put the call on speakerphone, so that Parker, who is currently putting his boxers on after our shower, can hear. She laughs at my stunned silence, and the sound makes Parker whip his head around to my phone.

"Ma?" He strides toward me and grabs the phone, cross-referencing the number and name on the screen.

"You've always been a private person, Parker, but for god sake. You couldn't have given me a warning before proposing on a national broadcast?"

Chewing on my thumbnail, I lift my eyebrows at him, waiting for him to answer.

"I told you about Carmie," he says, eyes narrowing in defense.

"Sure, sure. But you've failed to mention *quite* a bit of information. Like her name and that she is a student of mine and..." she's giving him a hard time, but I can hear the laughter in her voice. The happiness and joy.

"Carmie, I'm proud of you for that interview. You lived the phrase, *That which I own about myself, can never be used against me*. You finally owned it."

"Owned what?" I ask into the phone.

"Your pain. Which turned it into your power."

Smiling, I close my eyes and savor the moment.

"Mom, go away. We'll see you in Sedona when you come home from your client in Denver."

"Congrats, I love you both," she laughs and makes kissing sounds into the phone before hanging up.

The call ends and Parker wraps me in his arms. Not fifteen seconds into our silent companionship, my phone begins to ring. And ring. There's a brief pause, and then it picks up again. In my gut, I know who it is.

"Don't," he groans into my hair before taking a deep breath.

"I can't run anymore. You taught me that." I poke his ribs, even though my heart is sinking into my gut.

He sighs and walks back into the bathroom, leaving me alone.

"Yes, Carson?" I say without a tremor in my voice as soon as I lift the phone to my ear.

"This has to be a fucking joke, Carmela." His voice is so low that it gives me pause.

"My interview? Why shouldn't I make a statement about *my* life, Carson?"

"It reflects on our family! You fucking trashed us!" He's not a calm, cool, collected public servant. Carson is roaring into the phone and if I'm not mistaken, I hear a tumbler shattering against a wood-paneled wall.

Swallowing past my fear, I remind myself of who the hell I am. Even if every cell in my body is trembling and cowering.

"It is not my job to appeal to you, and it is not *your* job to find me appealing." The words barely come out between the lump in my throat and the mixed emotions churning in my chest.

"ARE YOU OUT OF YOUR MIND? Do you have any idea what you just did? Accepting a proposal from some uneducated piece of shit? Going on that broadcast? This will cost us the election! You fucked us! Royally!" He's yelling into the phone so loud that Parker stops moving.

Holding my hand up, I still him, praying he doesn't charge like a bull to give my brother what he deserves.

But like I said, I'm done running.

I am transformed by love. The love of my friends. The love of my fiancée. Most importantly—I am transformed by the love I've worked to cultivate within myself.

"Carson, if you and Dad lose the election, that is on both of you. Take some responsibility for yourself, for the people you are supposed to represent."

He's speechless, and I use the gap to say my parting words. "You were the person you needed to be to get this life. But somewhere along the way, you weren't the person you needed to be to keep it. That's on *you*."

After I hang up I go into my contacts and block him, my father, and triple-check that I have Seamus' number blocked as well. I leave my mom's contact open, but I know she won't reach out. She prefers to keep her place in the comfortable and numb existence; she'd never stand with me on my own.

Instead of feeling rejected, I feel free. With a deep exhale, I let the plush towel drop to the floor.

Parker grabs my phone, tosses it into our open suitcase, and tosses me onto the bed. All dread and heaviness evaporate from my soul the moment his warm skin presses down on mine.

There's no foreplay required with Parker because the best foreplay is reduced stress. My body feels open and willing for him because he's given me, in such a short time, the emotional stability, and honesty, I've always craved in partnership.

There were moments when he wasn't ready. There were moments when I wasn't ready. But there were never any games.

"Do you want to talk about it?" He asks, hands stilling on my face.

Shaking my head, I tilt my chin to kiss his jawline.

Kissing the corner of his mouth, just shy of claiming his bottom-heavy lip, I whisper, "You know, there was a time when I thought you were my rock bottom."

He pauses, before trailing his nose down my neck. "And now what do you think of me?"

"I think," I twist out of his reach, so he is forced to listen. "You were at rock bottom the same time I was. But instead of burying one another deeper, we stopped to lay a new foundation instead."

His eyes roam over my face, and I'm offered a half smile.

Lowering, he brushes my nose with the tip of his, and the gesture makes my heart melt.

"Do you regret proposing?" I whisper into the shell of his ear.

I'm terrified of the answer. But I owe it to my new self to ask. His weight drops onto my body for the length of his long, exasperated exhale.

Parker rolls off me and looks into my eyes. His words are slow. "Why on Earth would I regret proposing to you? I would marry you tomorrow if I could."

"Then why don't you?" I challenge, but my lips won't quite perform a smile.

"You can ask me if I regret proposing to you tomorrow, next month, or ten years down the line. The answer will remain the same. I am not someone who makes decisions lightly. If something I say or do seems out of the blue, that is because it took me months, possibly years, to decide on it. You, more than anyone else in my life, understand how much I keep under the surface before I let the world see it." His index finger trails down my cheekbone until it curves along my collarbone.

"I suppose anyone on the outside of this relationship might think it was impulsive of me to propose... but... I suppose it's because I'm finally learning to let go."

Nodding my head, I drink his appearance in. It's golden hour, the last final rays of the sun streaming in through thin curtains over the small windows. He's bathed in the light, like a portrait in a church covered in a brilliant swath of life.

"I love you intentionally, Carmela. I don't believe in soul mates or twin flames. Occasionally, I don't even believe in destiny. But I do believe in willing something to happen, grabbing the threads of fate, and weaving a new story."

My eyes water, but the corners of my lips finally curl up.

"I knit your name, and our story, right here..." he taps his chest in five slow resounding beats. "I knit your name. Not the stars. Not divine intervention. Not even God. And here, your name will always remain."

I close the distance between us and guide him onto his back. His lips mold to mine in a desperate plea, and I answer the call willingly. His hands travel up my thighs and waist as I straddle him. The blacks of his eyes expand in a slow build of heat and lust.

"I'll get you a ring, you know," Parker whispers, before intertwining his hand with mine.

An image of the 4-carat pear-shaped engagement ring Seamus forced on my finger appears, but I blink it away. Shaking my head, I tilt my head back and laugh.

"I don't need a ring." My chest squeezes in joy, instead of despair, and I love the feeling. He's about to open his mouth to argue, so I relieve him. "But, if you must. No diamonds." I squeeze his hand. He sends a pulse back to me.

"No diamonds. Not for my *ride or die*." He nods.

Our conversation was almost enough to make me forget about the full-blooded man *growing* beneath me. Sliding my claws down his chest, hard enough to leave faint red marks, I drag my hands into the waistband of the only piece of clothing between us. Looking at him from underneath my lashes, I catch the uneven rise and fall of his chest.

His briefs slide beyond his hipbones, but not low enough to free him, and I bend to drag my tongue in that delicious valley of muscle. It makes him shutter and arch his back in surprise.

"Little Red."

"Shh." I nip at his skin below his navel, over the trail of dark hair. With just one finger, I trace up and down his erection, over the fabric. His head tosses back, cords of muscle tight in his neck.

"I will do anything," he pants, "to get you to move a *little* faster."

"Beg." I hover my mouth a breath away from the head of his dick, which is straining valiantly against the fabric.

Parker groans, and if I were to look at him, I would see his jaw clenched, mind churning in stubborn defiance.

But I don't need to look at him. I could love him in the glow of the setting sun, the relief of the next sunrise—but I could love him in the valleys and shadows just as easily. I can, and will, love him in the dark.

"Beg, and close your eyes," I command, a small thrill making my heart gallop like a wild horse.

"Please, please, *please*." His last word is a prayer and a plea, all wrapped in one.

Snaking the tips of my fingers into his waistband, I pull, slow as molasses, until nothing is covering my destination.

It's not a surprise, the sight of him aching and hard for me, but it does feel like the first time. The first time when we are mutually connected.

Equal in our desire to worship the body and heart and story of the other.

Manhattan, November

" As you wish."
     Those were her last words before her cherry red lips and lowering her mouth until it was completely wrapped around me—in pure, unfiltered devotion.

Sweat now drips down my temples and my jaw aches from clenching it so tight. With my fingers tangled in her long, perfect, hair, I hang on for dear life as stars begin to pop and fizz behind my closed eyes.

"I need you, I need you," I pant before she uses her lips around me to *hum* in agreement. My hips jerk up, but instead of scaring her off, it only solidifies her reserve to move her wet, hot, mouth up and down...at a torturous and slow speed.

The more desperate I get, the slower she goes. She's matching the speed of the Earth's rotation, a long and natural journey from dusk to dawn. There's no rushing her. Not when I see a self-satisfied little smile bloom on her mouth when she takes a break.

Her hands grip me at the base and move with that same honey-in-summer tempo.

"This is, inconceivable." I sputter as her tongue reaches down to flick and tease the head of my cock.

"*I do not think you know what that word means,*" she quotes before crawling up my body, putting me out of my goddamn misery.

Turning my head, I notice the time on the clock and realize how long she'd been taking me for a ride on the edge of ecstasy. I deserve a gold medal, truly. A woman like her, a perfect mouth like that, and a story like ours? I bet you'd be hard-pressed to last ten minutes, let alone thirty.

With her knees bracketing my hips, my hands snake up the smooth contour of her thighs. Digging my fingers into her hips, I curl my upper body up so that I'm pressed as close to her as possible.

She wraps her arms around my neck and I can see myself through her eyes. The back of my throat swells, but I hold the openness of her gaze like a baby bird nestled in my palm.

I'll never crush her trust. I'll never forsake what she's given me.

"If I'm not inside you in three seconds, I'm going to lose my mind." I bite at the juncture of her throat and neck, eliciting a shiver to break across her perfect skin. Every cell in my body wants to freefall into the unknown with her.

"As you wish," she rises a few inches, and then sinks onto me, taking all of me, in one motion.

You know, I could give you the play-by-play here. How I never kept my hands to myself. Or how her voice only got rougher and sexier throughout the night. But I will tell you the only thing that matters: loving Carmela, the way that I do, is just like riding a bike.

It's second nature, effortless. No matter how long it took

for me to get here, the rush and euphoria of moving through the world on two wheels returned like it never left.

A woman I plan to marry the moment our feet find the red dirt of Sedona once more.

☆

W ell...nobody is getting married tonight. Last of all, me.

After a long flight, all I wanted to do was crawl into bed, *my* bed—with my future wife—but no. Man makes a plan and God spits out his beer and laughs his ancient ass off.

She's sleeping on my shoulder, lips slightly parted, a small frown between her brows.

"Hey," I nudge her slightly. "Wake up. We're home." She rouses at the word *home* and I don't bother hiding the way it lifts my heart into my throat. Smiling down at her, I intertwine our fingers and lead her to what I can only assume is waiting for us—a welcome wagon.

The moment we're dropped off in the driveway, I notice the lights streaming from the backyard and garage before she does. Leading her up to the steps, I drop our bags on the front porch and steer her around the property to the back.

I hate surprises.

But I love the look on her face once she rounds the corner and sees everyone filing out of the garage. I love the way her mouth opens, her eyebrows lift, and the way her lashes flutter." I make a mental note to plan a surprise for her birthday next February.

"¡Te felicito!" My mother screams at the top of her lungs, rolling her tongue and tipping her head back as she grants us with a loud howl.

She embraces Carmie first and I reluctantly drop my future-wife's hand.

318

Eden, Cillian, Landon, and the rest of the boys are laughing and walking toward us up the stone path. I expect a hug, a slap on the back, a fist bump—anything—but they crowd Carmie instead.

In the span of a few seconds, she's airlifted onto their shoulders and paraded around the lawn like the high lady of the desert. Her face is red in amusement and embarrassment. Those eyes of hers catch mine and I smile before letting my head tip back to release a lifetime's worth of laughter trapped in my heart.

My mother slides up to me and bumps my shoulder as we watch the men march Carmie around singing, "*We're going to the chapel!*"

"What if it doesn't work out?" I whisper. My eyes stay focused ahead, on the unfolding joy.

"What if it all does?" Her hand wraps around my arm and she gives it a tight squeeze.

"Your father..." she begins then takes a deep breath. "He was one of the greatest loves of my life. His moving on, transitioning into the next existence, does not take that away. Does not tarnish it. I miss him, I love him, but I am *relieved* for him."

"How can you say that?" I look down at her with a knot in my chest I thought I had untied.

She doesn't turn to face me.

"When you love someone, you don't have to agree with all of their choices. As I am sure you and Carmela will discover as partners. As hard as it is to accept, it was not any of our fault or our shortcomings as his family that caused his early death. He orchestrated it. But to tarnish the love he gave us before that, to forsake the *good* he did in this lifetime, as a husband and your father, is unacceptable. To rob yourself of a life filled with love in his name is equally unacceptable."

I swallow and nod my head.

"So, even if it doesn't *work out*...would you do it again if you had this time with her? Her love?" My mother asks and I feel the question like a skinny blade between my ribs.

"Yes." The answer is so easy it's almost stupid I considered any other reality.

"Parker? Are you feckin' kidding me? Carmie doesn't know how to ride a *bike*?" Eden yells from across the lawn.

Bending to kiss my mother, I head down the path and around to the side of the garage. To grab a surprise.

It was...in truth... meant to be an, "I'm sorry for being an ass on our hike" the other day gift. But this is so much sweeter.

"Is that for me?!" Carmie jumps up and down on her toes, trying to get a better view. Cillian points to his back, and she jumps on it gladly, before he runs down to meet me at the garage.

Of course, I knew she couldn't ride a bike. It was obvious that very first night I met her. She didn't need to confirm it for me. With an over-the-top white bow sitting on the cherry red frame, I can see her reflection in the polished metal.

"When did you have the time to buy this?" She breathes, running a manicured nail up and down the leather seat.

"After our hike."

Her eyes meet mine. For the third time tonight, I wish it was just us and my bed and the eventual rising sun.

"Be nice. You'll have me all to yourself soon enough," she laughs, reading my mind. "But where are the pedals?" Her hands go to her hips with a lifted brow.

I take a seat to show her how to balance on the bike. "Without pedals, you can learn to adjust your weight side-to-side without being afraid of falling. I lowered the seat as low as it would go so you can test the waters first." My hands run along the fresh rubber grips of the handlebars.

A small ache vibrates in my chest, a longing, for my dad to see this. The full circle of gifting someone their very first bike.

Carmie's hand is on my shoulder in an instant. "Will you teach me how to ride?"

"Stop babying her, Parker!" Cillian yells. "Let her go and learn like we did."

"That is all the proof I need that you have brain damage," I mumble.

"I can do it," Carmie gives me a gentle push. "Get off my present." She smiles and I want to swallow her smile whole.

"Alright, basics first. Then you can let these circus freaks teach you how to flip and throw tricks." I move off the bike and watch her take my place.

"First, practice getting on and off. Make sure for the first few rides you cover your legs and arms. Just in case. Good girl," I praise her, causing a faint blush to cross her features. "Now practice squeezing the brakes."

"If you are braking, you're not going fast enough," Cillian offers from the sidelines.

"Enough, Cill. Jesus," I mutter, but my lips quirk anyway. I can't wait to watch her hair fly behind her down a hill.

"Ok, like this?" Her hand pumps the brakes and Eden nods for me, before taking over.

"Just push off the ground and coast around a little without pedals. Yeah, just like that!" Eden jogs next to her as Carmie circles the garage on the sidewalk.

Her face splits into a wide grin and the world gets quiet for a moment. I imagine a life like this with her, where simple pleasures like learning to ride a bike bring so much joy it can't be contained. How she would find equal joy in teaching me something. Teaching our kids something.

"Don't look back, you're not going that way. Look ahead!" Eden shouts over her uninhibited laughter. She's squealing and lifting her heels off the ground, coasting along the small path.

Landon slaps my back and mumbles, "Thank God you

NIKKI LANG

pulled your head out of your ass. Or else you'd be forced to celebrate *me* proposing to her." He smiles at me and I huff a breath out in agreement. I pull him into a one-arm slap-hug that lingers. "Thank you."

I don't need to say why aloud. His patience, his stability, his tough love. I wouldn't be on the road to recovery and ready to race again—someday—without him.

He smacks me hard and then pulls me into a headlock. "Just don't get hurt again. I'm sick of you," he jokes.

My eyes trail Carmie pushing herself around the corners, her child-like glee ringing out into the night.

"Done. No more injuries. Just altars and first-place podiums."

You're a fucking slut.

How embarrassing for you.

I hope you kill yourself just like you killed your baby.

carmie

SEDONA, November

F inishing up my heavily annotated *Cheryl Strayed* novel, I set it on the coffee table in Black Panther Coffee Shop. I'm waiting for Lina to meet me here to discuss and I quote, *"What you were destined to do."*

"Hey, you look familiar!" A melodic voice finds me and I look up at the woman with a shaved head and large windcatcher earrings.

"It's...Willow?" I ask while rising, "From the psychic shop?"

"Yes! How sweet of you to remember. But, wait. I have something for you." She digs around in her pouch-like purse for a few moments. "Here," she extends the deck out to me.

"I...I can't take those from you." I look down at the worn-in tarot cards in disbelief.

"It would be a favor because they haven't worked right for me since our reading. I think they picked up on your energy and wanted a new owner." She shrugs without an ounce of resentment. "And," she begins, before looking around. "I had a dream about them. It's too hard to remember the details. But I know you're meant to have them."

A chill drips down my spine but I shake it away. "Thank you." I embrace them and hug her.

"I'll see you around, Carmie. Good Luck," she whispers into my ear.

"With what?" I ask, but she's already flouncing away on the coffee-bean-flavored wind.

I sit and play with the cards for a few moments. Shuffling, warming them, holding them close to my heart.

Everything feels so good, feels *so* right, for the first time in my life. I'm not hiding, lying, or pretending to be someone I'm not. And it seems like life is rewarding me for it.

Life rises to meet us, Lina tells us.

Starting with an easy three-card spread, I flip them over, left to right. I'm so focused and absorbed in reading the cards, I don't register my new visitor, plopping himself down across from me.

"Hello, Carmela. Nice ring you've got there. Oh wait, I don't see one." I don't even look up from the cards. I don't need to. That's the voice of the man I've blocked from my life. The one I was supposed to love and to hold, but left instead.

"Seamus." I lift my eyes and almost don't believe what I'm seeing. All of the hair on my body stands up in warning.

His eyes are red-rimmed and bloodshot. Hair, normally perfect and styled, is a true unkempt mess.

He sits in the chair across from me, but he's anything but still. Crossing his fingers underneath his chin, he makes a *tsk* with his tongue as he surveys the coffee table with my cards strewn about.

"Tell me, did your cards see me coming?" He whispers and I start calculating an escape route. I'm grateful for the midday lunch crowd filtering in and out of the shop... I don't trust this person in front of me.

"Did they tell you to leave me? Did your precious horoscope tell you that *Parker*," he spits the name the way someone spits chewing tobacco into an empty bottle, "is a better match for you? Hm? I want to know. I need answers, *now*."

Swallowing, the steel spine I've built for myself, vertebrae by vertebrae, begins to soften. It bends under his scrutiny.

"Seamus, I don't owe you an explanation beyond what I've been giving you for all of these months."

He stares at me without blinking.

It breaks my heart. But not in a way that makes me miss him. It's like I'm looking at my childhood home, but instead of it being inhabited by a new family, it's abandoned. There's no light on. It's falling apart. Darkness and dilapidation are all that's left.

Unnerved by the silence and the lump in my throat, I say, "Speaking to you about my relationship while you are in this state is a betrayal to my fiancé." I try to project calculated calm. "And over-explaining myself to someone so determined to perceive me in his image..." I swallow against the sandpaper in my throat, "is self-betrayal."

He nods his head, but he's not here. Not really. He's a ghost, made corporeal and dangerous by showing up in the flesh.

"What did you expect, Seamus?" I ask as slowly as possible.

"For you to come home. Come home to me." His words sound like a Molotov cocktail landing in that dead house, and catching ablaze. "Come *home* to me, Carmie. We were supposed to be together, forever." His voice isn't getting louder, but I can feel the frenetic energy between us, a shaky bridge over rushing rapids.

"Seamus, I can't do that. I won't do that." My thumb traces over the finger he slid a pear-shaped engagement ring onto all those months ago.

"Yes, you will. Or you'll have this on your conscious for the rest of your selfish life." His eyes harden as he leans forward, invading my space across the table.

Seamus places his palm on the cards and discretely ushers them off the table. I hear them falling to the ground as the rest of the coffee shop disappears. There's no more grinding, steaming, or laughing. There is only the unhinged man in front of me, locking me in place with his penetrating gaze.

"What will be on my conscience?" I barely choke out.

"Parker's untimely death. And you'll never be able to prove otherwise."

The words are spoken so softly but there's no mistaking them. The steadfastness in his threat. The willpower behind this last and futile attempt to get me to comply.

"I have a livestream planned for seven o'clock. It's up to you whether the world watches you take me back, with my name on your lips or you doom him to his fate. It's your choice. But Carmela?"

My thighs begin to tremble and I don't have the energy to stop it.

His hand presses down into my right knee and his lip curls up in an evil half-smile upon sensing my fear. "This will follow you around for the rest of your life. Should you choose the wrong option, it will haunt you."

"This is *your* choice!" I hiss at him. "This is not love, this is manipulation. This is *inhumane*, Seamus! How could you want this for either of us? I won't do it. I won't show up." I cross my arms and dig my nails into my skin.

"Very well," he says before flicking a piece of lint off his pants.

"I may, or may not," he drags the words out, "have put a contract out on him from your father's favorite rolodex of *cleaners*. He's paid, and there's no going back. Not without my word to call it off."

My mouth drops open and he finally relaxes.

"It might not be his first race, hell, maybe not even next year. But one day, you'll lose him as penance for leaving me. You won't expect it, just like I didn't expect my future wife to become such a selfish, entitled slut." He leans back and exhales a stale breath before clapping his hands together. Smiling, he adds, "I feel so much better getting that off my chest. Now, if you don't meet me at the coordinates I send to your phone, just remember what's at stake. Show up in something cute, too. I have a romantic gesture planned and everyone will be watching."

Rising, he pats my head like a good dog, before walking out the door as if it's just another Tuesday.

I feel the coffee shop tunnel out around me. Small dots plague my vision. My heart plays a game of tug war between stillness and hyper-speed. Seconds drip into minutes, which race into eternity.

Once I snap out of my delusion, a full hour later, I pick up my phone. Thanksfully, Lina texted me that she was held up at a birthing mother's home. I call the one person crazy enough to help me stop Seamus.

"Carson? I need you to bite your tongue, shut the hell up, and listen to me. I need your help."

carmie

SEDONA, November

W alking into the foyer of Parker's home, I drop my bag on the Spanish tiles. The tarot cards tumble out of the opening, fanning out all around my feet.

"I've been waiting forever, what's going on Little Red?" Parker shouts from the kitchen, the smell of garlic and olive oil permeating the air.

Looking around, I see a home between these clay walls. The art prints Lina has collected from the many cities she's traveled to for birth clients. The photos of Parker on his bike.

I don't want to leave this place. Not now, not ever.

I notice Parker in the kitchen, a towel slung over his shoulder and his sleeves rolled up. I take one last look at his hands. Smiling, I lean against the wall, and snap one thousand mental images of those hands moving the cast-iron skillet forward and back on the open flame of the stove.

He drops angel hair pasta into the olive oil and garlic sizzling away on the stove, twirling the noodles in the fragrant sauce. With intense focus, he uses tongs to pinch a serving and twirl it into a perfect nest on a plate.

Without even having to ask, I know that serving is for me. Because that's who Parker is. Who we both are. We're both givers, in our own distinct ways. Where my mouth never closes, his mouth is shut—but his love is *loud*. It's so loud I can feel it reverberating in the chambers of my now cold, little heart.

I don't move toward him.

He grates the fresh block of Parmesan over the bird-nest of garlic angel hair noodles. *Forward and back, shake, shake, shake.* How mundane, how domestic, and how heavenly to have finally found this type of love.

Only to lose it.

"You're freaking me out, Carmie. You've never been this quiet, or this still." Parker turns to face me with the block of cheese still gripped between his fingers, a small smile on his face.

It falls the moment he sees me, crying, against the wall. Turning the stove off, he abandons dinner and rushes toward me with a steady grace only athletes possess.

"I've only seen three men in your life reduce you to this state. So, tell me, which one was it? Carson? Your dad? *Him?*" His grip is tight on my shoulders.

He tries to make eye contact with me, but I can't. If I do, I'll lose all the resolve I've built for my plan and the few hours it took to come to terms with it.

"I have to go."

"Where?" He asks, bending lower to catch my downcast gaze.

"Back."

"No." His hand finds my cheek and he uses it to angle my face up. "No," he says again, louder this time. "No. I don't know what that fucker said this time, but no. No. I can't—no," his voice gutters out.

"I don't have a choice, Parker."

"Don't give me that bullshit, you *always* have a choice. Do not make the same mistake twice, Carmie. What are you thinking? Talk to me..." His voice softens but remains urgent. He knows time is slipping through his fingers. He suspects that an hourglass with our love inside has been flipped over. Grian by grain it slips away.

"I can't lose you again," he whispers, his fingers moving over my cheekbones and down my neck, until they grab me at the base of my skull.

A fresh wave of tears rains down my cheek. "If your Dad asked to see you before he died, would you go?" I ask.

Parker stops breathing. Even out of the corner of my eye, I see how his chest ceases all movement.

"Yes," he answers. "I would have done what I could to help him. Even if he was out of his mind."

He pulls me into his chest and wraps his arms around me, protecting me, from the undefined threat he knows is chasing me. It's here, in his embrace, I spill it all, spell it all out for him. Everything except my plan with Carson.

"I need you to trust me," I whisper into his shirt.

"And I need *you* to let me protect you." He squeezes me tighter. "He's not going to succeed in whatever backup plan he has. He's not going to hurt me."

Shaking my head, I squeeze my eyes tighter.

"You have no idea how powerful my dad is. He would never, ever, sanction something like this. Ever. But the people who have done contract work for him in the past are foreign intel or ex-military. They operate under a different set of values and morals. I don't doubt Seamus' intentions, and I don't plan to bet your life on it."

"Carmie, I, cannot, lose, you." Parker breathes the words out as if he's being punched over and over again in the gut.

"You aren't going to lose me, I promise." I reach up on my toes and kiss his chin. "Trust me. I have a plan."

"Why can't your plan involve me? Why?" His eyes burn a hole right into the fabric of my very soul.

"Because I need to pretend to be the woman he wants me to be, not the woman I've wanted to become. Have become. Because of you."

He shakes his head. "You became the woman you were born to be without me, Carmie. That was all you." Parker kisses the top of my head before stepping away. "I don't agree with this." He crosses his arms, but I see the crack in his resolve.

Smiling, I say, "Then consider this our first fight."

He barks out a cold laugh before saying, "I think we passed that milestone a long time ago."

We look at one another. A thousand words pass between us in the chasm I'm creating. Without thinking, I reach up, pull him down, and kiss him like my life depends on it. Like *his* life depends on it. I don't need to say, *I love you* because we've transcended that. So instead, I give him something I know he'll understand.

"Ride or die."

His eyes turn to molten whiskey before whispering back, "Ride or die."

"I need to grab some things, can you put those back in my purse while I get ready?" I ask him as I look down at the tarot deck, shattering the beauty of the moment.

He nods, picking up my purse, and with tender care, picks up the cards.

After I gather my things, he's back in the kitchen with my bag next to him and a plate of food waiting for me.

Shaking my head, I silently convey that my stomach can't

handle food right now. The nervous knot forming is spreading throughout my body, and I'm afraid I'll end up sick.

His hand is tight on my bag, almost as if he's unwilling to relinquish the last piece of me before I leave.

"Parker."

"You could get hurt." It's all he says and in those four words I hear it all. *You might not come home again. You might be underestimating his anger. You might be wrong.*

"I won't." I reach up to cup his face before giving him one last kiss.

Placing my hand on the bag, I tug at it and lift my chin.

"Ride or die."

His lips press into a tight line and he doesn't repeat it. But he doesn't have to. I turn and walk away, the bag on my shoulder feeling a little heavier. But I carry it for both of us. One last time.

☆

My car rolls over the loose rubble and gravel as I park at the trailhead. When I plugged in the coordinates, it read Bell Rock. One of the seven vortexes of Sedona.

Swallowing thickly, I look out the windshield and see him waiting with a smile at the start of the trail. He waves me over, and my stomach churns violently at how peaceful he seems. So at ease.

Looking around, I only see a few other cars parked in the lot. The small hope I had of Carson pulling through for me all but evaporates.

The sun clings to the horizon line as time drips and slides into slow motion. Sucking in a full breath of desert air, I grab my purse, unlock my car, and get out. My steps are so light, they barely leave prints in the red dirt. I'm a ghost, floating toward a dangerous afterlife.

"You look so gorgeous baby, come here," Seamus calls before wrapping his cold, damp, hands around my waist. "I can tell you've been eating well here," he pinches the skin above my hips before laughing and I resist the temptation to internalize his passive aggressive insult.

He stands in front of an old wooden sign that reads *Bell Rock Loop Trail* and looks incredibly out of place. It takes all of my focus to keep from rubbing my nose, a subconscious tell when someone doesn't like what they are hearing or what they are being faced with.

"Mhm." I give him an artificially sweet smile that makes my molars ache. I see it reflected in his envious green eyes.

"Shall we? I have something for you at the top. And Carmie, don't think I forgot about the alternative." He winks, then lifts his white dress shirt, showing me the matte black Glock in his waistband.

Nodding, I hold out a palm for him, and internally cringe when he laces his fingers with my own. I've done this hike before. With Fallon, Elyse, and Dee. The sun bore down on us, and we almost gave up halfway through the trek. I was so glad we didn't. By the time we made it to the top, my cheeks were damp with sweat and tears, an emotional catharsis I wasn't expecting to experience. I think, looking back, that's when a part of me *knew* how healing this place would be for me.

Nowhere to hide, nowhere to run.

Those six words found me in the middle of a meditation Elyse led us through as we rested against a great cliff face at the top of the mountain.

I thought I was running away when I moved to Sedona. But I was running to the only place on Earth that would force me, and then empower me, to *stop*. Stop running, hiding, placating, pleasing.

It's the desert, and it's Parker. I can't separate them.

They're intertwined, wrapping around one another, like a delicate and balanced ecosystem in my heart.

A red-hot fury coils in my belly, but I grip Seamus' hand as he leads me up the trail. Up the narrow trail of red rocks, past the scenic platforms and plateaus, and past the sign that mocks me.

Stay on the path, Healing in Progress!

He's a little breathless by the time we make it halfway up. We pause, looking out at the darkening crimson sky, and I vow to save sunsets for Seamus. *Endings. The closing of chapters. Goodbyes.*

Because my sunrises are for Parker. *Beginnings. The start of a new story. Good mornings.*

Seamus attempts to check his stock portfolio or his Bitcoin or whatever fucking fake means of wealth and status he clings to on his phone when I cover the screen with my hand and step into him. With a seductive smile, I ask sweetly, "Why don't we keep going to the top? I'm ready for that romantic gesture."

His left eye twitches for a moment.

"Why are you so willing to come with me now?" His hand slides up and down my arm, but it doesn't feel loving, it feels like a leash. An invisible collaring.

Digging deep and shuffling through the many faces and personalities I have chosen to wear over the years, I find the right fit. With my lower lip wobbling, I look up at him from under my lashes and purr, "I called Carson and realized the error of my wrongs. I think I need *professional* help. You were right..."

He sighs, before cupping my face and chuckling. "I *know*, Carmela, that's what I've been trying to show you. I'm so glad you came to your senses. We were meant to be together, don't you know that? Long before your father and my father set us up. Long before the world told us how important our union would be."

Bile rises in my throat as I slam my lips together and nod.

We climb, lunge, and walk up the rest of the path in silence. But it doesn't feel like the comfortable and confident silence I'm used to with Parker. It's the type of silence before an inhale. It's the sharp tip of a knife pressing between a rib.

My lungs work hard, but all of these months of training with Lina are paying off. Muscles I never dreamed of having are the only thing keeping me from sliding down the trail. It feels like a horror movie. One where if the girl isn't smart enough, she's the first to get killed.

Shaking my head and adjusting the strap of my purse, I make eye contact with the few straggling tourists making their way down the great vortex. Tourists, because nobody else is stupid enough to be out here in near darkness without headlamps.

I'm tempted to use my blinking morse code with them but stop myself. I don't need anyone else to save me.

Am I being stubborn to prove I can save myself? What if I miscalculated? What if I was being hopeful or delusional...what then?

The end is in sight, so I drown that thought out with forceful exhales as I use my hands to scale the next dusty boulder. Seamus is right behind me. His hands, as ugly as his heart, grip the grooves to pull himself up.

A small wooden sign and roped-off edges are in front of me. The finish line.

"Go on, baby, walk out." Seamus is tilting his head to the right.

Let me paint this picture for you.

This is the type of look-out that every single person who travels to Sedona will take a picture of or—quite literally—on. If, by chance, they are afraid of heights, they might skip it.

But it is *dark* out here. I can't see beyond that narrow ledge, with the miles and miles of scenery beyond it...and we're all alone tonight.

This spot. This predictable, unoriginal, spot, is where he intends to make some grand gesture. It should comfort me that Seamus wouldn't be stupid enough to do something as stupid as hurting me. But now I'm not so sure.

People can become different creatures in the dark. And I think, as I cast a sidelong look at him, I think Seamus has been in the dark the entire time I've been gone.

My legs begin to shake, and I suck in breath after breath as I stare out and then down at the five-thousand-foot drop. Down to the metaphorical first floor. Down to the flat, unyielding surface of the Arizona desert.

Looking left and right, seeking a hidden figure in the shadows, I close my eyes and force the tears away. My throat clogs, as I realize my backup savior, my backup plan, isn't here.

He isn't coming.

"Go. Now." Seamus has his gun out, and it's not surprising. He's beginning to shake a little as well. I wonder if I have time to get out my phone and make one final call before this goes south.

The hair stands up on the back of my neck and my vision blurs. Intuition is channeling into me so hard and so fast, I stop to put my hand out to balance. So many images are coming to me, flashing in my mind's eye, I can't discern what is happening.

All I see is red.

Stepping over a large gap between the rock surfaces, and ignoring the open maw of the abyss below me, I stabilize myself on the other side. He's right behind, with his ugly trembling hands. With every cell in my body, I know only one of us is going to walk away from this alive.

Yes, Little Red, you did miscalculate this.

Parker's voice in my head makes a small sob escape from my lips.

"We don't have all night. Let's go, baby!" Seamus presses the cold barrel of the gun into the small divot between my shoulder blades. Ironically, that's the place Elyse calls, *the sea of forgiveness.*

"I won't forgive you if you hurt me. Or him," I whisper before stopping on the small circular lookout.

It's so dark I can barely see the striped reds, maroons, and burnt oranges of the rock faces. I can't pinpoint the green shrubbery on the ground. All I see are the rising beams of a waning moon, the whisper-thin clouds, and darkness rolling in to cover our tracks.

He laughs, before kneeling and rooting around in his bag for his phone. "I never needed your forgiveness, sweet girl. It's irrelevant. I only needed you." His fingers continue to fumble through the pockets of his bag, and frustration over-takes him.

"It's here somewhere, hold on." His voice is strained. I can hear the hairline fractures in it spiderwebbing out into larger cracks.

Pulling out a blue velvet box, he cheers for himself before setting his phone on a small tripod. As he's trying to get a livestream started, I take the opportunity to slip my hand into my bag.

My fingers start brushing over the worn-in, tarot cards. Holding my breath, I keep my eyes on the back of Seamus' head and work faster.

If I can just find my phone, I can send a distress call, just in case he loses it.

Before my fingers find my phone, a sickening realization overcomes me.

"There's no service up here, fuck!" Seamus screams.

Exactly. Fuck.

The moment his phone screen goes black, Seamus catches my reflection rooting around in my bag.

"What the hell do you think you're doing?" He uncoils from his knee, like a cobra aiming to strike.

"I brought, a—" my voice fumbles and stutters. "I brought a gift for you too!" I say, praying my fear masked as enthusiasm is enough to trick him.

"Let's see it."

I stare at him for a beat too long. He lunges for my bag, but not faster than I can pull it away.

"Be patient!" I laugh with a manic edge. Men like to call women hysterical without realizing they are often the reason we're driven to madness in the first place.

My hand dips into the bag and instead of pulling out the tarot cards, my fingertips brush cold metal.

"It's dark, just give me a second," I say on an exhalation, before looking down in disbelief into my bag.

In case you need to be the wolf.

The blocky letters are scribbled on a small, orange post-it note. It's stuck on top of a silver handgun.

You wouldn't think it, but every woman in my family knows how to shoot. I wasn't trained to do this against someone my heart once loved...but a steady finger on a trigger, a solid stance, at this close of range? It's all I need.

"Alright, darling, here it is," I sing.

Time slows. It's as if this moment is initiating me into a club no woman ever asked to be in. I'm connected to a lineage of women who have been subjected to domestic coercion and violence. I am connected to *all* of their rage—and all of their pain. I am connected to the women forgotten by society. To the ones told, *you should've picked a better partner!* To the ones chastised with counter-claims of, *I know him, he would never do that!* I am connected to the victims and the survivors. I feel it all course through my veins and feel their fury at my back.

Dropping my bag, I step back so that I am unreachable, flip the safety, and aim the gun at the middle of Seamus' chest.

With blood roaring in my ears, and a twisted satisfaction at seeing surprise in his flared eyes, I open my mouth and let my inner-villain out.

"Alright, Seamus. Here's what's going to happen."

Carmie

Sedona, November

B eing a senator's daughter comes with many privileges. But only one of those, which is the most relevant during the unraveling of my current situation, might save my life.

How to handle a gun under psychological and physical duress.

We practiced for years on our family compound with former marines who were in special ops. Not only was I taught how to shoot, but how to defend myself if I were to ever find myself in a scenario where I needed to escape. It wasn't good enough for a D'Angelo to understand safe gun practices. We had to learn how to use them on the move, under pressure, and with our hearts lodged in our throats.

Like I said earlier, I was never allowed out of the country without my family or security for fear of being kidnapped and held for ransom. It happened and *continues* to happen to other adult children of American politicians. More times than I can stomach. Some come home. Many do not.

But I didn't bring a gun to Arizona. This weight is unfamiliar in my right palm. The butt of it, cold and metallic, is aimed at the one person I never in my wildest nightmares would think to aim it at.

Training, in any area of study, whether it's de-escalating patients or learning to protect oneself, kicks into high gear when adrenaline flows. So, as I stand with my feet firm in the red dust of *my* desert, I'm not afraid of what I might have to do.

For the first time in ages, I'm grateful to be a D'Angelo. That name alone, these experiences, will help me save myself and the people I love.

"Here is what is going to happen," I repeat as I lift my chin.

The desert darkens and brings with it a chill that prickles the sweat on the back of my neck. I'm silent for a few seconds, simply observing him. Seamus' hands are down at his side, his gun tucked into his waistband, but my eyes never leave his face. Those eyes, the boarded-up windows to his soul, are life-less. Cold.

I almost laugh. Didn't I always ask for my life to be like a movie? To be tossed and turned, surfing the high and low tides, all the way to my big happily ever after?

The action! The drama! The way two people find their way together in the end...*what an idiot.*

"We are going to walk down to the halfway point. You will have cell service at that elevation." I tilt my head toward the path behind us as I start to side-step to the wall of rock next to me. Protecting my back, I keep my hands steady and keep the gun aimed right at the center of his chest.

It's been a long time since I held one, but it turns out, it's just like riding a bike.

"You are fucking crazy," Seamus laughs, and the sound is a jagged piece of rock slicing into my memories. It's shredding them, one by one, with every second I am forced to listen.

"You will go to that plateau, call off the hit on Parker, and then you will be escorted back to your vehicle by the hidden agent Carson called in."

I'm lying, but it's worth it to see his face drain.

"Carson wouldn't do that."

"Wouldn't he? You threatened his only sister." I tilt my head again in an attempt to get him to move.

"He thinks you're a whore!" He screams, pulling the pin and detonating the remaining good memories that exist between us.

"It doesn't matter what he thinks. It's what he *did* despite it."

His jaw flexes and I can see his mind spinning like a wheel without an axle.

Every additional moment we spend on this dark stretch of mountain makes my blood rush with unease.

"Let's go," I say, louder this time, my voice amplified by the cavern below and around us.

His hands lower down to his waist and I catch the way his left one hovers near his waistband...

I aim at the ground three feet away from his right foot and my left index finger pulls the trigger. Absorbing the recoil, I flinch at the intensity of the gunshot echoing around us.

Seamus screams and jumps, his hands lifting once more.

"That is your only warning. You and I both know how accurate I can be when push comes to shove."

I'm referring to the Labor Day shooting competition from 2008. It's a story for another time. Let's just say, I wounded his pride in front of every single guest watching.

"I hate you," he seethes as I train the gun on him once more.

"Go. We have a downhill climb in the dark now." I try to appear confident, but my heart kicks at what will happen after I get him to make that phone call.

Seamus gives me a wide berth and begins to walk the trail. I follow, forcing my lungs to keep an even rhythm. We skid, stumble, and nearly lose our way down the winding mountain path.

I'm far enough behind him that he won't be able to overpower me and take my gun, but close enough I can hear him muttering and moaning.

There's no barrier between us and the stars. No light pollution. No billboards. Nothing. Those cold and distant stars above us are the only witnesses to our unfolding fate. I wonder if they're watching. If they designed our destinies and are waiting to watch their handiwork come alive.

After the longest passage of time in my life, I stop moving and shout ahead to Seamus. "Veer off to the right."

For added incentive, I cup my hand around my mouth and make a show of yelling out. "You can wait a little longer, you don't need to come out just yet!"

Seamus' eyes narrow on me and for a moment, one deadly moment, I fear he is about to call my bluff.

"Call him. Now." I say from my position on the path. I'm maintaining higher ground, just in case.

He slides his bag off his shoulder and I can hear the cadence of my heartbeat echoing in my eardrums.

"No service," he shrugs. I catch the way his left lip twitches down.

"Try again, speakerphone this time," I demand.

He dials and the blue light from his screen illuminates his features. It's a grotesque mask.

"I told you not to call this number again," a voice with a thick accent growls.

"I, ah, I need to cancel my latest, uh, online *order*." Seamus lowers his voice.

Whispering the words, "louder," I shake the gun in his direction.

"Do not swindle me, Сволочь. You *owe* me payment, job or no job."

Seamus swallows thickly. I don't recognize the word he used, but I know for a damn fact it wasn't a compliment.

"I will pay. Yes. *Yes.* Just cancel it," Seamus orders.

The man grunts into the phone before hanging up.

"Satisfied?" Seamus asks. His whisper may as well have been the blast of a starting gun. His hands move, lightning fast until his midnight black Glock is in his hand. It's damn near invisible, a shadow. You can't fly with a firearm. So that means he either drove across the country like a maniac or flew private.

But instead of pointing his gun at me—he's pointing it directly up, under his chin.

"WHY CAN'T YOU LOVE ME?" He screams into the night.

If I had to swear it, swear it on my life, I would tell you that every living thing in the desert paused to watch us.

Tears run from the corner of his eyes. I follow the movement for a brief second, reverting my eyes to the muzzle of the gun aiming into the underbelly of his chin for a kill shot.

"I WILL DO IT." His voice shakes at the edges, along with his hands, but I hear the desperate truth.

"Seamus, this—isn't romantic!" I start to cry. "It's traumatic!" The hysteria I've been holding back with a tight lasso is breaking free.

"You think this is love, but it's violence masquerading as love!" I scream with equal volume into the night.

"I would rather die than live without you." He drops to his knees, but the gun remains pressed, tight, under his chin.

I don't know what to do, I don't know what to do, I don't know what...

"WHY CAN'T YOU LOVE ME?" He half sobs and screams.

I know what I said earlier about training kicking in. But

this...this is different. There is nothing to prepare you for a moment like this. Such an unbelievable moment, where you are placed in the middle of one of those stories you hear passed around the campfire of female conversation—the unhinged men of our pasts and the lengths they go to.

Folklore.

But as my vision blurs and my hands begin to shake with a violent tremor, I realize they are more fact than fiction.

I lower my gun but keep my finger on the trigger.

"Please, come home with me," he pleads, one hand on his gun, one hand reaching out toward me.

But he's a dehydrated man in the middle of a desert—reaching for a mirage. He doesn't love *me*. He loves the idea of me. The *old* me.

"Seamus," I shake my head no, unwilling to contort myself and diminish who I've become, even under his threat.

"I called off the hit. I did that for you. Please—come with me. *For me.*" He pushes the gun harder into his chin, tipping it as if he were on his knees in church looking up at Jesus on the cross.

"You need help," I whisper.

He shakes his head in denial. "I need you!"

"I don't want a love like this," I say with conviction in my voice. "I want a love where two people, in their wholeness, choose to be together. Not two people who *need* one another in their brokenness."

"YOU! BROKE! ME!" He rises to his feet.

The gun drops from his chin, and just like a skilled sailor, I feel the current of the ocean shift. The wind is no longer at my back. It's in my face.

In slow motion, he raises the Glock. My arm lifts, a mirrored image of his. Two scorned lovers, in the middle of the desert, looking down the barrel of each other's gun.

Wub, Dub, my heart drums. It's so loud I don't hear the footsteps or ragged breath of a man approaching on the path.

"Little Red!" The voice is desperate and cracked. My eyes shutter for a moment, the need and desire to unravel into the safety of his arms is *so* strong. Too strong. As my eyes open again not a heartbeat later, I know that his presence is the catalyst of something horrific.

Seamus, too, recognizes the voice because his face splits into an ugly grin. He swings the gun toward Parker, never breaking eye contact with me. Then, after a pregnant pause, he pans the gun in a wide arc, back to me.

"If I can't have her..." His finger flutters on the trigger. "Nobody can."

"I love you," I whisper on the wind, my eyes on Parker, right before the gunshot ricochets into the night...and my world is plunged into darkness.

SEDONA, November

When I was young, I walked into my father's study late one Thursday night. I couldn't sleep, but he welcomed me with open arms. He was reading something from Helene Cixous at the time... "Blackness isn't black. It is the last degree of reds. The secret blood of reds."

It's all I can think of as I watch the color red disappear underneath the night sky. The way it drips, runs, and stains the dust, defies nature. There are no boundaries to keep it from moving. All it does is run.

With my heart on fire, I race up the final 100-meter climb and grab a crumpled Carmie in my arms.

My hands pat every surface of her skin and body. My hands search and prod.

Then comes the screaming.

That *sound* is far more agonizing than the silence I experienced while waiting for her in the airport. Her scream is worse than the sound of my bones snapping in Italy. The sound, echoing and bouncing all around us, is from deep inside her.

It's the sound of years and years and *years* of pent-up everything finally crashing to the ground. It's wild horses breaking free, the sound of their hooves on the open desert a chorus of thunderclaps. Freedom, but it's not joyous.

She shakes in my arms. Her voice gets raw and shallow.

I tuck her underneath my chin and rock her back and forth. Squeezing her. With minimal movement, I grip my father's gun in my hand and flip the safety. Tucking it into my back waistband, my hands find the back of her head and waist.

I pull her into my lap. All I can do is whisper, *shhhh*, over and over again.

Seamus is nowhere to be seen, from our vantage point at least.

Carmela pulled the trigger one second faster than him and it's the only reason her heart continues to beat. His shot went high and wide, his aim impacted by the shock of Carmie's bullet.

It saved her life.

She pulled that trigger in defense and watched as the blackish blood began to stain his white shirt, right below his left collarbone. When he looked down at the stain, his eyes didn't even look surprised.

He just stared at her, before stumbling back, and back, until his heels lost purchase. And he fell, down, the rest of the mountain.

There was no sound.

And even if there was, we wouldn't have heard it beyond the sound of Carmie dropping to her knees and tipping her head back in agony. I stood in silence for a moment as I saw her silhouette transform into that of a wolf howling at the moon.

That's when I raced to her, for fear she too had been shot.

But this isn't the type of pain I can cover and bandage with my hands. This is the pain of having to cut the thread of fate and choose herself. Nobody should ever have to be faced with this decision. Or the burden of what it feels like to wake up and remmeber they had to sever the life of another human being.

A tall, dark body steps out of the shadow on the path below us. "Carmela, your brother sent me," a thick, gruff voice calls up to us on the plateau.

"I'm going to need the gun, darlin'." He takes a few more steps toward us with his hands open and wide in submission. "So I can call this into local authorities and make a statement."

I lift my chin at him, cock my head before patting my back. He walks toward us, on silent and trained feet, before bending to extract the handgun from my waist. With a small black microfiber cloth, he wipes it down.

"This was self-defense. You can and will be honest. But I will also be adding in my credentials and statement to make sure this ends *tonight*, legally."

Carmie pulls her head away from my shoulder. "I'm not afraid to tell the truth. I don't want special treatment," she says through shaky tears.

He bends down, his knees cracking with age. His bald head catches what little light is available out here.

"I can't say where I worked in the government. That's classified. But I *can* tell you that I worked with your father for the last two decades. This is something that I will handle the logistics of. Not for your father. Not for your brother. I did this for *you*. A woman who never should have been put in that position." He stares at her.

Carmie is about to open her mouth to argue, so I press a light kiss to the corner of it. Whispering, I say, "You do not have to shoulder the lion's share of this pain or this story. Please, let someone help you Carmie."

When the day comes for my life to flash before me, I won't be seeing my career or the time I spent working. I'll be here, staring into those eyes, one blue and one green, with the ability to see heaven and earth at the same time. This is the only image I'll need before I say goodbye to this lifetime.

A small lift of her lips confirms she sees the very same sentiment in mine.

We rise, on shaking legs, before she nods to the ex-military, intelligence, *whatever* man. A man I will forever be grateful for.

I reach my hand out, and we spend the next few moments locked in a tight shake. Swallowing, I dip my chin and express my gratitude for whatever favor or strings are being pulled to make this happen.

In hushed tones, I ask him where the body is, and if we can avoid it on our way down. He nods in confirmation, before adding, "Wait by your truck for the authorities. I'll make sure you don't need representation."

Nodding, I turn back to Carmie to find her with her arms folded into her chest. I press my palm on her back, heralding us away from the scene of the crime. The scene of the horror movie she was forced to star in.

The reality that Carmie gets to come home with me almost consumes me.

Do you know how many women do *not* get to walk away after an altercation with an ex-spouse or partner? How most domestic violence will escalate until only one person remains?

My body shudders.

"Are you ready?" I ask, before touching the place behind her shoulder blades.

"For?" She raises her eyebrows at me.

With a sad smile, I press a kiss to the top of her head and say, "For a sunrise."

52 / BRIDESMAIDS

APRIL, Sedona

"I'm scared."

The words come out fast and I'm relieved at how good it feels to say them.

Lina puts both of her palms on my slick cheeks, and it's only then, when I feel her warmth and the direct penetration of her focus, that I realize I started crying.

So much has happened in the last year. But now isn't the time to ruminate on it or tell you every detail. Now is the time to help deliver Jasey's second baby.

Following the soft sounds of voices and music, I carry the heavy midwife bag into a hallway. The sound of running water reaches me, and I peek into an open door to my left.

It's been almost five months since I kissed my old life goodbye.

Parker and I were brought in for questioning after the fiasco on the mountain and I laid out the entire timeline of events (with receipts) for the investigators.

The retired guardian angel took care of the rest.

Seamus' mother reached out before the funeral and asked if I would be joining. It took me a few hours to decide, but I no longer allow obligation to guide my decisions in life.

I didn't go.

Plus, that favor from Carson was the last time I heard from him. I'm not sure I would be able to stomach seeing him at Seamus' funeral... my grief might implode at the pressure. Not over Seamus. But over the living and breathing and walking embodiment of how painful it is to lose a sibling.

There have been a few moments over the last five months where I reached out with a reconciliation attempt. Truth be told, I'm the only one putting in the effort. So for now ... we let it rest.

Lina is now kneeling next to the woman I've come to know as a friend, confidant, and fellow movement teacher—crying on the toilet. Lina is already pressing a cold cloth to her forehead and whispering soft words that don't carry to my ears. Jasey laughs hysterically, albeit broken up by groans of discomfort.

They had asked me to attend her first birth. But I wasn't ready then.

"Look away! It's—It's coming out of me like hot lava!" Jasey laughs and cries at the same time Lina does, and my heart stutters in my chest at the pure chaos and vulnerability in this situation.

Maybe I'm still not ready for this.

Tip-toeing backward out of the threshold, I almost make it when Lina looks up and offers me one of her knowing smiles.

"Carmie, please bring the bag over here for me."

Jasey, still seated on the toilet, doesn't even look my way. Her eyes are scrunched shut and sweat rains down her forehead despite the cool tile and night air blowing in from an open window. Her breathing shifts and Lina begins to count her through a contraction. *Dear God*, it looks miserable, but there's a determined set to my friend's jaw, and I'm taken back by the magnitude and strength she possesses.

Jasey decided on an informed homebirth for this baby and since she has no prior conditions that would increase the risk for a safe delivery...here we all are.

Lina, a licensed midwife, and me, a doula in training.

"Relax your face. That's it, the next wave will be easier if you keep that stubborn jaw of yours open and relaxed," Lina jokes. I'm awed by her ability to be so steady in this situation.

Lina has been a midwife for over *twenty* years. She's so talented, that she travels around the West Coast re-teaching breech positions to OB-GYNs and fellow workers within and outside of the system.

She's a radical, which is how I knew I wanted to keep following in her footsteps. The same ones that taught me to love my body to embrace my power, are now teaching me how to usher in a more peaceful world. Because it all begins with birth.

Kneeling, I hand Lina the bag, and she begins to pull out specific instruments. Embroidered letters adorn the side of it, reading *Make Birth Sacred Again*. Her hands pull out a pair of gloves, and she begins to work seamlessly and silently. I scoot back to give her space, while she takes the woman's blood pressure and uses an instrument to measure the baby's heart rate.

Before every assessment, before every movement, Lina asks for consent. She then grips Jacey's arm and helps her stand. It's only then that my friend, the laboring mother I'm in awe of, looks at me.

"Words can't describe," she sucks in a deep breath, "how overjoyed I am...to see you here." She smiles at me before eyeballing the door.

Jasey grabs my hand on her way out and waddles through the doorway, down the hall, and toward a bedroom. There's a pool set up, twinkle lights, and a cat in the corner, eyeballing everyone with an impatient glare.

"Where's Mateo? I thought he would be here by now?" Lina asks in a soft tone.

"He's, he's, at a fire. It's a small one, he said." Jasey labors to even hold a conversation and my palms are cold and clammy at the idea of her body withstanding *labor*. "He said that he'll be back soon."

"Alright. We will keep him posted, won't we, Carmie?" Lina throws me a look over her shoulder that I have no clue how to decipher, but I nod my head anyway.

Jasey starts crying out and her entire body goes rigid. She's bent at the waist, her forearms pressing down into the mattress.

"I can't do this anymore, Lina. I can't do it." She starts crying, but her body remains rigid underneath her robe.

Adrenaline floods my system, the urge to *do something* so powerful I fear I might rip my hair out if I have to sit here and witness my friend's pain any longer. I have to do something.

"This surge won't last forever, open your mouth and tell me how you really feel!" Lina's voice is full of loving authority and Jasey immediately submits to it without resistance. She turns her face into the mattress and screams so loud my eyes fly open and my heart stops beating for a moment.

Her entire body sags and Lina steps in to help her pivot to sit on the edge of the bed.

"See, I told you screaming would help." Lina has a small smirk on her lips like she's never been wrong a day in her life.

"I'm doubting everything," Jasey exhales the words. My heart cracks open at the raw pain emanating from her body. Her cat looks at me and then saunters into the closet with her tail flicking side to side.

"I just want him here with me. Why isn't he here with me? I can't do this without him!" Jasey drops her head back and prepares for what Lina calls another *surge*, which is a different way of saying a *mind-numbing contraction of the uterus.*

But words have power. So we use them with intention in birth spaces.

"I won't give you false promises—" Lina stays close to Jasey as she rides out the sixty seconds of intense physical pain. Once it's done, Lina speaks softly, "But I want you to answer me, how do you want to feel about your labor once your baby arrives?"

Jasey stands up and begins moaning, moving her body in shapes to try to alleviate the sensations. "I want to feel reborn," she gasps.

The words are cast out between us all like a spell. I can feel the magic burrowing its way into my bloodstream.

I hear the sound of pounding feet and a few moments later, a man wearing a navy blue *Sedona Fire Department* T-shirt emerges through the door and embraces my friend. I haven't had the chance to meet him yet, with his wild schedule and all, but I know he would hang the moon for Jasey if she requested it.

Jasey collapses into Mateo's arms and sobs while he strokes her hair and lowers them both to the ground. Lina nods to the door, and we walk out, giving them space to be with one another.

"It's been four hours, and she's finally fully dilated. What do you suggest we do?"

Lina's question pulls me out of my noisy head.

"I, ah, am not sure—maybe, we can..." I start.

Lina holds up her hand and I fall silent. The power and authority she radiates is a calm and yet equally strong antidote for the intense fear flooding my system.

This is a teaching moment.

"I'm not asking you to be a midwife yet, or even a doula.

I'm asking you to hold space and assist me. To keep this experience sacred. What do you think we should do?"

I chew on my bottom lip as I hear the strangled cries of another surge take Jasey away into a sea of pain.

"Everything." My eyes remain locked on the end of the hallway, and it takes all of my conscious energy to even out my breathing. "Or. Maybe...nothing?"

My eyes slide to Lina's, and I'm surprised to see joy and maybe even pride waiting for me.

"Exactly. *Nothing*. Do you know what I do for these women, Carmela?" Lina lowers her voice and guides me over to the sliding doors so I can see the stars.

"When I enter into a birth space, I don't worry about walking on toes or eggshells. Her pain isn't a problem for me to fix. Everyone in this culture is so focused on feeling *good* all the time they don't realize how stunted they become at handling any sensation besides *good*."

She pauses and places a hand on my shoulder. "Home-birth isn't for everyone. I'm not for everyone. But I'm not here to please people, Carmie. I am here to support and teach women *how* to navigate the sensations and feelings of birth. It's an initiation." Lina looks up at the stars, pauses, and smiles. "You know the myth of Hades and Persephone, right? Persephone did what many would not have been able to do. She fell in love with the underworld and knew she would never be able to go back to an existence without it. What Hades did wasn't a punishment or an act of cruelty. It was the initiation. Because of him, and because of the darkness, she became a Queen. She was reborn."

Chills sweep over my body and I close my eyes, imagining the Goddess of Spring bringing light into the dark.

"I guide women into the most dark and haunting place they can imagine. The underworld for them is the liminal space between life and death, between maiden and mother.

Fear—much like Persephone's mother, Demeter—wants to chain them to the smallest version of themselves possible. To tell them that they aren't powerful enough to do this. It wants to coax them into a mediocre and safe existence, one where they give their power and autonomy away."

Her voice gets lower and I'm sucked into the story.

"But I arrive and transport them to where they want to go. If they ask me to do something, I do it. If I sense with my intuition they need something, I act with their consent. I honor the rawness and natural process of birth. I do this so that the women I work with can return to Earth as a mother and as a woman uninterested in giving her power away. Ever again."

Moisture gathers in the corner of my eyes, and I can *feel* the difference between what Lina does for these women and what I did for my clients for so many years. She pats my shoulder and walks away.

Lina goes deep with people, and I went wide. She focuses on one transformative experience, keeping her interventions as minimal as possible. I tried to fix and solve everything at once so that I didn't feel as hopeless about my patient's pain. Hopeless about my pain.

Swiping at my eyes, I shake my head and return to the moment. I walk back toward the bedroom and am shocked to see Mateo standing in the birth pool, but Jasey is leaning against it, refusing to get in.

"No. No. The pressure. It's too much. It's TOO MUCH," she screams.

Something's wrong, we need to get to a hospital, we need to go—

Lina makes eye contact with me and my face must be giving me away because she *smiles* and holds up a finger to say, *just wait.*

"Come into the water, it's ok. I've got you baby. It's ok, I'm here..." Mateo uses soft words, his face set in a barely restrained mask of panic at witnessing the pain on his wife's face.

"No, I don't want the water. No, no," she pants.

"But," Mateo's face scrunches up.

"Mateo, she said she doesn't want it anymore, even if that was her plan. Trust it," Lina asserts.

He nods, but I think he wants to punch a wall in frustration. Or fear.

Jasey staggers near me and I resist the urge to grab her and throw her in the truck to go to a hospital. Then she opens the closet door...

She walks into the same closet her cat went into, keeping the lights off, and her labored breathing gets louder and louder. Her husband hops out of the birth pool and joins her.

Lina leans into the doorframe and asks with confidence I sure as hell don't feel, "Is this where you want to have your baby, honey?"

Jasey nods her head frantically and then she squats down. She opens her mouth and throws her head back into Matteo's chest behind her. He keeps whispering in her ear, "you're perfect, you've got this, I am so proud of you." His hands move underneath her arms and he interlaces his fingers with hers. He supports her weight as her cries of pain shift into something so unexpected.

Sobs of surprise and sobs of relief.

"She's coming!" Jasey cries out and her eyes open wide in surprise to lock on a smiling Lina.

"Yes, she is. Are you ready to be reborn, mama?" Lina crouches down with Jasey, and after three pushes a sound emerges from the closet. The sweet, sweet sound of new life.

Thirty minutes later, I'm tip-toeing outside onto the patio to get a breath of fresh air. I interlace my hands behind my head and laugh as tears stream down my face in awe.

M̲y phone vibrates in the scrub pants I'm wearing, and I smile as I take it out to see a photo of me and Parker, covered in red dirt, digging out his practice track for *Red Bull Rampage* in Moab a few months ago.

Today 9:06 PM

> How did it go? Tell me everything when you get a chance ... 👀

> I'll see you in a few hours, I promise. Expect a lot of yapping and jumping up and down and maybe...maybe a new plan for the next few years. 💨

> Wake me up when you get here. We'll make a five-year plan. Together.

As I put my phone away I catch the way my ruby wedding ring winks at me in the darkness.

Smiling, I shake my head and then tilt my eyes up toward the stars. I know without a doubt that my friend wasn't the only one reborn tonight.

53 / GOOD WILL HUNTING

Time is the only justice we have in this world. We all wake up, move, and settle down again within the same twenty-four-hour period as everyone else. It's a universal law. Our choices, habits, routines, and the people we surround ourselves with can move us closer to our target...or away from it.

But we all get those same twenty-four hours. And what we do with that time ends up being our personal religion.

My religion consists of two halves, creating an equal and harmonious whole. MTB and Carmie. Is it even a surprise at this point? And on this given Sunday, I'm going to church.

But what *is* a surprise, is how well I raced this season. I mean. Breaking every headline. Doubling sponsorships. Becoming someone my dad would be proud of.

And finally, bringing us up to date, a year and a half later... making it to the final day of the World Cup Finals.

My gloves pump the handlebars five times. But they no longer read, *Ride or Die*.

My promise with Carmie, and that catchphrase, no longer felt right after what we went through in Sedona last year. Carmie was the first to point it out after one of our weekly breath-work sessions together.

I still keep my dad's note with me, though. That worn and weathered notebook paper, folded and unfolded, yellowed with time, and softened with use. Tapping it five times, I mutter the song lyrics he wrote on it, and his parting words to me.

"'Tis better to have loved and lost than never to have loved at all."

The words used to haunt me, a mocking joke that only focused on what I lost. But I see and feel his words for what they are now. A goodbye, and an apology. The only one he could manage at the time. His truth was that he was grateful to have loved me for some time before losing everything.

Big screens are set up across the course for spectators to have a killer view while they stand, unblinking and breathless, watching their favorite athletes race down a mountain for three to five minutes.

Everyone is waiting for me down in the fishbowl at the bottom of the run, right by the podiums. My crew, but also Carmie, Elyse, Eden, Dean, Riley, Ian, Cillian, Tommy, Fallon, and a new addition, Lane. They all flew out for the weekend, and I've never known until now what it's like to have that many people in my heart along for the ride.

In my mom's case, she's watching her only child.

It was pure luck (or Universal design, in her words) that the US World Championships would be in Snoeshow Colorado this year.

The fastest riders? We go last.

I'm up here alone, waiting to ride, feeling the contradiction of time, slowing down and simultaneously speeding up.

Cillian and Eden asked if I wanted to know the time of

other competitors on the course today, and I shook my head no. Carmie calls that *growth*, but I always roll my eyes at her whenever she says it, which is only an indirect admittance of her being right.

But, like I was saying, it doesn't matter what the fastest time out there today was because I know, in my bones, it will be mine by the end of the run.

There's no sense of urgency, there's no *this or that*, do-or-die mentality. All I feel is confidence and a subtle current of pride for how far I've come.

Two minutes until the horn.

During my qualifying runs, I saw firsthand how brutal the Snowshoe course could be. Savage rocks. Unyielding roots all around the mountain. If I had to take my guess, two of Ireland's best are sitting on the podiums right now, waiting to see what I do.

It's time.

The wood roof and railings beside me fade away.

Feet on the pedals, ass lifted, I plunge down the starting ramp and onto the packed dirt. My eyes focus ahead on the neon green pegs lining the first stretch of the track, keeping the spectators and sponsorship banners out of my way.

I pedal hard downhill for eight seconds before I bank onto the narrow trail through the towering trees.

It's a short sprint after the trees until I hit the first ramp. I tuck while I fly, nothing underneath me but air. I cry out with a laugh when my rig and thighs absorb the shock of the landing, taking the next turn faster than I ever would in a qualifying run.

With the sun beating down on me and the drowned-out cheering of people around, my body breaks out in chills.

It's a perfect fucking day.

Tackling the next four technical and tight turns in the forest, I launch out and hit a wide-open stretch of dirt. I use it to my advantage and pump harder than my heart wants me to, more than my quads feel is possible, before gaining maximum acceleration toward the dirt ramp leading *into* the forest.

The sloping wall of the mountain is to my left, the trail is wide and winding around it. My face splits into what might look like a blur of maniacal joy as I take the next two minor ramps in the woods.

Roots, rocks, and the rest of the natural moguls cause my bike to shake at top speeds. Gripping my handles and squeezing my jaw tight, I navigate the boulders and raw earth underneath me.

Taking a corner too fast, I nearly hit the deck.

Six more turns down the mountain, I'm more than halfway there.

Passing over a narrow bridge of wood planks, I let it fly.

Racing off the mountain trail, my shoulder blades *ache* from controlling the way the ground threatens to knock me off with every turn, bank, and ramp. The dirt and flat track opens up in front of me and none of my downhill momentum matters.

I have to go faster.

Your time is almost too good to be true. Your luck is almost too good to be true. Your life is almost too good to be true.

Fuck that. I shut the thoughts down and get after it.

It's flat, then uphill to get to the last leg of the track. Which means pumping harder, and harder, until I can see the shade of the trees. The more I work on the toughest part of the course, the milliseconds I save toward the finish line.

Even though I've ridden this track many times before, my brain barely registers when I see the final *Red Bull* ramp in front of me. The noise of the spectators rushes back into my senses. Horns, bells, screams. It feels like coming home.

Hitting the wide blue and red ramp feels like a shot of

ecstasy blasted into my veins and I do something one year ago I would've considered stupid...

I throw a simple flip, watching the world from upside down in slow motion, before landing and sprinting to the half circle of fans, sponsors, and family at the finish line.

3:07.624

A career best. *A World Cup winning time.*

After I hit the brakes and drop my bike, I see Carmie in the stands crying and jumping and screaming like a lunatic. Lifting my palms to the sky, I let her read the bright red letters.

RIDE or FLY.

I beat out my competitor who loves to say, *If you're in control, you're not going fast enough,* by .046 seconds.

Yanking my goggles and helmet off, I head over to my woman. She's the only reason, after all these years, I finally know what it feels like to be the King of the mountain.

☆

After announcements, podium celebrations, and interviews, I'm free.

Everyone is waiting for me in the village, commandeering a large, outdoor picnic table under the setting sun. Riley sees me before anyone else, grabs the champagne bottle off the table, and sprints toward me.

He shakes it, and I scream, "NO! Riley!" But, he pops the cork and douses me in the sweet bubbles anyways.

Everyone at the table holds their breath, waiting for me to either punch him in the gut or wrap him in a hug. There's a lot of shit that went down with Riley over the last year...and there's an uneasy truce we've all been teetering on this weekend. But I look into his eyes and only see a friend.

Pulling him in for a hug, I smack his back as hard as I can.

Then I wrap my arm around his neck and drag him over to the table with me.

Carmie is on her toes, reaching up to kiss me. But instead of finding my lips, she drags her tongue up the column of my throat, catching the last drops of the champagne shower.

"Get a room," Riley coughs out from under my fatigued bicep.

Pushing him toward the table, I tell him to *Get the fuck out of my face*, before hugging and shaking everyone's hand.

Then Fallon. Who, unsurprisingly, doesn't get up to greet me. Not with her pregnancy nausea and sweat dripping down her temples. I bend to kiss her on the temple but don't miss the way Tommy narrows his eyes on me. She's due this summer and it's incredible to see my Carmela so passionate and excited for Fallon's home-birth.

But if there were sides in the *Riley Meltdown of 2022*, I suppose my chess piece would be firmly on Riley's side of the board. Not Fallon's.

Although it isn't my story to tell. That's a (long) one for another day.

Moving on, I clasp Dean in a quick hug, and then move on to Elyse, sandwiched between him and Eden.

God-damn it. Another story for another *day.*

Despite the untold stories and repressed feelings, we all spend the night together in good spirits. There's charcuterie, craft beer, whiskey, apps, and of course—crème bruele.

My mother leaves early, heading back to her new apartment in a cute Colorado mountain town, but not before pressing a ruby-red kiss to my cheek.

"Your father was with you today. I can feel it." She puts her hand on my heart and all I can do is nod. "Remember. Don't let your past overshadow your potential." She lifts my chin the moment it starts to drop.

"I love you," I tell her.

She tosses her hair over her shoulder and gives me an, *I know* look, before waltzing off to hug my wife.

Carmie gets up after dessert and stops just short of my seat. She scrunches her nose before taking a mini step back, "You, ah, have a unique smell right now."

"Like blood, sweat, and tears?" I ask, before grabbing her thighs and pulling her down into my lap.

Her candy-apple-smelling hair presses against my wet chest. I drop my nose and breathe it in while ignoring everyone within a two-mile radius.

Everyone, but her.

"Yes, my King. But also sticky champagne," she laughs, before squirming on my lap.

I bite her ear and whisper my version of *sweet nothing's*. Which are more dirty than sweet and more everything, instead of nothing. She goes still. I don't have to see her face to know it's the color of said apples, but don't worry, Elyse calls it out. Immediately.

A band begins to play outside, and Carmie turns to disarm me with one of her favorite weapons. Her eyes.

I know what they're asking, I *know* what she wants to do... and damn it...she's going to win.

"Come on, then." I pat her waist, and then her ass, as I set her on the cobblestones behind our table.

She leads us to the middle of the fray, this little blue-grass concert, before spinning in her tiny white T-shirt with my name and jersey number on it and loose-fitting ripped jeans. I'm missing half my jerseys, sweats, and hoodies now. But it's not something she'll ever hear me complain about.

She spins, and spins.

All I can do for a moment is watch and marvel at the woman she's become. An egotistical part of me wants to believe she bloomed in my hands, but I'm big enough to know the truth. When she moved here, a peony of a woman, she opened up to allowing Arizona and the magic of the desert to transform her.

Over time, she was no longer fragile. She bloomed, like a cactus flower, in the middle of the desert because she took the conditions given to her and made *life* from them.

Drawn to her, the way I'm drawn to my life on the bike, I take her hips in my hands and let her wrap her arms around my neck. We are the last to stand, and as night's darkness begins to fade, I walk with her hand-in-hand to our room.

But we don't go to bed.

I strip out of my clothes, rinse, and then pull her close to me once I'm dressed in my *Diamond Cross Ranch* T-shirt I got as a gift from my joint bachelor party with Tommy. Her skin is warm, and her muscles are relaxed as I lead her out the patio doors and onto the small landing.

Tugging on her hand, I bring her onto my lap as she curls up and nestles close. We don't speak. We don't even kiss. But I mentally stitch this moment into my very existence.

We're no longer two broken people, searching for something or someone to heal us. We're two people who stopped running, stopped hiding, and found one another when we were ready. When we were both whole.

I hold her on the patio, for every hour and every synchronized breath...until the sun rises and casts my wife, Carmela Radcliffe, in my favorite color.

Red.

And they all lived...happily ever after. Right?

ONE NIGHT IN CHARLESTON

VINCENT VAN GOGH, THE STARRY NIGHT

RILEY

LOOKING IN THE MIRROR, I can barely believe my reflection. My hair is brushed, the long golden blonde strands slicked back, and the tan from working outdoors instead of in a medic rig makes my blue eyes pop.

Lookin' like a handsome, little devil, Riley, I say to myself with a smirk.

Gripping the rim of the porcelain sink, I hear Elyse howling with laughter as she changes the music to one of her raunchy favorites.

Everyone is here for the weekend to help me and Ian settle into our new home and soak up God's Country. But what they don't know, is that they'll be celebrating something else in a moment.

Something historic.

Put it down in the history books, big.

Wear it like a Purple Heart until I die, big.

My Great Uncle Liam, one of my only living relatives from Ireland, used to tell me, *An áit a bhuil do chroí is ann a thabharfas do chosa thú.* Your feet will bring you to where your heart is.

Well, my feet, brought me to her.

371

Carley.

First, at Diamond Cross Ranch during Tommy and Parker's bachelor party. Now, in Montana, where Ian and I decided to live...coincidentally, in the same small town she relocated to as well.

Taking one last look in the mirror, I walk out of our small bathroom in the rented three-bedroom home right in the middle of this small mountain town and face the music.

Except this time, I'm not watching my friends propose to their wives.

I'm doin' it.

Navigating around the moving boxes in the hallway, I make my way outside onto the small patio. Carmie hung string lights in anticipation of tonight, the only person I confided my plans in. She has a Polaroid camera, ready to snap a photo the moment my life changes forever.

Come on, Riles. Come on. Don't puss out.

"Can I have everyone's attention? Where's Carley?" The two questions merge into one rushed statement as I look left and right.

Swallowing, I look into the wide-eyed and slightly surprised faces of my loved ones. The ones who stood by me when I completely blew up my career. The ones who bailed me out of more bar fights than I can count. The ones who I *know*, without a shadow of a doubt, will love Carley like I do.

Even if it is impulsive.

Even if it's too fast.

As if God himself was putting one ear in the clouds, witnessin' this moment, light pours from the cloudy sky and illuminates her heart-shaped face and long black hair as she walks through the open screen door.

Ian walks out behind her with a frown. Concern clutches my heart but I promise myself I'll get to him after.

Later.

"Carley, can you come here, please?"

We've been together a few months and it's been heaven. The type of love everyone around me seems to find. Lottery winners, all of 'em.

But now, it's my ticket that's showing the lucky numbers.

She walks toward me with that loud and in-your-face smile of hers, despite the hell her ex-husband put her through. There's a sitter for her kids tonight, and I wish so damn bad I could include them in this...

"Carley," I almost yell because I can't get a grip on the way my blood is pumping through my chest.

Kneeling, onto the cold pavers, I hold her hand and look into the face I haven't stopped dreaming about since she got out of her Ford Ranger and told us off for tailgating her too close.

Everyone shuts up when they see me, on my knees. Later on, but not soon enough, I would realize it wasn't the good kinda silence.

"Carly," I repeat again, forcing my throat to work and unglueing my tongue from the roof of my feckin mouth.

"My Ma, God Bless her soul, used to say something to me: *You'll know she's the one when it feels like your heart is lost at sea, but when you look at 'er, your heart catches a glimpse of land for the first time in ages. All you feel then, is hope.*"

Carley's dark eyes don't blink as she stands like a goddess, staring down at a devoted worshipper.

"I've been lost for so many years, Car." I shake my head, forcing myself not to get off track, to have an ADHD tangent. I lose that battle and forget my carefully planned speech.

I speak from the heart instead.

"Did you know, that in Irish, Carley means, *little champion?* That's who you are to so many people. At the therapy barn, at the bakery, for your girls..." my eyes begin to water and I resist the urge to pull away and wipe my nose. Damn it.

"When I look at you, that is who I will always see. A *little champion*. And it would bring me nothing but honor, pleasure, and happiness like I've never experienced in my worthless life, to champion *you* every single day we are together."

This is when I realize something isn't right. I feel a body behind me, but I'm not sure who it is. It's warm, and small, so most likely Elyse.

But I'm a stubborn son-of-a-bitch so I don't look. I squeeze Carly's hand tighter.

"I know you said you wanted someone to plan a future with. To take your life, and your daughters' lives, seriously. Someone who would grow up, and be a man."

Her eyes begin to water and for some reason, I can hear my third-grade teacher Ms. Delaney saying, *With* your *head? You're always going to be playing catch-up, Riley. Always going to be behind the eight ball.*

"Please, Carley. Will you marry me?" I choke the words out, barely audible, because my body must be smarter than my thick head. It must know, before I can figure it out, that something isn't right.

The snap of a camera goes off behind me, the flash blinding and jarring.

Carley's hand trembles in mine as she drops her chin to sigh. Her eyes close, two mountain rivers running down her face. She drops to her knees in front of me and begins to cry, something she's never, *ever*, done in front of other people before.

My heart stops and I hear the sound of the Polaroid being processed and tentatively ripped away from the camera.

Pulling my hand out of hers, I reach up to cup her now wet and cold cheek. The sun disappears and the sky darkens.

Her eyes move away from the ground.

And the man she looks at isn't me—it's Ian.

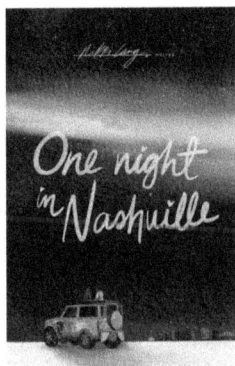

ONE NIGHT IN NASHVILLE

BOOK NUMBER ONE IN THE "ONE NIGHT ONLY" SERIES

☆

THIS ONE-NIGHT STAND DESERVES A SECOND CHANCE.

Dr. Fallon Avery is at the worst bachelorette party of her life. Matching shirts. Crummy bars. And the blister from hell, thanks to her bedazzled cowgirl boots.

So when she limps into the deserted men's room in search of respite, the last thing she needs is drummer Tommy Cunningham barging into her stall and giving her a) a bloody nose and then b) the shirt, quite literally, off his back.

Not that that explains why Fallon chooses to grab life by the shirtless stranger and have the hottest kiss of her life. Or why she agrees to a 'Say Yes Night' that ends in matching tattoos and...more.

But when Fallon uproots her life for Tommy, he breaks her only rule — no drugs — and before they know it, the ugliest parts of their pasts are threatening to break promises and hearts alike.

Maybe this wasn't meant to last longer than one night in Nashville...

<u>READ HERE TODAY!</u>

☆

Praise for "One Night in Nashville" —

"It's been a long time since I picked up a book that genuinely pulled me in, leaving me with nothing else I'd rather do than sit and fly through the story, the characters, the witty dialogue, the references, and details any lover of books and music like me would notice... and I found that and more with One Night in Nashville." — Sydney E

"I'M NOT SURE WHERE TO START WITH THIS ONE. First of all, this is Nikki's debut novel and honestly, it seems like she's been writing books her whole dang life! The second chance romance isn't always one of my top favorites, but Nikki wrote this one so beautifully. It's forever going to hold a huge piece in my heart."

— Maggie S

"I am in awe of Nikki's ability to write a raw, vulnerable, poetic love story that touches on the complexities of being human. Addiction, recovery, trauma, loss, grief. I would place a hefty bet on the fact that we've all dealt with at least one of these in our lives. She shows us that when we process and move through pain, lean into the support of our friends/communities, and face ourselves with honesty and compassion - that pain can become our medicine." — Catie M

CREDITS

Kyle ...
"After all this time? Always."
Harry Potter and the Deathly Hallows: Part 2

Mom ...
"I found out what the secret to life is: friends. Best friends." (Insert car crash scene in the parking lot here)
Fried Green Tomatoes

Dad ...
"Take these three items, some WD-40, a vise grip, and a roll of duct tape. Any man worth his salt can fix almost any problem with this stuff alone."
Gran Torino

Grandma Nancy ...
"Women, they have minds, and they have souls, as well as just hearts. And they've got ambition, and they've got talent, as well as just beauty."
Little Women
Thank you for saying and I quote, "I watch Outlander! I can handle these books." Thank you for passing on your love of traveling to me.

Liv ...
"Happiness can be found even in the darkest of times when one only remembers to turn on the light."

Harry Potter and the Prisoner of Azkaban

Thank you for being the Albus to my Harry. Thank you for being my light when I fumble around in the dark while writing. **These books would not exist without your magic.** That is not an over-exaggeration.

Catie ...

"My darling girl, when are you going to realize that being normal is not necessarily a virtue? It rather denotes a lack of courage!"

Practical Magic

Cat Rose ...

"Sometimes, the thing you want most doesn't happen. And sometimes, the thing you never expect does."

Love & Other Drugs

You championed this romance from the first page and every messy one during the process. Thank you for your friendship. Thank you for your honesty. Thank you for reading shitty PDFs. Thank you for giving me the gift of your time.

Mady ...

"So, good news...I saw a dog today."

Elf

Thank you for being the best sister-in-law so I can squeeze in a quick writing session and for also being the best co-conspirator possible.

The Women of Sedona Yoga Retreat ...

"You've always been crazy. This is just the first chance you've ever had to really express yourself!"

Thelma and Louise

There isn't enough room to express my gratitude and love for every one of you. My books wouldn't even be called the ONE-NIGHT ONLY books without you all helping me work through my doubts. Jess Ray. Shab, Julz, Maeg, Kim, Rona, Manon, Jess, Shirley, Anne. Catie. **Right people, right place, right time.**

Alyson ...

"And I didn't even know where I was going until I got there, on the last day of my hike. Thank you, I thought over and over again, for everything the trail had taught me and everything I couldn't yet know."
Wild

My Arics Baby ...

"I want to see my best friend's big sister, the girls from the soccer team, my next-door neighbor, real women who are smart and pretty and happy to be who they are. These are the women to look up to. Let's put life back into the magazine. And fun and laughter and silliness. I think we all - I think all of us - want to feel something that we've forgotten or turned our backs on because maybe we didn't realize how much we were leaving behind. We need to remember what used to be good. If we don't, we won't recognize it even if it hits us between the eyes."

13 going on 30

With special thanks to:

Krista West & Vigi with the entire Studio West Design Co. team — considering I have to spend half of my life online as an indie author, I am deeply humbled by how EASY you make design and marketing. Thank you for your support and love and constant "yes" attitude when I bring up something new ... love to you all.

Rachelle Grace — Your art moved me to tears and still does. Thank you for all of your faith and trust in me as a writer to give your art the story it deserves.

Mama Wilder — Thank you for inspiring me on how to become a secret third (worse) thing. I hope every woman in a vulnerable position discovers your non-profit and resources.

Kallie Caton of Birth Belongs to Women — You were the shining anti-establishment north star in my sky while writing the birth scenes, Lina's influence, and Carmela's character arc. Thank you for this movement.

Anjua — Mama Goddess Queen ... Pure Mvmnt changed my life. Without you, I wouldn't be the woman I am today and Carmie never would have had this journey. Thank you.

Mandy — Thank you for championing my characters and giving them a physical shape with your art! I am so grateful for you and this friendship we've found across all the miles.

My ARC readers — I can spend lifetimes writing stories ... but my voice would not exist in the world without you. I appreciate you. I adore you. You do the impossible in a world oversaturated with content and I hope one day we can all connect in real life as much as we do online!

Nikki Lang writes genre-bending, character-driven, love stories filled with intimacy and emotional depth. She loves to say that she is, "writing her heart out" with every book she publishes. Nikki will accept coffee, croissants, or compliments as acceptable offerings at her altar. She lives in the Midwest with her husband and daughter who remind her to "never lose heart."

Connect with Nikki at @nikkilangwrites on Instagram.